*Hawaiian
Crosswinds*

THE
DAWN *of* HAWAII
SERIES

BOOK TWO

Hawaiian Crosswinds

LINDA LEE CHAIKIN

MOODY PUBLISHERS
CHICAGO

© 2011 by
LINDA CHAIKIN

Edited by Cheryl Dunlop
Interior design: Ragont Design
Cover design: Studio Gearbox
Cover image: Getty images

Chaikin, L. L.
  Hawaiian crosswinds / Linda Lee Chaikin.
    p. cm. — (Dawn of Hawaii series ; bk. two)
  ISBN: 978-0-8024-3750-1
  1. Hawaii—History—19th century—Fiction. I. Title.

PS3553.H2427H39 2011
813'.54—dc22

                                    2011007483

We hope you enjoy this book from Moody Publishers. Our goal is to provide high-quality, thought-provoking books and products that connect truth to the challenges and opportunities of life. For more information on other books and products written and produced from a biblical perspective, go to www.moodypublishers.com or write to:

Moody Publishers
820 N. LaSalle Boulevard
Chicago, IL 60610

1 3 5 7 9 10 8 6 4 2

Printed in the United States of America

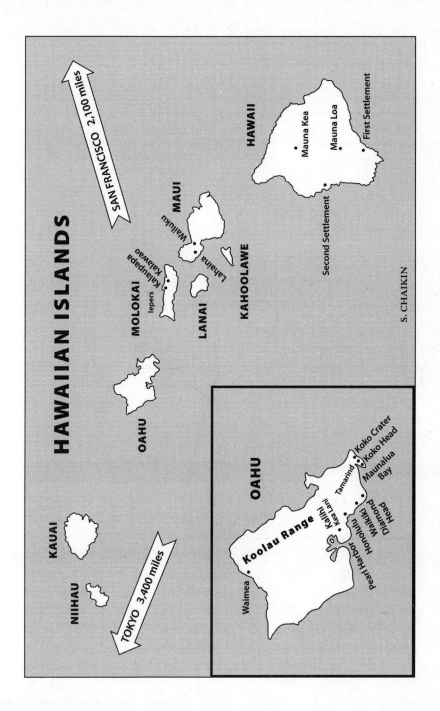

Contents

HISTORICAL CHARACTERS AND TERMS

Many of the characters who appear in *Hawaiian Crosswinds* are not fictional. Woven into the story of the Derrington and Easton families are real people who played an important role in the history of nineteenth-century Hawaii. The following lists include several of the more important characters and terms from Hawaii's colorful past. (Not listed are historical locations, buildings, and objects.)

CHARACTERS

Claus Spreckels — the sugar king from California.

Hiram Bingham — one of the first missionaries to Hawaii who helped create the Hawaiian alphabet, which was used to translate the Bible into Hawaiian.

John L. Stevens — American Foreign Minister (political) to Hawaii.

Kamehameha I monarchy — Kamehameha the Great conquered the other independent island kingdoms around him to form one kingdom, which he named after his island, Hawaii.

King David Kalakaua — who ruled over Hawaii for seventeen years until his death in 1891; the second elected monarch and the first to visit the United States.

Lorrin Thurston — member of the Hawaiian league and a grandson of pioneer missionary Asa Thurston.

Priest Damian — a Belgian priest who was ordained in Honolulu and assigned at his own request to the leper colony on Molokai in 1873, where he died in 1889 after contracting the disease.

Queen Emma Kaleleonalani — who in the 1870s had a cousin who was a leper at Molokai.

Queen Liliuokalani — the last reigning monarch of the kingdom of Hawaii, who was deposed in 1893; a musician and songwriter, she wrote Hawaii's most famous song, "Aloha Oe."

Walter Murray Gibson — King Kalakaua's controversial prime minister, who was eventually run out of Hawaii and died on his way to San Francisco.

TERMS:

alii — chief, princely

aloha — love, hello, good-bye

auwe — an expression of lament; alas!

haole — foreigner, especially white person; Caucasian

hapa-haole — person of mixed race; Hawaiian-Caucasian

hoolaulei — festive celebration

kahu — caregiver or nurse

kahuna — sorcerer or priest of the ancient native religion

kokua — helper; a person who would live with and assist a leper

lanai — porch, terrace, veranda

luna — overseer

makua — parent or any relative of one's parents

muumuu — gown, Mother Hubbard gown

Pake — Chinese

wahine — woman

Derrington Family Tree (Fictional Characters)

```
Ezra Derrington ======= Amabel
(missionary doctor)    |
                       |
            Jedaiah ======== Sarah Wilcox
            (minister)     |
        _____
        |                          |
   Ainsworth (sugar & politics)   Nora
        |
   _____
   |            |            |
Douglas     Townsend      Jerome ======= Rebecca Stanhope    Lana Stanhope
   |            |         (doctor)   |   (missionary teacher)  (Rebecca's sister)
   |       _____               |
   |       |         |               |
Candace  Zachary   Silas            Eden
```

Easton Family Tree (Fictional Characters)

```
Daniel Easton ======= Naomi
(missionary)    |    (missionary)
                |
         Nathan ======= Laura
    (sugar grower)   |
     _____
     |                        |
Ambrose ======= Noelani   Mathew ======= Celestine
                          (Matt)     |
                                     |
         Keno                      Rafe
    (Noelani's nephew)
```

Chapter One
Dark Omen

Hawaii
October 1892

*H*onolulu's *in for a storm*, Rafe Easton decided. The ocean murmured restlessly. Silhouettes of fringed coconut trees bent into the rising wind, their tall, slim trunks standing stark against the deepening skyline. Clouds tumbled along as if in a race for time. The usual mild trade wind besieged the island, a sure sign of a tropical windbreaker.

Rafe left Aliiolani Hale, the government building housing the Legislature to which he now belonged, filling the seat of Parker Judson who was in San Francisco. He headed down narrow King Street toward the Royal Hawaiian Hotel where he kept a suite of rooms.

The long day in the Legislature had ended with a personal victory that allowed for the legal adoption of Kip. "Thank You, Lord, for Your grace and that victory," Rafe said, finding comfort in the certain answer to his prayer.

The political battle for Kip was waged behind closed doors. Despite legal setbacks, by means of influence and power waged by Parker Judson, Ainsworth Derrington, and a handful of other Hawaiian titans, Rafe signed the agreement with the legislative authorities, and was now free to adopt Kip. Soon, the newborn he'd rescued well over a year ago would become Daniel Easton—named after Rafe's great-grandfather, one of the first missionaries in the Islands.

The wind buffeted the trees and maliciously tugged at his hat and his jacket. With relief he entered the Royal Hawaiian lobby with its handsome carpets, chandeliers, and lush foliage, and took the stairs to his suite.

Rafe decided to leave the baby in San Francisco with his mother, Celestine, rather than immediately return him to Hawaii. Since his marriage to Eden would not occur for another year, and Celestine wrote to him of her intention to remain at Parker Judson's Nob Hill mansion, he saw no reason to rush Kip back to Hanalei. In his decision, Rafe also considered his upcoming trip to Washington D.C. Celestine would keep Kip safe and well cared for until he got his green-eyed beauty, Eden, to the altar.

As yet, he'd said little to Eden about the success he'd been anticipating in the Legislature, and what it would mean, not only for Kip, but for her. They would enter marriage with a child two years old. Of course, it would come as no surprise since she'd been fully aware of his plans about Kip from the beginning.

Rafe drew his dark brows together thoughtfully as he removed his fashionable jacket and unbuttoned the crisp white shirt from around his neck.

He had hardly loosened his shirt when a rap sounded on the door. He opened it to find Ainsworth Derrington, white hat and black walking stick in hand. He was clothed as fashion prescribed in Honolulu: in a dazzling white duck-suit. He stood there, nearly as tall as Rafe, but as slim and straight as a lamp pole. His sometimes mysterious expression was in place and his deep-set blue eyes under tufted white brows were keenly focused on Rafe.

"I won't keep you long," he said, striding into the front room as limber as a cat. Rafe shut the door.

"Don't bother with refreshments, my boy. I'm on my way to dinner." Ainsworth turned and faced him, lowering his voice. "Truth is, I came to give you the secret location for the Annexation Club meeting tonight. Six o'clock at Hunnewell's beachfront house on Waikiki. You're expected."

At Hunnewell's? Rafe wasn't pleased.

"If I may say so, sir, a more secure location could be arranged here at the hotel, or Hawaiiana."

"Oh yes indeed, quite so. However, Thaddeus is busy writing the manifesto we're bringing to Washington and doesn't feel inclined to leave the beach house. You know writers, my boy, a strange lot. Once they get onto something it's not likely a hurricane could make them leave their typewriters."

Rafe clamped down on his impatience. "That's my exact point, sir," he said, too calmly. "Since Mr. Hunnewell's writing the manifesto, he's likely to have his office desk cluttered with important papers and names best kept concealed. He's not one to give attention to risk." Rafe was being very polite with words. "A houseful of guests moving about freely is the perfect place for a spy."

"Oh no, no. It's perfectly safe, Rafe. Perfectly. No need to worry there."

"If he leaves his writing lying about his desk the way he leaves legislation stacked on his desk at Aliiolani Hale, an opponent could find a gold mine of information. Again, sir, we're fortunate to have Hunnewell on our side, and I'm grateful for his influence on Kip, but you're well aware of his laxness."

"Yes, I'll grant you that one. One's discretionary habits do not always coincide with his intelligence."

"Perhaps if you advised that he at least lock his office door, he'd take the suggestion," Rafe said, keeping the bite out of his tone.

"Yes, I shall do so. No need to worry, Rafe, though your conscientiousness is commendable. Be assured there's no Benedict Arnold in the lot who will show up tonight; trusty men all."

It was no use. In some matters, Rafe found the rigid and experienced Ainsworth Derrington oozing with excess confidence.

"By the way, Rafe, I've been thinking of that lad, Keno. A good friend of yours, I know."

Ainsworth's mention of Keno was so far from the ordinary that surprise silenced Rafe. He stood looking at the patriarch, who stroked his silver goatee and watched him in return.

"I suppose he's taking the loss of my granddaughter Candace with painful heart."

"Assuredly," Rafe added with less bluntness than he felt. "He's in love with her. He has been for years." He added with a note of self-derision, "He and I share in common the fact that neither of us can bring the one woman we want to the marriage altar."

Ainsworth cracked a smile. "Yes, my sympathy about Eden. If I had my way she'd marry you now. I could still force it—" he looked at him evenly, "but as you've said, Eden must have her moment with Jerome and Rebecca on Molokai. Therefore, out of deference to your wishes, I've left matters with Eden alone, though I think Jerome's in error to want her working at his side."

"I do think it's necessary she participate, sir. It's for her good, not mine. If Eden's robbed of her moment with her father, as you put it, I know it will affect our future together. This is something she's got to learn for herself. I've known her since she was fifteen. She's been obsessed with Rebecca from that time on. You'll remember back, sir, when she believed her mother had been murdered."

Ainsworth winced and shook his silver head. "Dreadful. My fault, entirely. I've since repented of my silence about Jerome and Rebecca. I should have understood Eden better and seen where it would lead, and well—" He drew in an unhappy breath.

Rafe could see Ainsworth's emotions were genuine. "I bring it up to show that Molokai is crucial. I only recognized it myself recently. I don't want her to end up ten years from now believing I've cheated her out of something this important to her."

Ainsworth gave a nod. "Wise of you. You've a sound head on your shoulders. I've thought so for a long time. That's why I wanted you to marry Candace." Ainsworth's cool blue eye came up to meet Rafe's gaze.

Rafe remained unreadable.

"You could marry her sooner, and wouldn't have to worry about Molokai."

"Sir, there's only one woman I want."

"Eden, yes, an excellent choice. Noble at times . . . and most beautiful. Well, so be it. About Keno . . ." He walked a half-circle, one arm behind his back, a thumb and forefinger holding his chin thoughtfully. "I've been thinking. He is a fine young fellow. I can attest to that. One of the best. Yes," he drawled. "I do feel somewhat to blame for his unhappiness. I'd like to do something . . . er, beneficial for him—something that might breach the broken bridge, so to speak, and make the future shine a little brighter for him. Not that I want him to know I've done it, you understand. He is young, and hearts have ways of mending. I'd like to benefit him. So I've been thinking. . . ." He tapped his chin.

A faint stir of caution moved in Rafe's mind. Ainsworth was in many ways a man of strong and decent character. Why, then, did Rafe feel the need to be wary? *You're just too cynical,* another voice seemed to say.

"Do something beneficial?" Rafe repeated, watching him carefully.

"Land is what I was thinking about, Rafe. Sugarcane. A plantation of his own, cane workers in time."

Rafe looked at him with surprise.

"I've just the plantation land in mind, on the Big Island, actually, so that the two of you could be good neighbors. . . . I thought since you two are so brotherly that it would work out very well indeed. Perhaps you know of the section I have in mind, near Hilo."

Rafe did know, and agreed that it would grow productive cane.

"I can tell you, sir, that Keno would turn that section of land into a successful enterprise. He has it in him. He's dedicated, smart, and honorable. He wouldn't let you down." Ainsworth turned his gaze away and he did another half-circle on the rug, looking down as if he'd dropped something.

Rafe scrutinized the tall, dignified figure in white. "Now that you've brought Keno up, I'll admit to something," Rafe said. "The last few weeks I've been thinking about arranging with Parker Judson to have my partnership in Hawaiiana turned over to Keno."

He heard a surprised gasp from Ainsworth.

"I haven't mentioned it yet to Keno. I think I can convince Judson to go along with the idea. I promised Keno a year or two ago that as soon as I could handle the finances I'd back him in his own plantation. I was intending to bring it up to Judson in San Francisco. However, the sugarcane land on the Big Island is a better idea for a number of reasons. And I'll admit I'm not jubilant about giving up Hawaiiana. I've an emotional attachment to the place, since it was the first success I accomplished."

Ainsworth wore an expression that could only be read as shock, then dismay. He ceased his pacing and stared.

"I had no notion you had that deep of a bond with Keno!"

"He's a brother. We've been through it all together. The best, the worst. I want him to become successful."

Ainsworth was back to his habitual pacing, this time his slim hand on his forehead, deep in thought. Rafe watched him with another vague idea that caution was needed. He tilted his dark head.

"If you do this, sir, how would you arrange it financially?"

"Keno will know nothing of my involvement, or he would naturally refuse it."

Rafe considered. Would he? Because of Ainsworth refusing to let him marry Candace, perhaps he would.

"I think I could make him see reason," Rafe said.

That immobile façade was back. "I think it best I stay out of this altogether, Rafe. The land, the plantation, must all be arranged through a third party so that he will never know I had anything to do with his future success."

Rafe looked at him for a long minute.

"I was thinking you would make the best third party to bring it all to a successful accord. I'll have the land turned over to you, and you'll arrange for Keno to begin taking control of the property. Naturally, as my upcoming grandson through marriage to Eden, I can trust you explicitly. Plus, your friendship with Keno will guarantee his security in gaining control, and in time, ownership. We'll arrange matters with the lawyer, Withers, in the same way we handled the return of Hanalei. In due season Keno will marry a good Christian girl, have a family, and be a satisfied man."

After a perceptible pause Rafe responded. "Extremely generous of you, sir. However, Keno will naturally expect to know who the man is that's willing to give him such a bounty." Rafe added because of his own growing unease, "He's cynical. He doesn't believe in Santa Claus any more than I do." He looked at Ainsworth.

"Ah. He'll listen to *you*."

"I'm not so sure, not over a bounty that comes so magnanimously with no name attached."

"He trusts you, Rafe. If anyone can convince him to go through with this generous offer it's you."

Rafe began to worry. Keno did trust him, and he probably would go through with the offer if Rafe wanted to convince him. If it was indeed a genuine blessing, well and good. But if there was some shrewdness behind Ainsworth's generosity it would likely ruin Rafe and Keno's friendship.

_____୧୨_____

Twilight . . . In the Hawaiian Islands darkness descended rapidly. A sky wracked with angry vermilion splashed the distant steel-blue horizon of the Pacific.

Keno walked the dirt road leading away from the beach. He took the path inland toward a familiar cluster of ancient palms. In their midst stood the Bible mission church topped with a white cross, first founded by Dr. Jerome and Rebecca Derrington and now pastored by Ambrose Easton.

As Keno expected, a soothing glow of golden light burned in the front window. Aunt Noelani, always faithful to her tasks, large or small, lit the lamp in the front church window. For as long as Keno could remember she'd lit that lamp every evening. "Who knows?" she would repeat when he was a boy. "That light might be just what someone needs to remind them that Jesus is the Light of the world. And the world we live in is getting darker with time."

As a ten-year-old fatherless boy, who was half haole, the offspring of a British father, Keno felt isolated among unnumbered Polynesian aunts, uncles, and cousins while growing up. He regarded Ambrose as the true spiritual patriarch of his life. He knew Rafe felt the same.

Even so, his deep-seated struggle for acceptance and belonging continued. Disappointment in an earthly father, or the loss of one beloved, seemed to haunt more than himself. Zachary Derrington was the emotionally disturbed son of a *murderer*, while Eden Derrington's father was so preoccupied with his personal quest that he'd all but forgotten that he had a young, vulnerable daughter who longed for parental strength . . . until he'd returned to Hawaii a few months ago. Even now those tattered emotions affected Eden's relationship with Rafe Easton. And Rafe was not immune either. His anger over the injustice done to his father burned deep, though under heavy restraint. And the cool and beautiful woman Keno was in love with, Candace Derrington, lost her father at sea when a small girl, so that her grandfather Ainsworth was directing her future—mainly for his own cause.

Then this little church with its smiling haole pastor came into Keno's boyhood and drew him into the embrace of the great Creator God. It was through his pal Rafe Easton that Keno learned he could know God as *Father* because of the redemptive work of the blessed Son of God, Jesus. It was the same spiritual lesson Rafe learned after the death of his father, Matt Easton—that God has adopted us as His sons through Jesus Christ.

Keno paused on the sandy path to the church, a stone's throw from Ambrose and Noelani's homey bungalow. No mansion, this, but the warmest place in all Honolulu when someone needed a friend to trust. Ambrose was that friend.

Keno looked up at the dark sky. Even with a heart filled with gratitude, he mourned. No friendly stars shone tonight, only clouds and thick darkness.

Oh God—Father—I don't think I can live without Candace, he prayed in agony. *What am I to do?*

This evening he felt he needed every drop of hope and grace he could drink from the Monday night men's Bible study.

Rafe was usually in attendance, but tonight—well, he hoped Ambrose wouldn't ask him *where* Rafe was.

Keno entered the bungalow through the back kitchen door. He didn't notice Noelani anywhere about, though she couldn't be far. Something was cooking on the stove that made him hungry; it smelled like oysters from the pearl bed. And Rafe's favorite coconut cake was on the counter, as well, a sure sign Noelani expected him to drop by after the meeting. Noelani had loved Rafe as a boy and defended him whenever she could from the bullying of his stepfather, Townsend Derrington. Keno remembered how upset Noelani was when Rafe's lovely and gentle widowed mother, Celestine, married Townsend after Matt's death.

"She'll live to regret her choice in a man. Handsome, Makua Townsend is, but his heart needs washing and mending—better yet, he needs a new heart."

Noelani's "mama" love for Rafe caused her to take on the task of being Kip's nanny until Rafe smuggled the baby out of the Islands.

Pastor Ambrose stood in the middle of the sitting room with his Bible under his arm as though prepared to walk over to the mission church for the men's meeting. A man strong in the emphasis of the Bible, a soldier of much prayer, he stood with a solid frame and wide shoulders. Nonetheless, a heart problem kept him from the rugged Hawaiian-style kayak fishing he'd loved in earlier years. Throwing and hauling in the big nets was now hard on him. Years earlier he had been the one to encourage Rafe and Keno in their swimming and diving feats.

At first Keno thought Ambrose was praying, for he stood still, his head bent. It always amazed him that Ambrose prayed as much as he did. He even kept a prayer list he actually used! He would go for long walks on the beach and pray for the ones he'd written on a card. Keno often hoped he was on that list. Knowing Ambrose, he probably was.

But Ambrose wasn't praying this time. Keno noticed a deepening frown on the sun-weathered face and saw that his somber gaze was fixed on a sheet of paper in his hand.

Outside the bungalow the stormy wind made its presence known. The trees and bushes shook, and the weathered bamboo blinds rattled like skeleton bones.

Ambrose was so absorbed that he appeared not to have heard Keno's entry.

"Something wrong, Makua Ambrose?"

Ambrose turned to look at him, the frown remaining on his rugged features. There seemed to be what Rafe had called a moral intensity to the even gaze of his dark eyes. Those pastor's eyes now turned toward Keno, then stirred, as if awaking.

"Wrong, lad? Too much is wrong. When light is willfully rejected, darkness gains another stronghold."

Was he speaking of someone in particular?

"Will Rafe be coming tonight?" Ambrose inquired, folding the sheet of paper three times.

Keno ran his fingers through his wavy brown hair, a restless habit he couldn't seem to break. He shoved his hand in his trouser pocket. Here it came, the issue he'd wanted to avoid.

He and Rafe were as close as blood brothers, and loyalty brought Keno to a wider dilemma; he'd all but promised Rafe that he'd hold his tongue about the business tonight that had called him to Waikiki Beach. Though Rafe trusted Ambrose, he knew he would disapprove, so Keno still faced a problem.

Ambrose was looking at him as if he understood a spiritual tug-of-war was going on within. He must have liked what he saw, for his eyes spoke encouragement. He'd often said spiritual growth was the result of various trials. "No testing is too small when God's truth is involved, my lad. Don't wait for the big one, the lion's den, or the Roman arena—why, most of life's testing comes in the small things. And if you can't be trusted with the small truths, who will trust you with the big ones?"

Keno cleared his throat. It had become natural in these days of political division to cast a glance toward open lanais and doorways for unfriendly ears. He lowered his voice.

"Rafe's at a secret meeting."

"I rather guessed as much. Annexation I suppose?"

"They're all meeting at Hunnewell's house."

Keno hadn't decided whether Ambrose favored annexation to the United States or a continuation of the Hawaiian Chiefdom. Ambrose had been careful to keep the matter to himself. His congregation both favored and opposed, and he would say his calling was to teach the Word. "Its truths, if heeded, will give wisdom in all areas . . . including culture and politics. The Word already offends the proud sinner, so I shouldn't add yet another hurdle."

"Mr. Thurston's returning to Washington," Keno said. "Ainsworth Derrington and a few other big kahunas are going too. Even Rafe is tagged to go with them, since he's holding Parker Judson's seat in the Legislature."

"If Rafe expects to go with the Thurston group, then that may be the answer. They'll hold over a few days in San Francisco before taking the train to Washington."

"The answer?" Keno asked, bewildered. "To what?"

Ambrose tapped the paper he held, his solemn gaze fixed on Keno. "The answer to this telegraph wire. His mother sent it to me from San Francisco. She knew I'd get it to him safely. That meeting you mentioned, Keno. Can you take it to him now? It's important."

Keno glanced at his timepiece. "I'll go at once. They usually don't break up till around ten o'clock. If not, I'll find him at Hawaiiana, or the hotel. He's been using both lately."

Since Ambrose hadn't said what was in the wire, Keno refrained from asking, but guessed it to be troubling.

Noelani appeared from the kitchen carrying a tempting plate of small cakes. She was a big-boned woman, strong and healthy, with white hair worn in neatly coiled braids wrapped around her head and a cross on a gold chain around her neck. Her father had been a whaler out of Boston Harbor, her mother, Polynesian. She wore a typical Mother Hubbard gown, this one blue.

"You are going so soon? And where is Rafe? Again, he's not coming?"

"Keno will be back later," Ambrose told her. "Rafe might return in time. Better save those delicious cakes, my dear. We can't wait. I need to be over at the church in ten minutes."

Keno felt a grave stare coming from his aunt. "Did you tell your uncle what your ancient grandmother whispered to you about your haole father?"

Most of the time she treated him like a little boy. It usually amused him, but not tonight.

Keno affected indifference and tried to laugh. "Oh, that. I've been too busy to think about it, Aunt Noelani. I'd better go—"

Her dark eyes were unhappy. "Grandmother Luahine was wrong to tell you after all this time. It is a burden to bear. She's old. Too talkative." She looked at Ambrose. "Now there will be more trouble."

Keno felt the tension rise in the room like a thermometer in the noonday sun.

Ambrose stood still. Then looked at him with sympathy. He appeared to know what Noelani was talking about, even though Keno hadn't mentioned it to him.

"When did Luahine tell you, lad?"

Keno maintained his affectation. "Oh, a few days ago. I went over to see her. It was her birthday. Look, I don't want either of you to worry. Understand? It matters not to me. I'll never see him. He sired me—that's all." Despite his best effort, a strain of bitterness sounded in the low rasp of his voice. He tried the harder because of it. "Look, I'm going to say it. If any man's been fatherly toward me, it's you, Uncle Ambrose. I'll never forget what you've been. As for the other—I haven't given Grandmother's tale much thought." All the same, it did matter, deep in his soul. In fact, it made him *angry*.

Ambrose walked over to Keno and laid a hand on his shoulder. He said nothing, but the strength from his grip told Keno all he needed. Then he turned to his wife.

"I've got to be over at the church, Noelani. They'll be waiting. We'll all be back for refreshments in an hour or so." Ambrose walked out the front door, and Keno felt the rush of warm, moist air.

"Such words can only bring discontent," Noelani repeated. "And where there's discontent and roots of injustice, there will be *pilikia*—trouble."

Keno smiled deliberately at her repeated word of "trouble." He tapped his chest. "Not this guy, Noelani. I don't like trouble. You've nothing to worry about. My life will push ahead as usual." He wanted to add, *I've already lost what means more to me than anything else. There's not much more the Devil can hit me with.* Or so he hoped and prayed.

He walked over and put his arm around her shoulders, kissed her cheek, and left, shutting the door behind him. Outdoors, he was pummeled by the tropic wind snapping at the foliage and sweeping onward to produce havoc elsewhere.

He left the porch and the forebearing environment of the bungalow, a respite from the bitter winds of reality that too often blew with hurricane force, then made haste along the path toward the Waikiki beach house belonging to widower Thaddeus P. Hunnewell, the financially and politically influential father of Oliver P. Hunnewell, soon to be Candace's fiancé.

The waves foamed over the black rocks, some of them sweeping in close to his feet. He leaped from one rock to the next with the sure and steady agility of an acrobat.

Hunnewell, he thought with a touch of scorn. *Keno Hunnewell.* The names did not blend when linked together. He mocked aloud in the wind, "What about Keno *P.* Hunnewell, does that help?" No. He rejected it with contempt, as he knew the Hunnewells themselves would if they knew.

Nor would the fact that his biological father had been Philip Hunnewell, Oliver's uncle, make any difference to Ainsworth Derrington, or to Candace. Candace with her flame hair and cool blue eyes had sent him a letter two months ago written from her great-aunt's house on Koko Head. In the letter she'd "explained"—rather, *told* him—of her decision to bend with the wind of family compromise and marry Oliver P. She was doing this to please the Derrington family patriarch Ainsworth, who would make her his chief heiress if she would "wisely" comply.

Keno scowled. So, she had complied. So much for the Candace he had *thought* he knew, who left a fragrance of integrity in her passing, who had ignored his lack of birthright to the big Hawaiian sugar families, who had enjoyed the notion that he was half Hawaiian, who had said in the moonlight that his skimpy bank account meant next to nothing to her compared to his Christian character—and he had believed her.

Keno had tried to see her, taking his cousin Liho's boat out to Koko Head to Tamarind House, soon after he'd received her appalling letter, but she'd refused him. Her great-aunt Nora Derrington had stoically come to the parlor to inform him that her great-niece "Miss Candace is quite busy editing my manuscript, which must be completed and delivered to the publisher in November. She is unwilling to see you." She might as well have added "ever again."

He had written Candace several letters since the morbid rebuff in the parlor, but they'd been returned to him, unopened, in a large envelope. Not even Rafe had been able to influence her to see him.

For the past two months Candace had remained in relative seclusion, keeping her great-aunt company during her recuperation from the emotional shock of knowing that her nephew Townsend had callously tampered with her medication.

Since then Miss Nora had recovered her health and arrived at the Derrington sugar estate, Kea Lani, and Candace with her. Meanwhile, the day of Candace's engagement to Oliver was being arranged to take place before her grandfather Ainsworth boarded the steamer for San Francisco. The celebration would need a great fanfare and a mammoth *hoolalei*.

Anger and pain seized him. There had been no tropical sunset this evening, no blossoms heavy with love's promise. The wind off the Pacific was salty and damp, and Keno looked up to the starry heavens with hope, but they were blanketed by low hanging clouds.

*I*nside the beachfront house of sugar grower Thaddeus P.
Hunnewell, Rafe Easton stood near the lanai where the
same salty and moist wind entered from Waikiki. He leaned
there, arms folded, bored, looking across the large oblong room
furnished with rare native woods and decorated with potted
ferns. He half-listened to Ainsworth Derrington concluding his
long political briefing to a group of men that formed the new
Annexation Club, begun in recent days by the resolute Lorrin
Thurston. Rafe regarded Thurston as possibly the most perse-
vering advocate for the complex goal of the annexationists gathered here tonight. Men in the fight for the destiny of the Islands,
all loyal, or so Ainsworth believed. Rafe wasn't as certain. In
glancing at the sober faces of the varied gentlemen seated or
standing about the room, he persisted in his conviction that a
spy was sheltered among their ranks. Not that there was evidence
to lay his hands on. For all intents and purposes the men's zeal
confirmed them to be annexationists at heart.

What set Rafe on edge was Thaddeus Hunnewell's lack of

vigilance. Earlier, when the trip to Washington was planned, Hunnewell was commissioned by the highest members of the Reform Party to write the document they would present when they met with Secretary of State Blaine. Blaine, in turn, would take the manifesto to the desk of President Harrison, who was known to favor annexation of the Hawaiian Islands.

As Rafe understood it, the seven-page manifesto laid out in full detail each step planned by the Annexation Club for rapid success, in order that President Harrison could send a bill to Congress for ratification before he left office.

Thaddeus Hunnewell was a brilliant lawyer, an able politician, and a formidable spokesman, but like all of Adam's fallen race he had his foibles. At times Hunnewell came across as one deficient in the wisdom for discerning whether or not a man could be trusted. When betrayal did come, he was the sort of fellow who would always be shocked.

It had been easy for Rafe to learn that the important manifesto was here in the beach house tonight. Had Hunnewell taken any precautions? Was the document he worked on locked securely away? Or did Hunnewell believe, as did Ainsworth, that "none but trusty men" moved about the house this windy night?

Ainsworth's voice drove onward toward his political goal—

"And so, gentlemen, in order to establish these Islands on the foundation of liberty and justice, we *must* have the security that's based on the American Constitution and the Bill of Rights. I say, we *must* have annexation. It is our finest choice."

Ainsworth's familiar gold watch chain sparkled as he stood under the lamplight, as did the wedding band still faithfully embedded on his lean, tanned hand, though he'd been a widower for longer than Rafe could remember.

At the conclusion of his talk, Ainsworth inclined his hoary head with a "Thank you so much." His nimble fingers gathered his superfluous stack of handwritten notes from the table and he sat down again amid the semicircle of men, crossing his long legs at the knees and gazing at his spotless white shoes.

In response to the sober picture Ainsworth had painted of Hawaii's future, silence permeated the room as a bamboo blind rattled in a gusty breeze. As if on cue, several men started to speak at the same moment. A frustrated discussion ensued over "the queen's obstinacy" in not appointing one of their own Reform Party members to a position in her new cabinet.

Rafe recalled that the recent trouble had begun soon after Liliuokalani assumed the throne on the death of her brother, King David Kalakaua, in January 1891. Once seated on the throne she'd insisted that Kalakaua's cabinet, primarily men of the Dole and Thurston Reform Party, resign, in order that she might appoint her own men, leading some in Kalakaua's Reform cabinet to believe that they would be reappointed. Their expectations, however, were cut short, and a list of different names in support of a new Constitution was sent to the Legislature for ratification. The Legislature under men like Dole and Thurston had managed to gain enough votes to reject her appointees, and so the political chess game continued.

Thaddeus Hunnewell was pacing again, his leather oxfords squeaking on the polished floor. His son Oliver was late tonight, the truculent son who was accused of too little interest in Hawaiian politics.

"Liliuokalani is an obstinate woman," the lawyer named Withers said, shaking his head. "She'll continue sending the Legislature lists of men for confirmation who support overthrowing the '87 Constitution."

Hunnewell turned his sober countenance on the lawyer. "If she wins, our rights will be dissolved. We're not Polynesians, true; which is the main protest of the native Hawaiians, but we were born in these Islands. Never forget that, gentlemen! What more can the present generation of natives say of themselves than that? They haven't been here any longer than we have. The haole ethnicity of our fathers doesn't change the fact that we are true Hawaiians. Why, some of us here tonight are third generation, the Derringtons and

Rafe Easton over here." He gestured. "Are we to simply stand by and see the homes and businesses we built and sweated over surrendered to the whim of a gilded throne?"

"No!" came the unison of voices. Some of the men who'd been seated stood.

"Then we'll keep voting down her list of cabinet ministers," Hunnewell said. "One thing's on her mind by choosing these men. Annul the '87 Constitution, and with that, our rights as Hawaiians."

"We lack the needed votes, gentlemen," Ainsworth said, always the more serious and realistic of the leaders. "We may not be able to vote down the men she sends us next time."

"I tell you we can prevail if we gain a few men from the Liberal party."

Ainsworth pursed his lips. "A challenge. Is it possible?"

Hunnewell's smile was thin. "Wilcox and Roxbury can be won over." His eyes glinted. "I know Wilcox through and through. For a purpose that benefits his ambitions he'll join the Reform legislators. He can bring a few others with him too."

Rafe wasn't sure why, but something shifted his attention across the oval room toward the bamboo curtain.

From somewhere past the dusky perimeter of the room, out on the lanai, a lone lamp burned dimly on a Victorian style table, allowing shadowed corners to deepen as the sun approached the horizon. A curtain screened a landing with a flight of steps down to a cove. He glanced at his watch. It was still low tide, the cove accessible. He'd gone down those steps earlier that afternoon when Hunnewell had his house servants bringing refreshments near the beach.

Rafe fixed his gaze, seeking . . . for what, he wasn't sure. *Something there. On the lanai behind the bamboo curtain? A stealthy movement. Or just the wind moving the bamboo?*

The others, talking forcefully among themselves, their emotions now in a roil as only Thaddeus Hunnewell could stir them, did not notice anything awry. *Just as an eavesdropper would hope,* Rafe thought with cynicism. Like actors on a stage consumed with playing their roles, they stood beneath the circle of light, sometimes too self-assured, while an audience of one inconspicuously listened beyond the room's dark perimeter.

Again . . . a faint clacking of bamboo, a gush of air entering the wider spaces of the room.

Rafe moved unnoticed onto the lanai, and then to the screened landing toward the back stairs. Wayward wind or a spy, he intended to find out.

When Keno arrived at the Hunnewell beachfront house at Waikiki, the ornate iron gates that guarded the drive were shut against him. A glimmer of the sun's rays still illuminated Diamond Head, while the quick tropic darkness descended toward the waves washing onto Waikiki from the coral reef. Lurking shadows from coconut palms deepened.

He stood for a moment, gazing at the grand place, mingled with frustration and sadness. He seldom felt tested by jealousy, but it raised its ugly head as he thought of Candace.

If I was an esteemed somebody with a family name, I could have married her. What heiress wants to throw away everything to marry a hapa-haole with little in his bank account?

Jealousy was quickly followed by the hound of self-pity.

No wonder Ainsworth wanted his sweet Candace to marry old man Hunnewell's son. Why, look at what Candace will inherit. Money, handsome houses, land to grow even more sugarcane to maintain the Hunnewell assets. *And me, Keno? I have a hut on Hanalei and a trunk load of clothes, Bible books, and hopes! Not enough of the fine "stuff" in this life to impress anyone, let alone Mr. Ainsworth Derrington.*

Self-pity snarled into anger. Anger toward the Derrington patriarch for insisting the righteous Candace marry for loot and esteem from the circle of the elite. Yes, "loot"! Bags of it. Heaped up in the bank and drawing much interest.

Anger also gave a low growl at Candace for choosing to follow her grandfather's wishes when she'd told Keno on several occasions that she was more willing to go barefoot in the sand with him, "her handsome hapa-haole," than any son of Mr. Hunnewell.

He shook his head, still standing before the imposing gate of no admittance. He grasped hold of the cold, black wrought iron and rattled it in protest.

Wait . . . what was that? Was there someone there? He squinted into the shadows near the garden's inner wall, right inside the iron gate . . . just a shadow of a tree moving in the wind. . . .

It wasn't like Candace to behave this way. He couldn't understand her decision, so cold and pragmatic, so indifferent to him now when once she had loved him. Yes, she *had* loved him. He was certain of it. Now, she wouldn't even speak to him. On her return from Tamarind House, he'd waited for her to go out in her buggy that he might ride his horse and catch up with her, but instead of granting him even this small opportunity she rode everywhere with Oliver.

Yes, she loved *him*, Keno. Yet the lovely woman he'd thought so high and noble, so devout in her heart to the will of God, had turned her back to him for wealth and prestige. She had said so in the letter she'd written him, almost two months ago.

"I have freely made the decision to live up to the responsibility I have as a Derrington. I choose to do as my grandfather asks of me and marry Oliver. The engagement is upcoming. I know you will eventually understand this is the best decision for us both. . . ."

On and on the redundant explanation had journeyed down a spiraling path of empty words into a deep, dark well. Just standing before the Hunnewell gate heightened his frustration.

He doubled his strong fist and gently touched it against his other palm. His old sin nature would like to smash Oliver. Yes, *smash* him *hard*. Spoiled and selfish, having everything easy, everything he wanted—why, if it hadn't been for his rich father, little junior would have nothing—*stop it, Keno!*

His fist was not his own. He had surrendered it to his Savior—

like Rafe had when confronted by his bully stepfather, Townsend Derrington.

Keno shook his head wearily. Only the grace and the power of the Holy Spirit could control his runaway emotions. He frowned to himself. *Sometimes I think my emotions are worse than everyone else's.*

Maybe I shouldn't have come here tonight. Lord! Help me!

How easy to forget thankfulness. Why, even the Lord had not a place to rest His head when He came to earth. "The foxes have holes, and the birds of the air have nests; but the Son of man hath not where to lay his head." Awesome thought. *And I complain?*

He narrowed his gaze, hands on hips, lost in a stance he had so often seen of soul-brother Rafe when frustrated.

But then . . . despite the volcanic explosion that had crushed his dreams, Keno told himself to remember what he could not forget. The One through whom all things consisted and were held together also controlled the spiritual upheavals of those who belonged to Him. "He that openeth, and no man shutteth; and shutteth, and no man openeth."

There is a different Gate, an all-important Gate, and that one stands wide open to me.

Ambrose's words came ringing in his ears. "God is not indifferent to the loss and pain you feel. Discipleship means yielding to whatever His purposes might be. In the end, even when we can't understand, it will come out right, if not in this life, in eternity."

Keno bowed his head and, yet *again*, yielded himself anew to Jesus Christ.

A short time later he opened the gate and passed through it, and walked the paved path that circled the side of the house to one of the back entrances, telling himself that in his position—or rather, his lack of position—he would be expected to come by the servant's route.

My personal struggles are only for a brief time, but one day I will enter the Father's mansions and walk on golden streets. "And I won't be coming through the back door," he quipped aloud.

He heard no other sounds in the windy evening. He began to

whistle, hands shoved in his trouser pockets. He walked toward the back pathway. Movement from the yellow hibiscus bushes a few feet to the side halted him. *What was that?*

"Say! What are *you* doing here?"

That *voice.* He *knew* it. To his grief, it identified Oliver P. Hunnewell himself. *Oh no . . . Lord, help.*

Keno narrowed his gaze, making certain he hadn't imagined the voice he was growing to despise. The shadows were heavy here. He might not have noticed Oliver standing by the bushes if he hadn't spoken out.

Oliver Hunnewell came straight toward Keno. *If this were Spain, I'd suspect he was a bull with flashing red eyes,* Keno thought wearily.

Oliver was usually garbed in an expensive white jacket, trousers, watered-silk vest, a diamond stickpin in his lapel, and an expensive derby hat.

Tonight he wore dark clothing. He was tall, strong-shouldered, and his coloring fit his name, "Hunnewell," as he had honey-colored everything: hair, eyes, and mustache. It was one of those pencil mustaches that looked as if he'd spent an hour each morning artfully waxing it. He surged forward briskly, crunching fallen leaves scattered in his path.

Keno stood still. *Just my fortune,* he thought. Here was the rich prince, just returned to his father's castle to claim the woman Keno loved. Keno was bent on carrying her off to his castle, but the bride-to-be wasn't putting up a tizzy over being shanghaied.

Too bad the days of chivalry are no more. I would have challenged him to a duel to win her back. Life is so unfair.

Oliver stopped a few feet in front of him, sizing him up. Keno met his gaze evenly. *Go ahead, pal,* he thought, *try it.* Then a quick ache of guilt came with his next heartbeat. *Didn't you just pray and yield yourself to God? Remember who you are.*

Keno drew in a breath and cleared his throat. He tried to smile. "Why, it's Oliver! Hello," he said inadequately, the syllables nearly sticking in his throat.

Oliver's eyes fixed on him like a hawk on a sparrow. "It's *Mister*," he said, his voice striking the tone for a well-aimed insult. "But to you, it's *Makua* Hunnewell."

Keno clenched his jaw. *That's what you think, rich boy.*

"What are you doing on Hunnewell property?" Oliver demanded, lifting his rounded chin.

That chin. What a perfect target. Keno shoved his right hand back safely into his pocket.

Hunnewell property, is it? My mother's side of the family was walking here long before yours ever showed up. Keno swallowed the words before he unwisely trumpeted them into the wind. Every generation had to establish its own rite of passage. Responsibility was the key issue, not mere ethnicity.

"Look, I don't want any trouble. It's important I speak to Rafe. Is he still here? Pastor Ambrose Easton, his uncle, sent me to find him."

Oliver's mouth twisted. His cold gaze accused.

"Don't give me that rubbish. You're looking for Miss Derrington."

Keno gritted his teeth, his temper on the rise. "If I was here to speak to Candace," and he used her first name deliberately, "I'd come out in the open about it. I didn't think she was here, I've come to see Rafe. This is an all-male club meeting, isn't it?"

"That's none of your affair. You come out in the open? Rubbish. You sneak about peering into windows—"

"Now wait a minute. Don't make that kind of crack at me!"

"Now you listen to me," Oliver shot back. "Don't think I don't know how you've been *openly* making a fool of yourself with those letters you've been writing her. You've also been chasing after her horse 'n' buggy every time you see her go into Honolulu. Wouldn't surprise me if you weren't hiding in the bushes watching for her to go somewhere. She says you trouble and embarrass her."

Had she told him this? For a moment he almost believed him, then shook it off. Candace wouldn't flaunt another man's love for her. She wasn't like that.

"If I find you've been pestering her again," Oliver warned, "I'll have Marshal Harper haul you in on charges of harassment. Don't think I won't. I have a certain amount of influence here in Honolulu and in San Francisco," he boasted. "You'd be less of a fool to remember that."

Oliver turned on his well-made heel, striding toward the steps, his arms swinging at his sides.

Keno felt the blood pounding in his temples.

"What you should say is that your father has influence. You merely have family conveniences."

Oliver stopped. He swung round and faced him again. Even in the dim light of the Chinese lanterns his angular face said it all. He stormed back toward Keno, his open jacket swaying at his sides.

Then Keno remembered his last prayer. His lack of self-control sent a wave of frustration over his soul. *I've made a hash of it.* He drew in a breath and deliberately stepped back as Oliver stormed up. Keno held up his palm. "Now wait a minute. I didn't mean to speak out of line—"

Oliver smiled with scorn. His eyes seemed to shout that he was enjoying the moment. "Get out of here." He gestured toward the front road. "Before I forget I'm a gentleman and throw you over the gate. And stay away from Candace. She doesn't want anything more to do with the likes of you. I don't want to see you within a block of her, understood? If I do, I'll see you wincing for your impudent presumption."

Keno's injured pride clashed as a titan with restraint. A surge of anger filled the gap, causing his heart to thud like a war drum.

Oliver's mouth jutted downward in a satisfied smirk. "Go among your own people."

Among your own people! "Unfortunately, I'm with one of them now."

Oliver smiled coolly. "The sooner a dog learns he is one, the happier he'll be."

"Then, from one dog to another, it's time you learned that where mere Hunnewell blood's concerned, we share and share alike. Don't play squire of the manor with me."

The unfriendly smile had frozen on Oliver's astonished face. He stared, taken aback. "You're lying."

"I'm the biological son of *your* uncle Philip Pepperidge Hunnewell of Burlington, England."

"You're a lying hapa-haole."

"But your uncle Pepperidge didn't stay in the Islands long—he returned to his 'civilized' England when he found out he'd gotten my mother pregnant. I hear he's dead. But a Hunnewell I am, pal. Just call me Keno *P.* Hunnewell."

Oliver's face thawed as his emotions came to a boil again. A ruddy color emerged.

"You brazen dog. You won't impress Candace with such a blatant fabrication. She'll see right through you. That's what this is about, isn't it! A scheme to pilfer an upstanding name for yourself. What could you even give her in marriage? If you cared what's best for her, you wouldn't want her to go off barefoot and live in a hut. But *Hunnewell* you'll not steal, no, not by a long shot." Still gripping his white gloves he whipped them across Keno's face.

Keno blinked and turned his head aside, startled by the unexpected action.

The Victorian age gesture, though foppish to Keno, was understood to be disgracefully demeaning. A slap across the face with the dress glove of a lordly foe was as disrespectful a gesture as having your challenger spit in your face in a ballroom with nobles and ladies looking on. Keno would have preferred a fist.

Keno wrenched the gloves from Hunnewell's hand.

"Forget the gloves, pal." He flung them in the shrubs, and struck with his fist, releasing his bitterness in a teeth-jarring thud. Hunnewell reeled backward with a gasp, landing in a bed of twigs and yellow flowers, followed by silence.

～◌◌～

Ambrose's welcoming bungalow waited ahead, and yet Keno felt he couldn't go there now. How could he bring his sin and failure with him? How could he disappoint Ambrose? Disappoint Ambrose, yes, and what about his Lord?

Keno groaned. He fumbled in his steps. Guilt was a heavy shroud draping over his soul. *I have grieved the Holy Spirit.*

The sky was now a black canopy without a flicker of light. *Just like me. You miserable bloke. Why did you do it, why? You knew better, you knew you shouldn't have gone there, you knew your own sinful impulses—*

Fool, he rebuked himself again, lashing his soul. *You've given others ammunition to be scornful of Christians.* Oliver may be a believer, as the Derringtons insist, but he's lukewarm. Now Oliver can find another excuse to justify his disinterest in Bible study.

The wrath of man works not the righteousness of God. Even his hand hurt, so Keno told himself. The same hand that held his Bible when he taught a class.

And Candace will hear the worst details from Oliver. He'll be sure to make me into the instigator of this whole raw debacle. He'll exaggerate everything. And me? I've no audience with her to check his accusations. And what could I say if I did? That my action was justified because he insulted me?

You proved nothing except that you're a fool, a taunting voice seemed to say, as it floated along beside him. *It's the prince who has the land, the money, and the woman. And you? Hah! Even your reputation will be in shreds by the time you're out of this.*

You failed Him again. You're a miserable discard, Keno. You? An assistant pastor to Ambrose? Wrap yourself in shame. You'll never recover from this one . . . never.

*T*he wind stirred waxy green leaves, riffled through palm fronds, and softened the sigh of the sea. Rafe swung lightly over the rail and jumped down, his feet hitting sand.

The evening winds buffeted his loose shirt sleeves. The moon remained indistinct. Foaming wavelets at low tide were just beginning to ride their way up the white sand.

Rafe kept near the side of Hunnewell's large house and headed around back toward the garden and a secondary porch with a door. Where this entry might lead he had no idea. Chinese lanterns glowed on either side of the steps. The door was shut and the two windows facing the porch were dark.

He stopped. A silhouette on the porch moved from the shadowy door toward a railing beside the steps. There, revealed more clearly in the glow of the lanterns he recognized *Eden*. Eden Derrington, youngest granddaughter of patriarch Ainsworth, and the woman he remained engaged to marry—well, *sort of*. There was no date, only an engagement ring that seemed to appear when needed and disappear as if by magic.

Rafe couldn't explain his emotions, but seeing her here now utterly frustrated him. Though he was known for his suave affectation, Eden could rile him as no other. *Now what was she up to?* He stood with hand on hip and narrowed his gaze. Could she possibly have been the spy on the lanai behind the bamboo curtain?

Rafe knew Eden supported the monarchy, even as he had once supported Liliuokalani's right to the throne, but while the reasons for altering his loyalties were sound, he firmly believed Eden remained a royalist for the benefit of her father, Dr. Jerome Derrington, younger son of Ainsworth. Nora, her great-aunt, not only owned the *Gazette*, a newspaper firmly supporting the monarchy, but was also a friend of Liliuokalani. She might even be able to arrange a meeting between Eden's father and Liliuokalani about opening a research clinic on Molokai, where the leper detainment camp was located.

Rafe suspected Eden could be collecting information on the Annexation Club members for Nora to expose in the *Gazette*, or to give to Liliuokalani herself. He knew there wasn't much Eden wouldn't do for her father and his hopes for a clinic.

If so, Eden, I can't go along with your undercover work.

Eden spoke low to someone who must have been out of view in the shrubbery beside the walkway. Rafe couldn't make out what was said, and he came forward into the open.

She turned swiftly with a startled intake of breath and faced him.

"I'm not interrupting, I hope?"

"Oh! Rafe—why, hello. What a surprise to see you."

He turned the corner of his mouth. "A pleasant one, no doubt." He turned toward the shrubbery. "Who's playing hide 'n' seek among the hibiscus?"

A man stood and looked over his shoulder toward him.

"That you, Rafe? I could use a little assistance over here. We have a problem."

Rafe recognized Silas Derrington, born out of wedlock from one of Townsend Derrington's escapades on the mainland. Silas

resembled his father, though he wasn't as blond. Silas had arrived in
Honolulu in April and remained a divisive figure in the Derrington
family. His presence at Kea Lani continued to raise questions and
stir up resentments in his younger half-brother, Zachary.

Rafe walked over to Silas, who nodded toward the shrubbery.
Oliver Hunnewell sat on the ground with head in hand. Rafe
exchanged glances with Silas.

"He was out cold when I came across him," Silas said. "He'll be
all right, though."

"How would you know?" Oliver snapped. "I want a doctor. That
crazy hapa-haole tried to murder me."

Rafe shot him a glance. *Hapa-haole?*

By now, Eden had come and brushed between Rafe and Silas to
kneel beside Oliver. "I'm a nurse," she said briskly. "Let me have a look
at him. My father's not far away if we need him; he's working at
Kalihi Hospital tonight."

Rafe noticed with cynicism that Hunnewell gave in meekly to
her exam. He suspected he did so because she was so alluring. The
thought irritated him.

Rafe stood hands on hips looking down at Oliver scornfully.
"He looks okay to me. I've seen worse. You don't need to be babied,
Oliver. Tell us what happened."

Oliver glared up at him, baring his teeth. "One more crack out
of you, Easton, and—"

"Do be calm, Oliver," Eden soothed. She turned her dark head,
and her green eyes offered Rafe a cool rebuttal. "Patience, if you can
bear it, Mr. Easton. I know best how to handle this. He may have a
concussion."

His gaze held hers evenly.

Eden turned away and stood abruptly. "Let's get him in the
house with something to drink—hot tea, I think."

Tea. Rafe caught her reluctant eye.

"I don't want any tea," Hunnewell snapped, this time at Eden.
"I want a doctor—and a drink." Oliver got to his feet and swayed a

little. Rafe steadied him, but Oliver jerked his arm free, wiping his honey-colored hair back from his sweating forehead. He looked at Silas.

"What are *you* doing here?"

Hunnewell was suspicious of Silas? Interesting.

Silas lifted his brows. "Me? Why I came earlier this evening with Ainsworth Derrington, my grandfather. He wanted me here tonight."

Rafe picked up the defensive spirit in Silas's tone, and the association with *my grandfather*. Ainsworth and the Derrington name were as important in Hawaii as Hunnewell, maybe more so, and Silas was reminding Oliver of that, using his new position for all it was worth. Even Hunnewell appeared to back down a little.

Rafe wouldn't say it, because he didn't want to back Oliver, but he'd already wondered at the wisdom of Ainsworth's decision to bring Silas here tonight. Silas wasn't a Hawaiian. Having only arrived that spring, his loyalties couldn't be as settled as those born in the Islands. Rafe believed Ainsworth was trying to mold Silas into the kind of grandson he wanted in his line of heirs, just as he was pressing his will on Candace for political and economic gains.

Oliver's accusing gaze left Silas and swerved to land on Eden. As soon as he looked at her his features mellowed.

"I didn't expect to see you here tonight either. Did you come over with Rafe?"

Rafe was curious what her explanation would be and watched her carefully, folding his arms.

Eden remained outwardly calm. "Kalihi isn't far from here, you know. I had an hour off-duty and thought I'd walk over and see Grandfather Ainsworth."

Oliver appeared satisfied. Rafe was not. He might have asked how it was she knew Ainsworth was here, but not now. He wanted to get her away from the topic as quickly as he could.

"Let's get him inside. Whatever it is he wants to sip can be sent from the kitchen."

"I don't need any help," Oliver grumbled, glowering at all of them as though they were to blame for his sore jaw and damaged pride. "And I'll be sure to tell Candace when I see her how there's more than one hypocrite in Hawaii among the old missionary families."

Why make an attack on Christianity?

Eden raised her chin with that look of battle, but at the moment Rafe was more curious about what caused Hunnewell to bring up hypocrisy.

"Granted there are hypocrites, but what goads you into bringing that up now?" Rafe asked flatly.

"What goads me? Your crazy hapa-haole friend, that's what. He's a hypocrite and he's dangerous."

Rafe sized him up coldly. "On second thought maybe you should see the doctor. He'll give you something to put you to sleep. You'll feel better at sunrise."

Oliver's color deepened. "I'm not amused, Easton. It so happens your friend jumped me tonight."

"I assume you have Keno in mind."

"Yes. Keno. I was coming through the back garden when someone jumped me. I'm sure he tried to seriously injure me. He's dangerous. He's also been following Candace. Something must be done about him. He needs to be locked up. And I'm the man to press for it."

He's lying. "Keno would never jump you unless you provoked him, and even then he wouldn't come from behind. There's not a cowardly bone in his body. I know him too well."

"I tell you he was hanging around here spying from the bushes like a lunatic."

"Are you saying you saw Keno?" Silas asked.

"He couldn't have," Rafe scoffed.

"I didn't see him just then. I heard something out here and came to investigate."

Alerted, Rafe waited, studying him. Was he telling the truth?

"Someone was prowling around these grounds."

Rafe glanced at Eden's expression. What he'd expected to be there, was not.

"I came to the meeting late, after seeing Candace about our engagement party next week. The meeting here was well under way. I hesitated out front, thinking I didn't want to make a big entrance, so I thought I'd enter the house through the back lanai."

"And did you go there?" Rafe asked lazily.

"No. I saw someone peering in a window and—"

"The front of the house?" Rafe asked.

Oliver looked at him sharply. "A side window, but what does it matter? There was a prowler just the same."

"He could still be around here. Shouldn't we alert Mr. Hunnewell?" Silas said.

"He isn't. Keno knocked me unconscious and must have run off."

"It wasn't Keno," Rafe said.

"I should know who attacked me," Oliver snapped. "It was Keno."

"Sounds as if there may have been two men," Eden spoke up quickly. "Keno, but someone else, too."

Rafe looked at her. He didn't want her saying anything that might involve her with Oliver and Silas.

"Well?" Rafe urged. "What did you do then?" The more he could get out of him, if lying, the greater the chance that the details could derail him.

Oliver scowled at him. "I naturally went toward him to see who it was. Do you think a Hunnewell is a coward?"

"Perish the thought! I'm merely trying to learn what happened."

"Talk of spies for the monarchy was on my mind," Oliver continued. "As I neared the window, I called out. I surprised him and he ran off toward these shrubs."

Rafe was dubious.

"Well, that behavior got my suspicion up fast, as you can well imagine. I was determined to see who the man was. When I rounded this walkway and came near these shrubs here—" Oliver gestured to where they'd found him unconscious—"Keno jumped out at me. The coward didn't even give me a moment to defend myself. He struck me with something, a club, I think."

A flash of anger hardened Rafe. One thing Keno didn't lack was courage.

"Keno wouldn't jump you in the dark, let alone use a club. I don't think he was the man at the window either." *If there was a man at the window.*

"I agree," Silas said. "I haven't known Keno for long, but I admit being a little impressed with his character."

Oliver's face flushed. "Character! After slugging me? And he works at the mission church. Hypocrisy, that's what it is. Isn't he in line to follow Pastor Ambrose Easton? Yet he could have murdered me tonight. He's even deceived all three of you."

Silas drawled, "My cousin Candace may find a trifle bit of hypocrisy in you, as well, Oliver. That *drink* you want won't set well with her."

Oliver's mouth twisted. "I wouldn't sound so pious if I were you, Silas. I've heard New Orleans is a colony for drink and cards."

"Please," Eden said firmly. "Must you gentlemen insult one another?"

Rafe was more interested in the reactions going on and didn't mind the interplay. What had prompted Silas to defend Keno?

Though it was obvious Oliver had been struck, the story he was describing about Keno didn't connect with Rafe. If Keno had been here, what would have brought him? Not to spy, and certainly not to wait to clobber Hunnewell. There had to be something else.

"He said nothing to you? Didn't mention why he'd come here?"

Oliver pushed back his hair from his forehead impatiently. "I told you why he was hiding in the shrubs. I'm saying nothing more. You won't believe me anyway. I'll talk to Marshal Harper about this attack!"

Rafe turned to Silas, who was frowning and gazing in the direction of the beach.

"Anything on your mind, Silas?"

"I wasn't going to mention this, but perhaps I'd better. I saw someone tonight too. He was running toward the gate, but it didn't look like Keno to me."

Rafe studied him for a moment.

"When was this?"

"Say, twenty minutes ago? I came out to roll a smoke. A bit later I heard a big rumpus down in this direction. Most likely where we're standing. A minute or so later someone came through the trees near the front of the house, came as quietly as a little fox in slippers. He—or *she*—didn't see me at first."

Rafe noticed Eden tense slightly. She pushed a dark strand of hair from her cheek in a gesture he knew well . . . she did it when she was uneasy.

"I made a mistake with my cigarette. Whoever it was must have seen the glow, then the little fox took off running toward the beach. By then I thought I'd better have a look down this direction where I'd heard the rumpus. That's when I found Oliver."

"And Eden?" Rafe asked smoothly.

Her eyes swerved to him and narrowed. "I was just arriving."

"Yes, Cousin Eden appeared from the walkway here," Silas said.

Arriving from where? Rafe wondered. He would ask later.

"Eden tried the door on the porch there—to get some help— but it was locked. That's when you came along, Rafe."

Eden's face was veiled in the evening shadows and told Rafe nothing. He was sure all of them knew more than they were telling. That included himself. He wasn't going to give away the fact he had suspected someone behind the bamboo curtain. Not yet.

Oliver straightened his shoulders. "I've had enough of detective games. I'm going inside. I'll tell you one thing, Easton. I'm filing a charge against Keno with Marshal Harper. He won't get by with this kind of behavior. You can tell him I said so, too."

Turning, Oliver took hold of Eden's arm. Rafe was about to intervene but refrained when she assisted him.

"I'll see that my father comes to have a look at your bruises," she was telling Oliver. Silas followed, no doubt to join up with his grandfather and avoid further questions from Rafe.

Rafe watched the three of them walk toward the front of the house.

If Oliver did see someone peering in a window when he arrived, it couldn't have been Keno. And there wasn't a chance Keno would hide on the lanai to spy through the curtain on the meeting.

What had motivated Eden to come here tonight from Kalihi? He smiled a little; was she shocked to have seen him among all the annexationists? What would she do with that information? And had she intended not to be seen? Rafe thought so. Something had gone wrong. Most likely it was the dispute between Oliver and Keno or whoever was out there, and she'd been compelled to reveal herself to Silas. The nurse in her couldn't slip away and leave Oliver unconscious. She may have thought him seriously injured.

She was working tonight at Kalihi Hospital, she'd said. And Dr. Jerome was there also. Interesting . . . and just what were Dr. Jerome's thoughts on annexation? What, if anything, could he gain by garnering information for the monarchy?

What if Eden saw her father slip away and followed him, not realizing what he was up to until she discovered he was on the lanai listening secretly? A walk from Kalihi here to Waikiki was less than fifteen minutes. For the tall, lean Dr. Jerome it could be only ten.

But would Dr. Jerome work against his father, Ainsworth?

When it came to his zeal in opening his clinic on Molokai, Jerome would leave no stone unturned. Yes, Rafe decided soberly. Dr. Jerome could be included in the list of possible spies for the monarchy—*if* it could win him approval from the queen to open his clinic.

He made for the front gate and the road. Foremost in his thoughts was Keno's reason for coming here tonight. The rest could be pushed aside until later, after he'd spoken with Eden.

Keno was no fool when it came to spiritual wrestling with the pull of sin. He'd have understood from the outset that there was a solid chance he could meet up with Oliver here on the Hunnewell beachfront property. So what had prompted him to risk it?

Rafe left through the iron gate. Along the dirt road a smaller path he often used cut through clusters of swaying palm trees and scattered lava formations, to the *Wai Momi*—Pearl River—that the United States Navy was looking at with interest. Pearl River would make a tremendous naval harbor, he thought, but a lot of civil engineering would need to be accomplished first. If annexation was truly in Hawaii's future, Pearl River harbor would be a worthy prize.

He thought he knew where he could find Keno. The same place both of them went in time of spiritual need.

afe jogged along the water's edge on a large section of white sandy beach. There was no moonlight, and the stars that usually shone so brilliantly were now obscured. The waves thundered in, pounding over the low-lying rocks and splashing everything within reach. He took the path inland lined with tall, willowy trees swishing in the wind until he neared the mission church and his uncle Ambrose's bungalow. The lights gleamed in the church where Ambrose was holding a weekly men's Bible group.

The mission church spoke to Rafe of peace, for within rested the treasure chest of truth that would answer all debates and silence quarreling voices of strife.

Rafe hadn't gone much farther when he saw Keno. He hadn't entered the church but was sitting on a large black lava rock a short distance away. The lava rock was on a small mound that commanded a view of the church, the bungalow, and off in the distance, the white sand of the dry beach. Rafe could see he was spiritually browbeaten.

Rafe sighed. He waited for another minute and then climbed the mound to the lava rock. Keno glanced over at him, then went on holding his head as though he had a headache. Rafe stood, leaning against a smooth section of the stone, bracing his foot against the rock, and gazing off at the dark, restless sea, hearing the waves and the wind. Above the rock the dark palms rustled and shook. He remembered that when they were boys they used to climb here and watch for distant ships with binoculars, dreaming of their own ship one day and freedom to roam.

Below, the mission church was in picturesque view, white against dark silhouettes of tropical foliage. He took note of the open door and the lamplight pouring through, remembering the now almost traditional saying attributed to Dr. Jerome Derrington when he'd first built the church. The oversized door was placed in the center; for "Jesus is the true door that opens to forgiveness and access to the Father."

Rafe often thought that Jerome had made a serious error in his life when he'd made his decision to go off into researching a cure for leprosy after Rebecca's internment on Molokai. The decision had taken him away from his daughter Eden and the Derringtons, and sent him exploring exotic regions of the Eastern world. The arduous travels removed him from the work that had been his passion. Had he stayed in Honolulu and preached, his life might have been much more fulfilling—and his health stronger. Rafe hadn't said anything to Eden, but Jerome was looking haggard. Even so, better to try to stop a stampede of wild stallions than to stop Jerome from his quest for his medical research clinic on Molokai.

After a time Keno stirred. "Hunnewell tell you what happened?"

"Hunnewell has his story. What's yours?"

"Well, I thought I was being humble by taking the servant's route to the back entrance when I ran into Oliver. He accused me of sneaking around and he kept insulting me. I tried, but I just couldn't handle it. I'm not so humble after all, but proud. I clobbered him. Afterward, I understood how I ruined my testimony, so I took off. I came here to talk to Ambrose about it, but then I couldn't bring myself to walk into the Bible class full of godly men." He groaned, shaking his head and resting it again in his hands. "He's going to be mighty ashamed of his 'protégé.'"

"Don't you know him better than that?"

"Why shouldn't he be ashamed? When this gets around—" Keno looked down at the lighted windows of the church. "I'm his assistant—or I was. I'll be an embarrassment to him."

"Ambrose isn't the kind of pastor that needs to go around defending his reputation. He's an undershepherd to the Great Shepherd. All he'll worry about is restoring an injured sheep."

"Ultimately it's the Lord I've failed."

"The Lord is merciful. We have an Advocate with the Father. He's in the foot-washing business, remember?"

"Yes, but knocking people unconscious . . ."

"It wouldn't have happened if you hadn't already been wrestling with anger. I know, because it's one of my areas of spiritual warfare."

Keno understood Rafe's long journey of anger where Townsend Derrington was concerned. Even as a boy of twelve he had blamed Townsend for his father's death. There'd been a time soon after Townsend had married his mother when he'd suggested adopting Rafe and making him a Derrington, but Rafe had refused so vigorously that even Celestine had the courage to tell Townsend no, a stance she didn't take often enough when Townsend resorted to bullying tactics. Rafe had watched as Townsend eventually got his selfish way in marrying Celestine and wrenching control of Easton assets from her, and squandering them through the years. As Rafe grew into manhood his anger and dislike simmered.

"I'm in no position to lecture you," Rafe said gravely. "Except I know how dangerous anger can be when left unchecked. It can become one of Satan's strongholds to war against us."

Keno sat in the shadows, still holding his head.

"Strongholds make it easier for the Enemy to lay traps in our path. Both of us need to watch our vulnerabilities. We know sin crouches at the door like a lion, ready to spring."

"I could sense the lion crouching when I got angry, and he sure did injure his prey this time."

"Now he wants to see you crawl off into the wilderness of guilt and despair and lick your wounds. If you do he's won another battle. If we doubt that Christ can really cleanse us of unrighteousness, he has us out of the race and by the side of the road."

"You're right . . . I need to move on. Get the incident right with the Lord, then keep walking."

Rafe grew silent. They watched the activity down at the mission church, where the meeting was over, and some of the men had begun to drift out and over to the bungalow to greet Noelani and enjoy her little coconut cakes.

"But you know," Keno said, "the men down there are going to hear about me and Hunnewell."

"They know you. They don't know Hunnewell. They'll stand with you. If they don't, their fellowship would be superficial, wouldn't it?"

"Candace will hear about it."

"Candace will make up her own mind. But be sure Oliver's going to fill her ears with lies. He's already claiming you hid in the bushes and jumped out at him with a club. He's even talking of going to Marshal Harper."

Keno groaned. "Anything to make me a villain."

"Look here, Keno, it's also time to face the painful truth about losing Candace. The engagement is next week. She's going through with it."

Keno came to his feet, pacing. "She can't!"

"She will. She's the kind who'll walk barefoot over coals of fire if expected of her as a woman of honor. So will Eden. Well, you know how exasperating Eden is." Rafe stooped, then snatched up a piece of black lava and threw it. "She's going to Molokai with her father no matter what. So I've decided this will be the route of her emotional release. But it will certainly take patience."

Keno was deep within his struggle. "There's got to be more to

Candace's sudden decision than pleasing her grandfather."

"There is something more. I'm sure of it," Rafe mused. "Eden knows what it is."

Keno looked at him. "How do you know?"

"She looks away when I ask her about Candace."

Keno sank back down on the rock looking miserable. "*Women!*"

"You're not alone. Remember what I've gone through with Miss Green Eyes." He tried now to lighten the mood for Keno. "I've been thinking. If this was another time I'd put Eden on the *Minoa* and sail the Caribbean. We'd marry aboard ship. And there'd be nothing she could do about it."

Keno broke a smile. "That's an idea, pal. For both us."

"That's right. We'll take them with us and sail for Jamaica. I've heard land down there is cheap. Sugar grows as good as it does in Hawaii. We'll begin plantations and have dozens of sons to leave it to."

"A perfect plan." Keno stood. "And if this were the 1600s, as you say, we'd get by with it."

"Ah, those were the days."

"Maybe we'd get by with it now . . . ?"

Rafe looked at him, saw his serious expression, and laughed.

The moon unexpectedly came out from behind some clouds and sent a silvery glow on the grounds of the mission. The white building and cross gleamed like a beacon of hope, a lighthouse on a cliff in dangerous weather.

"We'll think about it. First, why did you go to Hunnewell's place tonight?"

Keno's lighter mood struck bottom again. His cautious expression warned Rafe. *Trouble ahead.*

Keno retrieved a folded paper from his shirt pocket and handed it to Rafe.

"Sorry, pal. We've been so busy with my problems I forgot about yours. Ambrose got this telegram tonight from your mother in San Francisco. Ambrose said it's important. So I went looking for you and walked into the Devil's campground."

At the mention of San Francisco the winds of conflict stirred to life again.

Rafe took the message, unfolded it, and read in the shaft of moonlight the words flashing the danger signal.

"Townsend is here. I believe he is watching the house. Parker Judson called authorities but Townsend gone again by time they arrived. He's still here in San Francisco. Parker has promised Kip and I will be kept secure. Even so, I'm uneasy."

He reread the message several times and then handed it to Keno to read.

In the tense silence, Rafe walked to the edge of the hill and looked off thoughtfully. The scene below would have made a pleasant painting to grace any wall. Stately palms, a neat white church, a centered cross trumpeting God's forgiveness, and men dispersing with Bibles in hand. Ambrose was standing in the doorway, his sturdy form outlined in the light from within. The sea breeze carried laughter that drifted up to the rock. All is well, the scene declared.

Except Townsend's in San Francisco.

Townsend, who had allowed Rafe's father to die from a fall he'd taken from a cliff, in order to gain his wife and his land. Townsend, who'd tried to gain Aunt Nora's estate by destroying her mind or body with a drug. Townsend, who had alerted the Board of Health about Kip's background on Molokai to heap revenge on Rafe for regaining Hanalei; and Townsend, who had set the flame to Ling Li's hut on Kea Lani because he'd suspected Ling of knowing about his reprehensible deed done years earlier to Matt Easton.

The words *Townsend is here* stared up at him as if dripping blood on the paper. At once the challenge to stop him gripped Rafe's emotions. Only the knowledge that his mother and Kip were secure within Parker Judson's house allowed him a reprieve from immediately packing his bags.

The crosswinds of conflict were beginning again, this time not against Keno but his own soul. He sensed the storm would be over-turning some structures built on sand before the tide turned back and the winds calmed, if they calmed at all.

Keno joined him on the hill's edge, handing back the telegraphed message from Celestine. His eyes were grave as they focused on Rafe.

"That lion you mentioned crouching at the door? I think he's licking his chops again," Keno said.

he men from the Bible study meeting had returned home. Ambrose's bungalow had settled down to a strained silence. Outside the door and windows, the rabid wind snapped and snarled at the tropical vegetation. In the kitchen Noelani was cleaning up the dishes left by the men's group, always her devoted duty in the sanctified work. "It's the one thing I can do. Dear Ambrose tells me how needful I am," she would say, and then she would smile.

Rafe paced the living room floor, one hand at the back of his neck. He felt a headache coming on. Keno leaned his shoulder into the wall, staring glumly at the floor. The windows rattled. A branch clawed at the side of the bungalow.

Ambrose's concern was fixed on his nephew.

"Let the San Francisco police track him down, Rafe."

"The way the Honolulu police handled Townsend from this end?"

Rafe was frustrated. The authorities were shorthanded, and slow. Townsend had outsmarted them easily enough. He must have used a disguise to board the steamer.

"Ainsworth wanted Townsend to escape from the Islands," Rafe stated. "He didn't want him questioned for fear the newspapers would run with the story and ruin the Derrington name. He put quiet pressure on the authorities to look the other way."

"You know my opinion," Ambrose stated soberly. "The authorities should never be left to the persuasion of the socially powerful, or its wealthiest elite, lest tyranny reign."

"Another reason for the US Constitution and Bill of Rights. But regardless of any argument made, they have your witness that Townsend admitted it," Rafe said. "He burned down Ling's hut to silence him on Matt's death. Harper has spoken to Ling. I've shown him the signed and dated letter Nora and Candace sent me. Townsend feared Nora would include details about Matt's death in her Derrington family history. That's why he tried to steal it at Tamarind House."

"But did he ever get the facts? He said nothing of that to me or Ainsworth that night at Kea Lani," Ambrose said.

"He must have gotten hold of Nora's writing the night Zach trailed him to Koko Head. Townsend considered her a threat when he saw that Nora felt it her obligation to present the truth in her book before she passed away. Then Ling became the next problem for Townsend. Ling was a witness to Matt's death. He had to silence Ling to undermine Nora's book. It was Townsend who burned down his hut; Townsend entered Tamarind House searching for Nora's manuscript to see if she'd told the truth about Matt; and Townsend walked away and let my father die. Townsend knew Ling was the only witness against him."

"What we don't have," Ambrose said, "is Townsend's confession about Nora."

"Or the heart medication," Rafe gritted, pacing again. "If we'd had hard evidence at the time, it would have supported Dr. Jerome's suggestion that a little arsenic could have been added."

Keno stirred. "I thought he and Doc Bolton both told the marshal they couldn't swear the medicine was poisoned?"

"They did tell him that," Ambrose said. "They had no other course, since poor, confused Nora tossed away the evidence. Afterward there wasn't much Marshal Harper could do."

Rafe wondered if Great-aunt Nora Derrington was as confused as she pretended. He had reviewed her folly far more times than he cared to remember, and he did so again now, with the result just as frustrating as before. Nora had destroyed the only evidence that could have proven she'd been deliberately poisoned.

"My dear boy! There's no reason for you to become livid with me about it," she told him when he'd questioned her soon afterward. "How was I to know the bottle would be crucial? All I knew was I'd become ill after the first dose of that dreadful medication Dr. Bolton prescribed. I've never set much regard on his prescriptions anyway. If it hadn't been for Eden urging me, I wouldn't have taken it at all. This time, I thought he'd genuinely erred, that the concoction had become rancid, and so I threw it away. Quite sensible, I assure you."

Whether it was or not, the deed was done. It was unfortunate that she had complained of medical incompetence, and refused to listen to Candace and see another physician. As a result it had taken two weeks before Eden and Dr. Jerome arrived at Tamarind House where they discovered just how ill she'd been. Arriving even a week earlier might have meant finding the bottle by the incinerator in back of the house. Rafe had gone there to search, but by then there was nothing but charred rubble.

Rafe poured himself some coffee. Hindrances and obstructions had hemmed him in for weeks. The failure to gather enough legal evidence to pursue Townsend had become a constant source of concern.

Now, hearing the details over again, along with the telegraph from Celestine in San Francisco, urged him to move forward on his own. If the Derrington family wouldn't opt for justice, then he'd take matters into his own hands when he arrived. He understood that his conviction worried Ambrose. Keno was right about the stalking lion out to devour. Rafe could feel its hot breath following him, urging him to become the lone avenger.

His mind veered off to Ainsworth. He had immediately taken advantage of the absence of the medication as proof that Nora was mistaken about poison. He'd urged her with great zeal to hold off filing legal charges against her nephew until after the trip to Washington. To others he said, "Nora is getting old, you know. She may have imagined the poisoned medication. We know she hasn't been in prime health lately. It's not surprising that she took to bed for a few weeks."

Whether Ainsworth actually believed this scenario was doubtful, and from the beginning he was looking for ways to delay the scandal from breaking in Honolulu, vexed beyond measure over how it would tarnish the Derrington name. "Especially now," he'd protested. "I assure you this is a crucial hour for the success or failure of the annexation movement. A headline of attempted murder by my son would be a gold mine for the monarchists."

Rafe understood Ainsworth's fears. Townsend's reputation would be used by the opposition and as a battering ram to topple the movement.

"As you say, we don't have Townsend's confession," Rafe said. "But then again he would never admit to putting arsenic in her heart medicine. When he saw what she'd written, that he'd walked away and left my father sprawled on the lava rocks, he knew his secret was no longer hidden, that Nora would unmask him. He had to silence her. And he would have if she'd been the sort to keep taking that medication. One more dose would likely have struck her."

When Townsend had showed up at Kea Lani, he denied everything Ambrose and Ainsworth put to him, then he became arrogant. He admitted deliberately setting fire to Ling's hut to silence Ling and his wife. He even admitted the worst—that he'd left Rafe's father to die in the lava bed where he'd fallen after an argument over Celestine. True, Townsend claimed he didn't think Matt would have lived anyway, but even if it wasn't premeditated murder—and Rafe had doubts about that—his action was willful contributory neglect toward manslaughter.

Rafe's chiseled jaw set. Townsend had wanted his father dead. He had wanted Matt's wife and Matt's land. And he got them, for a time. Now the choices he'd made along life's journey were slowly gaining on him. The clock was ticking. He lost the treasured Easton land and enterprise and the beautiful Celestine. And he risked murder to protect himself, and this time he'd failed to bring it off. What he might do next was the question that worried Rafe. *I must get to San Francisco.*

"As strange as this may sound, lad, it's you who might be the one in the most danger from Townsend. I believe he's always resented you, even when you were a boy. You were the smart one, the good-looking one, the inheritor of all things Easton, including Celestine's motherly pride and affection. And now Satan has filled his heart with hate. You're the one who has shined the light on him. And what's revealed isn't pleasant to look at."

A confident knock on the front door interrupted.

Noelani went to answer. Keno came behind her from the kitchen with a plate of coconut cakes and a mug of coffee.

"Evening, Noelani," a male voice said from the doorway. "Hate to trouble you this time of the evening. Weather's kicking up a storm, too. Thought I might get blown away. Say, is Ambrose still up? If he is, I'd like a few minutes of his time."

Rafe recognized the voice of Marshal Percy Harper. So Hunnewell carried through on his threat to call the authorities. Rafe smoldered. He caught Keno's eye. *Trouble. Hunnewell style. Be prepared.*

Keno sighed and set the plate down. Ambrose stood up from where he'd been sitting as Noelani, the lines in her forehead deepening beneath her white hair, led Harper into the room. Harper paused with a look of surprise on his brown face when he saw Keno. Rafe wondered if he'd expected Keno to have taken for the hills.

Keno came, coffee mug still in hand, looking for a place to set it down. Rafe offered to hold it.

Keno extended a friendly hand to Harper. "Evening, Marshal. Looking for me?"

Harper hesitated, then shook hands. "Hello, Keno. I'm surprised to find you here, I admit."

"On a Monday night after the men's meeting I'm always here, sir." He added, "I've nothing to hide."

"I hope not, son. Then were you here at the church tonight?"

A moment of silence pervaded the bungalow. "Well no, I wasn't."

"Where were you?"

"Wait a minute, Percy, if you will," Ambrose intervened. "We all know why you're here. I'd rather Keno kept silent than say too much until we know what charge, if any, Oliver Hunnewell has made against my wife's nephew."

"Sorry, Ambrose. I'm not liking this, but it's my obligation. Mr. Hunnewell says Keno trespassed his father's property tonight, hid in the shrubs, and jumped him, using a club, as he came along the walk. Had to do with Mr. Derrington's granddaughter, Miss Candace."

"He's lying," Keno said. "It was Oliver Hunnewell in the shrubs. I walked by going—"

"Then you were on Hunnewell property?"

"Sure, but I wasn't trespassing—"

"I sent him, Percy," Ambrose said. "An important message came to me over the wire from Miss Celestine. The message was for her son, Rafe. I asked Keno to take it to him. Keno wouldn't have been there if I hadn't asked him."

Percy Harper looked at Rafe for the first time. Something in his eyes informed Rafe that Harper was suspicious about more than Keno. Harper was close within the circle of trusted individuals around Liliuokalani. He and his wife even lived in a cottage near Iolani Palace property. The Reform Party hadn't wanted Percy Harper appointed as chief marshal, but the queen had pressed ahead and eventually won his appointment. Rafe had nothing against him; he seemed a fair fellow, but definitely against Thurston's annexation group.

"You were at Hunnewell's tonight?"

Rafe smiled disarmingly. "Let me see . . . there were several places on my agenda . . ." He tapped his chin. "Hmm, you know I'm thinking I need to be judicious about possibly betraying the confidence of some long-standing Hawaiian patriots. You should go directly to Hunnewell and ask who was visiting him tonight."

Harper eyed him. "You want me to ask Hunnewell? He's claiming Keno beat him up."

"I mean Hunnewell *Senior*. Yes, Marshal, he's the gentlemen to talk with. I think you'll find he'll tell you his son Oliver has been overly emotional these last few weeks. You know, the engagement to the Derrington granddaughter and all? Well, the ordeal has been wearing down on poor Oliver, if you know what I mean. I'm confident you'll find Thaddeus Hunnewell will make certain his son withdraws any spurious complaint against my friend Keno. Mr. Hunnewell's too smart to want an innocent, hardworking assistant to Pastor Ambrose brought up before the magistrate for an imagined evil by poor Oliver."

Marshal Harper considered Rafe. He pursed his lips and looked at Keno, then back to Rafe. "Is there something going on here I don't know about?"

"Why, no, sir," Rafe said. "We're hoping to keep Mr. Hunnewell Senior from a little embarrassment over his son. He wouldn't like it if the papers begin printing stories about Oliver, you understand, and about his guests tonight."

Harper's smile was cynical. "I'm getting the picture, Easton. But Oliver's mighty upset right now. Imagined, or no. If I don't at least bring Keno downtown for questioning, I'm sure to get some generous displeasure from Hunnewell *Junior* that's going to cause me a heap of trouble. And I assure you and Ambrose that I don't need that."

"I certainly understand those concerns," Rafe said with affected compassion.

Keno spoke up, "No wonder the Americans wanted a Bill of

Rights—and no arrests without some proof."

Harper scowled at Keno. "You're under Hawaiian law now."

"Hold on, friends," Ambrose intervened, stepping between Harper, Keno, and Rafe. "Nothing's gained by allowing anger to referee. Percy, I can assure you Keno's not the young fellow to hide in shrubs with a club. If he'd meant to voice his unhappiness over Miss Candace, Keno would do it face-to-face."

"Well, I've no bones to pick with that. I admit this whole thing surprises me. Still—"

"If you do bring him in," Rafe said, "it will just feed Oliver's pride. He'll think he can harass anybody he wants because he's a Hunnewell."

Harper sighed. "I'm sorry, Easton, Ambrose, but I've got to take him downtown for more questioning."

"Then he'll have a lawyer present," Rafe said evenly. "I'm coming with Keno. I'll call Withers on the Big Island. A boat can bring him over shortly."

A dignified female voice sounded from the open doorway. "None of this is necessary, gentlemen; I saw everything that happened from start to finish. I'll sign an affidavit if it's needed."

Rafe turned to the door. Eden stood there. Her dark hair was windblown, her lovely face strained and looking tired, but her green eyes were bright and concerned as she stared at Marshal Percy Harper.

She entered the room, and Noelani closed the door behind her. Noelani's aged face beamed at Eden, the girl she'd brought up here at the bungalow while Dr. Jerome Derrington had chased the wind seeking cures for the incurable disease.

Eden was still in her gray uniform with the white pinafore emblazoned with a red cross. Her cap, however, was in her hand. She was out of breath and Rafe thought she might have run most of the way to get here in time. It must have been some struggle in this wind. How had she learned Marshal Harper was on his way? He recalled that she'd gone inside the Hunnewell house with Oliver to tend to his "wounds." Evidently she had overheard Oliver send for Harper.

Before Rafe could respond to her arrival she came up beside Ambrose and faced Harper eye to eye. "Shall I accompany you downtown, Marshal, or would you take my testimony here?"

"Here's good enough," Rafe said, hands on hips, meeting Harper eye to eye with a message he couldn't miss.

"No need to go downtown, Miss Derrington. We can sit down here, and perhaps get this situation settled tonight. That is, if, er, I can just excuse myself for a moment? I need a writing pen and ink and some paper. Ambrose, do you have any?"

"Right over here."

Rafe drew up a chair for Eden, indicating for her to sit. Her gaze swerved to his. He lifted a brow with innocence, his smile disarming. "Always thinking of your comfort, my sweet."

Once she was seated, he leaned over near her ear.

"I appreciate what you're doing to protect Keno," he whispered, showing the reason he'd wanted her to sit, "but don't put yourself in harm's way. Yours truly wouldn't like it."

"Always bossy," she whispered back, smiling sweetly.

"Just looking out for your safety, darling—and mine." His gaze held hers soberly. "After you've convinced Harper, you and I need to chat. You can tell me what you were doing at Hunnewell's place tonight."

"And if I don't?"

He ignored the return challenge and looked over at the marshal and Ambrose exchanging words in a low tone. Straightening to his full height he told her, "I'll escort my ministering angel back to Kalihi. We can chat then, or are you finished for the night and going to Kea Lani?"

She released a breath and shook her head no. "Afraid not. I need to go back to Kalihi. I'll be helping Lana," she said of her aunt, "and Dr. Jerome." She always called her father "Dr. Jerome" when speaking of him to others instead of "my father." When she spoke of her mother it was always "Rebecca," sometimes Mother, but never would she address her as "Mum."

"You look exhausted," he said, concerned. "If Harper starts to badger you I'm going to clobber him. Then he can haul both Keno and me downtown."

She smiled. "If you want to help me, you can borrow Ambrose's buggy to bring me back later," she said.

"You're working too hard. I don't like it. You didn't expect to be seen tonight at Hunnewell's, did you?"

Eden said nothing. His mouth turned. "That's what I thought. You have guilt written all over your beautiful face."

"Really, Rafe! Go now, the marshal's looking at us. He may think you're passing me information."

"Just don't pass any to him. Nothing to put yourself at risk, darling. How about a cup of good Kona coffee?"

She smiled. "I thought you'd never ask. It'll help me face the dreadful Marshal Harper."

He spoke to Noelani, who returned with two cups of coffee fresh from Hanalei Plantation, one for Eden, the other for the marshal, who sniffed it appreciatively. "Ah."

A few minutes later amid the growling wind, Eden began giving her testimony to Harper, who sat across from her writing it down. Rafe stood nearby, lounging against the wall, listening intently, and watching Harper's response.

"Keno was hurrying along on the walkway, going toward the back of Mr. Hunnewell's house, toward the servant's and delivery boy's entry. He seemed to be in a pleasant mood; he was whistling one of Charles Wesley's hymns. Sure evidence, Marshal, that he didn't have violence on his mind. Suddenly to his shock, and mine, Oliver Hunnewell came out from behind the hibiscus bushes and demanded to know what Keno was doing there."

The marshal twiddled the writing pen between thumb and forefinger. "And what did Keno say to Oliver Hunnewell?"

"He said he'd come to deliver an important message to Rafe

Easton, that Pastor Ambrose sent him."

"And was Rafe Easton inside the Hunnewell beach house?"

Rafe saw the eagerness in Harper's eyes as they glued upon her. Eden hesitated.

Vigilant, Rafe fixed his cool gaze on Harper. Earlier he'd been sure in his own mind that Eden's presence at Hunnewell's had been a spy mission for someone. At first he'd thought she might be cooperating with the marshal himself, since his group surrounded Liliuokalani and fully supported the throne. Now Rafe knew better. The marshal wouldn't have blundered by openly asking her that question in front of Rafe. He'd have tried to gloss over her presence there and conceal what she'd learned. Yet he was putting her on the spot.

"I have no idea whether Mr. Easton was inside the house, Marshal. The first I saw him, he showed up to help Oliver Hunnewell."

Marshal Harper turned to Rafe, wrinkling his brow. "All right, Easton. Were you there tonight?"

"You just heard Miss Derrington. I helped free Hunnewell from his sprawling entanglement in the hibiscus bushes. So, I guess you might say I must have been there."

"Inside the Hunnewell house?"

"What has that to do with Oliver's complaint against Keno?"

"It has nothing to do with it," Keno spoke up.

Eden interrupted gracefully, "Marshal, may I please go on with my testimony?" She continued whether he was ready or not.

"I too, like Rafe, and Keno, was just arriving." She looked demure, even noble. Rafe kept his own feelings from display by lifting his coffee cup as soon as he expected Harper's eyes to shift over to him, which they did with curious intent.

"And what were you doing at Hunnewell's, Miss Derrington?"

Rafe saw her pluck her sleeve, then lift her chin slightly. His mouth tipped. He could read her actions like a book, but Harper couldn't.

"I had a break at the hospital. I needed fresh air, so I went for a walk."

And somehow ended up in the back garden of Hunnewell's house?

Rafe thought. Harper, however, was apparently satisfied.

"And you didn't see Keno jump Oliver Hunnewell and hit him with a club?"

Keno made a noise in his throat. Ambrose laid a hand on his shoulder to silence him.

"No," Eden said firmly. "That didn't happen, Marshal. Oliver Hunnewell was quite angry with Keno and using abusive language."

"Such as?"

"Oh—racist talk. Hapa-haole dog, mongrel, that typical thing. Keno should return to his own people and leave Candace Derrington to her better equals, like the Hunnewells. Keno announced that he, too, was a Hunnewell, that his biological father was Oliver's blood uncle, who'd returned to England. When Keno said that, Oliver's emotions exploded."

Harper dropped his pen and had to pick it up from the floor. "Hunnewell!" he repeated. He looked over at Keno. Keno gave a brief nod, appearing embarrassed by the disclosure rather than demonstrating pride. The marshal looked quickly back at Eden.

Rafe, however, showed not so much as a flicker of surprise. He already knew. Keno had come to him as soon as he'd heard it from his grandmother last week.

"Is this true, Ambrose?" Harper asked, turning round on his seat to look across at him.

"It is, Percy. Keno's Grandmother Luahine has recently sworn so, witnessed by a lawyer. I've only learned of Keno's biological father recently. Luahine was the midwife."

Harper looked over at Noelani, who stood near the kitchen, arms folded under her apron. "Noelani?"

"Yes, it's true. Keno's mother was my youngest sister, Pearline. She was the prettiest thing as a young girl. It was bad for her, though. It went to her head. Philip P. Hunnewell went for her in a mighty way and she believed him."

Keno conveniently slipped away into the kitchen, presumably to refill his empty cup.

"Pearline faced disaster in her life because she wouldn't come with me when Luahine wanted to bring us here to the mission church. On Sunday mornings she was always not feeling well, so we'd go off without her. Then we found out she was seeing Philip Hunnewell during that time." She shook her silver head sadly. "She called the baby Philip, only because she thought he would come back from England one day to marry her. Well, she died a few days after Philip's birth, and Mother Luahine renamed him Keno."

Harper was scribbling away. Rafe wondered if he even remembered why he had come. When he finished and looked up expectantly, Eden continued.

"Oliver was shocked, then horribly angry over Keno's disclosure. He lashed out and struck Keno across the face with his white gloves. I thought he was about to strike Keno again with his fist, when Keno struck back. Oliver fell into the bushes. It all took place quickly. The next minute Keno turned and left through the front gate. Then . . ."

Eden hesitated, and Rafe wondered why.

She looked uneasy, but then continued. "My cousin Silas Derrington appeared also from the bushes and trees and went over to Oliver. I joined him. I went to the porch door to get help, but that door was locked. A minute later Rafe Easton walked up and joined Silas in aiding Oliver to his feet. Well, that's all, Marshal."

Harper's pen scratched its way from paragraph to paragraph.

In the moments of quiet, Keno returned from the kitchen, sober-faced and silent.

When Harper concluded his notes he handed the testimony over to Eden to read. Rafe came up behind her chair and resting his hands on the back leaned over her shoulder to have a look for himself. Eden, after reading, handed it to Rafe. He ignored Harper. If he hadn't understood there was something more between them than acquaintanceship, he must have realized it now. He looked directly at Eden's left hand where an engagement ring sparkled boldly.

A minute later Rafe handed the testimony back to Eden, who

met his gaze. She appeared to read his thoughts, for she took the pen, signed her name, and dated it.

Harper stood to his feet, apparently satisfied.

"Well, we'll leave the matter where it is for the night. I'll report this downtown, have a conversation with Mr. Thaddeus Hunnewell in the morning, and be in touch."

Eden rose from the chair. He turned to her. "Thank you, Miss Derrington." He glanced for his hat. Noelani handed it to him. "Thanks for the coffee, Noelani . . . nice Kona beans you grow at Hanalei, Easton. You've got a winner on your hands." He turned to Ambrose. "Sorry about all this, Ambrose. This testimony from Miss Derrington is likely to settle matters. After Hunnewell Sr. reads this, I think he'll have his son shut the door on the matter. Well, I'm off." He put his hat on. Rafe opened the door for him and the wind rushed in and blew some papers onto the floor. "Storm's brewing. Good night folks, sorry for the trouble, but you know my duties. See you around, Keno."

After Harper left the bungalow, a relieved but still tense silence held them in its grip. Rafe turned to Keno. "So that's why Oliver boiled over. Got slapped with white gloves did you? Tsk, tsk, my good lad. What did you expect? One doesn't intrude into the ruling class, Keno. That's something which cannot be allowed. It's acceptable to have a haole father if one's poor, but a haole father with the name of Hunnewell and a middle initial of P?" Rafe arched a dark brow. "You've offended the elite pedigree of Oliver."

Noelani laughed. Ambrose affected a frown at Rafe. "Such sarcasm."

"But fitting," Eden said with a laugh. "You know what will happen now, don't you?"

"Of course," Rafe said. "The news will circulate Honolulu's better families that Keno is actually 'Philip' and his initial P is for 'Pepperidge.' The whispers will come round to Candace and—"

Ambrose cleared his throat. Rafe halted.

"Yes?" Keno said with enthusiasm. "And then?"

"Then," Rafe said dourly, "Ainsworth will also hear of it. He'll warn Candace it's all hocus pocus, and that she must go through with marriage to Oliver for the good of the Derrington name. And duty will call for the allegiance of our fair maiden Candace."

Keno put the plate of coconut cakes down on the table and stared at them with lost appetite.

Eden folded her arms and tapped her foot. "The humor ceased when you poked fun at my cousin Candace. She's very straitlaced and dedicated to the family."

"You're not suggesting, darling, she takes after you?"

"They are two of a kind," Ambrose said good-naturedly.

Eden turned to Keno. "How did you discover your father was a Hunnewell?"

"Grandmother Luahine told me last week. I was over at the hut to see her and about fifty other relatives—all Hawaiian, by the way. I think she believed she was giving me fodder to help win Candace. Having a Hunnewell for a father would turn things around for me, or so she thought. In reality it's made matters more complicated."

"I knew it wouldn't help Keno," Noelani said sadly. "I would have talked to Luahine first if I'd known she was about to reveal secrets. It's not as if the Hunnewells will receive him as part of the family, or suddenly give him an inheritance."

Keno straightened his shirt collar. "I'd no intention of mentioning it." He looked at Ambrose. "Anger loosened my tongue. You warned me, but I didn't listen well enough."

"We all can do better at listening, lad. There's not a one of us who can boast in our own strength before the Lord. If we do, it's likely we'll come tumbling down the hill," Ambrose encouraged.

"Anyway, I wouldn't force myself on the Hunnewell family," Keno said.

"Of course you wouldn't," Ambrose agreed. "You don't want to make Hunnewell or anyone else think you can be bought. When Abram rescued Lot and the king of Sodom from the enemy who'd taken them captive, the king of Sodom was thinking of paying

Abram for his deed by giving him the booty. Abram refused it. He wouldn't take as much as a shoelace from the king of Sodom. Blessing, true blessing, comes from God alone."

Eden stood to her feet and checked her watch. "I should start back to the hospital. Aunt Nora will want my help soon."

"I'll need to borrow your buggy, Ambrose," Rafe said.

"It's still hitched. I thought we might need it."

Keno came up to Eden, took her hand with eloquent display, and bowed deeply. "*Merci, mademoiselle*. Ah, but how can I thank you for coming to my aid? Henceforth, I am at your beck and call."

Eden laughed and retrieved her nurse's cap from the table. "I'll remember your pledge of chivalry, Keno. I may need it someday."

Eden's working beside Hartley and a father mesmerized by a belief in "herbal" cures for leprosy was indeed a matter that could lead to a wee bit of trouble. Dr. Jerome was a decent man, and Rafe didn't doubt his motives were to do good and honor God, but motives and deeds did not always bring an expected harvest.

Rafe walked Eden out the door and closed it behind them, pausing for a moment on the bungalow steps. The wind buffeted them and the sky was thick with clouds.

"We're likely to get drenched before we get there," he said.

They moved ahead to the horse and buggy, with Eden appearing anxious to be on her way back to Kalihi Hospital.

The challenge to win a confession from the prized beauty he had yet to fully capture would not be a simple task. Eden was never simple. As the wind whipped her dress and tore loose some strands of her hair from their pins, he decided the challenge was not merely stimulating, but worth every emotional moment it would demand.

Chapter Six
A Matter of Trust

*E*den listened to the horse and buggy *clip-clop* down the dirt road toward Kalihi Hospital. There was no moon tonight, and thick, low clouds promising rain were rolling in overhead. She heard the sounds of the sea and the palm trees swaying along the roadside in the muggy wind.

This was the first time she'd been with Rafe in several weeks. His work in the Hawaiian Legislature, the pineapple plantation, and the trips to Hanalei Kona coffee plantation on the Big Island kept him more than occupied.

Eden didn't know whether to be relieved by his seeming indifference to her of late, or to allow her feminine ego to become miffed by his lack of ardor. They'd already decided there should be little "ardor" between them, as marriage must wait for at least another year.

The tense silence between them persisted. Her apprehension mixed with concern over his silence. *He must be thinking of the message Keno brought him. What was in it?*

She glanced toward him, worried. Rafe wasn't the only one who had questions that needed answering. She had a few of her own and wondered about the correct time to bring them to the surface. Something important had surely prompted Keno to risk meeting Oliver tonight.

Despite the sultry night she shivered as she thought about the reason that had brought her to that garden. Rafe would think of questions that even the marshal had failed to follow through on. She had been surprised by how the marshal hadn't asked her the most important questions.

Eden turned her head slightly, and from beneath her lashes looked at Rafe, trying to guess his thoughts. Certainly not on her! She looked at the engagement ring on her finger and winced. There was no light, and the gorgeous diamond was as muted of its sparkling glory as she and Rafe were of romantic words.

She studied his profile, the strong cut of the jaw, the breezes that ruffled his wavy dark hair, the muscled body. So good-looking that Claudia Hunnewell, Oliver's sister, had said Eden was foolish not to "catch him" while she had the opportunity. "Don't you realize how many wealthy daughters of other planters have their eye on him? And here you go traipsing off to Molokai with your father." Eden's fingers tightened in her lap.

They just didn't understand her goals. Well, her cousin Candace did, to some degree. Though Candace had so many problems recently with her engagement to Oliver that she was preoccupied, spending most of her time at the Koko Head house with Great-aunt Nora. Candace had written her, "If my dear mother had been a leper on Molokai, and I'd never been able to meet her, I'd change many of my plans to do so. And as for working with Uncle Jerome, that's what you've been training for these years. It seems to me that postponing marriage for a year to fulfill a dream you've had since childhood isn't too much to ask. Rafe appears very mature about this. If you don't go before your mother dies, you'll always grieve that you didn't meet her. Later on in your marriage, you might even blame Rafe. No, it's better to get all of this worked out before you vow before God. Knowing Rafe's maturity, he thinks so as well."

Yes, Rafe Easton was a man that many women would be, and *were*, even now, setting their cap for, even ignoring the fact that he was engaged.

She looked at him again. Rugged, handsome, sound in the Christian faith, and his eyes, when they chose to meet hers—which presently they seemed not to want to do—were energetic beneath thick lashes.

The tension in his strong body could almost be felt. He wore what some would describe as a moody demeanor, but she'd known him too long to ever think of Rafe as moody or temperamental. He was one of the most unruffled and self-disciplined men she'd met— when he wanted it that way. And when he did, neither she nor anyone else could dissect his emotions. He was a master at placing them out of reach.

What should she tell him about the Hunnewell incident? She could not as yet bare her soul's secrets to him. She'd grown up keeping her emotions under lock and key and she could not easily surrender the key, not even to Rafe Easton, the one man, besides Ambrose, she *trusted*. She wanted that trust with her father, but as yet did not have it. But because she still didn't feel free to share her true motives with Rafe, there would be an unpleasant standoff between them, something she did not want but seemed unable to keep from happening. If only he would not insist on knowing *why* she had gone there tonight, but there was little hope of that!

Earlier, she had felt her heart sink when she'd seen him in the garden, knowing he'd recognized her on the Hunnewell porch. She had thought his sardonic smile would cause her to melt. *Why what a pleasant surprise, my dear Miss Derrington!*

Surprise, indeed!

If it hadn't been for Oliver goading Keno until that horrid punch in the jaw, she could have avoided detection altogether and slipped away from the back garden as quietly as she had slipped in—without being seen by Rafe or anyone else.

But then the worst had happened. How foolish of Oliver to call Marshal Percy Harper out of injured pride. He would recover from his debacle in a day or so. A bit of swelling, a smidgeon of black and blue coloring on his jaw, and a few pointed words from his father on the consequences of scandalous behavior. It was for Keno's sake she'd come forward to tell the marshal what she'd seen, and now she hoped to avoid an inquisition. She turned her head away from Rafe and sighed, looking at Kalihi Hospital.

They'd arrived, and not a word yet passed between them.

—⚬⚬—

Kalihi had begun as a small hospital three miles west of Honolulu, and surrounded on three sides by water. Eden discovered on her first arrival here that the Board of Health had at one time shut down the hospital and sent its lumber to Molokai where some of it was used to make coffins for the lepers—an item of history that disturbed her.

The new Kalihi Hospital and the Kakaako leper detention center were built on the waterfront between Honolulu and Waikiki. At Kakaako suspected lepers were held until diagnosed with the disease by the Board. There was also a small research laboratory where a team of doctors studied the disease. Eden felt fortunate to be working for her aunt Lana Stanhope, Dr. Clifford Bolton's assistant and fiancée.

The Kakaako branch was fenced with guards to detain the suspected lepers and keep them separated from the general population center only a mile away in Honolulu. After the Board's legal medical verdict they were either released or put on the boat for the one-way voyage to the leper colony. They would then arrive at the rugged coastline of Molokai where the boat couldn't dock and the waterway was rough and hazardous. In an earlier time they'd been literally dumped into the water to make their own way to shore or drown. Now smaller boats were let down from the leper steamer and rowers braved the waves to take the diseased as near to the black-rocked shore as possible.

Here in Honolulu, the blue waters of Kalihi Bay fronted the leprosy hospital on its west and south sides. Across the bay lay a large area and just past this was Ewa Field. Separating the two land areas was the natural anchorage called "the Pearl Lochs."

"The perfect place for a great naval harbor," Rafe commented. His first words since they'd left the bungalow.

Eden couldn't resist. "The United States Navy, I suppose?"

"Would you prefer the Japanese, or the English Navy?"

He was in a riled mood.

"Why can't it simply become the Hawaiian Navy someday?"

"That sounds pleasant enough, but reality demands its way. It would not survive for long among the world powers. Think of the future, not just 1892. The Pearl Lochs would eventually be taken by some empire, unless the annexation movement succeeds."

She decided not to argue. "Well, if I must choose one of those three, it would be the United States."

"It will be one of those whether we choose or not. That's why we need to support annexation while we still have the opportunity."

His smile was disarming. He stepped from the buggy, walked around, and lifted her down. His hands lingered a moment, resting on her shoulders, and his gaze was intense. "Tell me why you were prowling the garden area in Hunnewell's yard during a secret meeting of the Annexation Club."

"Really, Rafe! *Prowling?*"

Oh no. I knew this was coming, she thought.

"I'm serious, Eden." His eyes were bright with intent. "Do you trust your future husband or not?"

Startled by the implication, she paused, then: "Trust you? Of course I trust you!" Her voice had an injured edge to it.

"Do you? I wonder. If so, then trust me with your explanation."

"I can't." She withdrew from his hands and turned her back, looking at Kalihi.

"Then you don't trust me. It's as simple as that."

"It is not as simple as that. This is a personal matter."

"If we marry, your heart and life are laid open to me."

She turned, alarmed. *If we marry?* Why had he put it that way?

She'd never seen him so angry before. She'd been so busy recently at Kalihi, and with Great-aunt Nora, trying to arrange a meeting for Dr. Jerome with Queen Liliuokalani, that Rafe's changed mood came upon her unexpectedly.

"You speak of personal openness," she said, "but does that include your heart and life?"

"I've been open with you."

"Then what was in the message that Keno risked so much to bring to you?"

She saw his jaw tighten. "It was from Celestine in San Francisco. She recognized Townsend there, watching Parker Judson's house."

Eden couldn't silence the gasp that made all else she worried about momentarily flee. Her uncle Townsend, stalking Celestine . . . and maybe Kip too.

"Has Grandfather Ainsworth been told?"

"Not yet. But try to forget Townsend for the moment. I'd like to know what you were you doing at Hunnewell's tonight."

She couldn't bring herself to surrender all of the facts for fear he would jump to a wrong conclusion. Yet there was the seemingly equal danger of keeping silent and letting him think the wrong thing about her.

"Now, Rafe, you heard what I told the marshal."

"Yes, that you came for some fresh air. Come, darling, you can do better. I was surprised he accepted that."

"You talk of trust, well, why can't you trust me?"

"I trust your moral character explicitly, but your politics are allied with Great-aunt Nora's, and she's allied with Liliuokalani. If you were at the Annexation Club meeting tonight you weren't there to applaud. Though I can't be certain, I'd suggest you were there to gather information. Was it for Nora—to be handed over to the queen?"

She felt her cheeks flush. "Are you saying that I'm a spy? That I would deliberately work against you . . . as well as my own grandfather? He was there too—"

He smiled coolly. "Yes, he was there, as you found out later. But you told Oliver and Silas you'd come by to see Ainsworth. That gave you away. You had no idea he was there until you saw him from behind the bamboo curtain. Am I correct? I think I am."

She stepped back. For a moment she couldn't find her voice, perhaps because she didn't want to. Her stiff, unsteady fingers clasped her nurse's cap.

"If you are accusing me of some evil, then say it plainly."

"Were you on the lanai tonight?"

The crackling tension between them held steadfast. She turned her back.

Rafe took hold of her shoulders and brought her round to face him again. "So you were there, spying?"

She tightened her mouth and met his gaze evenly.

He released her. "Stubborn, aren't you, *darling?*"

"I am not a spy. That should be sufficient."

"Who sent you then? Not very considerate of whoever it was to let you risk yourself to disclosure, like a pretty little thief peering in a window?"

"Oh!" she exclaimed.

"Was it Nora? The queen—our very own 'lily of the stars'? Or, perhaps, let me guess! Perhaps the honorable Dr. Jerome?"

She clenched her hands. "Speaking of trust, you're behaving as though you have none in me!"

He studied her face for a long moment. She saw an anger in his eyes she'd never seen before. It devastated her.

His hands slowly disengaged from her shoulders; he stepped back from her. Somehow this simple act spoke more concretely than any words he may have chosen.

He kept speaking of not having her trust. Trust, she knew, meant so much to him. From the time she'd known him he'd always been the one she could turn to. Now, he thought she didn't trust him—

"Very well, Eden. There's little use going on like this. We'll leave matters unsettled between us until you decide you can trust me. In the meantime, I've work to do at the hotel. The Legislature meets tomorrow."

She froze for a moment, feeling some relief that the horrible showdown between them appeared to be shelved. Any relief died, however, as she considered *unsettled between us*.

"You're angry with me," she said quietly. "What do you mean, 'We'll leave matters unsettled between us'?"

"Sometimes, darling, I don't think you're ready for the sacrifice of marriage."

She drew back, stunned.

"You haven't the kind of trust needed in the man you say you're willing to build a new life with," he stated. "Your emotions are tied to Jerome. Marriage is about love, trust, commitment, and loyalty to one man above all others, your husband."

"Rafe," she cried, a thin edge of alarm to her voice. "You can't mean this—"

"I do mean it. I've always come last with you."

"That isn't true!"

"I'm convinced it is, Eden. There's little room in your heart right now except for Jerome, Molokai, and Kalihi Hospital. Well, darling, you can have them to your heart's content. They are *all* yours. But I don't come with them."

She stood, unable to move or gather her wits, watching helplessly as he walked around the side of the buggy.

"But Rafe," she called feebly, her voice breaking, hardly above a choked whisper.

"Good night, Eden."

"Wait!"

"When you're ready to trust me as a woman should trust the man she expects to marry, you know where you can find me. But I won't wait long, not this time. I don't intend to be around much longer. Two weeks at the most."

She watched through blurred vision as he got into the buggy and flicked the reins.

The horse drew the buggy down the road into the shadows and out of view.

An *ultimatum*!

—⁂—

Inside Kalihi Hospital, her ears filled with the roaring wind and the slashing rain on the windowpane, Eden thought her heart would splinter like glass and explode into a thousand pieces.

When she reached the nurses' retreat, a small room off the main hall, she was so emotionally exhausted that she nearly stumbled inside. She was relieved to see that Lana wasn't there. She had time to be alone, to think . . . to recover.

Still . . . he insulted everything between them when he simply rode away without offering a clearer explanation for his anger with her.

It hurt deeply that the one man she loved more than any other accused her of not trusting him. But Rafe told her that he would allow her to fulfill the dream of a lifetime of struggle—to meet her mother, and to work alongside her father in his research clinic for a year—though he was not at all pleased with the decision.

Eden felt the old dismay sweep through her like a gale.

Well! If that's the way he feels about it, then so be it. I'll let him go just as coldly as he turned and walked away from me.

She looked at her image in the small mirror above the wash basin, searching her face as a stranger might. A girl stared back, pale except for the emotional pink in her cheeks.

She pressed her lips together firmly. She was sorely tempted to stamp her feet in frustration. Instead, she pushed aside a dark curl that had come down in the wind at the back of her head. *Be calm.* Her fingers trembled. A sign that not all was right in her heart.

She loved him.

She smothered a cry of rage and, grabbing the big yellow flower from the bowl, crushed it and hurled it in the trash container.

A saintly missionary was she? Self-controlled and forebearing? Oh how wrong they were who believed this! Perhaps Rafe was right after all. She wasn't emotionally ready for marriage. She wasn't ready to be a suffering missionary on Molokai either. Only Christ knew her weakness and failure.

She turned away from her image, her hands gripping the table, allowing the tears to break as a fountain. Thank God no one was here to see her fail like this.

―⸿⸮―

She walked to a chair and collapsed dejectedly into it, allowing the tears of frustration to follow their course.

Life without Rafe was unimaginable.

The wind slammed the rain relentlessly against the windows.

After leaving Eden at the hospital, Rafe returned to the Royal Hawaiian Hotel. He had settled on the idea of reserving his own suite soon after he discovered that his responsibilities in the Legislature, along with political strategy sessions with the Reform Party, often called for his personal presence and the necessity for late hours. A nearby suite reduced the need for time-consuming boat trips to and from Hanalei on the Big Island.

He was in a grim mood as he entered the room. No matter how strong the emotional bond with Eden, he was determined to restrain his emotions and press onward toward the crisis in San Francisco. He had a calling of his own to solve and he meant to accomplish it. With cool deliberation he emptied his pockets—and dropped the clutter on the table with a deliberate clink.

The clock was ticking. He walked across the polished floor with its thick rug to the writing desk.

He must wire a message to Parker Judson in the morning. Tonight, he would send one to Ainsworth Derrington and pay the errand boy to deliver it at once.

Confident of his decision he wrote swiftly. His bold handwriting darkened the white stationery.

Dear Sir,
As you will be at Iolani Palace in the morning to meet with the queen,
it's important I speak with you as soon as you arrive. Ambrose
received a wire from Celestine. Townsend is in San Francisco. He's
been prowling about Parker Judson's house. My mother and the boy
Kip are staying with Mr. Judson, as you know. Action on our part is
essential. I have decided to accept your earlier suggestion to join you
and members of the Reform party on the trip to the mainland, but I
plan to remain in San Francisco while you and Thurston go by train
to Washington D.C. to meet with Secretary of State Blaine.
Rafe Easton, Royal Hawaiian Hotel

Earlier, Rafe had sought for a way to decline the trip to Washington in order to fulfill his obligation to supervise the plantations and attend the Legislature, but because he held Parker Judson's seat he'd been requested to join the Thurston committee. He now recognized a door of opportunity. The steamer would first stop in San Francisco. Thurston and Ainsworth were to meet for a day or two in the Bay city with the controversial California sugar king, Claus Spreckels, before boarding a train for Washington. Rafe could take care of the adoption of Kip and look into the matter of Townsend.

He went downstairs. The chandeliers and lamps were all aglow like a cache of reflective diamonds. Having sealed the envelope and paid the errand boy with the promise of more upon his successful return, Rafe went back to his suite.

As he opened the door, across the room he glimpsed a man beginning to rise from a chair. The lamp beside the chair was dimmed, and a tall potted banana plant cast large leafy shadows. The man crouched, then grabbed the back of the chair.

Rafe already had his jacket off when a familiar voice said clumsily, "That you, Rafe?"

Rafe halted, exasperated, leaning a shoulder against the door. "Do you have to hide in the shadows like that?" he growled.

Zachary Derrington, Rafe's stepbrother through Celestine's marriage to Townsend, and Eden's blood cousin, blinked as he finally managed to turn up the lamplight.

He and Zach were nearly the same age. They grew up as opponents due to Zach's perpetual warfare. Matters had changed between them since Zachary had come to Christ almost two years ago, but the tension occasionally remained as an old holdover.

"Oh. Sorry." He frowned. "Well, the door was unlocked," he said defensively. He pointed to the lamp beside the overstuffed chair. "You're the one who lowered this light—" he stopped, and smiled ruefully. "I should have spoken up. Sorry."

Rafe laughed. "Have a seat."

Zach, a tall, fair young man with a cleft in his chin, looked more like his father, Townsend, than did Silas. Throughout Zachary's young adulthood the rivalry to win Eden's affections away from Rafe was relentless, and until recently, bitter. At the time, Zachary did not believe that Eden was his blood cousin. When the fact of her birth to Jerome became obvious, Zachary did an about-face and was now fixated on marrying Bernice "Bunny" Judson, Parker's niece.

Even when Zachary was troublesome, Rafe looked out for him, granting him latitude. Since childhood Zachary had manifested disturbances of one sort or another, some troubling enough that he'd been under a doctor's care. Fortunately, since his troubled soul had come to Christ, he'd shown extended periods of a more genial personality. Now, however, with so much anxiety over Silas, and Townsend's bullying, there were new episodes when he became distraught and used the medication prescribed by Dr. Bolton.

"Wind too heavy for the houseboat?" Rafe asked with a sly smile.

Zach had taken to spending much of his time living on his boat rather than going out to Kea Lani, much as Rafe had taken a suite at the hotel to avoid the same longer ride past Kea Lani, the mission church, and to Hawaiiana.

For Rafe there was a second reason that he rarely stayed at Hawaiiana now. He had built what was called the Great House for Eden and it would be a very long time before they lived there together, if ever. He disliked entering the silent domain that echoed with his footsteps.

Zachary groaned. "That wind is murder—and speaking of murder," he looked up, his silvery-blue eyes tense, "I've got something important to talk about. That's why I came. Got any coffee?"

Rafe tilted his dark head and his eyes measured Zach. He rang for coffee, then turned his attention back. Unless he'd seen Ambrose or Keno in the last hour, and it wasn't likely, he could not have heard the news that Townsend was sighted in San Francisco. What troubled him then? He couldn't be serious about murder.

It was only when Zach moved a trifle clumsily into the light that Rafe had his answer—or part of it. He noticed damp dirt smudges on Zach's fashionable shirt front and, worse, what looked like dried blood on the collar below his right ear.

Rafe moved over to where Zach sat in the chair and drew the lamp closer. "What happened?"

Zach touched the side of his golden head. His icy blue eyes reflected bewilderment. "I've got a knot on my head the size of a coconut."

"I can see that. How did you acquire it?"

"I'll explain—I need that coffee first . . . you don't realize how my head throbs."

Rafe narrowed his gaze. "On second thought, we'd better brave the wind and visit Dr. Jerome again."

"No!" He snapped to his feet. Zach's impulsive response came as if a Chinese firecracker exploded in the room.

Rafe considered Zachary's relationship with his uncle Jerome, and knew it to be on solid footing. No trouble there, at least that Rafe knew about. Jerome was even sympathetic toward Zachary's concerns about the arrival of Silas, which Zach saw as an outrageous intrusion into his life.

"I'll—be okay." Zach touched his head again. "This isn't worse than being thrown from that stallion. Thought I'd broken my neck that time."

They both had thought so. Rafe and Zachary were horse enthusiasts, and enjoyed breeding fine horses. Now that Eden posed no jealous threat, they enjoyed friendly competition over who had the best stallions and mares.

"Sit down, Zach. There's no ice here, but I can ring to make sure."

Rafe did so, and decided he owed it to Zachary to hear the facts, keeping Zach calm and his own doubts restrained. His decision came to an abrupt halt as the bellboy delivered the coffee.

"Sorry sir, no ice. But the manager says pouring wine on a cut will help it heal faster."

"Bring a bottle."

"Yes sir. I brought one."

When the boy left, Zachary was still sitting, leaning his head in his hands. Rafe used the wine to clean the wound behind his ear and temple. Rafe was relieved that he hadn't been keen on going down to Kalihi Hospital where Eden was on duty, or calling for Jerome to come to the hotel.

Rafe poured the coffee and handed him a cup, ignoring Zachary's eye wandering over the wine bottle. They'd come to physical blows once when younger, again over Eden, after Zachary had come from some wild party on the beach. To his credit, Zachary hadn't touched the bottle since Eden brought him to Christ.

Rafe learned through the years that the wisest attitude when dealing with Zachary was a restrained demeanor, even when Rafe felt anything but coolheaded. He lifted his cup and sampled the coffee made from his own Kona coffee beans, which had been sold to the hotel and brewed by the chef.

Rafe had given a generous sample of his Kona beans to the hotel manager. Compliments had come from the guests on the "wonderful coffee flavor" and now management requested regular orders of beans from Hanalei Plantation. He tried to ease the tension by casual conversation until Zach was ready to explain what happened to him.

"I've been thinking I could hire someone to market the coffee to the other hotels, including those in San Francisco."

Zachary gave a brief nod, looking glum. "Good idea. I wish now I had taken my education in agriculture. Grandfather gave Silas management rights of the sugar. Says he knows it better than I do. And my journalism for Great-aunt Nora doesn't appear to be going anywhere. Unless I could inherit the *Gazette*, or buy it from her to establish my own paper, I don't know where I want to take the future. If it wasn't for *Silas!*"

"Silas can't impede you. No one can, unless you give up. Maybe it's time to reconsider your future by surrendering it to the Lord. Maybe He has a different plan."

Rafe walked over to his luggage and dug out a small bottle. *Kalihi Hospital* was typewritten on the label. He looked over his shoulder at Zachary. If he refused to see Dr. Jerome, then he needed help.

"Here, take two of these with more coffee." He tossed the bottle to Zach.

Zachary scowled and squinted to read the writing on the bottle. "What are they?"

"Eden gave them to me a month ago. They stop a headache, dead."

"Sure it's not more of what Nora took from Dr. Bolton?"

Rafe looked at him sharply. "What? Why did you say that?"

"Poor joke. Sorry."

"No, I mean, why did you think of Nora's medicine bottle?"

Zachary rubbed his forehead, holding the bottle. He frowned, turning it over in his hand again and again.

"Same kind of bottle . . . same kind of white pills . . ."

"Wait, you *saw* Nora's medicine bottle and what was inside?"

"Sure. Both at Hawaiiana when Eden brought it to her from

Kalihi, then again at Koko Head."

"At Koko Head," he repeated. *But that was impossible—if Nora tossed the bottle as she said she did.* "They were pills?"

"Pills. The bottle was sitting on her bedstand at Koko Head. I picked it up and shook it. They rattled. She got upset."

Rafe's heart thudded. He walked over to the chair. "She was in bed?"

He nodded. "She was still sick from that overdose we blamed on my father," he said of Townsend, his voice tightening with resentment toward his father as he spoke his name.

Rafe considered the new information. "This then was before Eden and Dr. Jerome arrived with you on the boat?"

He nodded briefly and winced, hand going to his head again. "'Leave that alone,' Nora snapped at me. Almost bit my hand off when she snatched the bottle away. She stuffed it under her pillow."

Rafe stared at him, but his mind saw Nora at Tamarind House—heard her claim to throw away the medicine because it was "rancid." Could it be Nora had retained the medication after all, and concocted that story of tossing it? It would fit Nora. No dim "little old lady" was Nora Derrington, but smart, quick on the uptake, and independent in her decisions. If she had suspected she'd been poisoned and kept the medication—

Zachary obediently popped two pills in his mouth and swallowed.

Then Nora must still have that incriminating bottle.

Zachary looked at Rafe, troubled.

"What did you mean a minute ago about the need to call for Dr. Jerome—*again?*"

It took a minute for Rafe to put a clamp on his excitement over learning about the medicine bottle and bring his mind back to the problem at hand. He walked over to the table and picked up his coffee cup. He stared at it, calming his emotions. After a moment he explained the Oliver-and-Keno incident, safely defusing the moment's intensity.

"Oliver's a strange fellow," Zachary mused. "He's very pro-British, you know. I've wondered why he didn't take his education in England instead of Harvard."

Rafe glanced at him. "Thaddeus H. wouldn't like it too much if he knew his son preferred the Union Jack."

"I'll say! He doesn't know. Sometimes I don't think Oliver even loves my cousin, but his father approves of the Derrington name, just as Grandfather Ainsworth approves of Hunnewell. The engagement is next week you know. Candace is a cold fish about the whole thing."

Rafe thought the same. "There's something suspicious about that engagement. Why was it she pressed ahead to see Keno these last couple of years and didn't care what others thought about it? She's one woman who makes up her own mind about things, regardless."

"True."

"Yet suddenly, she breaks off with Keno, refuses to see him or even respond to his questions, and is going through with the engagement to Hunnewell next week. Doesn't that ring false to you?"

"Now that you put it like that, yes." Zachary leaned his head back against the chair.

Rafe glanced at the time. "Okay, Zach. Let's have the facts. Before those pills send you to slumber land. What happened to you?"

"Right." Zach drew in a breath, drank from his cup, and began.

"You know how I'm suspicious of Silas being involved with the gambling cartel. You know it, everyone does. Grandfather Ainsworth and Great-aunt Nora are upset with me about it. Well, I've got facts now. Not exact proof yet, mind you, but that will come too. Just you wait and see the fireworks I'm going to unleash before this is over." He told Rafe about following Silas earlier in the evening.

His ice-blue eyes hardened.

Zachary leaned forward. "I'm going to talk Nora into sending me to San Francisco as an investigative reporter for the *Gazette*. I'm going to dig up everything I can about Silas and his rosy past as a journalist."

I'd better not mention Townsend is there now.

Rafe stood looking down at him, arms folded. "You'll have difficulty convincing Nora to send you. As you say, she's supportive of Silas. She won't like it if she thinks your intention in going there is to stir up more trouble."

"I've got another reason for going, too. One she *does* support."

The sudden wistful expression on Zachary's face tugged Rafe's mouth into an amused smile. Bernice "Bunny" Judson, of course. Zachary was right, though. Nora did approve of his interest in Bunny rather than Claudia Hunnewell.

"So," Rafe edged him back on the trail. "You followed Silas tonight to a gambling house in the Rat Alley district. You say Silas didn't go inside. He stood around for a while, then walked toward Kalihi Hospital." Rafe managed to sound casual.

"Right. Then he stood around some more, just as if he were waiting for someone."

"You're certain this man was Silas? You saw his face?"

"I didn't need to see his face. It was Silas. He even looks like a gambler."

"I don't know what a gambler is supposed to look like. You didn't see his face but you're sure it was Silas."

"Certain," Zachary stated coolly. "I just told you so."

Zach's *certainty* had been proven wrong before. He'd been certain some two months ago that it was Silas who'd secretly entered Great-aunt Nora's house on Koko Head to steal the manuscript she was writing on the Derrington family's beginnings in the Islands. The man, it turned out, was not Silas, but Townsend. Rafe decided it was pointless to argue with him about it now.

"All right. So Silas stood outside the hospital. Then what?"

"Maybe five minutes later out walks my uncle."

"Dr. Jerome Derrington, right?"

"Of course!"

"Just want the facts straight. Go on."

"I would if you wouldn't keep harassing me!"

"Here, have some more coffee." Rafe poured, trying not to scowl.

"So out walks Uncle Jerome."

"Was Jerome alone?" Rafe asked smoothly.

"No."

Rafe's gaze shot to Zachary's.

"Another man was with Jerome, a medical colleague, I think, though I can't say for sure.

"At first, I just thought Uncle Jerome was going home to Kea Lani, that he was merely walking out with a colleague. Then they'd separate and go their own way. It was about the usual time he leaves his research and returns to the plantation. So I took it for granted Silas had come to meet him and they'd go home together in the family coach."

"Did you see the Derrington coach?"

"No, but I thought it might be parked down the road. The idea is, that isn't what happened." Zachary quickly gulped his coffee. He was getting excited again.

"Instead, Silas moved back behind the palm trees. He didn't want to be seen."

Rafe thought back to the Annexation Club meeting at Hunnewell's. Silas had arrived with Ainsworth, but there'd been definite gaps of time when he could have slipped away and walked to Kalihi Hospital where Zachary believed he saw him. Perhaps Silas even had time to visit the gambling den at Rat Alley, though that would be more difficult. His return to Hunnewell's would easily go unnoticed, especially during the cookout meal they'd had on the beach, when the men were coming and going from the house to the cook-pit near the shore.

Rafe remembered that someone else had been late in arriving, in fact, very late, and that was Oliver. His father had become irritated.

"So Uncle Jerome comes down the hospital steps, and off he goes walking quickly. But not alone. The medical colleague is with him. They take off at a brisk walk for the houses near Waikiki. *Then*

Jerome is not returning to Kea Lani yet, I thought. *He's just out for a stroll with his friend.* I would have forgotten the matter and gone my way except for Silas."

"He follows his uncle?"

"Yes, and he didn't call out for him to wait, either, so he might join him in the stroll. He trailed him, not wanting to be seen. My hackles were up by then. I wondered why, so I went after the three of them, making sure they didn't hear me following."

Zachary stopped and scowled. "I know what you're going to say, that I shouldn't have been following my uncle and Silas like that."

Rafe was not thinking that at all. He was wishing he had been there to gather the facts for himself.

"Keep in mind it was Silas I was watching, not Uncle Jerome," Zachary said stiffly.

"You don't need to make excuses. Just go on, Zach."

"All right. Next thing I realize we've walked to the Hunnewell beach house. There's a thick wall of trees that line the wrought-iron fence, as you probably know. A man comes out from those trees. By now it's dark. Still, I see he's Oriental, Chinese, dressed in some fancy garment that may have been silk."

Rafe was now intently listening. "The Oriental was alone?"

"Yes, but off down the road I glimpsed several other men standing by a hackney. I may be fevered, but I'd insist they had *swords!*"

Silk and swords. The two together told Rafe the Chinaman was no ordinary sugarcane worker, or vegetable seller hawking his wares on the Honolulu streets, not even a proprietor of a gambling den in Rat Alley, though he likely had come from there.

"Jerome and this silken Oriental stand and talk in low tones for a good ten minutes."

"Where was Silas during this time?"

"Well, that's just it, he wasn't anywhere to be seen. I lost sight of him as we neared Hunnewell's house. He must have gone through the gate into the garden, or through some other little opening in the wall. I never saw him again."

"But Dr. Jerome was just ahead, and so was the medical colleague, and the Chinaman. The three of them were standing near the trees. Is that still correct?"

"Sure! The three of them were standing and talking, or arguing."

"Then one of them would have seen Silas enter through the gate into the garden."

Zachary scowled. "Silas could have stepped behind some bushes, just as I did when approaching, then entered through a small opening. But I think he went through the gate, because that's where I was clobbered. Just as I entered a few minutes later. He was hiding there in the shadows waiting for me."

"Wait, Zach. Get back to Dr. Jerome. So Silas wasn't in view after Jerome and his colleague met up with the Chinese man."

"No!"

"You couldn't pick up anything they said, not even a word, a name?"

"It's windy tonight and those palm fronds were moving and shaking just as they are now. Nor could I get as close as I would have liked."

"Anything stand out about this Chinese fellow except his guards and garb?"

Zachary rubbed his forehead. "Nothing."

"Ever seen him near the gambling joint you mentioned?"

Zachary rubbed his hand over his eyes. "Never."

Rafe moved about. "What about near one of those Chinese lending shops, a bank?"

Zachary hesitated. He drew his brows together. "Well . . ."

Rafe came back and looked down at him. "Yes?"

"There was one of those lending shops on the same street as the gambling den . . . wait! . . . but, no . . ." He shook his head and winced. "No, I don't remember seeing him there. One thing for sure, he couldn't have been a cane worker in those clothes. He was nothing like the old man you have on Hanalei."

"Ling Li. All right, go on."

"There isn't much more. They talked, and I got the impression, though I couldn't hear anything, that the Chinese man was angry."

"All three men were angry?"

"I had the impression Jerome and the colleague were entreating him. Then the Chinese man turned toward the waiting hackney, and the guards assisted him."

Rafe walked over to the large window and looked below to the darkened street. A few people were still moving about bucking the wind, but for the most part they had scattered like sheep, the shops closed and boarded up.

The first raindrops fell slowly, followed by a blinding flash of light across the sky, then a deep grumble of thunder. The rain squall broke into a deafening torrent, whipping and lashing the window. Rafe thought of the worst storm he'd ever experienced. It was on the *Minoa* in the Caribbean. A few times he'd thought the creaking ship was either going to sink or break up in the mountain-sized swells.

Rafe thought of his favorite Psalm 29, the voice of the Lord in and over the storm, both natural, and the spiritual upheavals of the world, nations, and individuals. He'd memorized it years ago, and he found his mind wandering through his favorite lines.

> *The voice of the Lord is upon the waters:*
> *the God of glory thundereth. . . .*
> *The voice of the Lord is powerful;*
> *the voice of the Lord is full of majesty. . . .*
> *The Lord sitteth upon the flood;*
> *yea, the Lord sitteth King for ever.*

Rafe drew the double shutters closed, then the thick drapes. If all went well, they'd still be on dry land in the morning.

Zach had spoken of another medical person with Dr. Jerome. He must have been talking about Hartley. Rafe's thoughts turned a corner to Herald Hartley, the medical assistant to Dr. Jerome Derrington.

From the time when Hartley first arrived at Kea Lani in the early summer months, Rafe had entertained his private suspicions concerning him. Rafe was game to admit to his personal reasons for not liking Hartley, but there was much more to it than the masculine dislike he felt because of Hartley's keen interest in Eden, and Dr. Jerome's apparent hope that his daughter and his medical assistant might somehow come together.

It was Dr. Chen's journal that first gave rise to Rafe's suspicions of Hartley. The Chinese researcher had kept a medical journal for the twenty or more years of his Far Eastern travels into Nepal, India, and China. It was the journal that Hartley had carried away in his suitcase from San Francisco's Chinatown, along with the news of Chen's unexpected death. Hartley had brought both the journal and the news of Chen's demise to Dr. Jerome at Kea Lani.

True, Rafe did not set much faith in the herbal cures that Chen must have believed in all these years, and saw no reason why anyone would steal it. But among that particular group of medical researchers in the world of medicine, Dr. Chen was a credible force. It was clear that Dr. Jerome believed in it, even if the Hawaiian Board of Health did not. And that Hartley believed in Jerome.

Rafe turned away from the shuttered window and looked over at Zachary, but decided not to say anything of this now. While Rafe had no idea just how or why they could be allied in motive, he found that he couldn't shake the suspicion that this incident tonight at Hunnewell's gate between Dr. Jerome and the Chinaman in silk was associated in some way with Dr. Chen.

"The medical colleague you say left Kalihi in the company of Dr. Jerome tonight," Rafe said. "I suppose he was Herald Hartley, his assistant from India?"

Zachary was staring forlornly into his empty cup. "Hartley?" he repeated as if the name had slipped between the cracks of his memory. Then: "Oh, him," he said with a tone of dismissal. "No, it wasn't Herald. I'd never seen this fellow before."

"It wasn't Hartley!"

Zachary seemed a little surprised by Rafe's passionate response. "I didn't see Hartley. Rather a bland sort, isn't he?"

Sly was the more likely, Rafe thought.

"He blends into Dr. Jerome's shadow is the way I sort of think of the fellow," Zachary said, refilling his cup. This time he added a lot of milk and sugar. Rafe watched the ruination of his superb Kona blend as it became more like "British tea."

"Herald would have made a dandy valet for my uncle," Zachary continued. "Oh, no sir! Oh, why yes sir! Very well, m'lord Derrington!"

Hands on hips, Rafe watched him too gravely. "I think, old chap, that bash on the head may be settling in now."

Zachary cast him an offended look. "To get back to the sobriety of my experience, then. Uncle Jerome and the unidentified colleague entered Hunnewell's garden through the big gate. I waited a full minute to make sure I didn't run into them, then followed. No sooner did I pass through the gate, and under some poinciana trees, intending to walk up to the front door as bold as you like it—bam! Something exploded in my brain. That was it. When I came to I'd been drug over beneath a tree, close beside the gate wall—forgotten, like a dead rodent."

"Very telling." Rafe listened as rain threw itself against the panes, and the wind whined and screamed around the corners of the hotel.

Whoever did it actually drew more attention to himself than if he'd ignored Zachary entirely. It would have been wiser for the person to have acted as if he were coming from the house and given him a friendly greeting.

The attacker must have reacted out of sudden, mindless fear. That worried Rafe. It was the kind of impulse that proved dangerous when a person believed himself cornered. Townsend possessed that kind of emotional trigger, but Townsend was in San Francisco.

And Eden had been in that garden. He knew a flash of frustration born from a different kind of fear. She might have been injured moving silently about the thick tropical shrubs.

Rafe regarded Zachary pensively, walking to the overstuffed chair where he sat slumped. "Let's go over the time again." He looked at his timepiece.

Zachary drummed his fingers on his chest, thinking. "Let's see . . . it was a few minutes after six o'clock when I followed Silas to the gambling den."

"And when you followed him to Kalihi?"

"I don't know exactly. Less than an hour had gone by."

"That would make Dr. Jerome's meeting with the silk-clad Chinaman around—?"

"Ten after seven. I looked at the time."

Rafe wasn't as sure, but he thought Silas and Ainsworth entered together around 7:15. If so, that did give Silas time enough to accomplish what Zachary claimed. And Hartley? Both Hartley and Dr. Jerome could have come to Hunnewell's property and no one would have noticed.

Zachary leaned his head against the back of the overstuffed chair. "What do you make of it?"

"I don't know," Rafe said shortly. "What I do know is that Silas was at Hunnewell's tonight. He was there in the garden when Oliver and Keno had their trouble. What I don't like about this, besides your getting bashed, is the fact Dr. Jerome was there, evidently not telling anyone of his presence, not even Ainsworth."

Rafe did not mention Eden.

"Silas is up to mischief," Zachary said. "But not Uncle Jerome. Yet I can't understand his being at Hunnewell's tonight, meeting with the Chinese fellow."

Rafe kept his suspicion to himself.

"It had to have been Silas who knocked me out."

Rafe was not as sure. "Look here, Zach. I want you to say nothing of what happened tonight to anyone until we can look into it. Keep all this out of the *Gazette*."

"Don't worry. But if Great-aunt Nora knew, you and Grandfather would be on the front page tomorrow. And I'd likely get a bonus for putting you there."

Rafe looked at him for a moment and mused: *And if the queen knew the annexationists' secrets? What manner of bonus might she give?*

"Can you agree to silence? Or will you be going to Ainsworth?"

"My grandfather wouldn't believe much of anything I told him anyway. Like I said, I'm going to try and interest Nora in my investigative journalism in San Francisco. There's plenty I can dig up. Silas has boasted of his newspaper work there, and also in Sacramento. Well, I'm going to take him at his word for once and see if that's so. I want to know what he was up to in sunny California. And I'd just as soon not have Silas know I've been following him around Honolulu."

Rafe remained silent about Townsend, not because he expected Zachary would be hurt by the current news. He had shown little distress over his father's earlier act against Great-aunt Nora. He'd never experienced affection from his father. Townsend had pummeled Zachary with abusive words long before Silas arrived. Silas just made the situation worse.

It was Townsend's nature to be abusive, as Rafe had also experienced as his stepson. But Rafe, unlike Zachary, hadn't been damaged by Townsend's criticism, nor had it caused him to attempt to win Townsend's praise. The abuse hardened Rafe against the man his mother had unwisely married. He didn't care what Townsend thought of him. Oddly, as Townsend discovered that, he respected Rafe more. The people Townsend treated well were those more powerful than he, those he thought might be able to enhance him.

Rafe decided to let Ainsworth break the foreboding news of Townsend to Zachary tomorrow.

By now, Ainsworth would be getting the message he'd sent to

him at Kea Lani if the errand boy had gotten through before the storm hit hard.

The medication was beginning to work on Zachary, making him nod his head. The rain continued, and the tropical wind wracked the trees, scattering the flowers along the walks.

"Better get some sleep now, Zach. The weather isn't letting up."

Zachary mumbled something and went over to the big Chesterfield sofa, where he sank down with relief and drew an arm across his eyes. This was not his first time on his stepbrother's couch. He mumbled: "Who was that Chinese fellow . . . wore silk and embroidery . . . why would he meet with Uncle Jerome?"

Rafe looked over at him. He had his own ideas but kept them buried. Dr. Chen and the journal fit the Chinese puzzle. The question was whether the meeting tonight had been on friendly terms, or an unpleasant revelation for Dr. Jerome. What troubled Rafe was the knowledge that Dr. Jerome entered the Hunnewell garden afterward.

He flexed his jaw. Eden knew, of this he felt sure, but Eden was not willing to *trust* him with the truth.

Chapter Eight
Winds of Allegiance

The worst of the storm had blown over by morning, though the clouds still covered the sky with gray and the wind came in strong gusts. Palm fronds and broken pieces of shrubbery littered the street in front of the hotel when Rafe came down to the lobby that boasted of undisturbed quantities of orchids and banana plants. He decided to call for a hotel carriage to take him to the meeting at Aliiolani Hale where he was to meet up with Ainsworth. Zachary was still recovering from his head injury, but Rafe thought the worst was over, and had ordered breakfast sent up to the room.

Rafe had crossed the lounge toward the doors when a bellboy came scurrying up.

"Message for you at the front desk, Mister Easton."

Rafe glanced toward the hotel clerk, who motioned toward the message slots behind him.

As Rafe walked toward the desk a woman standing there turned to leave, and as she did she looked straight at him. She wore a strange garment, all black, with a head scarf decorated with symbols of the zodiac. She had her eyes painted to make the lashes black, and her lips were red. She saw him looking her over and must have supposed he found her attractive, or it was the other way around, for she boldly stared at him, the corners of her mouth turning upward.

"Good morning, sir," the clerk said as Rafe stopped at the front desk. "A message arrived for you only minutes ago."

The woman turned and walked slowly away.

Rafe took the envelope and stepped aside to read it.

Rafe, you do have a right to know what I was doing at the Hunnewell house last night. Darling, I do trust you. I must talk to you. Will you meet me at the Beretania church this afternoon? Despite the weather, they are going through with the tea and luncheon planned to raise donations for a new church building. Great-aunt Nora will be there with the queen. I'll wait for you on the green. Yours ever, Eden

A faint smile turned his mouth.

He turned to leave when again he saw the woman, but this time a man walked beside her. A gloomy looking fellow, tall and skinny, also wearing black, with a sleek top hat.

The hotel carriage brought him to the front of Aliiolani Hale, the government building housing the Legislature on King Street across from Iolani Palace. He stepped down and paid the driver. "Wait for me. I won't be longer than an hour."

The rainstorm of the previous night depleted itself, but the muggy weather proved more uncomfortable than Rafe recalled for this time of year. He lowered his hat against the diffused sunlight and glanced about. The street was muddy. Again debris lay everywhere, as though a mild tornado had cannoned through. The northeast trade winds needed to flow over the Islands again.

Several prominent carriages belonging to key leaders in the Reform party were arriving out front of the building. He recognized the familiar Derrington carriage with its *D* on the door. Rafe quickened his stride to reach Ainsworth before he entered the white ornate building.

Rafe opened the carriage door for Ainsworth Derrington. "Good morning, sir."

The patriarch's weather-tanned face was haggard, as though he'd spent a restless night. Rafe felt sympathetic. It must be a horrendous burden when your son becomes Cain.

"I received your message, Rafe; most disturbing news." He shook his silver head as if in overwrought dismay.

Rafe held the door. The distinguished figure, agile and garbed in white as usual with his panama hat in hand, stepped down nimbly.

"I am shocked. I fully expected Townsend to remain somewhere here on the Islands until we could quietly locate him."

"We should have watched the steamers."

"I've called a family meeting for tomorrow to discuss the matter, and what we can do."

Rafe bit back his impatience. What was there to discuss? The reasonable thing was to notify the San Francisco authorities to put a warrant out for his arrest. Yet, it was not so simple since Nora had not filed a complaint against her nephew. All that may be about to change if Rafe could verify what Zachary told him last night with reference to the medicine bottle.

If I had that bottle!

He'd already debated the wisdom of whether or not to inform Ainsworth now. He'd decided to hold back until he first arranged to speak with Nora alone. Despite Ainsworth's proper show of alarm, Rafe expected him to go on urging restraint, even with the added information coming from Zachary.

"If Nora won't file a criminal complaint," Rafe told him, keeping his voice calm, "then I'm going to San Francisco to handle this myself. I'm going to track him down. I can't take the risk. Townsend already guessed, if he's clever and smart, and he is, that Celestine has left the marriage and won't come back to him. You know the results of his anger. Once it gets out of control he can explode into a rage. I suspect that's what happened between him and my father that day. His anger snapped and he lost self-control. . . . Rubble is the only thing left."

Ainsworth groaned. "I saw the tendency in his childhood. When he was a youth he was out of control. I desire this ugly matter to be settled as soon as possible. We'll take no chances with Celestine and the boy. I'll not stand by and see your mother harassed. That, I can promise you."

Rafe remained cautious, though he believed the genuine conviction of the words. Ainsworth had always frowned on Townsend's carnal life in the Islands and had more than once threatened to disinherit him for gambling debts and womanizing on the sly.

Ainsworth took firm hold of Rafe's shoulder. "I tell you, Rafe, if any of this shameful news gets to the newspapers the hope of annexation is all but lost. Townsend—a member of the Legislature, and of our own Reform Party—arrested on charges of attempted murder! Can you see that in the Washington and New York news journals? Unfortunately his deeds won't be treated as an individual crime, for which he is wholly responsible. The enemies of annexation will see to that. Any wind of scandal connected with the names of those in the struggle will undermine if not destroy our political and moral cause!"

Rafe wasn't sure a death-dealing blow to annexation would necessarily follow. He didn't doubt that some would snatch any opportunity to send this kind of information to Washington. A message from London to the White House would come, accusing them of backroom deals with a criminal faction in Hawaii. Even President Harrison, who favored annexation, would likely back off.

Thaddeus Hunnewell appeared on the steps with other Reform legislators and beckoned Ainsworth and Rafe to the meeting.

Ainsworth grasped Rafe's shoulder as they walked toward the building, his eyes showing genuine concern. "I know, my boy, I know. This is most difficult for you. Very difficult indeed, for both of us.

Together we'll handle this wisely. Justice will not go unsatisfied. I only ask for caution. Not for Townsend's sake, but for the future of Hawaii."

Rafe would indeed be cautious, but regardless of the consequences, he was moving forward on his own.

—∾—

Thaddeus Hunnewell waited for them in the chamber. His sunbaked skin tinted by a rise in blood pressure, he marched about the foyer waiting for them.

Hunnewell hurried toward them. He might have been auditioning for the part of the grim reaper, Rafe thought, preparing himself. Thaddeus H. was sweating. He drew out his white cloth and wiped his face.

"I've blundered," Hunnewell said in low voice. "After the meeting last night someone broke in my office and stole the manifesto I'd been working on for the US State Department. There's not hide nor hair of it anywhere. Shocking! I can't understand who would do such a dastardly thing."

After a brief discussion it was agreed that the stolen manifesto should not be brought up in the meeting. They gathered a few minutes later in the cloakroom with a half dozen others in attendance. Before Hunnewell spoke he took Rafe aside.

"You can tell your friend that my son showed more bluster last night than good sense. Oliver won't be making a legal case out of the unfortunate circumstances that trapped them both into an incident we wish had not occurred."

"Keno will be relieved to learn that, sir, and so am I."

"I've told the marshal to drop the case. I hope that will suffice."

"I think Keno should find your decision quite satisfactory."

He slapped Rafe on the shoulder. "Come along, now. We've important matters to discuss."

The meeting began at 11 a.m. after some preliminary small talk.

Hunnewell, his face drawn, began his discourse, leading a compelling charge against the monarchy, and raising a lively response from his audience. According to Hunnewell, Liliuokalani had once again refused to cooperate with the Reform Party in the choice of qualified men for her cabinet.

"The queen is refusing to appoint even one of the Reform Party's men to the new cabinet. It's the height of stubbornness, and it won't strengthen her cause on the throne."

"It's a constitutional principle," the lawyer Withers stated.

"Just so," Ainsworth agreed.

Hunnewell looked at each man present. "Gentlemen, I have it on trusted word from one who knows that the queen is even now overseeing the writing of a new Constitution."

Dismay spread through the group, which turned to frustration and anger.

"I knew we couldn't trust her," Withers said. "I've thought from the beginning of her reign that this was her goal. Was she not angry with Kalakaua for surrendering, as she claimed, his sovereignty to the missionary party?"

"The missionary party," Ainsworth repeated with genuine frustration. "She should know better than that, and she does. She herself claims to be a believer. But it serves the opponents' political purposes to twist the truth and blame the missionaries for anything in politics they don't approve. It's a dangerous game for Christians, and yet the opponents use it every time."

"I believe Liliuokalani and those around her planned this change in the Constitution before her brother died in San Francisco," Withers continued.

Murmurings of agreement followed. Hunnewell went on: "It's been suggested that she's been meeting with certain advisers over this for some time now. And I know who these men are."

Rafe looked at Hunnewell. "This action of the queen's shouldn't surprise us," Rafe said. "We know she disapproved of King Kalakaua for signing the '87 Constitution limiting the powers of the monarchy."

"All true."

"Well, then, gentlemen. I know where I stand," Rafe said. "And I think I know where most of you do." He looked at each man, trying to be patient with their hesitation. "Except for holding meetings and decrying the state of things, what do we plan to do about it?"

Tense silence stalked the room. Some moved uneasily in their chairs and glanced at Ainsworth, wondering if he would tell Rafe to keep silent.

"Gentlemen, I propose the inevitable, that we dethrone Liliuokalani and form a Republic, or become a territory of the United States."

"Dethrone her?" came from the side of the room with a gasp.

"Why not?" Rafe asked bluntly. "Isn't that what we've been talking about for months? Even before she took the throne? True—we haven't been using that word, but we all know what is meant by annexation. Did she not swear to uphold the '87 Constitution when she took office after Kalakaua?"

"She did indeed," Ainsworth said with a slight smile, looking around at the older men. "Well? Gentlemen? The younger generation has spoken. We are ready for a decision. She is deliberately failing to keep her oath to uphold our legal Constitution, and as a result we have the legal right to dethrone her." Hunnewell swerved his head toward the lawyer, Albert Withers. "Well? Albert, do we have your approval?"

"Well," Withers drawled, "technically speaking, Thaddeus—" he drummed his fingers and pursed his heavy lips.

"Technically speaking, Albert, will only get us off the issue. She swore to uphold the Constitution, and now she's secretly planning to toss it to the flames and replace it with another." Hunnewell, riled at last, paced, hands in pockets.

"If the Islands become a territory of the United States of America we will be under a solid Constitution, protecting our homes, businesses, and properties from arbitrary rule, yes, and even outright future confiscation according to the whims of a queen, or some new king—as yet unborn—" and here he deliberately stopped and looked around at those gathered.

"She never intended to uphold the present Constitution," Rafe said. "Now she's stepping back from her oath, claiming it's what the native Hawaiians want. If Hawaii doesn't become part of the United States soon, some day in the future it will find itself absorbed by Japan, Russia, or Great Britain."

"Quite right," Ainsworth said, resting his hands on the handle of his walking stick as he leaned against the back of a chair, sober and restrained. "I believe she has been secretly gathering men, her firm supporters with legal backgrounds, to help her draw up changes that will weaken the '87 document. At a time of her choosing she will bring it forth and demand a vote of the Legislature to approve it."

"Never!" Hunnewell said fiercely. "It's treason!"

"According to her," Rafe said, "treason took place in '87 when King Kalakaua signed the Constitution."

"She swore to uphold it, and we will never accept a weakened Constitution that takes away our right to vote on the laws of the land."

"But, to dethrone her," Edwards the businessman questioned uneasily, his voice resonating in the room, "considering the reaction of the native Hawaiians, how could it even be attempted without an uprising?" He shook his head with doubt.

"But there won't be an uprising if annexation is brought about rightfully through peaceful means," Rafe said.

"Make up your mind, Edwards," Hunnewell said. "You say you want annexation, well then my good fellow, annexation demands that the Islands come under the laws of the United States. We cannot be a territory while retaining a sovereign that places our Constitution at the mercy of her whims."

"Even so, how could it be accomplished?" Edwards questioned. "She'll not simply lay down her crown and walk away, nor will those who energetically support her."

Hunnewell paused in his pacing to gaze down at Ainsworth.

"Well Ainsworth? Out with what you know, my man. How could we dethrone the queen and keep Honolulu from an uprising?"

Rafe looked at Ainsworth, suspecting the man knew something . . . or rather, someone.

Ainsworth, his deep-set gray eyes meeting the others with grim resignation, spoke quietly. "Very well, gentlemen. I have it from a reliable source that Captain Wiltse of the *USS Boston* will assist if necessary."

Rafe recalled what Eden had said some time ago about Silas. How he'd mentioned in front of Great-aunt Nora, Zachary, and others, that the American ambassador Stevens was sympathetic with annexation, and he also supported Thurston, Dole, and the others. Stevens privately assured Ainsworth of the landing of American troops if they should be needed to protect the Reformers in the overthrow of the monarchy.

The men looked at one another. A new confidence bolstered the wary.

Rafe committed himself by stating openly, "Should that hour strike, then I, for one, will align myself with the red, white, and blue, with the hope of seeing it flying over Iolani Palace. If not, gentlemen, then the next generation may be under the Japanese, Russian, or British flag. The Islands are a treasure, and on our own we're not strong enough to protect it; we will need the backing of a nation like the United States. I am confident Hawaii will be far safer in the hands of the US Constitution and Bill of Rights than with the emperors, czars, and kings."

"My sentiments exactly," Hunnewell said.

Ainsworth gave a deep nod of his head. "Just so, just so."

The others gave the same assent. Edwards also nodded. "If, as you say, there is no bloodshed."

"We all want that," Rafe said. "And we must ensure the use of all possible restraint. But freedom doesn't come without a cost. If we enjoy liberty without cost, it's because someone else has paid the price."

Ainsworth rose to his feet and looked at each man present. "And now, gentlemen, an announcement. The Reform Party leadership has agreed to sponsor Lorrin Thurston and others—Hunnewell, Easton, and myself included—to send off to Washington D.C., to meet with Secretary of State Blaine. We will depart a week from now. With that, this meeting is adjourned."

Rafe looked at his timepiece. He was to meet Eden in ten minutes. He left the cloakroom speedily before Ainsworth or anyone else could summon him and returned to the hotel carriage.

"To Central Union Church. Make haste."

⸺ ҩ∙ҩ ⸺

On Beretania Street, Eden Derrington stood near the front lawn of Central Union Church awaiting the arrival of Rafe Easton. She carried an umbrella in case the clouds decided to break again, and although it was culturally taboo for a woman to run in public, she was ready to risk a frown from the other ladies and make a dash for cover, quite unwilling to ruin one of her finest dresses.

Today the ladies of the congregation were giving a luncheon to raise money for the building fund, and Queen Liliuokalani, whose private residence, Washington Place, was just across the street, was gracious enough to attend with some of her aides and friends. Great-aunt Nora was with her, always a strong proponent for the monarchy, and would be walking with her entourage. It was Nora who'd been able at long last to arrange the meeting tomorrow at Iolani Palace for Dr. Jerome to discuss a research clinic on Molokai with the queen.

Eden drew her dark, winged brows together. What would Rafe think of the arranged meeting, especially after she told him about what she'd seen last night at Hunnewell's garden?

She grew tense and uneasy again. Was she doing the right thing in telling Rafe? Well, she certainly was where her own interests were concerned. But . . . she pushed her anxiety away, refusing to look it square in the face until Rafe arrived.

She had the next twenty-four hours free. She had worked with Aunt Lana Stanhope until four o'clock this morning, arose late, and come straight here to the church. For once Eden was not wearing the typical gray nursing dress, white pinafore with the red cross, and nursing cap. It made her feel outright pretty again to be wearing one of her fashionable dresses with puffed sleeves, tight wrists, and high Victorian neck, all adorned with eggshell-colored Brussels lace and modified pearl buttons. She had chosen the dress color of a mint green because Rafe always complimented her when she wore that color. He said it brought out the green of her eyes and the auburn shades in her dark brunette hair.

She walked restlessly along the edge of the lawn. She glanced back at the church steeple. The big clock was striking the hour. The sun was out from behind the clouds and a cooler trade wind began to blow across the Island. She removed her wide sun hat with its ribbons, then put it back on again in a restless habit, perturbed with the events of the last months. Everything had seemed to go wrong that could. And now her uncle Townsend was in San Francisco, no doubt spying on Rafe's mother and Kip.

She paced up and down the walkway along the emerald lawn. The wind tossed against her and ruffled the lace on her dress, but she did not feel anything. The crème ribbons on her sun hat tossed in the breeze.

Eden looked over at the church again. Activity stirred as Queen Liliuokalani arrived to participate in the luncheon. Great-aunt Nora walked along with the pastor and an entourage welcoming the queen, while children sang in Hawaiian and offered an array of flowers. Eden had already informed her great-aunt that she would be meeting Rafe Easton, and to cover for her in case anyone should notice her absence. She didn't think they would, not with Liliuokalani present.

Eden left the front of Central Union and walked forward across the green to where some palm trees stood straight and undisturbed by last night's windstorm.

"The righteous shall flourish like the palm tree," she quoted Psalm 92:12.

"Despite the badgering windstorm of last night, these palms remain unbent. Nor will I be uprooted or broken in two by the trials of life, but depend even more on the strength and protection of the gracious Lord." She had prayed much about this meeting with Rafe and believed the Lord wanted her to confide in the man she loved and expected—*hoped?*—to marry next year. Marriage was built on truth, trust, and forgiveness. Eden remembered Noelani saying to her once, "You have to have plenty of all three to keep a strong and congenial marriage. If you start hiding things from each other it won't be long before the Devil's also convinced you it's okay to lie too."

She looked up the street, hearing the smart *clop* of horses' hooves, and recognizing a fine carriage from the Royal Hawaiian Hotel approaching. The driver drew up to the edge of Beretania Street.

Eden watched as Rafe Easton opened the door and stepped down, telling the driver to wait. He looked across the lawn and saw her.

Eden walked forward to meet him.

Rafe Easton walked forward and Eden went to meet him. The way he looked at her from across the street suggested he liked her appearance. Of course, this was why she had taken such pains to look her best, though tired from last night's work at Kalihi. Relieved, she hurried toward him.

He wore a spotless white shirt, a handsome jacket with brass buttons that reminded her of a naval jacket, and matching trousers. She could feel her face flush upon seeing him.

"Rafe!" She reached a hand toward him.

The inevitable dark brow lifted. "What a pleasant invitation." He took her hand between his warm, strong ones and her heart sang again.

"I accept, gladly." He drew her toward him in a firm grasp. Cupping her chin, and ignoring everything going on around them, he planted a brief kiss—not on her lips, but her forehead.

"Disappointed?" His eyes teased.

"You ought to be ashamed to ask."

"I'm not." His smile was disarming. "A proper kiss is an art."

"Really, Rafe!" she said with a little laugh. She stepped back, fixed her tilted hat, and cast a hurried glance over her shoulder toward the church, wondering if anyone had noticed. The luncheon crowd was assembling, full of pleasant conversation, smiles, and alohas.

"You're a bit late," she said with contrived severity as she waited for her cheeks to cool. He was not late, but she said so because it made good cover.

"All right, my sweet, I have dropped everything to come at your beck and call."

"I believe it's the other way around."

"I admit I wouldn't come running for just any woman. Well . . . except, maybe, Bunny."

There was the faint mischievous look in his eyes again. She should have been warned by it, but responded too quickly.

"Bunny. Such a silly name for a grown woman."

"What! You mean to tell me you don't think it's, well, 'rather cute'? Zach does."

"*Bernice* sounds much more sensible," she said stiffly. "I don't know her well. She gave me a cold shoulder when she was here that Christmas. Probably because she was flirting with everyone from Oliver and Zachary to—you." She stopped, noticing the glimmer deepen to satisfied amusement. Why, he was deliberately provoking her!

"I've always heard a rose by any other name . . ." he began too smoothly.

She folded her arms, eyeing him.

"We have, I believe," she said loftily, "something more important to discuss than Bunny."

He smiled. "I'm delighted you see it that way. You don't want to talk here, do you? There's not enough privacy—or did you expect to go to the church luncheon?"

"Let's go somewhere else and have something to eat." Eden was not a bit hungry, but presumed that he would be since he had attended a meeting at the Legislature that morning. And the fewer people about when she unveiled her story, the better.

She had dropped her hat in a gust of wind. Rafe snatched it before it blew away and settled it gently on her head. "We've a choice: lunch at the Royal Hawaiian, or one of the other hotels."

She didn't want to go to such a public place. "Do you still have Hawaiiana open?" she asked, thinking of the Great House. Actually, Eden had a good reason for wishing to go there rather than dine at one of the fancy hotels, though normally she'd have opted for the Royal Hawaiian.

Mention of the pineapple plantation caught Rafe's attention. "The house? It's open. Keno is staying there in my absence. He's the best man I could possibly have managing the pineapples for me right now, and I can trust him explicitly. He's living in one of the first-floor rooms. Noelani comes over in the afternoons and helps take care of his needs."

The Great House would have been Eden's now to enjoy if they'd married two months ago as first planned. Whether they would live there in the future remained unsettled. Now that Rafe had control of Hanalei, it appeared as if the stately plantation in Kona country was his priority. She wasn't sure which plantation she preferred, though Hanalei had impressed her with its matchless view and its Easton family history, and because it meant so much to Rafe. Once her term on Molokai was finished she could be happy anywhere with him, as she'd told him already.

"Let's go to Hawaiiana," she said.

He gave her a slanted look, a trifle surprised by her choice. "Hawaiiana it is, then, but do you mind telling me why you wish to go there?"

Rafe took hold of her elbow as they walked on together across the green toward the waiting coach.

"Candace is returning this Sunday to take over the Chinese Christian women's Bible group," Eden explained. "I thought I'd tell them good-bye and make sure everything in the hut is ready for Candace."

Eden had taught the previous two months since Candace had been at the Koko Head house with the ailing Nora. That was over now, since Nora returned to Kea Lani, and Candace was anxious to return to her Bible teaching.

"I've told them I'm going away to Molokai for a year, but they didn't expect me to leave the class yet. But it will be good for Candace to reunite with them again, even if Oliver doesn't like her doing so." The fact that Oliver was against Candace's service troubled Eden. She had never believed him a committed believer, even if Zachary did.

Rafe helped her inside the pleasant hotel coach and spoke to the driver, then climbed in and sat opposite her. The coach moved off down Beretania Street toward the Pearl River area.

"I'm sure his irritation is over the possibility of her coming into contact with Keno on Hawaiiana," Rafe said. "Even so, it doesn't say much for his Christian convictions. It does show Candace he doesn't consider the work important. He'd rather see it fall apart and the Chinese women go untaught than risk an encounter with Keno."

"Rafe, I'm worried. Maybe I shouldn't judge him, but I've always had a suspicion he isn't genuine. This will be crushing to Candace. She's so dedicated, and she needs a husband who's as zealous, or more so."

"Because she is, as you rightly say, zealous, she ought to know better than anyone he's an empty talker."

"Then you don't think he's genuine either?"

"No. You're right about not judging someone's inner motivations, but the fruits of character and the deeds of everyday life can be seen with the eye. You heard Oliver lie and defame Keno. He was willing, and even desirous, of seeing him hassled and put in jail for a few weeks. But I saw Thaddeus Hunnewell this morning. He's told the marshal to drop any charge against Keno."

"Wonderful!"

Thaddeus Hunnewell was from one of the old families, in which the titles, the wealth, the bloodlines, and the patriarchs and matriarchs were revered and ruled the family enterprise, especially when land and wealth were involved.

Eden's father, Dr. Jerome, though Ainsworth's beloved youngest son, had almost nothing to say about the Derrington enterprise, due to Ainsworth's own adherence to the laws of patriarchal dominance. Once the line was crossed by a marriage undesired, Ainsworth did not forgive or forget. He had mentioned only last night at dinner that "dear Millicent Judson Beacon has borne George Hampton Beacon Jr. four healthy sons."

It did not take Eden long to guess why her grandfather would tell the news to Dr. Jerome at the dinner table. Ainsworth was thinking that Jerome's wife, Rebecca Stanhope Derrington, had only produced one child—a *girl*—and not even his *favorite girl* at that. And if Jerome had listened to him years ago and married Millicent Judson rather than Rebecca Stanhope, Jerome would be much better off today having four sons. Ainsworth evidently believed that the robust Millicent had produced these sons on her own initiative because she had come from the Judson family.

I do have one positive feature going for me though, Eden thought. *Grandfather Ainsworth is absolutely jubilant that I'm going to marry Rafe Easton. Rafe supplants even the well-regarded merits of a Hunnewell.*

Taking into account Townsend's fall, Jerome should have inherited the Derrington crown jewels, but had suffered loss over his choice of Rebecca instead of Millicent Judson, and for becoming a doctor wandering the East instead of entering Hawaiian politics and doing more to enhance the Derrington estate. As a consequence of being Rebecca's daughter, Eden had been shown scant favor as a child compared with either Candace or Zachary.

But she was not resentful. God gave her Ambrose and Noelani, and it was through their witness and godly character she learned of the greatest Treasure of all, Christ Jesus. *I wouldn't exchange this legacy for the entire Derrington enterprise.*

In fairness to Grandfather Ainsworth, however, he had rejoiced in his youngest son's homecoming after such a lengthy absence, even though it was his granddaughter Candace who was chosen to wield the golden key for the next generation of Derringtons. Now Candace must pay for the honored position by sacrificing a marriage based on love for one arranged.

Eden remained distressed over the reason Candace agreed to marry Oliver. It was a secret that only she and Candace knew: Grandfather Ainsworth had promised Candace he would arrange for a secret land opportunity for Keno if she would marry Oliver for the good of the Derrington family. He would not only leave her his main heiress, but would do good to Keno as well. Eden knew her cousin too well to believe she would have agreed to the bargain if it hadn't been for the *consequence* to Keno if she didn't cooperate.

Grandfather had stated that if Candace refused to fulfill her responsibility to the family he would use his power in the Islands to see that Keno was banished from Honolulu. Eden had little doubt that their grandfather could and would fulfill such a threat. Evidently Candace believed it as well.

It troubled Eden that Dr. Jerome did not even have the money to pay for the printing press that she and Ambrose wanted to bring to Molokai for children's Bible stories. It surprised her to learn recently how lacking in finances Jerome was. A loan for the printing press might be gotten from Rafe—though she had not asked him yet. She glanced at him. It was also Rafe's ship, the *Minoa*, that they would ask to use to haul the press to the island. So far, she hadn't dared mentioned either of these needs to him.

Eden looked out the coach window at the blue seascape and wondered if it was ever right to break a pledge. Specifically the pledge she'd made to Candace to keep silent about her reason for marrying Oliver.

I should never have vowed. I shouldn't have permitted her to insist on my silence. It puts me in a very awkward position.

I'll talk to Ambrose about vows, she thought suddenly.

She watched Rafe tap his chin as he sometimes did when

pondering. She had always found the action attractive, though she couldn't say why. He would be amused if he knew. He seemed to think many of her responses were amusing. When he did, she tried all the harder to appear older and wiser. For a minute she allowed herself the indulgent pleasure of enjoying his masculine good looks, knowing that someday they would be hers. She liked his sun-bronzed skin, the chiseled jawline that spoke to her of strength of purpose, the muscled body—then she realized how easy it was to allow her desires to become undisciplined, and even more so because they were engaged. Somehow it seemed all right to be a little lax, but an engagement ring was *not* yet a wedding ring. In fact, the need for caution was exceedingly great. They were in love, they *knew* they were in love, and they knew marriage waited.

Quickly she looked away at the diamond engagement ring before he noticed the romantic glow that no doubt warmed her eyes. It would not be fair to him either, she thought. How long since she had read her Bible? Days, now, because she'd been so horrendously busy at Kalihi. Too long. She'd discovered early in life that relying only on Sunday church was not enough to keep her in fellowship with God. She needed time alone in the Scriptures. It was then that He spoke to her heart, using the Word itself. No wonder, then, that she was seesawing too near the edge on many issues, whether it was Rafe's sexuality or her bouts with frustration. Of all the memories she cherished of Rafe through the recent years, the one that influenced her most was having seen him so many times alone on the black lava rock near the mission church, reading a small black Bible.

Chapter Ten
The Wicked Spies Upon the
Righteous to Kill Him

A jumble of palm fronds and broken ferns from yesterday's storm hindered passage over the road tracking northward as the coach bounced over muddy ruts. The view of the Pacific Ocean along the coastline was dotted with fishing barks and boats. Eden saw large dark fishing nets spread out on the white sand, and the Hawaiian fishermen busy mending them in preparation for their night torch-fishing expeditions. Others were working in a taro field where a battered wagon was being loaded.

They rode past a papaya grove where a number of contracted Asians were laboring. Bungalows built on stilts or rocks above ground soggy from mountain runoff emerged amid green slopes and more distant fields.

The Easton pearl beds were not far away. Eden was pleased that Celestine had regained rightful control from Uncle Townsend, and that they would soon be under Rafe's control. It was jurisdiction over the pearl beds that had fed the trouble between Townsend and Celestine when she'd insisted last year that her son rightfully inherit what his father had worked hard to attain. Remembering that Townsend was even now prowling San Francisco heightened her worry. She'd been praying over Celestine and Kip since Rafe had told her the news.

Within a short time they rode past the Derrington Kea Lani Plantation, and some distance beyond it—actually walking distance, which she'd covered on foot several times—to Rafe's Hawaiiana.

The pineapple plantings had flourished these last few months, the green slips growing into strong bushes that Rafe said would produce the sweetest and plumpest pineapples anywhere in the Pacific. He could market the pineapples to the mainlanders, and was still deciding how to accomplish it with Keno and Parker Judson. His notion of "canning" the fruit seemed to Eden a bit challenging, and she did not see how such a complicated task could ever be accomplished, but she had learned a long time ago not to underestimate Rafe and Keno. They could get together and come up with some of the wildest plans she had ever heard of, but she loved to sit and listen to them as she had in the old days when Candace had been with her, and Rafe and Keno would come to visit them at Kea Lani.

The rich Hawaiian soil beneath the bright sunlight smiled on the pineapple slips, as had the rain and all the rest of God's blessings. Grandfather Ainsworth scolded himself every morning at breakfast because he had not taken Rafe seriously when he'd had the opportunity. Instead he'd given his son Townsend the nod to try to run Rafe out of Hawaii. Rafe had left Honolulu, but returned two years later with a treasure from French Guiana.

When in San Francisco two years ago, Grandfather Ainsworth tasted one of the new variety brought back on the *Minoa*, and even though the fruit wasn't fresh, he admitted to Parker Judson that he'd made an error in not backing Rafe Easton. It was then that Parker Judson had contacted Rafe and made an offer of partnership too generous to refuse, and so the business relationship had grown into a friendship.

The pineapple bushes were thriving in their new homeland, and so was the sugarcane.

"Ainsworth was telling Silas this morning that there are deep rumblings of trouble from the native population over too many non-Polynesian workers being contracted," she said.

"I can understand that," Rafe said thoughtfully. "Trouble is, the growers have little choice. We'd have no men to labor in the fields if we couldn't contract them. But the natives have a legitimate complaint; at the rate we're bringing the Asiatics in to the Islands they could change the balance of Hawaiian ethnicity in another generation if they stay on to settle. But actually it's Wilcox who's stirring up the racial issue. He's a hothead. He's telling the Chinese and Japanese they have the right to vote along with the Hawaiians. It plays well for his power base."

Eden refused to come to any firm decision. "Well, the workers aren't citizens of Hawaii just because they're laboring here," she mused. "They were contracted with a certain thing in mind, to work. When the contract is fulfilled aren't they to return with their wages to their own nation?"

"That was the original idea, but most of them aren't going back. The native Hawaiians find that a possible threat, since they'll be outnumbered. Ultimately it all comes down to annexation. Without it, in the kind of world we live in, Hawaii will be lost in another forty years. We might as well come to grips with it."

"But you know what Liliuokalani would say," Eden said quietly. "The native Hawaiians want their monarchy. They don't want annexation to the United States."

"I'm sure a good many of them would vote against annexation if it were put to them today, especially with Wilcox haranguing them as he does, and the queen promising a return to the old chiefdom and the rule of the alii. But fortunately we don't have to face that vote now. There's time to show them it's the best thing for Hawaii as a whole. Times have changed. A few rulers from the noble alii can't protect Hawaii from the growing bullies coming of age in the Pacific. I'm confident the Hawaiians can eventually be persuaded and vote to be aligned with America if we can explain the reasons why it's so crucial for the future. In fact, Thaddeus Hunnewell was writing a manifesto on this very topic to present in Washington when the group from the Reform Party meet with the leaders there. Unfortunately," he said with a scowl, "it was stolen last night from his desk in the library."

"Stolen," she said softly. "Oh Rafe, what if it ends up in the hands of Queen Liliuokalani?"

His riveting gaze searched hers as if to ascertain whether her surprise and alarm were genuine. She felt a warm flush begin to brighten her cheeks. *So that's what he thinks. That Dr. Jerome may have taken it?*

"If it ends up in the hands of the queen," he said smoothly, "she may soon be telling an executioner to sharpen the ax."

—⟋ᘐᕬ⟍—

As the coach neared Hawaiiana Eden saw many Chinese workers in the fields. She knew life for them in China was no better, perhaps worse. Of their own will they'd boarded the contractors' ships for Hawaii. Some, bringing their families, signed contracts to work for a certain wage and a certain period of time on Hawaiian plantations. Many came for the benefit of wages to send back to large families in China. When their contracts expired, the majority remained. They signed new contracts or began their own agriculture, and some set up shops in the Iwilei area of Honolulu. A familiar sight in the Islands, especially Honolulu, was the sellers of vegetables and fruits. They were seen trotting along the narrow streets busily calling out their wares, carried in baskets on the ends of a long pole draped over their shoulders. Many of those who were financially able imported goods from their ancestral countries to sell to their fellow Chinese: precious silks—loved by many haole women too—and also classic chinaware, a certain mixture of tobacco weeds, and herbal medicines considered strange to the haole mind-set.

They also smuggled in opium. The drug cartel within China sent their "kingpins," the leaders, to the Islands, some posing as workers for easier dispersal of opium among the Chinese on plantations. King David Kalakaua had signed over the sole right of opium dispersion to one particular kingpin from China who had paid him more than seventy thousand dollars.

Along with opium came its enslaving twin, the addictive game of gambling. A cartel was working secretly to bring casinos into the Islands from the mainland to hook even more unwise Hawaiians and haoles into risking their money while spinning wheels and shuffling cards. Many Chinese highly esteemed "luck and fortune," and gambling of all sorts went on privately among the workers, both on and off the plantations, every day of the week. Chinese money lenders prospered through usury, while the Christians in the Reform Party fought against the legalization of drugs, gambling, and prostitution, many of the cartels run by secret kingpins.

The palms and ferns rustled alongside the road. At last, the Royal Hawaiian hotel coach turned from the dirt road toward the plantation house in the distance. Across the sun-drenched acreage that reached far back toward the Koolau Mountain range Eden scanned the distant hills of green foliage contrasting with dark boulders and streaked with garnet and mauve. Mauna Loa was robed with a mist today after last night's downpour, but the variegated shades of green, purple, charcoal, and blue remained visible.

The house stood a princely structure of white surrounded by sage-green coconut palms and a wide lanai. The driver stopped under the shade of several large crape myrtle trees in lush magenta bloom.

Rafe opened the coach door and assisted Eden from the coach to step into the mottled sunlight. She looked up at the lanai, wondering if Keno were home for lunch, and if Noelani was at work in the cook room.

She left Rafe speaking with the driver, whom he told to return the coach to the hotel since he had decided to stay in his house tonight. House servants kept up the cleaning, but with Celestine gone and Rafe mainly at Hanalei, the cleaning help only came on the weekends. On arriving, Eden was surprised to find the front door open several inches. Keno must have been in a dreadful hurry earlier this morning.

Eden entered the wide hall ahead of Rafe, and was greeted by the sounds of near silence: shrubs rustling in the wind, and a creak or a snap of wood responding to changing weather. She became conscious of a disturbing and inexplicable sense of unease. There were no cooking sounds from the back of the house where Noelani would have been working if she were here. So, then, no lunch? Both Keno and Rafe would be more disappointed than she, since she rarely bothered eating at noontime. Her appetite was small, one of the reasons for her willowy figure that made her the envy of many.

Eden swept across the hall toward the parlor, her favorite room in the house, because Rafe had it designed with her in mind.

The room was walled on three sides, while the fourth had an archway with intricate wrought-iron scrollwork on the screen doors. The last of the sunlight had faded from the room, but the curtains were still closed against the lanai and the room seemed airless. Eden tucked her brows together. Odd, the front door being left open, and yet Keno hadn't bothered to open the screen doors to allow fresh, cooling air into the room.

Eden walked there and drew open the curtains, allowing the gusts to sweep in with welcome relief. The screen side accessed the lanai that faced an enclosed garden of delicate ferns and flowers. Her favorite tree was the poinciana, with blossoms in lush crimson, and an aged hau tree with a plethora of sunny yellow blossoms.

Odd, she thought again, scanning the garden area below the lanai steps. She had an impression that someone should be around somewhere. Perhaps Keno was here after all, or even Noelani, gathering some flowers for the lunch table.

But—Eden narrowed her lashes, straining to see where a shadow fell near the white gardenia blossoms. Something else white stretched out from behind the leafy, waxy leaves—*no, it couldn't be*—but it was. A man's leg in a white trouser, with his foot thrust outward.

Alarm shot a burst of energy through her. *It's Keno!* She surged forward onto the lanai, lifted her skirt, and rushed down the steps and across the garden walk to the gardenias.

The man lay facedown on recently dug garden loam. He wore a white jacket and trousers, one arm folded beneath him, the other reaching forward, the fingers of the hand claw-like. It was not Keno.

Eden dropped to her knees beside him and felt the outstretched hand, discovering that it was still limp, the flesh warm. The man was rather stout; he may have only fainted from the heat. She felt for the pulse in his wrist, nothing. She put her finger just behind the top of his ear near the temple, but again nothing. She bent over him again, cautiously turning his head enough to peer at his face. As she did, she drew in a sharp breath.

She sprang to her feet, staring down at the dead Chinese man.

The sound of footsteps leisurely crossing the lanai caused her to look up. Rafe came down the steps to the garden and walked toward her. He stopped—

The next moment he had crossed the garden walkway in several brief strides and his hands were clasping her shoulders.

"Darling, what's wrong?"

Eden turned her head toward the flowering bush, and Rafe's eyes followed her gaze. In a moment he was stooping beside the body. He lifted the man's shoulder until he could see beneath him to where his chest had lain on the soil. He released the shoulder to fall back down.

Eden heard him sigh.

"That's him," she said in a tight whisper.

"What do you mean 'that's *him*'?"

"The man I saw last night with Dr. Jerome," she whispered. "The man who came to Kalihi Hospital yesterday evening. The man that brought Jerome to meet another Chinese man in front of Hunnewell's garden!"

Rafe looked at her sharply. "He *what?*"

She nodded. "Rafe, he hasn't been dead for more than a half

hour. It may have been heart failure."

"No," came his terse voice. "There's a knife under his left rib."

He rose to his feet, frowning, looking down on him. "You say this man brought your father to a Chinese man near Hunnewell's?"

Eden's hand went to her throat. "Yes." She gazed down at the man on the ground.

"Interesting, I think, that he's Chinese as well as the other man."

"Somebody murdered him?"

"As you rightly point out, and probably not more than half an hour ago. Furthermore, in my garden . . . now what was he doing here?"

Eden had no answers, not that Rafe expected any. She glanced about the garden, feeling a slow tingle rise along the back of her neck. The shadows among the thick ferns and shrubs grew menacing.

"He wore rings," Rafe mused.

Eden followed his gaze to the dead man's hand and saw pale circles around two of the fingers. "Was robbery the cause of his death?" Eden asked.

"Perhaps merely an afterthought. Come inside." Rafe took hold of her arm and steered her quickly toward the lanai steps. "You better tell me everything you know about last night, darling. We haven't much time. I'll need to send for the marshal."

"This is dreadful! Why would it have happened?"

"Why does anything evil happen in this life? Come, I need to know everything."

Chapter Eleven
Wicked Discovery

*R*afe led Eden to a comfortable chair to gather her wits while he went off to the cook room. Eden heard an unearthly racket. He returned soon with coffee and a plate of bread, meat, and fruit.

"How can you eat with that poor dead man out in the garden?" she protested.

"Not a dead *man*, darling. A dead *body*. The man's soul has been taken away to where he'll be for a very long time. Anyway, I'd have thought you'd be accustomed to dead bodies by now. Some that are worse looking than this one."

"Well, to some degree," she said, "but this man—or this *body* if you must be technical—seems different. He was alive last night with my father. I saw him."

He bit into his beef sandwich.

Her stomach felt queasy. She was exhausted.

"Hand me the sauce, please," he said. "Keno should be here shortly. Let's get to the point, darling. This is going to be a busy day."

Eden looked at him coolly and sipped her coffee, but even then her throat was dry and she hardly tasted the flavor.

"So Dr. Jerome was at Hunnewell's, prowling about the garden with this man," he began. "Did you know him at all?"

"No. I hadn't met him, but I'd seen him previously, even before last night."

"Where was that?"

She tried to remember. The details remained hazy. "I believe it was right here at Hawaiiana."

His gaze showed surprise. "It appears I'm not as informed about what's taking place on my own plantation as I thought."

"Oh!" She looked at him, just now remembering. "The door was open a few inches when we arrived."

He paused, interested.

"I thought Keno and Noelani were here," she continued. "Since they're not, maybe Keno left the door open for the man to come in. Perhaps he knew Keno as well as my father."

His coolly observant gaze fixed on the garden area. Losing interest in his sandwich, he stood, holding a napkin. "I wonder . . . if he knew Keno, that would change everything."

What did he mean to suggest by that? Doubtfully, she followed his glance outdoors.

"Meaning, that if he came here with Keno's knowledge he would have expected to meet with him on some matter of importance." His forceful gaze came back to Eden. "You think you may have seen him here before? Interesting. I'm acquainted with the men and their families on Hawaiiana, and I don't remember him. With a white suit and rings on his hand, he's likely not a field worker. Nor would an assassin usually stop to remove rings unless they're valuable."

"Assassin?" she asked uneasily. "Is that what you think?"

"That's my guess. I may be wrong, but it looks to me as if someone trailed him here with a purpose to kill him. Taking the rings was an opportunistic theft."

Eden shuddered and glanced uneasily toward the garden again, and then to the outer hall. She moved toward him. "How do we know he's not still in the house, hiding somewhere? The man hasn't been dead for very long. The murderer may have been inside when I entered. I had the strangest feeling when I came into this room." She looked around.

Rafe caught up her hands, bringing her eyes to his. "Steady your nerves, darling. There's no one here now. I had a quick look around when I went to the cook room."

So that's why he pretended to be so hungry. He hadn't said anything because he hadn't wanted to alarm her.

"Had the murderer been here when we arrived, he would have slipped away while we were in the garden."

Yes, that made sense to her. "An assassin," she whispered, "but why an assassin?"

"Maybe from an opium or gambling cartel, who knows? We've got to think before I send for the marshal." He looked at the time. "Keno should be here soon. I want to hear what he has to say about this."

Eden's mind raced to the man who'd been with Dr. Jerome last night. There'd been two of them. The dead man in the garden who'd met him at Kalihi, and the one in lordly silk waiting with a hackney. Opium . . . gambling!

"So the assassin could have trailed the man here."

"Right. Then the victim realizes he's in big trouble and bolts for the garden, fleeing for his life. The assassin overtakes him and kills him."

"But what did he do to warrant assassination? If it's opium—"

"That's what the police will want to know. If Keno can identify him we'll be moving in the right direction. Now, darling, I want you to go over the details leading to what happened last night."

Eden moved restlessly about the oblong parlor. She feared to bring her father into the dark dilemma. But the more she tried to cover his tracks, the more muddled it all became. She must trust that her father had done no wrong, but she must trust Rafe even more. She turned quickly and looked across the room at him. Sunlight streamed in touching the rich woods of koa, teak, and mahogany. She was aware that Rafe watched her, looking calm despite everything. She found his eyes disconcertingly observant.

"How about it, Eden? I think you'd better tell me everything please, right from the beginning and without leaving anything out."

She gave a relenting nod of her head. "It's true, what you suspect about Dr. Jerome. He *was* at Mr. Hunnewell's. I followed him there into the garden."

⸙

While Rafe listened in silence, Eden told him everything that had happened on the evening in question. Rafe listened attentively, but sometimes Eden had the odd notion he already knew most of the facts.

"Where I'm concerned it all began an hour earlier at Kalihi," she told him. "I was on a break from working with Aunt Lana and Dr. Bolton in the leper quarantine area. I came into the nurses' lounge. From the open doorway I could see out into the corridor near the front entrance to the hospital.

"My father had entered the corridor from another location. Before I could call to him to join me for coffee, I heard his muffled voice speaking to someone else in the corridor. It turned out to be the dead man."

"The Chinese fellow now dead?"

"Yes. Dr. Jerome said something like, ' 'Oh, why hello,' but I can't recall the name, his voice wasn't clear."

Her words caught his interest. "Are you saying Dr. Jerome was friendly to him? You didn't recognize any antagonism in your father's voice or manner?"

Had he suspected intimidation? She hesitated, wondering how to explain the change in her father's emotions without giving the wrong impression. "No, there wasn't any antagonism, not at first."

"Not at first, but later?"

"It might not have been antagonism, Rafe, but worry."

"Did you pick up any other exchanges, or even a word?"

She shook her head. "The voices were too low. I knew he couldn't be a patient. All our patients are suspected lepers, awaiting diagnosis. They're not permitted to leave the fenced area. So his presence there seemed unusual to me."

"You saw the man's face, right? Because you just now recognized him."

"Not at first. He had his back toward me. He wore—well, you know, what he has on now." She glanced toward the lanai. "I saw his face as he walked past the lounge to leave with Dr. Jerome a few minutes later."

"It's the same man. You're certain."

"Yes. It's him." She rubbed her arm uneasily. "I did catch sight of someone else, a woman, waiting just outside by the front entrance, but I couldn't say definitely she was with him."

"A woman," he pondered, gazing off. "What was she doing?"

"Looking in from the outside steps. She didn't stay in view long. I caught the merest glimpse of her face. She wore black, and something over her hair. A scarf, most likely. It partially covered her face. I do recall strange red designs on the scarf . . . I couldn't make them out."

His gaze caught hers with interest. "Zodiac signs?"

Curious, she searched his face, then shook her head. "I don't know. It happened too quickly."

"So Dr. Jerome left the hospital with the Chinese man and the woman?"

"Not with the woman. And I don't know whether she was Chinese. I have an impression she was not."

"Then, you saw your father and the Chinese man leave Kalihi together and walk to Hunnewell's beach house. What about this feline in black clothes?"

She smiled ruefully. "A carriage waited for her alongside the road."

"A nice one?"

She paused, considering. "Come to think of it, yes." She added, surprised, "Very much like the coach we used today from the Royal Hawaiian Hotel."

A spark of interest showed in his eyes. "Ah. You didn't happen to see a pale, gaunt-looking fellow with her? Also in black?"

She wondered why he asked that. Had he seen the woman and man together somewhere?

"I couldn't say. The sun had already set and it rapidly grew dark. I didn't see her again. It was curious, though, why she would be at the leper facility. The way she behaved on the hospital steps was almost clandestine."

Rafe looked on, composed and unreadable. "What then? You followed your father?"

Eden felt defensive, though she still believed she did the right thing. Even so, she plucked the lace at her sleeve. "Yes, I followed, and I shall tell you why. When he first greeted the man, he was amiable. Then, as they began to converse, his mood changed. Distress was written over his face, and the stark alteration worried me."

"But he left with the man willingly?"

"Yes, I'd say he was anxious to go with him. He usually won't leave Kalihi when he's on duty unless called away by some major concern. So when I saw his distress, and how anxious he was, I knew something must be wrong. I followed them toward the Hunnewell beach house. It came to me then that perhaps Grandfather Ainsworth had sent for Dr. Jerome. Someone in the annexation meeting might have become ill, even Ainsworth himself—"

"Hold on, my sweet. We need a detour at this point. Just how was it you knew your grandfather was at the annexation meeting—or rather, at the 'secret' meeting?" he said with a wry tone.

Eden turned and smiled for the first time. It was rather fun to checkmate Rafe with surprises, since she so seldom was able to do so. She had another surprise in waiting, too. One about Oliver.

"Oh, quite simple, really," she said, baiting him.

He narrowed his gaze under dark lashes. "Simple?"

"Yes, Candace told me about the meeting."

"Candace," Rafe repeated. "How did she find out about Thurston's new Annexation Club?"

"Oh, she knows quite a lot, now, thanks to a certain person."

Rafe's bracing gaze caught and held hers. "Are you going to keep this certain person a secret?"

"I don't keep secrets from you," she said with a look of innocence.

He smiled, and taking hold of her arm, drew her close. "Are you taunting me, my sweet?"

She laid her palm against his chest and pushed away lightly. "Earlier in the afternoon Candace stopped by to speak to Aunt Lana about the wedding—you did know Lana Stanhope is marrying Dr. Bolton in a few weeks?"

"Yes. Let's see . . ." His dark eyes smiled. "There was something about a honeymoon at Kalawao leper camp."

She narrowed her lashes.

"Very nice couple," he said meekly. "All right. How did Candace know about the meeting?"

She smiled. "Why, Oliver himself told her."

"Oliver!"

"Yes, he'd made plans with Candace two weeks ago to come to dinner at Kea Lani last night, then Mr. Hunnewell interrupted his plans. So Oliver had no choice except to inform Candace he wouldn't be able to come. Well, when she wanted to know why, he had to explain, didn't he?" She tried looking naive.

"Oh but of course he'd need to explain. A woman's curiosity and intellect must be satisfied at all times."

"And naturally Oliver told her about the Annexation Club meeting."

"Well, that was exceedingly discerning of him. Needless to say, she'd then wish to know who would be in the club, so I suppose he passed on even more interesting tidbits."

"I see you understand," she said sweetly, keeping a straight face. "After all, Candace had invested her time in a perfectly fine dinner, and gotten a new gown, only to be disappointed."

"Don't let Keno hear that she was disappointed," Rafe said.

"I doubt that she really was. But at least she felt somewhat compensated for a spoiled evening by hearing interesting tales about the club Oliver was invited to join."

"Ah, yes, I can see Oliver would make a top-of-the-line secret agent. He'll trust his secrets to the trade winds to ensure Candace understands."

"Speaking of secrets, I've another to offer if you care to hear it."

Rafe cocked a brow. "You've earned my full attention."

"Well, it's Oliver's, actually," Eden said. "Did you know he supports the Hawaiian monarchy?"

Rafe lost his bantering mood and became alert. His quick gaze searched hers.

"Did he tell you this?" he asked briefly.

"Yes, he knows I support Great-aunt Nora's work for the monarchy. Either Nora told him, or perhaps Candace. At any rate, he mentioned it to me recently. He couldn't be more open about his own support of the queen. I don't know if this means anything, but he also said he 'has nothing but respect for the British Empire.' He doesn't have the courage to explain how he feels to Mr. Hunnewell."

"I don't suppose he would, when his father is one of the chief architects of annexation in Honolulu. Especially when Hunnewell trusts that his son has the same convictions he does. Knowing Hunnewell Senior as I do, I imagine there are few secrets kept from Oliver—" He stopped abruptly.

Eden looked at him. She recognized the engrossed look on his face. An idea had struck him with full force.

"What about?"

He turned his attention on her. "That rather shakes things up, doesn't it? In fact, we need to add a fourth member to our list of possible spy suspects for Liliuokalani. Well done, my sweet. I withdraw my remarks about Oliver's naïveté. It looks as though it may rest with some of us. In which case he's clever enough to deserve being watched."

Anything that had to do with Oliver worried her because of Candace. "You think he was in the garden waiting to contact someone when Keno happened to show up?"

"Now that Oliver's been identified as pro-monarchy? It could be. Something was stolen from Thaddeus Hunnewell's desk last night. Something important to the annexation cause. The question of who took it and why is complicated by the fact that Oliver is one of several who might have various motives."

"Liliuokalani couldn't have a better spy, could she?" Eden said.

"He's right in the mix of things. You've given me something to think about, darling. So who among our motley group of possible spies was in the garden when Dr. Jerome arrived with the Chinese man?"

"Silas," she said, "my father, the Chinese man, Zachary, Keno, Oliver, and myself. Oh! And *you*."

"Ah. I would be a valuable spy for the queen, would I not? Like Oliver, I'm allowed into the deepest, darkest meetings with those rebels Thurston and Dole. Furthermore, I'm the least suspected. That is the Devil's way, isn't it."

"Also, until the telegraph from Celestine, you'd planned on going to Washington D.C. with Mr. Thurston and Grandfather to discuss secret details about possible annexation. Yes, you would be a very profitable spy for Liliuokalani."

"How did you know about 'secret details' to be discussed in Washington D.C.?"

"Grandfather mentioned it this morning to Silas."

"Did he? Rather reminiscent of Hunnewell and his son Oliver, isn't it? Trustworthiness is assumed because of family position. But let's move on, darling. Zach says a second man of Oriental descent was waiting in the shadows of Hunnewell's fence, near the west wall. Did you happen to see him?"

"Yes, he and Dr. Jerome talked for several minutes. Then he became angry, turned, and hopped into a hackney."

"Angry. That may be important when we keep in mind the victim out back. And like Zach you heard nothing of what was discussed?"

"Zachary?" She narrowed her lashes. "What about Zachary? And why is it I suspect you *already know* what I witnessed last night?"

Rafe appeared to hesitate, then to make up his mind. "All right. You've promised to be candid, and you are, so I'll meet you on level ground." He poured coffee into his cup.

"After we parted last night in—shall we say in no good humor?—Zach waited for me at the hotel. He'd been knocked unconscious as he came through Hunnewell's gate by a phantom with evil intent. He awoke under some trees by the fence, but by then the annexation meeting was over and things had quieted down. That's when he showed up at my hotel room blaming Silas for all the evils of the world, including the knot on his head."

"He was attacked by the same man who killed the Chinese?"

Rafe considered. "I don't think so."

That roused her suspicion. "Then someone at the annexation meeting would need to have struck him down."

"Maybe not. Any number of people from the outside could have done it. Hartley, for instance."

Herald, the medical assistant who worked with her father, had taken a reprieve from his duties for several days from the Big Island claiming he needed a rest. But Eden was not aware that he had any motive. She was about to say as much when Rafe continued.

"Silas, also, is a possibility—though your grandfather made him a member of the group, I don't consider him a true annexationist. He's too much a newcomer to care about Hawaii's destiny. Right now he's on a wave to please the honorable patriarch with his dedication to all things Derrington, much to Zach's frustration."

Eden agreed about Silas. He was a difficult man to understand.

At times he came across as humble and genuinely thankful for the embrace he'd received at his homecoming from the "distant unknown," but at other times he seemed as clever and shrewd as biblical Jacob before he'd become Israel, a prince with God.

"Even the dead man in the garden may have struck Zach," Rafe was saying, "since you say he was with your father. And yes, the assassin. He first may have followed the victim from Kalihi to Hunnewell's, failed to get him there, and trailed him here to Hawaiiana." He looked over at her. "I'll omit the other honorable man among us besides Ainsworth, the dignified Dr. Jerome. Although he was there with the opportunity, I can't see him bashing Zach. Jerome is mixed up about Molokai," he said lightly, "but he's a decent man, a true Christian."

Eden smiled ruefully. "Thank you," she retorted. "I'm pleased you're giving my father some leeway, because unfortunately, what I have to say about him leaves precious little."

His dark brow shot up. "Interesting indeed, coming from your sweet lips.

"Shall I go on?" he suggested casually, and did, without waiting for her response. He leaned against the back of a tall winged chair, arms folded, and appeared as though discussing the weather. "So then, earlier, Zach followed Dr. Jerome from Kalihi Hospital on a jaunt to Hunnewell's, where—"

Eden stiffened. "Zachary followed my father?" she asked with a hint of indignation. "Why?"

A hint of cynical amusement reflected in his smile. "I suspect, darling, for the same reason you did, though Zach didn't think the man with your father was the man outside, but Silas."

She shook her head and moved about restlessly. "He's usually wrong about Silas. It makes little sense for Silas to bring Dr. Jerome to Mr. Hunnewell's house."

"Perhaps, but for that matter, why would the Chinese bring your father there to meet the man in Oriental silk robes?"

Eden lapsed into disturbed silence. She'd already asked herself that a dozen times without a suitable answer.

When she kept silent Rafe proceeded with disciplined restraint. "Zach followed them on foot from Kalihi to the beach house. I suspect you did the same?"

Eden looked over at him. His head was tilted and his gaze said he was assessing her motives.

"I followed him from Kalihi, but why didn't I see Zachary?"

"Yes. I wondered about that myself. He claims he didn't see you either—no, wait. Let's just say he failed to mention whether he'd seen you there. He may have decided to keep it from me, knowing my response. Especially after that crack on the head he took. Not a very mellow place to be wandering around alone, my sweet. In any event, he stuck like jam to his explanation that Silas was behind it."

Rafe set his cup down with a *clink*. "I'll need to ask Zach why he kept quiet about seeing you. I don't think he intends to get the law involved, since it was his uncle Jerome he followed, but all that's changed now with a murder on our hands." He scowled. "The Chinese would need to be bunged off here at Hawaiiana! Loads of new trouble, now." He finished his coffee. "I can't allow this to keep me in Honolulu. Not with Townsend in San Francisco. I need to be on that steamer." He looked at her. "But I can't just take off unless I'm confident you're safe. No more wandering about the midnight garden."

She smiled. His concern made her feel loved. "I promise to be indoors and fast asleep by ten o'clock. At least we can tell the marshal we were together at Beretania at the time the man was killed."

"I just don't care to have the marshal's investigative work slow me down." He looked at her. "Let's forget both of them for the moment. I want to get back to Dr. Jerome and the corpse in our garden before Keno arrives."

The word *our* struck her heart; even in that sober moment it renewed a sense of belonging with him. She was not alone in this debacle, they were in this together. In a much smaller way, *belonging* to Rafe was to her symbolic of the peace and joy that swept over her soul when she remembered and considered that she belonged to Christ. The eternal God was *Abba Father*. Even in the midst of death, yes, even *murder*—like the first murder with Cain and Abel after the Garden of Eden. Whether one's particular time to live in a world in rebellion against God took place in period of revolution, war, great sweeps of persecution, or the unknowns waiting at Molokai and San Francisco, as believers in Christ, she and Rafe could find His grace sufficient.

He cocked a brow. "Darling? Are you awake?"

Eden blinked and looked across the room at him. He narrowed his eyes, watching her.

She smiled and sat down on the edge of the settee.

"I was thinking of *our* mysterious garden," she murmured, "our life, you see, *our garden*, as it were. I was thinking that so many things can happen in our garden, and that we're 'gardening' together. Does that make sense? And that our True Father will oversee us, and bless if we continue to trust Him."

Rafe walked over, and clasping her hands, drew her up from the settee to stand close.

"This is not the wrong *place*, but it is the wrong *time*. Even so you're right, Eden, my love. It's you and I together, no matter what. Dead body and all." He brushed his lips against her temple.

A tear came to her eye. "It's sad about the poor man, terrible."

"Let's get back to the living." He gave her hands a little shake. "So Zach didn't see you leave Kalihi Hospital. However, he did see your father leave. When you got to Hunnewell's you saw him meet with another Chinese man wearing silk. All that is correct, right? But you heard nothing of what was spoken because it was a noisy, windy evening. Then what happened next?"

"My father entered the front yard through the big gate, along with the dead man. A minute or two later I too slipped inside. Once I was in the garden I saw Dr. Jerome ahead of me, but I didn't see the man again . . . until a short time ago."

Rafe took a turn about the room. "Our guest under the gardenia bush could have been the one who clobbered Zach, though I'm not yet convinced." His intent look told her something badgered him. "Logically, you should have been the one struck from behind as you entered the gate, not Zach."

"Yes, so I thought, but could Zachary have misled you about being knocked unconscious?"

"I took a close look at his head. If it had been his purpose to mislead it would've been to try to pin it on Silas. He'd been clobbered all right. There's no getting around that. But it's a trip through a maze to figure out just when he did enter the gate. If he was as close behind Dr. Jerome as he claims—entering within two to three minutes afterward—he would have seen you, or you'd have seen him."

"Unless he came through another way," she suggested.

"He claims he entered by the front gate. All right. So much for that. So you didn't see anyone else in the garden when you first entered except Dr. Jerome?"

She kept telling herself she had nothing to hide, that she had volunteered to come and speak the truth. That she wanted a resolution as much as Rafe did. And there was no accounting how Rafe looked at her. Those eyes of his, so resolute, had a way of making one wilt, or warm.

"No, my father was there, alone." She put her palm to her forehead. "It was all I could do not to go to him. He walked up and down the walkway near the hibiscus bushes, in distress. I felt so sorry for him. He must have made a decision. What it was about, I don't know. He walked quickly toward the back section of the garden."

"Toward the back lanai?" he repeated.

"Yes. The back lanai. There's a stairway from the garden up to a porch-like area that connects to one of the parlors. That's where he went. I know of the area because Claudia had me come to the house recently. We all met in that very same parlor as the Annexation Club last night. I remember the back porch, and we went down those steps into the garden area."

Claudia was Oliver's younger sister and for all intents and purposes she was engaged to Zachary but without an official announcement and ring. Ainsworth kept maneuvering and so did Mr. Hunnewell, but Zachary kept up his elusive dance.

Silence followed the revelation on Dr. Jerome. She had expected a strong reaction from Rafe to what appeared an act of willful eavesdropping on her father's part. She had been embarrassed by his action, and when Rafe said nothing untoward, or even registered surprise, she was taken aback. His eyes were inscrutable.

There was no turning back now, so Eden continued.

"Dr. Jerome stood there in the darkness on the lanai. There was a bamboo curtain between where he stood and the lighted room. I could hear voices coming from within. An argument was under way, or so it sounded. I think it was Mr. Hunnewell speaking. You know how his voice booms in that kingly sort of way? Well, if he was trying to be secretive, one wouldn't have thought so. My father just stood there on the lanai listening—" She turned from Rafe and walked across to a window to look out, to calm her emotions. The clouds were still rolling by toward the higher mountains, and gusts of strong wind still blew.

Rafe didn't hurry her, and she went on again, "However, I didn't stay to see what he did, or whether he met with anyone. I was disappointed, upset—so I hurried off toward the front gate intending to return to Kalihi."

After a perceptible pause, when it was clear she had no more to divulge, Rafe walked up behind her. Her heart beat faster with the feel of strong but tender hands on her arms.

"I don't know why your father stood on the back lanai like that, listening. He could have walked in the front door with Ainsworth and been received with more credibility than Silas. Jerome is a Hawaiian, even if he's been gone these many years, while Silas, in my opinion, has almost no believability when it comes to zeal for the Islands. He only arrived from the mainland in April."

Rafe waited a moment. "Eden, you're certain you've no idea why Jerome went there?"

She shook her head. "No. What you said about his attending the meeting with Grandfather is correct. He could have. I've heard Grandfather try to discuss politics with him on many occasions and my father rarely becomes involved in the discussion." She turned, her eyes anxiously searching his, and finding restraint. "So why did he go up there? Why was he so distraught? Why stand in the shadows and—and eavesdrop!"

He looked at her steadily. "Perhaps it was necessary not to be seen by anyone. His disinterest in Hawaiian politics could possibly serve as a cover."

Eden tensed. At first her emotions balked. "I don't believe it of him."

"I say it, darling, as a possible scenario, not as a fact, not even something I necessarily believe. What we do know is that he *was* there on the lanai."

Yes, and *she* was the reluctant witness.

Rafe went over to the table and poured coffee into his cup. "While he stood there he must have heard Hunnewell and Ainsworth both calling for the overthrow of the Hawaiian throne. There was even the mention of the American Navy. Of Captain Wiltse of the *USS Boston* lending assistance if necessary, if bloodshed broke out. From the beginning I'd thought it reckless to be meeting the way we did. With so little caution taken."

Eden watched him. Did he believe her father guilty?

"Why did you come out to the garden?" she inquired suddenly. "The meeting was underway."

"I believed there was someone standing behind the bamboo curtain. I'd intended to go around the back way and surprise whoever it was, but that's when I met you hiding on the porch."

"I wasn't hiding—exactly," she said, embarrassed. "I'd gone there for help, but the door was locked. Then I heard your footsteps approaching. So I stepped back in the shadows so as not to be seen."

He smiled faintly, a brow inching up. "No matter. Well, you're right about Thaddeus Hunnewell. He might as well have used a bullhorn to warn the queen a meeting was happening. Though he's a smart and talented lawyer, he lacks insight into human character. I told you he was working on an important paper for the Reform Party. It was stolen last night. Far as I know he did nothing to safeguard his work during the meeting."

"And when you saw me in the garden, you thought it was me behind that bamboo curtain."

He leaned his shoulder to the wall, watching her. "The perfect spy, a medical nurse, always at the scene when needed, limpid green eyes and all."

Eden lowered her lashes.

"I could see you playing the role of a spy for Dr. Jerome, or even for your Great-aunt Nora," he continued, growing more serious. "Nora could bring the information you provided to the queen to win favor for Dr. Jerome's clinic, or your father might bring it himself."

Would she spy to gain the clinic on Molokai? After all, she was a supporter of the Hawaiian throne. She wasn't ashamed of her allegiance to the Hawaiian monarchy. Could she spy then? To a certain extent perhaps—but . . . she didn't think she could betray other honorable men that she respected like Sanford Dole, and least of all her grandfather. And Rafe? *Never*.

Steadying her voice with an effort, she said, "Rafe, I assure you, I was *not* working with Dr. Jerome last night as a spy."

Rafe looked at her a long moment. His vibrant gaze softened and warmed. "Your words are well spoken," he said gently, "and accepted. I rushed to that conclusion too quickly, didn't I?"

She stared at him, surprised and mollified.

"You admit it?" she said quietly. "You believe me?"

"I do. You've denied it and I take you at your word. We're in for some rough traveling, if we can't trust one another when we're married."

Her heart was warmly moved.

"Still, though," he tapped his chin thoughtfully, his brisk gaze scanning her with interest. "You'd make a very good one."

"Why, thank you, Mr. Easton. Such compliments, coming from *you*, will soon have me in a swoon."

"I thought only my kisses would have that effect."

Eden wisely kept silent.

"Rafe, seriously, I can't see Dr. Jerome spying for the queen. Unlike Grandfather Ainsworth and Nora, he's not involved in politics. Without Nora to arrange an audience with the queen he'd never be able to see her. He has no open door into the Blue Room."

He folded his arms, leaning there, and watching her. "Your point is well taken.

"Then again, if he'd been there to aid the monarchists, it wouldn't be out of personal zeal for a political belief, but to win approval for his clinic."

Eden sighed and sank onto the settee again. "Yes," she said wearily.

"Then, again," he said, "even if the clinic does come closest to his motivations, I can't see him holding the annexationists' feet to the fire with his father Ainsworth heartily involved in the political movement, and Candace prepared to marry a Hunnewell. Could he betray his family to gain approval of the clinic?" He gave a brief shake of his head. "I don't believe it's in him. He's dedicated to his cause, and if you'll pardon my saying this, darling, a trifle obsessed over it."

She lifted her chin slightly, but was too relieved by his words to be offended. If the truth were known, she too, believed her father a "trifle" obsessed over the clinic, and sadly, over an impossible cure for Rebecca. She had been inclined to overlook these weaknesses because she had her own reason for going to Molokai to meet Rebecca from afar, and to serve.

"Even so," Rafe continued, "Jerome's far too decent a Christian to think the end justifies the means. Ambrose told me your father was meeting with him several times a week now to pray for God's provision for the clinic. He's obviously looking to the spiritual and not the political to provide."

A giant millstone was lifted from Eden's shoulders as she realized Rafe had come logically to the end of his suspicions and did not believe Jerome guilty of spying to fulfill a personal cause. Eden stood, feeling stronger and more hopeful than she had at any time since last evening.

"There's more involved than the politics of annexation versus the Hawaiian Chiefdom." He straightened from the wall. He gazed out the window. "I doubt if all those involved are playing the same game. We may be on the wrong track trying to tie all the events and the individuals together into a singular cause."

"Meaning," she said, "that annexation or its counterpart is one cause for some of the actions last night, but that opium and gambling were quite another, and that they both somehow merged?"

"Exactly. There may be a third reason for some of what happened, too. The Chinese man in silk sounds to me like what Ling has called a 'kingpin,' a ruler. After speaking with Dr. Jerome in a manner that can only be described as clandestine, the kingpin departs in his fancy hackney. Who is he and what did he want with Dr. Jerome? Most likely the kingpin is a ruler in the cartels."

It was making sense to Eden, but she continued to struggle over why Dr. Jerome would be connected.

"Zach insists he trailed Silas to one of the Chinese gambling dives in Rat Alley. There, Silas met with the kingpin. Then Silas went to Kalihi to meet Dr. Jerome and bring him to Hunnewell's to meet the kingpin. Now, as far as the details go Zach probably has it right. But I rather think the man he claims was Silas was our unwanted guest outside under the gardenia bush. In what way was he involved earlier? Surely not in the annexation question! So why did he show up at Kalihi last night to bring Dr. Jerome to Hunnewell's? Certainly not to introduce him to Hunnewell! But to bring him to speak with the silk-clad kingpin. Was there a message from the opium trader to Jerome? You seem to think the kingpin was angry. If so, why? What was the message? Anyway, with that said, darling, you can see why I no longer think Jerome was spying for the monarchy to gain the clinic's approval or otherwise."

Eden gazed at Rafe for a long moment as she weighed in silence the possible validity of his scenario. So, then! Rafe had come to the conclusion that Dr. Jerome, the Chinese kingpin, and the murdered man were isolated from the doings at the Annexation Club! Great relief winged its way through her soul. Her respect for Rafe leaped forward as she understood more fully that his motivation for trying to discover the truth had never been to undermine her father's credibility.

She rebuked herself. *How could I have possibly thought I needed to be cautious with Rafe!*

"The Oriental opium trade here in the Islands reaches even into San Francisco's Chinatown," Rafe said. "I know this through Ling Li. He's mentioned it to me several times. San Francisco may well be the cause of our third motivation for some of what happened last night." He looked at her for a moment as if deciding something. Then, "It's most likely the trail to and from San Francisco that's connected with Herald Hartley and Dr. Jerome."

She stared at him. "You don't think Dr. Jerome is in any way involved in opium," she said, horrified.

"No, darling. I'm convinced Hartley is chin-deep in the suspicious goings-on with Dr. Chen and the medical journal he brought to your father some months ago. Was Dr. Jerome involved? Maybe not, but if what I think is correct, he may know about it now after last night's meeting with the Chinese in silk."

Eden was at a loss for words. The mere mention of San Francisco's Chinatown awakened an unpleasant memory in her mind. Dr. Chen, an associate of her father in medical research into leprosy, seemed to step from the fog, and with him there emerged something unpleasant. Something she did not care to think about, that had seemed not quite honest. It was her father's assistant Herald Hartley's explanation of Dr. Chen's sudden death in Chinatown, and of his medical journal arriving in Honolulu inside Herald's satchel, a gift from Dr. Chen to Dr. Jerome. An old fear half-buried lifted its gaunt face once more and demanded to be heard. *Dr. Chen* and the journal. *Dr. Chen who had died unexpectedly, having made an error in consuming one of his own poisonous herbs for his various avenues of research.*

"Rafe, are—are you going to say anything about all this, and what I've told you?"

He lifted a brow. "To Dr. Jerome?"

"Well, to Jerome, or to Grandfather Ainsworth—Mr. Hunnewell, any of them."

He folded his arms. "No."

"No?!" She stared at him. As she did, a faint smile loitered around his mouth. "But . . . I thought—" she said, and stopped.

"I know what you thought, my sweet. That I said all this to build a case against him, and now that I have, that I'm going to follow through to humiliate my future father-in-law. You don't know me yet, do you, Eden?"

She searched his face, taken aback.

"I may ask Ambrose to talk to Dr. Jerome, or I may have the opportunity myself if it seems wise, but I don't want you present. He'd never forgive me for dragging out anything unpleasant that may reflect on his character, not with his daughter beholding it all."

Again, he was acting with wisdom, she thought. Maybe Rafe was right, and she didn't know him quite as well as she had thought? She looked at him, handsome and often enigmatic, and wondered.

"Let's go on," he said quietly. "You turned and left your father on the back lanai. You hurried away and came upon—? Keno and Oliver."

"Yes. I ducked behind some shrubs. They were talking. Oliver was rude, even obnoxious to Keno." She let out a breath. "Keno hit him. Oliver landed in the bushes. Keno was upset and turned and left, going toward the gate."

Rafe gave her a moment, then pushed on.

"This is important. After Keno left, how long until Silas showed up?"

"Maybe a minute or so."

"He spotted Oliver in the bushes, then what?"

"Well," she reluctantly admitted, "he gave a chuckle, as though amused. I stepped out and he must have heard my footsteps. He quickly stooped to have a look at Oliver. If I hadn't made my presence known there's no telling what he would have done. I've a feeling he would have left Oliver in the bushes and went on about his own business. I don't think he likes Oliver Hunnewell. But by then Oliver was already stirring. I walked forward and asked Silas if Oliver was hurt."

"Was he surprised to see you?"

"You know Silas. He's almost as unruffled as you are. He asked me to please go for Mr. Hunnewell. He said that the door to the library was open from the side porch. So I went up the steps to enter the house, thinking I'd call for one of the servants to locate Mr. Hunnewell, but Silas was wrong, that door at the porch was locked."

His interest sharpened. "He thought the way was open? That's curious."

Eden saw nothing curious about it.

"Thaddeus Hunnewell uses the desk in the library for his writing," he said. "The manifesto I told you about would have been sitting on that desk." He turned toward her. She must have looked tired, for his eyes softened and he looked apologetic.

"I'm afraid I'm wearing you out. Just a few more questions, darling, I promise. Are you up to it?"

She smiled. "It isn't your questions. I was up late last night."

He went to the table and poured her some coffee. "You went into the house with Silas and Oliver. Did Dr. Jerome go indoors from the back lanai, say to have a look at Oliver's injury?"

She took the cup and walked toward the breezeway, then stopped, remembering what was out there under the gardenia blossoms, and turned back. She looked at him. He stood watching her as if alert to her struggle. Her heart thumped uncomfortably.

Now it was coming, the *personal* part that *she* was involved in, the action she'd taken that now made her flush with embarrassment.

She had been unwise in her fears concerning her father and did a foolish thing. She cringed, remembering. She did not want to admit it to Rafe, though she had confessed it as sin to God, but it looked as if she must confess to the man she was going to marry and spend the rest of her life with.

She began the explanation slowly to work up to the reasons for what she had done.

She held the cup between her palms and looked into the dark liquid. "If my father did come inside from the back lanai, I never saw him. When Mr. Hunnewell came in to see Oliver, I saw an opportunity to slip away. I went to the parlor where the annexation meeting had taken place. The gentlemen had all either gone home, or were with Mr. Hunnewell who was asking Oliver questions. I stepped out on the back lanai, but Dr. Jerome was no longer there. When I returned to Kalihi later, he was there working, as though he'd never left."

"And Oliver?"

"Oliver continued his tantrum over Keno 'attacking' him, as he put it. I knew it was a lie. But how could I say otherwise then? So when he insisted on calling Marshal Harper to come to Hunnewell House I knew I would need to defend Keno, even if it meant giving away my cover. I waited until after the marshal spoke to Mr. Hunnewell and Oliver, and when he left for Ambrose's bungalow, I slipped away. You know the rest."

"When you first went inside the house with Oliver and Silas, who went for Mr. Hunnewell?"

"Silas."

"Did he come back with Hunnewell to see Oliver?"

She considered. She hadn't paid much attention. "No, he didn't come back, come to think of it. Mr. Hunnewell arrived within a few minutes. The men from the annexation meeting came along with him to see what had happened to Oliver. We were all in the library. There was a great commotion, everyone talking at once. I didn't see Silas there."

"Then if Silas had wanted, while the rest of you were taken up with Oliver, he could have gone back to the now empty parlor where the meeting had occurred. He could have stepped behind the bamboo curtain and spoken with Dr. Jerome?"

Rafe's voice was deceptively casual. The implication, however, was anything but that.

"Yes, he could have," she agreed.

"Did you go first, or did Silas?"

She thought. "Silas. I first attended to Oliver."

Rafe walked up. His voice was quiet. "And now. Earlier in the garden you had mentioned calling for Dr. Jerome to come and have a look at Oliver."

She felt the warmth beginning to rise.

"Yes, I did."

"Why did you say that when you *knew* Jerome wasn't at Kalihi but on the back lanai?"

She tried to stare calmly back at him but her gaze veered aside. "I wanted to establish an alibi for him in front of you and Silas, and then with Mr. Hunnewell and the other gentlemen—because I repeated the same thing to them. Everyone heard me. I—pretended to send a message to him at Kalihi." She bit her lip. "Then I told Oliver that Dr. Jerome couldn't come. He was in the midst of treating a patient, but that I would go to Kalihi, and bring Lana back with me. That much, I did intend to do, but Oliver said he was feeling better. I knew he wasn't seriously hurt and didn't need a doctor."

"I see."

She winced. She could read nothing in those two simple, quiet words, but they might have been daggers. The flame of humiliation burnt her cheeks, and she whirled round to confront him, defensive. "So there! You forced me to tell you. Are you satisfied? Now I suppose you're ashamed of me," she accused, and all at once her wall of defense crumbled. "And with good cause," she said bursting into overwrought tears. "Yes, I *lied*! But I've already confessed to the Lord—"

Rafe, in one swift unexpected movement, crossed the broken

bridge between them. In two strides, he reached for her, but she slipped free. He caught hold of her and pulled her into his arms, holding her fast.

"Darling, Eden. I don't live under an illusion. If I fell in love with you because I thought you were without sin, then where would I be in the relationship? I'd be out in the rain. You couldn't bear to put up with me."

She wet his handsome jacket with bronze buttons with her tears. "I've confessed to the Lord—"

"Yes, I'm sure you have," he soothed. "It took a sacrifice on your part to decide to tell me the truth. Do you think now that you've trusted me, I'm going to hold it against you?"

Eden stood there hurting, yet knowing she must place all that was between them—with all of the questions, and the misunderstanding, and the hope of a future together—into the gentle hand of God. *I love this man. And love hopes all things. Endures all things.* . . . Under his gaze, her eyes misted.

"Besides," Rafe said, "I didn't insist on the truth to catch you in some fault, but because I needed to know what happened. When we make that marriage vow, Eden, it's for better or worse. And you might as well know that I still think I'm getting the finest girl in all Honolulu, and the most beautiful."

"Rafe." She came to him with sudden relief, and he held her tightly. He buried his face in her hair. His lips brushed her temple, her throat, and then he was kissing her, passionately, and she found herself clinging to him, returning his kiss.

"Nothing must ever come between us," he said.

"Nothing," she whispered.

He held her ring finger to his lips for a tender moment. "It stays put this time. There'll be more struggles, but we'll commit to working through those times." His hand closed tightly over hers as he pressed her palm again his chest. "Until death do us part."

She clung to him. "No, darling, not even then, because I'll love you forever."

"You're going to Molokai to meet Rebecca so you can write her life's story the way you've wanted to," he said. "We've settled all that at Hanalei. And I'm going to San Francisco. In a year we'll meet again, right here in Honolulu, and we'll have Ambrose marry us. That's a promise and nothing will interfere. Agreed?"

She nodded, at first unable to talk. He gave her a light shake. "Say it."

"Yes! Yes!" She would marry him now, at this moment if he asked her. They could go to Ambrose, and no one would ever know until the ceremony was over. It was on her lips to speak it but he bent and was kissing her again.

Somewhere in Eden's fevered mind a door slammed. Or was it a dream? The voice of Keno whistled loudly from far, far away. He stomped his feet.

"Oh, why, what a surprise! Hello everybody," he said in a loud, innocent voice of feigned surprise. "I'm not interrupting anything ... serious?"

Rafe finally released her. Eden stepped back, holding to the back of a chair. Rafe dug into his pocket and handed a cloth to Eden. "Here. Handkerchief."

Eden's fingers trembled as she wiped her eyes. Rafe turned toward Keno, who wore the look of smiling noble innocence. Rafe smirked. "It's about time you showed up. We've a dead body in the garden with a knife to the heart ... expertly inserted. I need to know if you recognize him. He's Chinese. Around forty years old. Rather stout in the belly."

Keno froze as if trying to decide if Rafe were somehow jesting, but after hearing the physical description, he drew in a deep breath. He ran his fingers through his hair.

"I'm afraid it sounds like Sen Fong."

"Then you know him?" Rafe asked with alert interest.

"If it's Sen, the answer's yes. He was waiting in the old field bungalow at five this morning," he said of the hut used for Rafe's office. "He looked fairly done in. Said he wanted to talk. The *luna* came up just then to get his orders for the day and I didn't have time for Sen. I told him I'd meet him here at the house at lunch, to come inside and wait, that it would be safe."

"Safe?" Rafe repeated. Eden too, looked at Keno quickly.

"Did he say he wasn't safe?" Rafe asked.

Keno glanced toward Eden. "I'll explain. Better show me where he is first."

"Rafe, that was the name I was trying to remember. Sen Fong. Dr. Jerome spoke it in a friendly way last night at Kalihi. 'Oh, hello, Sen Fong, what are you doing here?' or something of that nature." She looked quickly at Keno. "Now I recall Ambrose having mentioned that name, too."

"Ambrose?" Rafe turned to look at her. "If he has anything to do with this Sen Fong business, we've been working with the wrong assumption."

"If you mistook Sen Fong for anything but a new convert to Christ, then you've been barking up a wrong bush," Keno said.

Rafe stood, one hand on hip, scowling to himself. "This changes everything."

Eden sank into a chair. "Yes."

Keno looked from one to the other, curious. "Trouble?"

Rafe nodded to him, then gestured to the back garden. "First, we'd better make sure he's the man you're telling us about."

The wind played aggressively through the ferns and palm fronds, tumbling white blossoms along the garden path as long, silvery clouds swept overhead.

Rafe felt the wind surge as he stood beside Keno looking down on the body.

"Yes, that's Sen Fong." Keno stooped beside the body and lifted the white jacket. "Mighty sharp knife."

"Expertly used. Looks like the assassin had plenty of practice." Rafe took the small rug he'd grabbed from the back porch on the way out of the lanai and spread it over the deceased. Now that he knew Sen was a brother in Christ, he felt differently about the remains.

"His worries are over now," he said. "What do you know about him, Keno?"

"Well, I didn't want to talk before Miss Green Eyes. It's not a pretty story. Ambrose knows all the details."

If the man was a new Christian, then Ambrose was likely to have had something to do with it, Rafe decided, then thought of

Sen Fong going to Kalihi to bring Dr. Jerome to meet the possible kingpin. Perhaps Dr. Jerome had something to do with Sen's conversion as well?

"Then we need to talk with Ambrose. You'd better go for the marshal. The longer we keep a murdered man in the garden the more questions we're in for."

Keno shot him a glance. "Have you forgotten how anxious he was to arrest me last night? Oliver's lies have me in a poi pot. Now I'm supposed to show up reporting a murder victim who's been knifed in the heart? Oh no, pal."

"You're out of the pot. I spoke with Thaddeus Hunnewell earlier. He intends to drop the inquiry into last night. He doesn't want any bad publicity over Oliver any more than Ainsworth wants the newspapers digging into the facts around Townsend. But I'll send one of the boys for the marshal."

"Hunnewell dropped the inquiry? Whew! Thanks for taking it on. I thought I might be cleaning commodes out at the Oahu prison for the next decade."

Rafe sent one of the younger Hawaiian servant boys downtown for the marshal, writing out the message and sealing it so the boy couldn't spread the news to his friends along the way that "Makua Rafe got dead man in his garden—with knife in heart."

Rafe asked Eden to remain at the house to meet Marshal Harper and show him out to the garden. However, the real reason for asking her to remain was on account of Keno's earlier comment that Eden should not be burdened with the details surrounding Sen Fong.

Ambrose was the man to talk to, all right. He had an empathy with the Chinese sugar workers on Kea Lani and Hawaiiana because of the small Bible meetings that were being established. Rafe had been involved in the groundwork when he'd lived here on the pineapple plantation, but now that he needed to spend time at Hanalei or downtown Honolulu, the classes here were led by Keno under the administration of Ambrose.

Twenty minutes later, Rafe and Keno arrived at the mission church to find Ambrose at his pastoral work in the church office. The door was usually left unlocked for anyone who cared to enter to sit in the pews, read their Bible, and pray in a quiet, undisturbed environment, or just to slip away to be alone. Rafe came here often. He liked the silence. There were no interruptions except for the lonely breezes in the rustling palm trees. Something about the sound of the wind in the trees moved him spiritually, though he couldn't explain why.

Ambrose had heard them enter and so came to the door of his office. He stood with the light behind him emphasizing his solid Easton frame.

"Well, lads," he said with some surprise, "come in." He walked toward them and the pews, for the office was too small to receive the three of them comfortably. He searched their faces, and they must have announced trouble, for he gestured to sit in the front pews.

"What brings you here, Rafe? Isn't there a meeting with the queen this afternoon?"

"Tomorrow," Rafe said. "Soon after Nora brings Dr. Jerome and Eden to Iolani to get the clinic approved." His voice told nothing of his inner feelings on the matter of the clinic's certain approval, but Ambrose already knew that he wasn't pleased, even though he'd yielded to Eden's desires on the matter.

"Ah, yes. Jerome was here asking for prayer about the clinic. Looks as if Queen Liliuokalani is near to approving it. If it does gain her nod, he's planning to leave for Molokai within a fortnight."

Ambrose's gaze showed Rafe no sympathy. He knew him too well for that. From childhood Rafe had never wanted sentiment from his father's elder brother.

"We need to trust the Lord on this" was all Ambrose said. He went on casually, "First, Jerome's trying to raise needed cash for medical and food supplies. They'll need wood too, for the building that will go up. I told him the congregation would be pleased to do what they could. Unfortunately it's not going to be nearly enough. Herald has nothing to spend, so I'm told, and Eden's wages from Kalihi and the allowance Ainsworth gives her will hardly fit the bill for the three of them."

Rafe never ceased to be amazed at how little Ainsworth's younger son received in allowance from the family wealth stashed in Spreckels' bank. If a reason were required to spy for the monarchy, Jerome's need for money to build the clinic and support the research supplied the motive.

But Rafe no longer believed this to be a credible explanation for why Dr. Jerome was there that night. As Rafe had admitted to Eden, her father's obsession over his clinic could be questioned, but his sincerity and Christian faith could not. Dr. Jerome wasn't in the best of health, as Rafe had easily noticed the last time he'd seen him, and yet he pushed ahead doggedly in his work at Kalihi, and was assisting Ambrose with the teaching of Scripture on the plantations.

"There's also the financial need for a printing press," Ambrose was saying.

Rafe realized some time ago that Eden wanted to ask him for a loan to buy the press and help build the clinic but couldn't find the courage. He could easily alleviate her dilemma of asking him outright, but that would have spoiled the game. He found it ironic that he may be the one to sponsor Dr. Jerome's clinic on Molokai.

"When was Dr. Jerome here?" Rafe asked.

"Less than an hour ago."

Keno shot Rafe a look.

"Why?" Ambrose asked, as if he smelled trouble brewing. "Were you wanting to speak with him about something?"

"Not exactly . . . do you know Sen Fong?"

Ambrose's countenance changed, but not for the better. Rafe noticed the lines of worry. Ambrose removed a pair of small spectacles from his front jacket pocket and cleaned them with a white cloth. He was thoughtful, taking longer than necessary to polish the lenses. He slid them on, then ended up ignoring the reason he put them on by looking at Rafe over the edge of the rims.

So, his uncle was debating whether to tell him what he knew. Rafe waited with a disarming smile. He almost always got around his uncle.

"Well, yes," Ambrose admitted at last. "I know Sen. And I know his background."

Rafe looked at Keno and gave a brief nod.

"He's been murdered," Keno announced. "His body is over at Hawaiiana, in the garden. Knifed."

Ambrose remained silent for a long moment, followed by a weary sigh.

"Very well, then. Let's talk. Why don't you close those windows, Keno. Then come over here and sit down, both of you. Though Keno knows most of this already."

"That bad, is it?" Rafe asked, as Keno went around shutting windows against any possible eavesdropper.

"Well, not entirely bad where the plantation workers are concerned. With the leadership of Dr. Jerome some headway's been made in working with the sick. We've slowed down the gambling and the opium sales among the Chinese on Kea Lani and Hawaiiana. Sen Fong was a top distributor in the Islands. Better have a seat. This will take a little time to explain."

⁓ ᳂ᳲ ⁓

Rafe and Keno sat in the church-house pew across from their uncle with the sunlight pouring in through the side windows. Rafe listened in speculative silence while Ambrose gave details of what had been transpiring while Rafe was away, taken up with Hanalei and life in the Legislature.

"The opium cartel out of Shanghai has infiltrated every plantation in the Islands, and the abuse among some of the cane workers and their families has increased," Ambrose told Rafe. "As you well know, King Kalakaua opened the door wide for a particular opium lord to be given the sovereign right to supply the sugarcane workers, the gambling dens, and prostitution houses."

Rafe was not naive about the vices of the Islands. Even when a boy he'd come across cane workers on Kea Lani smoking opium, and the culture had not changed.

"Naturally, the Hawaiian king and his government received money in return for the right. One kingpin outbid the others and paid a great bundle of money for the sole right to supply this addictive deception," Ambrose went on.

"As you're aware, the opium run isn't new," Ambrose said. "What is new is how they've infiltrated. They've managed to place themselves right in with the contracted cane workers and their families. Keno has seen this. And now they've established strongholds right on the plantations. The leaders' huts are used as depositories for the opium until it can be dispensed and sold, not only in the fields, but Honolulu and mainland San Francisco."

Ambrose shook his head and stood with righteous anger. "Is this what Hawaii wants? Thousands of her people preyed upon by the greedy and powerful, smoking the drug and lying about the beaches, streets, and gutters, in a deceptive stupor with wasted lives and destitute families? God cannot bless such corruption!"

Ambrose was right, of course. The opium and gambling cartels were growing more powerful, and like Goliath, they rumbled intimidating threats to the cowering.

"Little by little, step by step, they are gaining strongholds. We can stand against this form of deception in the one way we have been enabled—by not being ashamed of the true Light of the Gospel of Christ," Ambrose said passionately. "And so this brings me to Sen Fong."

As Ambrose looked down at them, Rafe's mind leaped backward in time to when he and Keno were boys being taught by Uncle Ambrose to love truth and stand firm against youthful temptations. Ambrose would pick up his old worn Bible, wave it under their noses like an Old Testament wave offering, and say with calm, precise passion: "This Book is the foundation of life for now and always.

If you think otherwise you're in deep trouble, boys. Every book," and he'd tap the Bible, "yes, even the sacrifices in Leviticus, is the Word of God and is profitable for our learning."

Rafe was aware of Keno shifting in the pew with a sober expression. He was still pricked by having clobbered Oliver last night, and having the marshal show up at Ambrose's bungalow.

"Sen Fong was one of the kingpins in Oahu," Ambrose said. "He was distributing to Kea Lani, to Hawaiiana, and to Hunnewell's plantation—"

Rafe, quick on the uptake, interrupted— "Hunnewell's?"

"Yes, Hunnewell's, Collier's, Palmer's, Dutton's, all of them."

Hunnewell's. Rafe thought of the Chinese man in silk who'd waited near the tall iron gates of the beach house, which apparently had become a familiar territory.

"Jerome and I have been holding campaigns in Oahu, working with the willing plantation owners to bring the message of Christ to the workers. The results have been encouraging. Chinese have come to Christ on every plantation where we've preached. And Jerome's been treating the sick among the workers, while he informs of the evils of opium and gambling addiction, and they're listening."

"And Sen Fong came to Christ through one of these campaigns?" Rafe suggested.

Ambrose smiled for the first time. "That's what I'm saying, Rafe—a victory, despite the murderous outcome. As you'd expect, our actions haven't gone over well with the cartel. The light of truth is a direct threat to their racket."

Rafe took in the news with calm consideration. It was as he expected.

"Sen Fong came to a recent meeting to spy out the dangers we presented to the cartel. I was speaking in the fields of Hawaiiana for several days, and Jerome was teaching the medical dangers of opium. Well, after a few days the Word penetrated his soul. The Spirit worked, and one night, quite late, Keno brought Sen to the bungalow door. Tell him what happened, Keno."

"I had some curiosity about him from the beginning," Keno admitted. "I knew he didn't belong to any of the Bible groups I was involved with. I asked him if he were a Christian, and he said yes. Well, I thought, I don't believe he is. But that's what the meetings are all about, bringing sinners to the Savior. So let him get close and feel the holy fire! Well, he did. He came to me a few days later. He was afraid of being seen, and while he didn't tell me who he was afraid of, I thought I could guess. He asked me to bring him secretly to Ambrose and Dr. Jerome. I did, and Ambrose took us in. Sen asked that Dr. Jerome be there, so I went gallivanting off to locate him. It happened to be his night away from Kalihi, so I was able to find him at Kea Lani. It took some doing to get one of the house servants up and moving. But at last, Dr. Jerome came downstairs. He came with me here to the church, and he and Ambrose must have talked with Sen for over an hour. I fell asleep in the back."

"Three hours," Ambrose corrected. "I've not seen such a case before. Sen paced the floor like a caged hyena. Questions, questions, questions. In the end he was praying with me and trusting in Christ. He was truly repentant, but besides that he was convicted about his work and vowed not to have anything more to do with dispensing opium."

"He was in grave danger from that very moment," Ambrose said.

"He knew too much," Keno added.

"The main kingpin viewed him as a threat," Rafe ventured. "Sen would know all of their routes, opium stashes, middlemen, and the top kingpin in the cartel. So he had him killed by an assassin's knife."

"After he was baptized, his public confession of his faith made him a martyr in the making," Ambrose said.

Rafe smacked the pew in front of him and stood. "If I'd been around I may have been able to get him out of Oahu."

"And be shanghaied to work on the Great Wall of China," Keno cracked. "It's bound to need repairs by now."

"It would have been worth the risk."

"Well, truth is, I did send you a message," Keno said unhappily.

"I was going to have him meet us at Hawaiiana. When you didn't respond, I figured—"

"I didn't get the message," Rafe said. "Where did you send it?"

"Hanalei."

"I've been at the hotel the last two weeks."

"Don't, lads, don't," Ambrose said, holding his palm outward, a pleading look on his rugged face. "God is in control of these mysteries of life. The missed appointments, the lost opportunity, the shipwreck, the heart attack . . . that's where our faith in Him is tested. How strong is it? Having rescued Sen Fong from a lost eternity, for a reason known only to God, Sen's violent death was allowed. Even so, I assure you, evil has no permanent triumph. That's our confidence through this life of trials. All things work together for good to those who *love* God. So don't blame yourselves for a message gone awry."

Rafe walked over to the window and opened it. He needed fresh air. A rush of fragrance from flowers Noelani had planted came to him on a breeze that carried birdsong.

"I remember now that Sen had mentioned that he'd warned Dr. Jerome the kingpin didn't want him intervening in their work."

Rafe turned from the window. "Sen told you that, when?"

"Just yesterday."

The very day Sen brought Dr. Jerome from Kalihi to meet with the Chinese man in silk.

Rafe shot an inquiring look at Ambrose. "Why was Dr. Jerome singled out? You do most of the preaching."

"Sen thought it was because they'd heard Jerome founded the mission church. He's also been more vocal in using the Board of Health to try and defeat the opium bill in the Legislature."

Sen Fong's visit to Kalihi was beginning to make sense to Rafe now. Sen must have been sent to tell Jerome a kingpin wished to speak with him at Hunnewell's. Perhaps it was the top man himself who had opted to meet with Jerome. What was the message given? Both Eden and Zach had suggested the kingpin grew angry, but the anger may have come only after Jerome declined to cooperate. Did he then tell Jerome to end his vocal campaign against them? He may have been asked to encourage the queen to pressure her Legislature to pass the opium bill when he met with her tomorrow. Had there been an incentive? A large bribe? Or a warning with a promised scorpion's sting!

Whatever was said or threatened had distressed Jerome. Eden saw him in the garden pacing and upset. Then he had gone up to the back lanai, but why? Only Dr. Jerome could explain that, and why it was Sen Fong had disappeared in the garden, since Eden hadn't seen him again.

Had Sen Fong then gone after the kingpin, following him to the gambling den? It was only a guess on Rafe's part, but Sen may have thought it his new Christian duty to confront the top opium leader over the way he'd treated Dr. Jerome, a decent man who was trying to help the Chinese people. He may have tried to explain to the kingpin why Jerome refused to cooperate with the cartel. Whatever was said or done, Sen was murdered the next day.

Rafe turned to Ambrose. "I believe Dr. Jerome was warned last night at Hunnewell's to cease his crusade against the opium bill. The warning's likely to extend to you as well. It could prove risky for both of you, though they usually avoid moves against a haole—but where money's concerned, who knows."

"Hold on there a moment, lad, what did you say about Jerome being warned at Hunnewell's?"

Rafe told him about Sen Fong and Jerome outside Kalihi Hospital, and Zachary being knocked unconscious as he came through the gate, but he did not mention Eden, or Jerome up on the back lanai.

Keno gave a low whistle. "Now who would have clobbered Zach, and why?"

Ambrose too looked worried for the first time. "Did you look at Zachary and actually see where he was hit?"

Rafe knew why Ambrose would ask such a question. He did

not put it beyond Zachary to work himself up into such an emotional storm that he would end up somehow laying the blame on his arch competitor, Silas.

"I examined him. There was a cut all right, and it fit with his explanation of what happened. He was groggy when I found him in my hotel room." He turned to Keno. "When you left Hunnewell's after meeting Oliver, did you see anyone around the garden or outside the gate?"

Keno stood frowning, staring down at the floor. "I'm not sure."

"Not sure?" Rafe's interest quickened.

"I thought there may have been somebody. Possibly a movement of someone nearby when I first entered but . . . well, it was dark, and windy. The bushes and palm fronds were moving. After leaving Oliver my mind was in turmoil, it all happened so quickly. I'd hate to suggest someone was sneaking around when I first arrived. I can't be sure."

If there had been someone nearby after the fiasco it might have been Silas. Despite Zachary's obsession with Silas, it did look as if Silas or even Oliver may have been near the gate when Zachary entered. Rafe had little choice but to put the matter aside for the present.

"I'd like to stay and look into all of this," Rafe said, trying to keep his frustration under control. "But the steamer leaves Honolulu on Sunday morning for the mainland."

Rafe looked at Ambrose evenly. "Have you been warned the way Dr. Jerome was?"

Ambrose looked undisturbed. "No. Not a peep. It wouldn't do them any good anyway. I think they know that. I don't want you worrying about me, lad. If the Lord's not finished with me yet in the work we're doing here, they're wasting their time."

"When a strong man armed keepeth his palace, his goods are in peace." Rafe quoted the words of Christ.

Ambrose nodded soberly. "That, too. And so I shall."

Rafe thought of Hiram Bingham, the first missionary to

Hawaii. Most of the whalers hated him for hindering their sexual conquests in Hawaii. One night several had gotten drunk and followed Hiram when he left the king's house. They'd planned to kill him. But a Hawaiian Christian had learned about it and also followed Hiram. When the time came for the drunken whalers to jump the missionary, the Hawaiian had beaten them off. The whalers had also tried to burn Hiram's bungalow down, and a church. The opium and gambling cartel reminded Rafe of these whalers. They didn't want Ambrose and Dr. Jerome reaping spiritual fruit among the Chinese sugarcane workers from the teaching of Christ.

Rafe snatched up his hat. "The marshal's been notified by now of Sen Fong's murder. I'll need to go back to the house and give him my report."

"He'll want to talk to me about this, and to Jerome as well," Ambrose said.

Ambrose was right. The marshal wouldn't ignore the fact Dr. Jerome was with Sen Fong last night. "If Dr. Jerome can identify the kingpin, the marshal will need to go to the gambling house in Rat Alley," Rafe added.

Keno looked at him. "Why Rat Alley? There are gambling dens all over Honolulu."

Rafe considered what to say. "Zach claims he followed Silas there. That's where he met with the kingpin who was waiting for Dr. Jerome at Hunnewell's."

Keno groaned. "Double trouble. We're all going to be made into Peking duck before this is over."

"Where's Eden?" Ambrose asked, concern in his eyes.

"At Hawaiiana."

Ambrose searched his face. "How much does she know about all this?"

"Too much. As usual, she's in the thick of it. She found the body."

*W*hen it comes to forgetting what Townsend did, some memories don't deserve to be buried—not yet.

Rafe felt the wind tugging at his jacket as he stood on the burial ground at Hanalei by Matt Easton's gravesite. Raindrops met his face as he looked off toward the beach where dim foaming lines of surf washed ashore. Not far away was another grave, that of his grandfather, Daniel Easton.

Two men, two legacies, Rafe mused. "My father knew how to multiply the land's produce. My grandfather knew how to look up at the stars and see the Lord's footsteps moving silently through eternity. I am the restless heir of both men, and God will hold me responsible for the pathway I've taken. I can't live any way I choose, then expect special treatment to be handed to me from God just because Daniel Easton lived a godly life."

⌒⌒

Early each morning Eden and Herald Hartley left Kalihi Hospital and walked the short distance to Dr. Jerome's makeshift laboratory at the Kakaako branch of the hospital, near the entrance to Honolulu's harbor, where the suspected lepers were held for diagnosis.

The Kakaako branch stood on a sun-drenched shoreline of mostly mud flats and a few withered tufts of parched, yellowing grass, for when the south wind blew, the sea water was pushed all the way in and left the area soaked with salty brine. Suspected lepers were restrained here for long periods until the doctors could determine whether the sores and blotches that afflicted the patients were due to leprosy or another disease of lesser consequence. As Eden knew, most of the patients held at Kakaako would be diagnosed as lepers. When this decision was reached they would be quickly boarded on the leper ferryboat bound for Molokai—the settlement of no return, where they were outcasts for life.

Thank God the witness of God's mercy is there, Eden thought. The leper colony of doomed individuals was a picture of all humanity without the redemption found in the work of Christ on the cross.

"I've thought about the justice of detainment," Herald Hartley was telling Eden as they left Kalihi Hospital porch and walked toward Honolulu harbor to Kakaako. "Though I understand how your sensitive nature may be easily offended by this facility, what does it really matter if some of these ignorant people here do not have leprosy now?"

"Well, it matters to them. And it's unfair to label them as ignorant."

"Well, quite so. However, even if some of them are afflicted with other tropical skin diseases, they're also dangerous to the healthy."

"But that's not fair, Herald."

"Regardless, it's still true that they are dangerous! If not leprosy, they have tropical rash-itch, or tuberculosis of the skin, or a later stage of syphilis. So what happens? We determine they are free of leprosy and they're released to return home with great relief and tell everyone they are clean. But are they clean? They're even more dangerous for spreading the diseases they do have! So, again, compassion becomes counterproductive. We must approach these issues with strict adherence to the law."

"You sound dreadfully callous. Almost as if you're not speaking about individuals—each one unique, made in God's image. Doesn't that tell you how precious they are to our Creator?"

"Oh, quite, quite. However, we have little choice but to deal realistically when it comes to disease. So we must keep them contained in cages or—"

Slowly she had been growing impatient with the young man in recent months. As her father's secretary, Herald Hartley had been his supporter and vocal defender, but as his medical assistant, he displayed uncaring attitudes that she noticed coming to the forefront. The more comfortable he had begun to feel around her, the more he showed a side to his nature that sometimes sounded almost heartless. She now sighed as she considered working beside him day after day at Molokai.

This morning, however, despite his usual arguments about the strengths and weaknesses of medicine, Eden noticed that he lacked his usual vigor. His tan face was haggard. His shoulders stooped a little under the white medical apron.

"At least we will soon be off for Molokai," he said. "Dr. Jerome is certainly pleased with the prospects awaiting us tomorrow with Queen Liliuokalani. Miss Nora has provided your father a splendid opportunity. A delightful lady, Miss Nora. Very practical. No emotional nonsense about her."

Eden turned her head and looked at him. Would he imply that she was an emotional creature? It was true about Great-aunt Nora, though. She had showed a bright spirit that morning after receiving a message from Iolani Palace confirming Dr. Jerome's appointment with Liliuokalani tomorrow afternoon. "Not a thing to disturb your confidence, Jerome," she had said to him at breakfast that morning. "She's sent a message to me promising she'll let nothing interfere with the upcoming meeting tomorrow, not even the pesky members of the Reform Party she's due to meet with before you."

Ainsworth, Mr. Hunnewell, and Rafe Easton were included with those "pesky" Reform members that Great-aunt Nora had singled out without realizing she'd done so.

Dr. Jerome had seemed to have confidence in Nora, and he'd assured her he was leaving the matter of the clinic's approval tomorrow to "the grace of our Lord's purpose," before leaving the plantation house with Eden for Kalihi. He was now at Kakaako at his makeshift research lab, where he was seeing the leper detainees one at a time, carefully watching every blemish and rising.

Eden, however, noticed that her father, as well as Herald, had been withdrawn and thoughtful recently, especially since the news of Sen Fong's murder yesterday. Sometimes she would come upon him standing and looking out a window at Kalihi with a frown on his forehead, his hands folded behind his back in a reflective stance. Herald also appeared to her to be tiptoeing about, jumping with a start when her father turned suddenly to speak to him.

When she asked Dr. Jerome what worried him he merely smiled tiredly and patted her shoulder. "Eden, my dear, you've enough on your mind already."

"Is it Sen Fong's murder?" she asked quietly. Almost immediately, Herald had dropped a vial, spilling the contents on the mat flooring, and her father had reacted impatiently.

Afterward, Dr. Jerome had looked at her, his deep-set eyes grave. "Yes, Sen Fong. His murder is still a terrible situation for the living. He had a family in San Francisco. . . . I've written them to try to bring some comfort and hope. I don't know whether Sen had time enough to share his conversion with them by letter, but I've explained in as much detail as I could what took place in his mind and heart, and why he became a Christian. Let's pray that when they receive my letter they will seek to know more and respond as he did."

She would have liked to ask him more questions, but he'd obviously wished to avoid the details, and with another pat on her shoulder he was gone, walking briskly back to the research lab to join Dr. Bolton in a laboratory test.

Now, as Eden walked with Herald down to Kakaako she frowned to herself. Her father knew more than he was disclosing about Sen Fong. What had happened when he met with the Chinese kingpin in front of Hunnewell's?

They neared the Kakaako holding station. Herald paused abruptly, his long fingers tugging unconsciously at the linen tie string around his middle. A muscle at the corner of his bottom lip twitched as it often did. Eden followed his gaze toward the section of sparse struggling turf in its sandy location to a certain good-looking young man in a white shirt with wide sleeves and dark trousers. He stood watching them.

"That's Easton," Herald said, nothing in his voice.

"Yes, I'm expecting him," Eden said cheerfully. "As a member of the Legislature, Rafe Easton can bring the plight of the detainees before the others. That's my hope, at least."

Herald gave a nod, but his manner lacked any enthusiasm. Instead of offering to lead the way and elaborate the dire needs to Rafe, he skirted the issue.

"Dr. Bolton said the government can't afford to grant any more funds to the Board of Health. Well, I'll be about my business. I've much work to do this morning. See you later, Eden," Herald said and he walked off toward the building.

She looked after him, holding back her impatience. A moment later Rafe walked up. He looked after Herald.

"In a bit of a hurry, isn't he," he stated.

"I rather think he's avoiding you," she said with a brief smile.

"I have that effect on some people." His gaze warmed as it came to rest on her, causing her heart to beat faster. "Just as long as you don't sprout wings and take off, my dear Miss Derrington."

"Oh, I'd never do that, Mr. Easton; I need an escort for the fancy dinner-ball at Iolani," she parried lightly.

"There's nothing like being needed."

"Seriously, is there any news about Sen Fong?"

"Nothing but our past suspicions. Mine haven't changed. The

marshal is watching the gambling dens, following a suggestion he may find something, but I doubt he'll come up with anything to identify the assassin. Now . . ." He smiled. "Why am I being escorted to Kakaako?"

Her eyes met his. "Money."

"That's what I thought. How long is this tour? Afterward, I'd like to have a little chat with you on a few matters."

"It won't take long." Eden walked on toward the Kakaako Leper Detention camp, explaining the desperate needs to Rafe as they walked.

"I've spoken to Dr. Bolton about things, but it's way beyond him, and it's no one's fault, really. The funds just aren't available."

Kakaako was not a new or pleasant camp for the suspected lepers to wait out their verdicts. The area was like a wasteland, absent of trees and foliage, and there was no shade except by the sides of dilapidated huts on posts. They had been constructed on stilts because the strong south wind often brought the sea rolling in across the mud flats, flooding the area. The situation only encouraged idleness, adding to the squalor of the detainees.

No words were needed for Eden to explain her concerns as they walked slowly past unclean holding cages with suspect lepers wearing blank expressions, as if they had long ago given up all hope.

"If God's Word could convert an opium kingpin like Sen Fong, then it could do a work here as well," Rafe commented as they walked back toward Kalihi Hospital. "Liberty begins with a heart reconciled to God. What the lepers need most is hope, hope from the Bible that transcends their situation. I'll ask Ambrose to begin a ministry here. At any rate, I'll bring up the needs in the Legislature again. The last time they voted it down. Even if they won't allocate more money to the Board of Health, we'll get publicity in the newspapers, and maybe some interest from charitable institutions and individuals. And let's get Zach to do a big write-up in the *Gazette* on the urgent needs. Maybe Parker Judson and Celestine could do something in the mainland to interest the American churches. In the meantime . . ."

Eden brightened. "Rafe, those are wonderful ideas. I'll talk to Ambrose and Zachary at the family meeting tomorrow. There are also some nuns here," she said quietly. "Walter Murray Gibson brought them, and built them a handsome nunnery, and a small hospital on Molokai."

"With Priest Damien having gone to Molokai years ago, it probably encouraged Gibson to bring in the nuns. If Gibson ever thought that brought him any merit, it didn't do his character any good. He remained a corrupt political official until they ran him out of Hawaii."

As Walter Murray Gibson was leaving he had nearly been lynched by some of the people from Honolulu who had heard about his financial dealings, but Sanford Dole had rushed down to the wharf and saved his life. Gibson, then boarding the steamer for San Francisco, had died on the way.

They'd reached the lawn in front of Kalihi, a much more pleasant spot for conversation, with rustling palms, leafy banana trees, and blossoming bushes. Rafe stopped and faced her, taking hold of her arms. He smiled. "And now for good news. Kip is going to be secure. My reason for entering the Legislature has met with surprising success. I've obtained legal permission to begin adoption proceedings for Kip, though I'll need to go through the San Francisco agency."

Eden caught a breath. "Oh, darling, that's wonderful news." Unable to contain herself she hugged him; then, a little embarrassed over her exuberance, she gave a little laugh and was about to step back when his arms tightened.

"Not so fast." His vital gaze held hers. He kissed her lightly. "The full reward will be collected another time. Am I to assume by your delight that you still fully agree to becoming his mother?"

"Darling, I'm looking forward to being his mother," she said firmly. "Those green eyes of his—" She stopped as soon as she spoke and then rushed on, hoping he hadn't noticed, but that would be unlike Rafe, and a brow lifted curiously.

"What about his green eyes?"

She tried to shrug it off, to steer him away, and said lightly, "Oh, well, I have green eyes and I shall be his perfect mum." Even that didn't succeed, because he was linking Kip with her.

The thoughtful silence held them. *Oh no, if his thoughts begin to move toward that possibility....* She saw a curious spark in the depths of his gaze. She anxiously tried to think of something else to say to detour his thinking, but her mind seemed to freeze. Inevitably, she waited for the next question: Rebecca has green eyes, doesn't she?

It seemed an awkward minute had passed in silence before he spoke. When he did, his voice glossed over the question, leaving it unspoken as though nothing had occurred. But she knew he'd been remembering her mother Rebecca . . . Molokai . . . the baby left on the beach . . . a woman hiding in the rocks who refused to reveal herself and had run away when she saw that he'd rescued the infant from certain death.

"Yes, you do have provocative green eyes," Rafe said. "I've always thought so."

She rushed in. "And so, darling, when will you bring Kip to Hanalei?"

"I thought I'd wait until we're married and settled, 'adjusted' to each other is the way Ambrose put it." His eyes flickered with amusement. "I don't know whether I'll ever 'adjust' to you or not, but I'm anxious to find out."

"I shall be the perfect helpmeet for you," Eden said piously. "But why must you adopt Kip in San Francisco?"

"A safeguard. He was aboard the *Minoa* when I first docked there after French Guiana."

Eden remembered. She'd been attending Chadwick's Nursing School when Great-aunt Nora arrived with King Kalakaua's entourage staying at the Palace Hotel. Eden had gone to the hotel to meet Nora and have dinner with a large group of people the king was entertaining. She'd met Rafe at the hotel, and what a shock it had been. The next day she'd visited him on the *Minoa* to see and taste the new pineapples he'd brought back. Parker Judson, also in San Francisco, at the time had shown great interest. Eden had discovered Kip aboard and had unfairly thought ill of Rafe. And Rafe had stubbornly refused to convince her the baby was not his biological child. What a drama that had been between them! That was when Grandfather Ainsworth was trying to get Rafe and Candace to marry.

Eden instinctively laid her palm on his arm as if he might slip away from her heart again.

"And so Kip will remain with Celestine in San Francisco until after we're married and *adjusted*," she said, clearly getting the plan laid out in her own mind. She wouldn't mind at all if Kip was to be with them from the very beginning of their marriage, but if Rafe preferred to wait she wouldn't protest. Kip was in wonderful hands with Celestine, one of the finest ladies with Victorian conduct that Eden knew. Since it had been Rafe's idea to adopt Kip from the beginning, as well as Rafe's scheme to snatch him away to San Francisco to prevent the Board of Health from sending him back to Molokai, Eden accepted the plan he wanted.

And what if her suspicion about Kip and Rebecca turned out to be right? How would Rafe react to the news?

As soon as I discover the truth on Molokai I shall send him a message by the supply ship, she thought, and asked, "When will the adoption officially take place?"

"It will take six months, then I can sign the final legal paper."

Time enough to meet with Rebecca and to get the facts back to Rafe. And if she were wrong about her nagging suspicions? Well then, Rafe need never be bothered about it.

"And now," he said, "you have something you'd like to discuss with me before I leave for the mainland? Perhaps you're hesitant to bring it up because of modesty?"

At first she thought he spoke about Sen Fong and the suspicious happenings of a few days earlier at Hunnewell's, which unfortunately remained unsolved and as murky as ever, perhaps worse, as the days moved on. Then it struck her that perhaps she hadn't been as subtle as she had thought when it came to the problem of raising the money to buy the printing press. Dr. Jerome was much concerned over the need for a loan to pay for supplies and the construction needs for the clinic. She had entertained the notion that she might get a loan from Rafe, but couldn't bring herself to ask.

She drew in a breath and decided that she would approach the matter with the straightforwardness Rafe appeared to like from her. He disliked coyness, or the feminine art of wiles.

"It's about the printing press," she said. "I've mentioned it before. Rebecca first brought it up in the letter I received several months ago. Perhaps you remember?"

"I do. Ambrose has spoken of it as well. Rebecca knows of a discouraged young lad there who still has good use of his hands. Ambrose says you want to teach the patients there to print children's books, even some Bibles. And both of you are hoping Ambrose might teach him to run the press, and create a paper for the colony. The press is your idea, I believe. I'm not surprised, my sweet. I expected as much. Your heart is moved by spiritual needs and hopelessness. You see, darling, I do pay attention to your interests."

Eden couldn't keep her surprise from showing. She'd thought she might have to go into long detail to explain why the printing press was needed and important.

"Ambrose has also suggested that maybe you would consider the use of the *Minoa* to bring the press to shore," she said meekly.

"Where do you expect to get a printing press?"

"Well, Ambrose mentioned one could be bought in and shipped from San Francisco."

"That would take months. I assume helping this boy find a purpose in life is somewhat urgent. Why not buy one from your Great-aunt Nora? I'm sure the cause will appeal to her. Don't worry about the money."

"From Nora . . . ?" she said, bewildered.

"If I recall correctly, she ordered a new one for the *Gazette* a year ago and isn't using it. Since she's obviously in no hurry, I'll buy it from her and she can reorder when she's ready."

Eden broke into a smile. "Of course! I remember now, it was Zachary who talked her into buying it and she was quite displeased about it afterward because of the cost. Darling, that's wonderful. That press must be better than any I could have wished for. And does this mean you can actually deliver it?"

"To see such a happy smile and have your eyes light up? Yes. When I return from San Francisco, or else Keno can deliver it sooner. Ambrose can go with him and set it up. And yes, my sweet, I shall loan the money to build the clinic. There must be a satisfying reason for sponsoring a cause which I've opposed all this time, but I just can't figure out what it is," he said wryly.

"Oh darling! You will? Oh Rafe, I shall never forget your generosity! I love you so much."

"I knew there was a reason—*that* must be it."

She laughed. "Wait till my father learns it's Rafe Easton who'll loan him the money to build the clinic. He won't know what to think about the change that's come over all of us."

Rafe smiled. "I think he'll know what to make of it, all right. A wise man signs a peace treaty with his soon to be father-in-law."

She supposed her father would also prove wise enough to make peace with Rafe. It wasn't lost on her that in the end, Rafe's favor put Dr. Jerome in his debt.

"Speaking of Keno," he said. "Strangely enough, Ainsworth is offering him land on the Big Island to grow cane, and a financial loan. I've had a look at it. It's decent sugar land. Trouble is, Keno isn't of the sugar-king mentality; he's pineapple or coffee."

Eden looked at him quickly. She had spoken to Ambrose about vows and he'd given her his wisdom on what Scripture taught. He had mentioned Jephthah who had made a rash vow to God, and because of it his daughter had remain unmarried to serve in the tabernacle at Shiloh all her life. In those days for a Jewish woman to remain unmarried and childless was a shameful fate, and so Jephthah's daughter had mourned what would befall her because of her father's hasty vow. There were other rash vows as well, but the worst, in Eden's opinion, was wicked Herod. In order to keep his rash vow he had ordered the death of John the Baptist! Ambrose hadn't told her what to do. He'd left the conclusion to her. Eden had made up her mind. How could she keep the truth back from Rafe when their upcoming marriage was certain? She couldn't!

"Do you think Keno will accept the agreement?" she first asked.

"I haven't told him. Ainsworth has asked me to play the third party and to keep it a secret from Keno. There's something about the plan that makes me uncomfortable. I'd rather everything were in the sunlight when it comes to Keno. He trusts me, and I plan to keep it that way." He looked at her. "I'm not insulting your grandfather by any means, as I think by and large he's a good man. But there's something more behind his offer. He isn't the sort for philanthropic deeds without a solid reason for doing them. Keno's been ignored by your grandfather—even when Candace was out beating the drums for his merits. Now that she's broken off with Keno to marry Oliver, why would Ainsworth decide to be his benefactor? Rather intriguing, don't you think?"

She *felt* the discerning gleam in his gaze.

"You're right," she admitted. "There is something unseemly. And I know what it is."

He looked at her intently. "I thought you might."

"I couldn't speak about it before. Candace was adamant about vowing my silence. I acted rashly and have relented. It's been troubling me ever since. I've talked to Ambrose about breaking a vow, but I didn't explain what was troubling me."

"You were wise to discuss it with Ambrose and come to an upright conviction. I think I know what's behind Ainsworth's unusual generosity, yet I need to hear it from you."

"Grandfather means well by Candace, and I suspect by all of us. As you say, he's a decent man, but well, he does have stringent ways as you know when it comes to ruling the Derringtons." She frowned. "There's no excuse for the way Keno's been treated, and he's manipulating Candace. I can't see any other way to explain it."

"Then he's rewarding Candace by granting Keno plantation land if she'll marry Hunnewell?"

"Yes, but there's more. If she doesn't marry Oliver, then he's stated clearly that he'll run Keno out of the Islands."

Rafe's jaw set. She saw anger in his eyes as she'd expected. Rafe had himself experienced banishment from Townsend similar to what Ainsworth had warned would happen to Keno. A few years earlier when Rafe had worked for Nora at the *Gazette* he'd written editorials supporting the monarchy that had made her grandfather livid. He had feared Rafe could turn the planters against annexation. Ainsworth had given Townsend permission to harass Rafe and run him out of Hawaii. So much had changed since those early years that Rafe was now a dedicated annexationist. Townsend's threat to run him off the Islands had been greeted with a challenge, but Rafe had already intended to go to sea. He left for French Guiana, only to return one day with the means to thwart the Derringtons. Now, of course, Ainsworth's feelings toward Rafe were the very opposite, and it was Townsend who had to leave Hawaii due to his own sinful ways.

"But Candace knows Grandfather can send Keno away, and would do so if necessary," Eden went on.

"I challenge that," Rafe stated. "As long as I have anything to say about it, Keno isn't going anywhere. If necessary I'll convince Parker Judson to let Keno buy into Hawaiiana. I mentioned something of that idea to Ainsworth when he came to me about the land on the Big Island."

She was not surprised. She had the horrible notion that if Ainsworth moved against Keno there would be a standoff between Rafe and the Derringtons that would lead to an iron-clad dispute.

"Well, Candace took Grandfather seriously, and in order to see that Keno has the opportunity to fulfill his dreams she agreed to the ultimatum. The land, she thinks, will make up for Keno losing her, and that he'll find someone else to marry."

"Very sacrificial. But unwise. We're not going to allow Ainsworth and Thaddeus Hunnewell to ruin their chance for happiness by recreating a new Romeo and Juliet scenario. Keno's mad about her. He'll never get over losing her. I know him too well."

"What will you do?" she asked urgently.

"I'll make certain this scheme is brought out into the sunshine, my sweet. Keno's going to know the reason Candace has been running from him, and Ainsworth will be told there's no deal on his bribery plan. Keno's going to get his own plantation all right. But not from Ainsworth. There's no question about Keno getting land. He and I made an agreement before we went to French Guiana that I'd back him financially. We've been waiting for Hawaiiana to begin producing. But I don't need to wait for that any longer. The Easton legacy was turned over to me, and soon the pearl beds, so there's enough to back Keno now."

She couldn't restrain her response. A smile struggled to her lips. "That's what I was hoping you'd say about standing up to Grandfather. He thinks most highly of you now. If you insist on standing up for Keno, then I've a notion Grandfather will relent."

"On a marriage with Candace?" he asked doubtfully. "I can't see it."

"Perhaps you're right about the marriage, but if Candace decides Grandfather won't be able to ruin Keno's future in Hawaii, then, well, I think she may revert back to being the Candace we both know. What are you going to do?"

"There's still a few things that don't fit. I'll need to look into them before the steamer leaves on Sunday. I do know that I won't be duping Keno into accepting a land grant, however grand, as a result of losing the woman he loves."

Yes, that's right, she thought with a shudder. If Keno ever discovered the deceit that was played upon him, he may come to hate the very soil he walked on, knowing the price that was paid by the woman he loved and lost. Rafe as the third party would be seen as part of the deceit. She was relieved that Rafe had recognized the serious risks and stepped back.

Her anger wanted to rise up against her grandfather's conniving ways, but she kept telling herself Ainsworth probably didn't mean to harm, but to strengthen. What he appeared not to understand, or perhaps refused to deal with, was that family blessing did not grow from pragmatic manipulation to gain wealth and influence, but from incorporating God's revealed truths into lives and relationships.

For Eden, the more she matured the more disturbing it was to discover the erroneous mind-set and actions of the dignified patri-arch, the son of an early missionary.

"Sometimes I don't understand Ainsworth," she commented wearily.

Rafe looked at her, taking note of the burden she felt for her family.

"After all, he was raised the son of a wonderful missionary."

"One would think that children reared by godly parents would turn out the same way," he agreed. "We know it doesn't always happen that way. Samuel and his sons are an example of that. While Samuel was loyal to God and to Israel, his sons, as corrupt judges, took bribes and were part of the reason Israel gave for wanting a king to rule over them, which God said was rebellion against Him. I was thinking of something similar to this just recently at Hanalei."

She looked at him, curious.

"I did something I haven't done since the actual funeral took place years ago. I went to my father's grave," he said. "I thought of my grandfather, also a missionary like Ainsworth's father. My grand-father, his son Matt, and I were all very different. Our parents or grandparents may have walked with God, but we are not less responsible for our decisions, and God isn't going to eradicate the consequences of our actions just because we came from a Christian family. Nations founded on righteous principles are also not guar-anteed the safety and blessing of the next generation."

Eden normally assumed her dignified and sometimes over-powering grandfather, so brilliant in the ways of sugar business and politics, was a seasoned saint who should also be wise in the ways of the Bible and prayer. Eden thought of the painting of godly Jedaiah Derrington above the stairway at Kea Lani and realized that all that Jedaiah was could not guarantee his son Ainsworth would follow his footsteps.

"I've no appetite for the luncheon yet. Let's walk, shall we?" Rafe suggested.

"Did Grandfather Ainsworth tell you there's to be a family meeting tomorrow evening about Townsend?" Eden asked.

"He told me. Though I don't see what good it's supposed to do us. Townsend has stepped beyond the boundary of what his father may think of the matter. I would like to have the authorities handling him." He gave her a sober look. "You might as well know I wired P.J. this morning. He's mentioned the Pinkerton Detective Agency to me before. I've asked him to go ahead and hire a man. I want Townsend tracked down. The sooner he's brought in for questioning by the law, the sooner we can all get on with our normal lives."

"Grandfather isn't likely to approve, but I do think it was a wise decision. It should help Celestine feel more secure, too."

"You're right. I'm not going to have my mother so frightened that she fears to leave the house with Kip."

"Could it be he thinks she doesn't know about the attempt he made with Great-aunt Nora's medicine? Maybe he thinks she'd receive him in the house. He is her husband."

"It's Parker Judson's place. He calls the shots on who comes in and who doesn't. But you have a point. Townsend may believe he can get by with it because Celestine is unaware of what's happened."

"Rafe," she said, pausing to look at him. "You don't think he'd—well, try and do harm, do you?"

She wondered whether she should have brought it up when she saw the hard glint in his dark eyes.

"Townsend bears a dangerous nature. Like Cain, he's riled by jealousy. He perceives a right to be Ainsworth's inheritor. And he actually thinks he has more right to my father's estate than I do. Reasonable or not, one who thinks that way may do most anything to defend *his rights*."

Eden, mulling over Rafe's description of her uncle, thought he was correct. Townsend had always been a fighter for what he said was his, but little of what he claimed had been earned, and he showed no thankfulness to God, because he was "merely possessing what was his." For years Rafe had said Townsend was responsible for Matt's death, and while she may have agreed to some extent, she had never grappled with the awful conclusion that Townsend was dangerous.

"Harm Celestine?" he said thoughtfully. "He worries me, and I've no confidence in his character. He has at times displayed an unhealthy jealousy for his wife, and he has a ruthless manner that slowly destroys the other person."

Eden shuddered thinking back over incidents between her uncle and Rafe's mother. In the past she and others thought, *Well, that's Townsend for you, that's just the way he is.* She knew she would pray more often that when the confrontation between Rafe and Townsend came, Rafe would be wise and willing to commit the outcome to the law. And what was most important to Eden was that Rafe come out of the situation unsullied, his fellowship with the Lord undisturbed by carnal wrath.

May it be so, O Lord. Keep Rafe from stumbling into vengeance and tragedy.

*C*andace Derrington unpacked her portmanteau and hung her evening dress in the guest chamber closet at Hunnewell's beachfront house. She was here to have dinner tonight with Oliver and his widowed father, Thaddeus, who was even now preparing for his trip to Washington D.C. Other guests would be present, including her cousin Zachary—reluctant dinner date for Claudia Hunnewell—and also the British commissioner and consul general in Hawaii, James H. Wodehouse, and several members of his staff, their wives, and a few assistants.

Candace was surprised upon discovering that the commissioner would be guest of honor at the dinner.

Now why would the British commissioner come here? The question held her interest for some time until she had opportunity to meet with Oliver for a brief walk on Waikiki after lunch.

Oliver didn't appear to mind her questions. His breezy laughter merely strengthened her conviction that he believed women, even smart women like Candace and Great-aunt Nora, should keep their footprints out of politics.

"And why shouldn't the British commissioner come to dinner?" he asked with a forebearing smile twisted on his lips. "There's no accounting for the oddities of friendship, my dear Candace."

My dear Candace. She loathed the way he put it. *Don't trouble your feminine intellect with such deep concerns, dear.*

Marriage to Oliver would have its stresses and strains.

Keno never spoke to her like this. Keno saw her as a *woman.* He was romantic, funny, charming, and treated her well. Candace with her finishing-school manners, her education, her interest in Greek. He appreciated her accomplishments and never felt threatened as though they might infringe on his manliness. He accepted and loved her for who she was. It didn't make him feel diminished that she liked Greek.

"True," she said, deliberately pushing back, "but it does seem strange. Your father, I mean."

"Indeed, how so?" They walked along the white sand, casting long shadows on the beach, their wide-brimmed hats appearing to touch.

"Well, I would think it obvious as to what I *mean*," Candace said. "Is your father not a staunch ally of Misters Thurston and Dole? Your father's quite prepared to pack his bag to go to Washington to sell annexation of the Islands to the American president."

"He is, yes."

"Well, in spite of all that, Mr. Wodehouse comes to sip tea with him. Mr. Wodehouse who hotly disputes annexation? He thinks that if such a diabolical event as annexation should ever occur, he would much prefer Hawaii to become a British colony. Doesn't it seem peculiar then, *my dear Oliver?*"

Oliver smiled patiently, as though she had become too upset over the latitude permitted in a man's world, and needed to calm down, so he artfully changed the subject.

When later that afternoon Candace continued to think about the situation, she went to the desk and wrote a brief message. She sent it by one of the serving boys to Eden, at Kalihi Hospital.

—⟋ॐ⟍—

Eden received the message and read with interest.

There's a dinner party at eight o'clock here at Hunnewell's. After the concerns of three nights ago, guess who's coming to dinner? The British commissioner. I find this unusual, don't you? With Thaddeus Hunnewell a strong annexationist, and Britain against American annexation of the Islands? Anyway, Alice has complicated things by catching a cold, and we need a dinner partner for Bill Wallace. Can you come? I'm sure Rafe won't mind as it's nothing to do with romance. Here's your opportunity to sit in and observe. You may have something of interest to pass on to your handsome fiancé next time you see him.
Candace.

Eden went to Aunt Lana and asked if the evening off was possible. When Lana arranged it, Eden quickly wrote Rafe a message at the Legislature.

—⟋ॐ⟍—

Darling, would you mind terribly if I share in a candlelight dinner with Bill Wallace (and a dozen others) at Hunnewell's tonight? Candace has asked me to come. Alice has come down with a cold and someone needs to keep poor Bill company at the table over roast chicken. I'm sure you're quite sympathetic toward him.

Oh—and my reason for going? Guess who else will be there? The British Commissioner Wodehouse. After your suspicions over a certain missing piece of information we discussed yesterday at Hawaiiana, I may be able to pick up an interesting tidbit here or there that you can use—even from Bill.
Yours ever, Eden

⸺⚬⚬⸺

Eden watched from the front door at Kalihi as a Hawaiian boy came scurrying up the steps.

"Message from the Legislature for Miss Eden Derrington."

"Thank you."

Eden opened the envelope and read in Rafe's handwriting—

⸺⚬⚬⸺

No dinner at Hunnewell's. No candlelight. No sympathy for Bill Wallace.

R.

⸺⚬⚬⸺

Eden scrunched the paper. She quickly wrote a message to inform Candace.

⸺⚬⚬⸺

Candace smiled, receiving Eden's brief return message: *Handsome fiancé is totally unsupportive.*

"Then I'll be the one who observes the happenings," Candace murmured.

Later that evening at Hunnewell's, Candace Rosalind Derrington stared coolly back at her reflection—auburn hair brushed straight back into a chignon, sharp blue eyes, a sober face, high cheekbones, and slashing brows. Tonight she dressed in a deep blue silk gown, with high neck and cuffed sleeves fringed with lace.

She reflected on the news that Oliver had unexpectedly brought up this afternoon during their walk on the beach. Evidently displeased with her questions, he'd decided to discuss Keno. Oliver told her how he had "caught" Keno on the property the other night "sneaking" about the darkened garden, hoping to spy on her activities.

"He had thought tonight's dinner party, with you in attendance, was to be held two nights ago," Oliver explained.

To Candace the worst part of all this was to learn that Oliver and Keno had "physically tangled." She was not the sort of girl whose ego spiraled upward to learn that two men had fought over her. It seemed hideous actually, and then Keno almost getting arrested. She was thankful to Eden for coming forward in Keno's defense, and to Rafe for confronting Thaddeus Hunnewell over Oliver demanding Keno be prosecuted, as if he were some sort of underling!

Candace snapped her hairbrush down on the vanity table. She found nothing flattering about two men slugging it out while she supposedly stood in the background, breathlessly prepared to swoon over the victor, who would ride her off into the sunset.

"Absurd," she murmured to herself dourly. "If either one of them ever considers me a bag of produce to fight over and then sling across his saddle as booty, well! They'll have a shock coming—I'll box both their ears."

How pleasant it would be just to sneak aboard the steamer leaving on Sunday with Grandfather Ainsworth, then hide in San Francisco with Rafe's mother, Celestine. It wasn't that Candace considered herself a victim of her grandfather's ploy to have her marry Oliver. She had voluntarily cooperated with his patriarchal family law. When he'd told her he would run Keno out of Hawaii if she married him, she knew that somehow, some way, he *would*. "We need the Hunnewells and they need us," he'd said. "Just like we need the Eastons, the Judsons, and the Doles. We must bond together. This mind-set is key to the future of the Islands. That's what it's all about, Candace, saving the Hawaiian Islands and making them a part of the United States."

Was it? Though she could exhibit a strong will to box the ears of Oliver and Keno if necessary, such was not the case with Grandfather Ainsworth. Perhaps she inherited too much of his personality to oppose him.

It must be the father figure, she thought with a sigh. Both Eden and I desire a *missing* father/daughter relationship, a stable authority figure, and though we know it's found in a personal relationship with our *true* Father God, we still seem to respond emotionally to a "little girl" need.

It was silly, actually, she thought, coolly impatient with herself. I'm a grown woman.

But still . . . wasn't it much the same deep-seated need that troubled Zachary? The rejection and ridicule he'd received from his father, Townsend, through the years had left parts of his self-image tattered. And Rafe Easton? His forceful personality felt the need to *defend* his father and to protect what he had established at Hanalei.

She and Eden had discussed their similar needs just a week ago, and later Eden had written down two Bible verses and placed them inside Candace's Bible.

Now, before going downstairs to a dinner she wished she didn't need to attend, Candace returned to her vanity case and brought out the Bible that had belonged to her father, Douglas. She removed the folded piece of stationery. Yes, there they were, the two verses Eden had written, John 20:17 and 2 Corinthians 6:17–18.

"I ascend unto my *Father*, and *your Father*."

She knew that Jesus spoke this to Mary Magdalene as she wept at the tomb. She was the first one to whom Christ showed Himself alive after His crucifixion—a woman.

"And I will welcome you, and I will be a *father* to you, and you shall be sons *and daughters* to me, says the Lord Almighty."

Although she knew the word *sons* in the Bible was often generic, she especially loved this verse because of its mention of "daughters."

In a moment of rare emotion, she did what she had seen Eden do. She raised the verse to her lips and kissed it.

***

Candace stepped out of the Hunnewell guest bedroom into the quiet hallway. Something was all wrong about the notion of Keno sneaking around in the garden, she thought with disdain . . . to spy on her! She knew him too well to believe that. As Great-aunt Nora would say, "Such poppycock!" Candace wrinkled her brow as she came down the stairs. Keno was not the sort of man to be peeping into windows. If he'd wanted to confront Oliver, he would do it openly.

Her jaw set. He had wanted to confront *her*, but not trusting her own heart, she had kept away from him. He was so straightforward and humble he hadn't even thought of that being the reason for her standoffishness. Perhaps that was best for him.

Keno may not have prominence in Hawaii, but he did have something more valuable than land or sugarcane—the same that Rafe Easton had so much of—character. Both men were dependable and morally strong, which had impressed her from the beginning, as it had Eden. He and Rafe Easton were so much alike in that regard that they might have been twins. She supposed that was the main reason for their friendship. Rafe had taught Keno much of this when they were in their teens. Keno even had a similar physical appearance—dark hair, muscular build—

I will not think about Keno, she thought through gritted teeth, coming firmly down the steps. *For his own good, I will not think of him.*

Soon now, Grandfather Ainsworth would arrange a land purchase for him. Then one day Keno would forget her . . . at least to the degree that it didn't hurt so deeply to remember.

She lifted her head. *He will meet a lovely girl—he deserves a lovely girl. Someone sweet and submissive who supports his life's plans. Let him marry and have children.*

"And Candace Rosalind Derrington? He will forget me faster if he believes I was unjust with him, that Oliver's name and money mean more to me."

She squared her shoulders. *I'm being sacrificial, I know. Some will call me foolish. But that's because they don't really love. They want a man to meet all their needs, but—*

Greater love hath no man than this, that a man lay down his life for his friends. Sacrificial good for the one *loved.*

And Oliver—her heart gave a thump. "Well, even if I don't love him I can learn to like him. I'll be able to respect him as the father of our children, at least. I *must* be able to do that. I'll try to make him a loyal wife. Perhaps someday, yes someday, I can learn to love him. Not like Keno, of course, but there are different kinds and different stages of love."

The house was a scenic one. She had always enjoyed coming here with Eden to visit Claudia. Claudia and Zachary were downstairs in the entry hall now. They were exchanging heated words, but keeping their voices low. Candace slowed her descent.

Zachary, a tall and fair young man, was always correctly dressed with manners to match when he wanted to impress, which presently he no longer wanted to do.

Claudia Hunnewell had ebony hair, and was rather plump, and spoiled. "Well if that's how you feel about it," her voice floated up, "I shall tell Father."

"Now, Claudia, this isn't the time to start a controversy. I'm going to San Francisco. My job with the *Gazette* demands travel."

Candace coughed gently and came on down the steps, pausing on the bottom stair, hand on the newel post.

"Hello, Zachary. Is Grandfather Ainsworth coming this evening?"

"He was invited, but had to turn it down."

It was obvious to Candace that her cousin wished he could have done the same.

"He's at Kea Lani, resting up for the voyage on Sunday," he concluded.

"Come, Zachie, we need to talk," Claudia insisted, taking hold of his arm. She ushered him across the hall into another sitting room.

The weather had cleared after the big storm of two days ago, and the evening was typically Hawaiian, the moon reflecting on the calm sea, and the breezes refreshing. Candace moved toward the outer screened lanai that stretched down toward Waikiki beach. The other guests were arriving and beginning to congregate before dinner in the parlor. She could hear their voices exchanging pleasantries, and now and then someone laughed.

I need a few minutes before I can face them, and Oliver, she thought wearily.

She walked along the lanai in the direction of the beach and stepped through the door, keeping to the walkway and avoiding the sand on either side.

The sea was a mere sigh, its low tide inching onto what would be in daylight sugary white sand. A lone cloud, *lonely* like her own heart if she even for a moment allowed her mask to fall, winged its way across the face of the moon.

She stood staring out into the dark—out to where the crosswinds struggled for preeminence. Darkness settled in like a veil. A breeze swept past touching flowers and leaves with a gentle hand.

Her eyes wandered to the poinciana tree where Oliver told her Keno had stood the other night before coming up to the window. She blinked hard. For a moment the scene was repeating before her eyes. A flare from a match sprang up. Someone was standing there. Almost in a dreamlike trance she started in his direction. Keno?

"When can I expect the manifesto?"

The British voice, low and articulate, shook Candace to her senses, and to an abrupt halt.

"I was prepared to retrieve it from his desk the other night. Everything was arranged. I was foiled at the last minute. When I opened the folder it was empty."

Oliver's voice!

"Any idea who it might have been?"

"Yes. Trouble is I can't be certain," Oliver said.

The man with the British accent murmured something that blew past her. She grasped one or two of the words from the wind— "careful," "much at stake."

"Who'd ever suspect the son of one of the strongest annexationists in Hawaii? Not my father, anyway. He'd back me to the bitter end."

She caught a glimpse of Oliver beneath the tree talking to someone whose back was toward her. He must be one of the assistants of the group who'd arrived with the British commissioner.

"If Easton's friend recalls having seen you come from there—"

Oliver's voice turned derisive. "After last night who'd believe him, if he did? They'd be inclined to think he was making it up. He wants revenge over my becoming engaged to Miss Derrington. His blundering arrival was a stroke of luck, even if I did need to take it on the chin."

"What of his claim to the Hunnewell family?"

"Perfect rubbish," Oliver snorted.

"His father was indeed a Hunnewell, your uncle Philip."

"Rubbish!"

"I say! My dear fellow. It's up to you whether you accept the facts. You asked me to look into it. At any rate, your uncle is dead now. The chap was caught in an elephant stampede some fifteen years ago while hunting ivory in Rhodesia."

"And the woman?"

"Hawaiian. A lovely girl. Dead, as well."

"Who knows of this? What of my father and Ainsworth Derrington?"

The man's voice cut through the wind, "Who can say? . . . depends on whether he intends to bring the matter up before a lawyer."

"That would open the door to all kinds of trouble."

"Mr. Hunnewell won't wish the subject to receive public scrutiny. The sooner you wed Miss Derrington, old chap, the better your position to inherit both the Hunnewell and the Derrington estates. Just remember, old Derrington's a stickler. If you don't please him he can easily turn the reins over to Easton. Quite a head on his shoulders I hear, and he's to marry the doctor's daughter."

The wind huffed again, shaking the palm fronds with a dry crackle, as though in disapproval of two conniving men below.

The Englishman said, "Our absence will be noticed. Better go in to dinner."

"Not together. You go first. I'll follow shortly. I want to enter with Miss Derrington."

Candace turned and ran back to the lanai, stepping into benign shadows and slipping out of view.

he day after the dinner at Hunnewell's beach house, Candace drove her buggy along the dirt road returning to Kea Lani plantation from her morning visit on Hawaiiana. She had gone to the pineapple plantation in order to meet with the Chinese Christian women's group. It was good for her heart to reunite with them in prayer and encouragement before resuming the class this Sunday for the first time in several months. The women received her back with many smiles.

One of the women at the prayer meeting had asked about Hui, Ling Li's wife, a strong presence in the group before their bungalow went up in flames, set by Townsend. Rafe Easton had transported the Li family over to Hanalei on the Big Island to safeguard Ling's testimony about Townsend. Candace assured them that Hui and Ling both were doing well.

She was sober and reflective as she drove her buggy back toward Kea Lani. She thought about Oliver and what she'd overheard last night at Hunnewell's—as well as what Oliver said about Keno. And this afternoon there would be a family gathering to discuss Uncle Townsend and Celestine's telegraph message from San Francisco. She doubted it would go well. Nora had stepped back from filing charges against her nephew, and her grandfather wasn't likely to advocate for bringing the law in when the Derrington name was at stake.

And now, there was this murder of the Chinese man named Sen Fong, which she learned about early this morning when she returned to Kea Lani. The women's group told her that though they knew who Sen Fong was, they knew nothing of who might have killed him. Candace believed them; their loyalty to Christ made their witness secure. There was one thing of particular interest, though. She'd noticed the youngest member of the women's group, Luli, a relative of Ling Li and their main translator into English, had not come today. When Candace inquired about her, the women seemed a little uncomfortable. Perhaps she should mention this to Rafe, since the horrible deed had occurred on his plantation, and since Luli might be cautious in coming forward to tell anything she might know about Sen Fong's death. She loathed bringing trouble on the women. Still, civic duty called her to do what she could to help bring a murderer to justice.

As Candace drove the buggy closer to Kea Lani, thinking of the family gathering, she saw someone ahead walking along the side of the dirt road.

As she drove closer she recognized her cousin Silas. He was walking and swinging a walking stick as though he were leading a band of trombones, horns, and drums. She rode past him before stopping, and waited, looking back as he came trotting up with a pleasant smile. *Silas*, she thought curiously, *is a strange person*. Like Eden, she could not make up her mind about him, despite Zachary's dislike of his half-brother.

Silas doesn't appear the least concerned about the family meeting over his father, she thought.

He was a pleasant looking man with chestnut brown hair in his late twenties, older than she, but not by many years. When he first arrived he'd had a well-trimmed goatee, and was now clean-shaven. She thought he looked better without it.

"Good morning, Cousin," he called. "Thanks for the ride; it's a wonderful morning." He climbed up into the buggy beside her. He had the same light blue eyes as Zachary, and while of a husky build, he showed no interest in strenuous outdoor activities like Keno and Rafe. Silas was fashionably out of place on the Islands with his crisp white linen shirts, well-polished shoes of the highest fashion, and dapper hats and walking sticks. She glanced at his walking stick with a heavy silver handle in the design of a wolf's head.

He noticed her looking at it, for he smiled rather ruefully and laid it aside. "Not exactly typical of Hawaii is it?"

"Wolves make me think of the great Northwest," she said, giving a flip to the reins. "Have you ever been there?"

"Me? Oh no. I'm not much into wilderness traveling. I—er, won that walking stick in Sacramento in a wager before I came here to Honolulu. Nice, though I'm not exactly thrilled with the handle, not that I've anything against wolves." He smiled at her.

Candace did not return her cousin's smile but looked straight ahead. Zachary had told her all about his gambling interests. According to her grandfather, Silas had turned his back on all of that. She hoped it was true. She rather liked him, but then again, there seemed something not quite right about him. Or was she too judgmental?

"You should come to the mission church on Sunday," she told him bluntly. "It could do you good."

Silas chuckled, but there was no humor in his tone. "I'm sure it would. As it does so many other well-dressed hypocrites, like my dear old father, Townsend. Here he is, my old man," he said flippantly, "and I learn he may have done in Rafe's father and poisoned Nora. Amazing! Going to church in his Sunday best clothes really helped him, didn't it?"

She considered his statement, though she was more surprised by the depth of the sneer in his voice. She wasn't used to seeing him break out of his amiable and suave demeanor to unmask a bitter nature.

"Well, I'd better apologize for that one. I shouldn't have offended you."

"You didn't offend me. I've known for a long time that my uncle is untrustworthy. What I didn't know was that if pushed, he could become a dangerous man. My faith isn't so weak that a bit of well-deserved criticism of hypocrites undermines it. But as to your consideration of hypocrites, why not discuss the very worst ones? Don't forget that Judas was with Jesus, hearing His wisdom and seeing many miracles, just like the rest of the disciples, and yet it didn't help him, did it? So if someone has a heart like Judas or Pharaoh of Egypt, it might even be hardened by hearing the Truth."

"You mean that?" he said with a slight taunt.

"Absolutely. It's more a matter of whether you love truth. So you need not apologize for expressing any honest doubts." She met his ironic gaze evenly before turning her attention back on the dirt road.

He smiled and looked at her a bit slyly. "Well, you've turned my objection on its head—certainly something to consider, but not on such a gorgeous day." He sighed and looked up toward the blue sky. "No wonder you annexationists will fight tooth and claw for this Island. The longer I'm here, the more I want to stay."

She looked at him thoughtfully. He did appear to be settling down into the Derrington family. When he first arrived, she had the impression he wouldn't remain long, that he'd come for a singular purpose, and when done with it, whatever it was, he would be on his meandering way.

"Well, you won't be the first. But you speak as though you think you may need to leave." She glanced at him. "From what Grandfather says he's quite pleased you're in the family and becoming more established every day."

He sobered. "He's been more than fair with me. A decent man. If my beloved half-brother has his way, however, I'll soon be booted out to sea for shark food."

Candace kept silent on Zachary.

"Now who could that be ahead of us?" he asked, giving a nod up the narrowing reddish dirt road.

Candace had already seen the man astride an auburn horse and her breathing tensed. *Keno.* She tightened her mouth and silently prayed for strength.

"Better slow down," Silas urged with amusement in his voice. "He's stopping in the middle of the road. I'll get off here, this is convenient for me. We're at the crossroad for Kea Lani and the mission church. Thanks for the ride, Cousin."

"You needn't go," she said stiffly.

Silas glanced toward the muscled young figure on horseback and his eyes twinkled. "Oh yes, I do need to go. It looks as if Keno's been expecting you to ride by here. Good day, lady," he said with a bow, stepped down, and strolled off toward the turn in the palm-lined road.

Did someone tell Keno she would be on the road alone?

Candace watched Silas for a moment and then turned toward Keno as he rode toward her.

"Good morning," Keno called. "I'm not blocking the way, am I?"

She smiled ruefully. "Oh no, you wouldn't do that."

She noted that he had a relaxed and disarming way about him. He was quite handsome, too. Now that she knew who his father was she could see the Hunnewell in him that previously she had thought was the blood of a Scottish whaler. His shirt was open and he wore, of all things, an old Texas-style hat with a cockily planted feather at the side. Her heart stirred. She felt an awful pang and her hands gripped the reins. It was Keno who had brought her to faith in Christ. Before that she had gone to church, but had had no personal relationship with Christ as Savior and Lord, nor any interest in the Bible, except to carry it to Sunday service and back home again where it went into a drawer.

"I'm in quite a hurry, if you don't mind," she said, keeping a grip on her emotions, and her voice as cool as she could.

"I won't keep you long. If I'd known you were at Hawaiiana I'd have joined you."

I didn't want you to join me.

"I just found out from Rafe, you went there to meet with the women," he said.

So that was it. Rafe Easton. How did Rafe know? Eden must have told him she was taking the women's Bible class again.

"So he's up at Kea Lani already?"

"He's mighty anxious. The steamer leaves Sunday. He wants Mr. Derrington to do something about tracking down your uncle."

"Yes, and I don't want to be late for the meeting."

"Look here, Candace, I've got to talk to you. I guess you heard about the other night and the trouble with Oliver?"

"If the marshal came to arrest you for trespassing on Hunnewell land and attacking him, did you think I wouldn't hear about it?"

"I suppose Oliver told you I was hiding in the bushes waiting to pounce like a cat on a rat!"

"Oh yes, except he doesn't consider himself the rat."

"No, I don't suppose he would."

"He says you nearly broke his jaw."

"I could have busted him, all right. He was—" he stopped short and pushed his hat back from his forehead. He looked ashamed. It was this character trait of humility and yielding to his Lord that she loved about him. In her eyes it increased his masculinity. Oliver with all his smiling arrogance was less the man. Keno didn't realize what his desire to be obedient to God did to her heart. She had already spoken with Eden about the trouble between Oliver and Keno, and Eden had explained the details, even some of the words Oliver had used.

"I was wrong to hit him," he said.

She bit her tongue to keep from telling him he wasn't to blame as much as Oliver was.

She tipped her head, scanning him. "I hear you're a Hunnewell, too. That makes Oliver your cousin."

He winced. "I'd as soon have a snake for a cousin. How did you find out about my father?"

Candace thought of all she had heard last night. Her heart

thumped. She still had not made up her mind what to do about it. If she told Keno, he would surely insist she tell her grandfather. She needed time to consider what Oliver had meant by his strange clandestine words without Keno urging her to act at once.

She ignored his question and said, "Oliver takes the news quite seriously. I think he's worried you'll go to Mr. Hunnewell."

"What's he afraid of? Does he think I'm suddenly proud because a Hunnewell fathered me? I'd just as soon have it be a whaler. I don't need his name to make me feel like a man. I know who I am. And knowing who my true Father is brings all the confidence I need to face anyone in this life."

Candace was gripping the reins so hard they pressed into her sweating palms. She stared blindly at her lap, fighting back the volcano of emotion spilling at her heart's door.

"Would you think better of me if I gained the Hunnewell name through the court, and got some form of inheritance from the family? Well, it wouldn't make me sleep any better. Philip Hunnewell didn't want me for a son. He fled like a spineless coward to his fine English home. Let him stay there. I wouldn't waste my time trying to earn his acceptance. I don't want his name. I don't want to meet him. Ever."

Her heart thudded in her ears. She was not a woman who cried. The more emotional the pain, the more she steeled herself against showing it. She could have cried out, *I don't even like the name of Hunnewell!*

"Tell me the truth, Candace, that's all I want! Do you love Oliver? Tell me you do and I promise I won't trouble you again!"

She opened her lips and no sound came. A cramp constricted her throat.

"You belong to *me*. You told me that yourself. You told me you loved me that night, do you remember? Have you forgotten that night, Candace? Well, I haven't. Were you telling the truth? If you lied to me—if you *lied*—then go ahead. Marry Oliver."

She couldn't take anymore. She flipped the reins and the horse jolted forward toward the turn that led to Kea Lani.

*S*ilas Derrington whistled as he strolled along the pathway that forked toward Kea Lani. In the distance the white plantation house stood on a low rise facing toward the sea. *A mighty good-looking plantation,* even seeing it from afar. Reminded him of the plantation homes around the mainland's old South, especially Vicksburg, Mississippi, and his own Louisiana. He didn't do much talking about his Louisiana background. He wanted to keep his connections with New Orleans as far removed from that bloodhound Zachary as he possibly could.

He smiled wryly. *Nice young man, otherwise, or could be, if he'd lay off the half-brother jealousy. Would be kind of nice to have a brother, if the guy didn't relentlessly hate the sight of me. And why? What have I taken from him so far? A job managing the sugar production that Zachary hadn't wanted anyway. So what was his problem?*

If anyone has a right to resentment it's me! I'm the one rejected and cheated by the Derringtons. I belong here as much as Zachary, Candace, or Eden. Was it my fault Townsend didn't marry my mother?

He smiled to himself, amused by the standoff between his

cousin Candace and Rafe's friend Keno. He rubbed his chin. Maybe not so amusing the other night, however, when Keno had flattened Oliver. Not that he minded the British sympathizer getting a firm lesson in humility.

Silas chuckled, swinging his walking stick. If Oliver had known he'd be picking himself up off the ground he may have thought twice about his tactics.

Silas stiffened his jaw. That incident with Keno was planned, of course. Oliver had lain waiting, as the old saying went, "to pick a bone" with Keno. He'd needed an alibi. Well, he'd stirred things up all right, and made a big alibi, not that it would do him much good now, since Oliver failed to accomplish his task for the British.

Oliver had planned to steal his father's secret seven-page manifesto, written for the upcoming trip to Washington. The policy document was to find its way ultimately to the desk of President Harrison, who favored annexation of the Hawaiian Islands.

As Silas understood it, the document laid out in full detail every step planned by the Hunnewell-Derrington committee to bring events together for the rapid success of annexation.

Mr. Hunnewell would be astounded if he discovered the truth about Oliver's underhanded ways.

Silas shook his head. What a plunge into the muck of disappointment for poor old Thaddeus! His own son, a spy for men surrounding the British commissioner. Oliver, who was boasted about, promoted to success at Harvard through no sweat of his own, spoiled by easy riches, had turned out to be an ungrateful son to the man who'd done it all for him. But as yet, old Thaddeus didn't know.

What did the British want the document for? Undoubtedly to send it to London to embarrass the American government. The British powers that be would delight to put pressure on the US Congress to denounce the secret cooperation between members of the Reform Party and the American president. Harrison might have no choice except to back away from annexing the Pacific Islands.

In view of all that, Oliver had his mission laid out for him last night. He was to create a diversion. The more trouble and confusion Oliver caused, and the more people suspected of possibly spying on the Annexation Club meeting, the better. The fiasco of confusion gave more reasons to Thaddeus Hunnewell and Ainsworth Derrington to place the blame for the document's theft on the Royalists, rather than someone inside the club.

And Oliver himself? What was his rationale for cooperating with the political treachery? He needed nothing. He was already a wealthy young man, an only son, the sole inheritor of the great Hunnewell bounty. He was permitted by the social norms of the day to tread in his father's footsteps all the way to the Legislature to take possession of power he hadn't earned and didn't deserve.

More than likely Oliver's reason for joining the Brits wasn't to receive anything tangible from them, but to keep something buried. Some sin he wanted covered up that they knew about. *So what else was new?* Silas thought with scorn for the rich. Or he could be so misguided as to feel a thrill when the old Union Jack waved in the winds.

Could the arrogant Oliver P. Hunnewell have a secret he needs to keep locked away so his father doesn't find out? An undisclosed incident back in the States may well damage his present plans if unveiled in the newspapers—just the way the Derringtons were willing to hush up Townsend's actions. For Oliver it might be something he didn't dare let Candace discover.

Why was Oliver aiding the expansion of London's empire over and above the United States? Only Oliver knew. Somewhere along the way he had made a decision to support England. Then again, politics aside, Oliver had a sound reason to keep any scandal hushed up from Ainsworth. There was all of the Derrington inheritance and land that he would rake in through marriage to Candace. A man would need a strong reason to risk losing it to the possibility that Ainsworth might learn he was against annexation!

"The elite," Silas murmured sneeringly. He knew all too well the insults paid to the socially inferior. Oh yes, Oliver had meant every cutting word he'd used to slice through Keno's self-respect the other night, even though the fracas had been planned and Keno had walked into a bull's ring by mistake.

And so Oliver had responded to the task given him that night without a missed step. If it hadn't been Keno, who would it have been? That it had turned out to be Keno merely worked in Oliver's favor. He could add a little vindictive poison to the commotion already planned.

He curled his lip and swiped his walking stick hard against a bush in his way.

"What about you, Silas? You've been able to cover your bitterness toward the Derringtons pretty well, indeed, since coming here to Honolulu. You've been the smiling, amiable cousin from afar who bears no grudges that your childhood and youth were ones of neglect and abuse.

"How self-righteous of them to condemn me for being a gambler. They didn't need to hang out in the dives of Louisiana as a boy, waiting for a handout to get something to eat. What else would I learn but a deck of cards, a quick 'cheat' to get ahead? And all while the Derringtons lolled about in their *Hawaiian paradise*." He whacked at another bush.

He glanced at the time. There remained an hour before the Derringtons were to gather at Kea Lani at Ainsworth's request to discuss Silas's wayward father, Townsend.

Silas came to a fork in the road. To his right was the road to Kea Lani, while on his left was Ambrose's bungalow and the small church with its cross and open door.

⸺ ᥆᥈᥉ ⸺

Ambrose was in his church office sitting at his desk writing with one hand and leafing through his Bible for the verses he wanted with the other. He paused and glanced up when a board creaked near the open door. Silas Derrington leaned in the doorway, a tired smile on his face.

"Don't you ever get tired of reading that Book?"

He looked like his father, except he was more elegant, more limber and fashionable than either his father, a professed boxer, or Zachary, an outdoorsman. If Zachary was hoping that Silas was falsely claiming to be Townsend's firstborn, he was wrong. His credentials as a Derrington were evident to the eye.

Ambrose smiled, removed his spectacles, and leaned back in his squeaky old chair. He motioned for Silas to enter and have a seat in the small chamber. The breeze blew in through the one window open toward the sea.

"The answer to your question, my lad, is no. There is nothing stagnant about knowing Jesus Christ. I continually learn of the goodness and greatness of God each time I give my sincere devotion to the Word." And he quoted, "More to be desired are they than gold, yea, than much fine gold; sweeter also than honey and the honeycomb."

Silas smiled ruefully. "I'll take your word for it."

"Don't ever do that. Taste and see for yourself that the Lord is good. God keeps an individual relationship with each of His own. Don't trip on that box of books, lad. They just came in today. I've not had time to unpack them."

"The question remains of where you'll put them," Silas said, stepping over the box and finding a small foothold of empty flooring to ease himself into a cane chair.

Ambrose laughed. "A trifle cramped, all right."

"With all the money the Derrington family has in the Spreckels bank," he said, glancing around, "I'd think they'd get together and build you a bigger church. They all claim to be religious."

Ambrose took note of the vein of resentment in his tone. Was the bitterness for the Derrington name or what he thought hypocrisy? He decided it was the Derrington name. Now what was the root of it? Ainsworth was making Silas a top manager of the sugar manufacturing and paying him double what he would normally pay one outside the family. He had also been embraced into the midst of the family as a full-fledged member, with the assurance of a bigger future inheritance. What continued to feed the resentment?

"A larger and finer building has already been suggested, but Dr. Jerome, and Eden as well, wish to keep its historic reputation. I admit I do too." Ambrose went on to briefly explain how Jerome and Rebecca had founded the church here, and how the first Hawaiian who had come to faith in Christ was Noelani's mother.

"Until her conversion, the Hawaiians wouldn't venture to within a yard of the front step. I had superstitious trouble with the Hawaiian leaders just a few years ago when a hurricane came through. They insisted the storm came because we worshiped Christ instead of the gods of their Polynesian myths, Kane and Pelee, the primary spirit. They insisted I bless all of their animals and fishing nets so no harm would come to them in the hurricane. If they lost their animals and nets, their spirit god was deemed the stronger and the true."

Silas's eyes reflected interest. "What happened?"

"By the grace of God the storm blew through. Their livelihoods were saved. More importantly the true and living God was glorified as the Creator. The people began to come on Sunday in larger numbers. Since then they've sincerely turned to Jesus as their only Lord and Savior."

Silas changed the subject as soon as an opening came.

"I've been out walking this morning. I came upon my cousin Candace returning from the Easton plantation. Isn't that where a Chinese man was found murdered this week?"

Ambrose sadly noted the pretentious attitude of ignorance that Silas displayed. Silas already knew who Sen Fong was, yet he was suggesting otherwise. Ambrose knew this to be true because of something Sen had told him, something Ambrose would not repeat because it had been given to him as a man of God.

"Yes, his name was Sen Fong," Ambrose said quietly. "Eden

found him in the garden at Hawaiiana's house."

"An ugly discovery for a fine girl like Eden."

"She's a nurse and she has seen worse."

Ambrose believed Silas had stopped here today by chance, but after he'd gotten here had decided to see if he could discover how much was known about Sen Fong's background. Ambrose decided to come straight to the point. Silas remained connected in some way with the gambling cartel, he was sure of that, but what of the opium dealers? Ambrose hoped he was wrong.

He folded his arms on top of his desk and leaned forward with a level stare. "Did you know Sen Fong?" Ambrose asked outright.

Startled by the bluntness of the question, Silas stared.

Ambrose was heartened when he saw the struggle Silas went through in order to not lie to him.

"Oh well, you know, I'd seen him around now and then."

"Now and then," Ambrose repeated, still meeting his gaze squarely.

"Actually," —and Silas pulled at his earlobe, glancing about the room— "well yes, that is, I knew who he was."

"He was in the opium cartel. He told me about it."

Silas glanced at him sharply. "He told *you!*"

"Sen became a Christian a few weeks ago." Ambrose leaned back comfortably.

Silas nearly choked out his unbelief and shock. "Sen Fong a Christian! That can't be."

"Why do you say that, lad?"

"Well! Sen Fong was a terrible man. He was an opium dealer, all right, and a lot more, including a murderer." His light-blue eyes narrowed. "He killed a Chinese once. I don't know what it was about."

Ambrose showed no shock. He told Silas of the Bible campaigns on the Oahu plantations. "He came here late one night with Keno and asked for Dr. Jerome and me to answer his questions on the merits of gaining forgiveness of his sins. I showed him through Scripture that Christ Himself is our merit, our righteousness. He is made unto us everything we need as corrupt, leprous sinners. He is made unto us wisdom, sanctification, redemption. Sen Fong exchanged his sin for a robe of righteousness that night."

Silas moved uneasily. Again he changed the subject.

"Then Keno and Jerome know about his involvement in the opium?"

"So does Rafe."

Silas let out a breath of what may have been despair, or perhaps relief, and leaned quickly against the back of the chair.

"I see." He was thoughtful. "Yes, I think I understand now."

"Understand why he was murdered?"

Silas remained silent and pensive. He stared at the Bible on the desk.

Ambrose went on quietly, "We think his coming to Christ was the reason the kingpin had Sen murdered."

At the word *kingpin*, Silas swerved his gaze to Ambrose. A glimmer showed in his eyes. He seemed surprised or troubled that Ambrose knew the term, though he said nothing to prove he was thinking that.

"What makes you so sure it was the opium dealers?"

"Sen Fong was a kingpin himself. I know that because he told me so. He wanted to be free of the evil, and of the men who lorded it over him. He had a new Master now. He told me he would be in danger, that he knew too much, but little did I realize how soon, or how violently they would move against him."

Silas shifted in the cane chair. His blue eyes had turned cold and angry.

Why is he angry? Ambrose wondered. *And at whom? At me? With the cartel?*

Silas leaned forward and his gaze seemed to grab hold of Ambrose. "You say 'we' believe this about the opium dealers. Who are *we*, you and the marshal?"

"I don't know what the marshal thinks. He hasn't said much to me yet. I was speaking of myself and my nephew, Rafe."

"What does Rafe know about this?"

"Probably about as much as the marshal. He's put a few ideas together that make sense."

He sank against the chair back. "It's atrocious about Sen Fong. Makes me angry thinking about it."

Ambrose came to the conclusion that Silas was not involved in Sen Fong's death at the hands of the opium cartel. He too was upset by the murder and perhaps had come here to find out, in a round-about way, whether the law believed the cartel had committed the atrocity. If Silas was still involved with gambling, would this injustice to Sen Fong help to turn him away?

"It was done for money," Silas murmured more to himself than to Ambrose.

"Why do you say that?"

Silas looked at him. "Ah, yes, money," Silas repeated with some disgust. "People will do anything for money. I include myself. I acknowledge my weakness. But murder? No. Money is the root of all evil. You see? I do know something about your Book."

"A good start, lad. I'd like you to begin coming to the men's Bible study on Monday nights. The Bible, however doesn't say that *money* itself is the root of all evil, but that man's *love* of money is the root of *all kinds* of evil. A gold piece sitting here on my desk—if I had one—" and he smiled, "would be neither good nor evil. It would be neutral. It's what a man might do in order to take that piece of gold from my desk, and what he'd use it for if he had it in his possession. It could be used for good, or evil."

"And Sen Fong was murdered because he chose, as you put it, a new and better Master. So then, 'they,' whoever was behind it, and the assassin who pushed that knife under his ribs, were together in the deed. And they did it for money."

"Yes, and in the long run it was more of a tragedy for them than Sen Fong."

Silas looked at him with doubt. "How do you come to that conclusion? Sen Fong is dead. They walk away free."

"Not forever. '*Fret not over the man that brings wicked devices to pass, for he will soon be cut down like the grass, and wither as the green herb.*' From this life's standpoint, yes, it was probably tragedy, since if he'd lived he may have been able to lead others to the Light that he had found. Then again, there's the issue of God's sovereignty at work. Nothing takes Him by surprise. Sen's days on earth were cut short. But Sen was ready to step into the presence of God. We never can be sure when our own time is up. Sen was ready. He was clothed in the righteousness of his Savior, Jesus Christ. Eternity is out there, Silas. The crucial question is are you ready?"

Silas shifted uncomfortably in the chair. He avoided Ambrose's eyes and looked at the time. "You're right," he said in his offhand way, and stood, "time is catching up with me. It's time I removed myself from here to Kea Lani. If I'm late my grandfather will hold it against me."

Ambrose walked with Silas to the front door of the church.

Silas smiled. "Thanks for the Book information. I'll give the matter some thought when I have a more convenient time."

"You know Silas, I read something of that nature before."

Silas looked around for his hat and walking stick. "I must have left my stick in the buggy." Then, with a suave "aloha," he was gone.

Ambrose looked after him with a note of sadness. Silas strolled on his way toward the fork in the road—whistling a meaningless tune.

*I*n a gesture of determination, Rafe jerked his hat lower and tramped along the edge of the pearl lagoon. The full moon climbed above the blue-black water, causing it to shimmer with diamond sparkles. The fringed silhouette of coconut trees stood along the water's edge where he emerged from the beach. Kea Lani was not far ahead. He intended to find Great-aunt Nora and discuss the prescription bottle, which she'd told everyone she mistakenly threw away. Thanks to Zachary's slip of the tongue, if it was that, Rafe knew differently. The challenge would come in convincing Nora to turn the prescription over to him. He must talk to her alone while Ainsworth was busy elsewhere. Rafe didn't put it past him to wrangle Nora into either keeping it hidden or releasing it to him.

The wooden building stood across the road on a gardened plot of land once owned by the Derringtons but now part of a larger acreage sold under his stepfather Townsend to Parker Judson.

When Rafe agreed to a partnership with Parker Judson, he first went out of his way to negotiate with Judson to allow the historical church to remain untouched on its own plot of ground, along with Ambrose's bungalow.

Rafe had built Ambrose and Noelani a bigger and better house close to his own plantation house on Hawaiiana, but Ambrose always returned to the little bungalow beside the church. Not that Rafe blamed him. It was easier to work on his sermons and other activities close to the church.

Also, Ambrose wasn't much for fancy houses. "I want to live on a par with my congregation. You know as well as I, Rafe, that most of them are Hawaiians. The wealthy planters and their families usually go to Kawaiahao church," he said of what was considered the church of the royals near Iolani Palace.

Rafe made his way past the pearl lagoon. As he'd mentioned to Eden at Kalihi, the financial matters of the Easton estate were now in the care of the family lawyer. The pearl bed was again Celestine's and she was in the process of granting Rafe legal jurisdiction. For Townsend, this loss, along with losing Hanalei, was the root of his present wrath. In his arrogance he had convinced himself he had the right of control to bleed the Easton assets dry. Rafe couldn't prove it, but he believed it was only after losing control of the Easton estate that Townsend had made the decision to harm Nora Derrington, his aunt. Silas had come to Rafe recently and mentioned he'd overheard a bitter argument between Townsend and Celestine near the time when Eden had brought Great-aunt Nora her medication from Dr. Bolton. Townsend had disputed Celestine's right to turn all of Matt's legacy over to her son and there'd been the sound of Celestine being struck.

"I didn't tell you at the time. I was afraid you'd tangle with Townsend," Silas said. "Not that the cad didn't deserve to be roughed up. Miss Celestine's a mighty gracious lady and she deserves so much better than Townsend. After the move against Nora and now with him in San Francisco, I thought it would be wise to tell you."

Rafe's jaw flexed. Thinking of Townsend striking his mother and allowing Matt to die sent his blood pounding.

The mission church was ahead among the swaying palms near Ambrose's hut, where a familiar light glowed an evening welcome in the window.

Rafe frowned as he continued his walk. He crossed the yard and took the steps to the front door. It was after eleven o'clock when he quietly tapped on the door. He often arrived at this late hour, coming straight from Hanalei. He leaned his shoulder into the door a moment, troubled, considering his decision to find Townsend. He looked back down the steps toward the small mission church and felt a pull on his heart as the Hawaiian wind brushed his face and the moonlight illuminated the cross.

Ambrose was expecting him, and opened the door, his sun-tanned fatherly face and keen ebony eyes appearing doubly dark below silver hair and rather long bristling brows. Those brows looked as though they were windblown. Rafe smiled. "Evening Ambrose."

"Ah, come in, lad."

Despite the humid weather, Rafe had rarely seen him in public without his knee-length frock coat over a starched white cotton shirt. An old gold watch chain persistently hung from his pocket. From childhood Rafe and Keno both had often been amused because the watch never keep accurate time. Ambrose was always ten minutes late behind the pulpit and kept the Hawaiians ten minutes past the service hour. The matter had become a tradition. There was always what Rafe called a freshly bathed, minister-like quality to his uncle that brought out the best in Rafe's behavior. Ambrose had had him memorize much of Psalm 119 when Rafe was twelve years old, quizzing him on occasion on certain verses—"*Wherewithal shall a young man cleanse his way?*"

"*By taking heed thereto according to thy word,*" Rafe had answered.

Ambrose had smiled, satisfied, and patted Rafe on the shoulder. "You'd better," he had warned.

Ambrose now stood in the doorway and beckoned him inside. Rafe entered, noting the open Bible on the arm of the big chair beside the glowing lantern. Ambrose usually "soaked up" the Scriptures, as he put it, before he went to bed, memorizing verse after verse. As boys, he and Keno had once tried to guess how long Ambrose could go without saying memorized verses.

"I smell coffee."

"It's on the stove. Eden stopped by after she left Kalihi today."

"I saw her this morning."

"So she said." Ambrose followed him to the kitchen where Rafe was pouring himself a cup. He spied a plate of cold chicken and helped himself as Noelani expected, though she was now fast asleep upstairs.

"Yes, Eden said you'd been exceedingly generous."

"Don't weigh my motives. They're self-beneficial."

Ambrose cracked a smile. "So I gathered. Well, Eden is very pleased."

"The medical journal that Dr. Jerome believes to be a treasury of sound medical research on leprosy doesn't impress me. I don't believe leprosy can be cured with exotic recipes of rare herbs from distant, exotic lands."

Ambrose sighed, looking troubled about Jerome. "No, Jerome's launching his little boat into a strong headwind, I'm afraid. What worries me most is how he's going to react when his dreams fall apart. I've word from Molokai that Rebecca is growing weaker by the day."

Rafe tensed. "Does Eden know this?"

Ambrose shook his head and sank into the chair. "No one knows. Rebecca asked her kokua to say nothing to Eden. She's hoping to live to meet her. After that—"

Silence filled the bungalow. Rafe worried about Eden's response.

"Jerome is walking into a storm to say the least," Ambrose said. He looked over at Rafe, who stood leaning against the kitchen counter holding his cup.

"Even so, lad, I think you're doing wisely when it comes to Jerome and Eden. Giving him an interest-free loan to build the clinic and buying us Nora's new printing press deserves our gratitude. And what's more, I think you'll get it double from Jerome. He's going to be enthralled. By the way, Eden informed me you'd have Keno deliver the press aboard the *Minoa?*"

"I'll arrange it before I leave."

"Good. There's a poor young lad there who could use a little hope and adventure. Rebecca sent word about him. Starting a little paper will put some enthusiasm in his life. I'm hoping to help him see the love of the Lord through this."

"So Eden told me. Bibles and children's Bible stories as well. Do you have everything you need?"

Ambrose's eyes sparkled with humor. "I'll make sure to send you the charges."

"See that you do. I'll be talking to Nora tomorrow. I don't think I'll have any difficulty getting the press from her, but the other reason why I need to see her isn't likely to endear me to her kindly heart."

Ambrose sharpened his gaze. "Oh? Why so? I'd expect her to be pleased about getting her money back on that expensive press Zachary ordered. He said she was cranky with him about it for weeks."

"It's not talk of the printing press that will upset her, but the prescription bottle she said she threw away after she was poisoned."

Rafe explained what he'd learned from Zachary, and what he hoped to accomplish in his meeting the next day with Nora at the Kea Lani family meeting over Townsend. When he'd concluded all that Zachary had revealed, Ambrose shook his head thoughtfully.

"That news is very dangerous, Rafe. Just be grateful to God Townsend isn't in Honolulu to find this out. I tell you, I'd be worried about her safety and *yours.*"

Rafe was surprised by the gravity of his uncle's response. "Where Townsend's concerned I can take care of myself. There's a part of me that would be pleased to have a dust-up with him."

"That, Rafe, is what worries me."

Rafe didn't want to discuss it. "You're right, though, about Nora. Maybe even Ling." Rafe drew his brows together. "Maybe I can get her to understand her position. She's holding evidence that could put Townsend behind a chain link fence for many years."

"To say the least," Ambrose stated, looking at him anxiously. "Who else knows of this bottle?"

Rafe gave a shake of his head and bit into the chicken. "Just Zach, as far as I know. He either let it slip out to me deliberately, or he doesn't see the total value of the information. That's hard to believe, though. Zach isn't dense. He has a normally suspicious nature."

"So you're inclined to think he wanted to let you know."

"That's what I'm thinking now."

"Why he didn't tell you sooner is curious, though."

"Zach is like that sometimes. He and I get along well, as you know. Though, even now, at times, he backtracks. He's been under duress lately over Townsend and Silas. He's defensive about it."

"Well, you know him better than any of us. You always were protective of him, even when he didn't realize it."

"At least he comes to me now, when he's in trouble. That gives me a chance to try and step in before he makes matters worse for himself."

"And others."

"Yes." Rafe frowned. "That prescription bottle—I've got to get hold of it tomorrow. I want to take it with me to San Francisco."

"Rafe, it might be wiser to let the authorities handle it, with Townsend, I mean."

Rafe knew what Ambrose feared would happen. That Rafe would lose control of himself and decide to reap vengeance on Townsend. Rafe wasn't too sure, himself. After learning from Silas that Townsend had dared to strike his mother, Rafe could see what swelling tide of testing might be awaiting him. He hadn't told Ambrose what Silas said, knowing it would convince him even more that he should stay far afield of Townsend. Rafe told himself he'd already settled the issue. His anger was under control.

Townsend had always been an oppressor. If cornered there was no telling what he would do. Rafe gritted his frustration. It would be a long two or three weeks on the steamer to the mainland.

I must get to Parker Judson's on Nob Hill. I'm going to find Townsend.

And when he did? Rafe would think about the outcome later. He finished the chicken.

"If nothing else, Rafe, a discreet private detective could be hired to track Townsend down and gather evidence," Ambrose said.

Rafe looked at him. "That's what I wanted to talk to you about. Parker Judson sent a wire today. He's suggesting a man he knows from Pinkerton Detective Agency. Naturally, Ainsworth will be opposed. He's already asked me to wait until we have both arrived in San Francisco. He'd like to track Townsend down himself and have a 'chat.' It's all I can do keep my tongue civil when he speaks in that fashion. He's utterly frustrating at times."

Ambrose shook his head with sympathy. "Yes, Ainsworth took a wrong route years ago. He never found his way back to where his father Jedaiah had pointed out for him. Ainsworth became too busy building the Derrington enterprise to take much time considering whether or not he was building according to God's specifications. People won't believe it, lad, but money and privilege can be a curse. Far better the generation of young people who must strive and work and go without than those who've had indulgent parents who put too much on their plates. They're actually destroying them. Instead of men, they're making spoiled children. They'll grow up soft and compromising. Pity the generation who is left to such leadership!"

Ambrose had suggested a private detective agency months ago when it looked as if the Derringtons were going to step back yet again from the issue of Townsend, just as they had years ago over the death of Matt Easton.

When Rafe had first talked to Ambrose soon after the trouble occurred at Koko Head over Nora's illness, Ling's hut going up in flames, and the slowness of the Honolulu authorities, Ambrose again suggested to Ainsworth and Nora they hire a detective.

"Oh we will, we will," Ainsworth had replied. "First, Ambrose, I need to find Townsend and discuss this with him. I want to know what it's all about." And Nora had sat mute and sober, refusing to meet Rafe's gaze or even look at Ambrose. Little had Rafe known at that time that she had the prescription locked away.

"If anyone could recommend a dependable detective agency," Ambrose suggested calmly, "it would be Parker Judson. He's right there in San Francisco."

He thought of Celestine, and Kip . . . and Townsend. The steamer wouldn't leave for several days. He decided to send a telegraph wire to Parker Judson in the morning. Three weeks was too long to wait to hire a detective. Rafe would ask Parker to hire a man immediately.

Rafe would take no chances when it came to Townsend and his bouts of rage. When his temper exploded he became an out-of-control instrument of evil.

"I'm sending Parker a wire in the morning. Ainsworth won't like what I'm doing, but this time he'll need to face up to the truth."

The next morning Rafe left the Royal Hawaiian Hotel and caught a hackney for the telegraph office on Bethel and Merchant street, and told the driver to wait. He walked inside the small room.

"I want to send a wire to San Francisco."

A minute later he wrote to Parker Judson:

"Leaving Honolulu for SF this Sunday. Don't wait for me to arrive to hire a Pinkerton detective. See if you can get one to track down T. D. now."
R. E.

he next day Rafe rode his new auburn stallion from the stables at Hawaiiana to Kea Lani to attend the meeting Ainsworth had called. He arrived an hour early hoping to locate Great-aunt Nora and insist on a private meeting. He knew Nora well from the two years he worked at the *Gazette* before he left the Islands on his voyage. She favored him then, and did all in her power to keep him running her newspaper. Rafe once entertained the idea of becoming a journalist and a writer. He even wrote the article on why Rebecca Stanhope Derrington had been sent secretly to Molokai, and dug up enough "scandalous" information, from Ainsworth's viewpoint, to use it to force him to explain the truth to Eden about her mother. Rafe felt at the time that he had to do it for Eden. She was certain Rebecca had been murdered. When Ainsworth discovered this he said, "I had no idea she thought such a thing."

"Sir, you'll need to explain the truth to her, or I will," Rafe had said. And so the mystery of Rebecca had been solved. But the idea of becoming a journalist and starting his own newspaper had died when he returned to Hawaii with the pineapple slips. Now it was on

Zachary that Nora had pinned her hopes to bringing her beloved *Gazette* out of near bankruptcy. Rafe had an idea about the *Gazette* too, but now was not the time to confront her with it.

Except for Zachary, it appeared that the others had not arrived yet, which was what Rafe had hoped for. As he entered the front entrance hall he heard Zachary's voice in the parlor. Rafe walked to the open oval doorway and paused there before entering. His gaze swept the sunny room with its open lanai, handsome wood furnishings polished to a sheen, and Zachary on the stage carrying out some emotional display to convince Great-aunt Nora of something.

Rafe smiled to himself as he saw her. Nora sat in a white winged-back cane chair. He gazed at her: silver hair in a bun at her neck, tall, too thin, dignified, crabby, but secretly owning a heart full of love for her wayward family members. *Like a frail and aged queen,* Rafe thought. Her thin hands rested calmly on the chair arms, and as was typical she wore no rings, bracelets, or jewelry of any kind. "It gets in my way." Her sharp gray eyes under white lashes followed her nephew to and fro. She wore a Victorian dress of dark blue and white lace down to her ankles, up to her throat, and tight at her thin wrists.

Zachary was saying, "Now look here, Nora, how do you expect me to be the upcoming journalist of the Hawaiian Islands if you don't give me the opportunity I need to dig up the truth and put it out there for all to read? Rafe's going with Grandfather to San Francisco. It's only wise I go along as well. I need to report on any annexation meetings Grandfather and old Hunnewell have with the American government." He stopped pacing and came up to her royal throne. He rested his hands on either side of the armed chair and bent down to look her in the eye.

"You want the facts of what Thurston is up to? You want them laid out in the *Gazette,* don't you, Auntie?"

Auntie! He's really buttering her up. Rafe folded his arms, watching.

"Well of course I do. But who'll run the *Gazette* while you're away? I haven't the strength to go downtown every day. Silas could do it, but he's apparently lost all interest in journalism since Ainsworth put him in charge of the sugar."

The mention of Silas hardened Zachary's face. "Silas was never a journalist. He's nothing but a gambler."

"I won't hear such bosh." She slapped the arms of the chair and leaned forward. "You need to grow up, Zachary. It's time you accept your brother and mend relationships. This is reality. We need one another. You need a brother."

Zachary threw up his hands helplessly. "To bash me on the head again?"

"Oh, what rubbish. It must have been one of those rabble-rousing annexationists. You should have called Marshal Harper at once to raid Hunnewell's beach house."

Rafe's mouth tipped at the corner. He reached over and tapped on the parlor doorway.

"Good afternoon, Nora."

"Come in, Rafe. I've just been telling Zachary I'd be pleased if he went with you and the other annexationists to keep an eye on your rabble-rousing. But who can I get to run the *Gazette* while he's away?"

"I'll find someone," Zachary said moodily.

"Ambrose has a second love for journalism," Rafe said, walking up beside her chair and taking the thin, frail hand she offered. "I think you can get him to run the *Gazette* while Zach's away."

"Ambrose certainly knows the business," she agreed. "Isn't he hoping to help a leper boy with a start-up journal of sorts on Molokai?"

"In fact, we'd like to buy that new printing press and take it off your hands. Ambrose and Eden have plans for it at Kalaupapa."

"That's the best news I've had all week. This hasn't been a good week, with that murdered Chinese man discovered in your garden, Rafe. Murder and mayhem are enough to upset the young, let alone a woman of my particular age."

Rafe, in spite of himself, felt affection rise for the vinegary lady.

"I was taught that getting old meant wisdom," Rafe said, and then caught his error but it was too late. She pounced on him with a rebuke.

"*Old?* Posh! My soul is as youthful now as it was at twenty. And, young man, I'll remind you I was quite a good-looking girl in my day."

Rafe smiled. She amused him most times. "I've no doubt, madam."

"And I'll have you know I could have had a number of the finest men in the Islands. But none of them stirred my romantic fancies. Actually," and she cast him a side glance, "I rather liked your grandfather Daniel."

Rafe lifted a brow. "What happened?"

"Oh, he married a missionary girl who came out from Boston, I believe it was."

"His loss, surely."

Nora laughed. "Diplomatic, aren't you. Zachary ought to learn some of your manners." She looked over at Zachary, who stood amused by the conversation between his great-aunt and Rafe.

"Now as for you, young man. No wonder you can't get Bernice Judson's heart. You're not well mannered enough. You need to be suave and charming."

Rafe looked at him.

Zachary's mouth turned. "It isn't my manners; when it comes to Bernice, it's Claudia Hunnewell and Grandfather's meddling. Claudia's already running to him, complaining that I won't give her an engagement ring before I leave for San Francisco. I expect I'll be reprimanded today on offending Thaddeus's daughter."

"Claudia," Nora scoffed. "That girl is a goose. Silly. No mental sagacity."

Rafe was convinced Nora had a special "Granny" kind of affection for Zachary, though she rarely displayed it. Dexterous, impatient with nonsense, she lived for her historical writing, debating and defending the truth as she believed it. Nothing upset her more than what she thought was "the ordinary people's lazy refusal to search out the facts" of what was happening in the world, especially concerning the fate of the Islands.

"Why don't people think? Why do they want the silly things of life? So they end up deceived."

"If Ambrose will take over for me, then there's no reason why I shouldn't go to the mainland."

Nora gave a nod of approval. "Very well, if Ambrose is willing, then perhaps it's wise for you to gain firsthand knowledge of what Thurston and his Reform group are up to with the American government. I'm sure," she said, her voice cryptic, "Rafe won't tell us."

Rafe caught Zachary's eye. He wanted to be left alone with Nora. Zachary must have remembered what he'd told him the other night at the hotel about the medicine bottle, because he glanced from Rafe to Nora, and then walked over to the doorway.

"Grandfather will be arriving soon," he seemed to warn by suggestion. "I think Doc Bolton is going to be with him. Strange, why Bolton is coming. I wonder what he has on his professional mind?" He went out and they heard him going upstairs to his room.

Rafe closed the double doors to the parlor. Nora raised her brows. He walked back to her chair and looked down at her gravely.

"We haven't much time before the others arrive. I want to talk to you, Nora. It's crucial."

She sighed. "I thought you may have come to me about Townsend."

"You know he's been seen in San Francisco. You've experienced just how dangerous he can become. If he finds out you still have the prescription bottle, tablets intact, and didn't throw it away as you claimed, he has a very sound and urgent reason to try a second time to silence you."

She looked at him a long moment in silence, showing no shock at the disclosure.

"What of Ling? of Eden?" Rafe reminded her. "Townsend set

the bungalow aflame by a willful act. Silas is a witness. And you were poisoned. It nearly took your life. No light thing, that. It's a willful attempt at murder. We have no right to excuse evil just because it was a Derrington, and your blood nephew."

Nora rested her forehead on her palm, her elbow on the arm of the chair. "I know that. That's why I wrote about your father in the Derrington history book. I've no intention of protecting Townsend."

"You told Dr. Jerome and Bolton that you'd thrown the prescription bottle away."

"Only because Ainsworth wanted to protect the family from the sharks in the newspapers. He pleaded with me to hold off just until he could locate Townsend here on the Islands and speak with him. I promised him I would. I'd no intention of ridding myself of the prescription. I knew it was secure, and it still is. At the right time, as needed I shall produce it."

"In the meantime he's roaming the streets of San Francisco watching my mother. You know how jealous he is of her. Now he's in a rage because he feels she's turned against him in my favor. Knowing his nature I'd suggest that even now he's steaming over Parker Judson."

Nora looked at him quickly. "Parker Judson? What has he to do with any of this?"

"Nothing, but try and convince Townsend of that. She's staying in his mansion on Nob Hill. She has a baby boy that she's become happy to care for. Do you think Townsend's mind will not jump to conclusions? Not that Kip belongs to Celestine, naturally, but that she might be falling for Judson, and he for her?"

Nora frowned and closed her eyes. "I had not thought of it, but now that you mention it, yes. I can see how he would."

"I've wired Parker Judson this morning to hire a detective to track him down. Ainsworth won't be happy about my action; he still wants to wait. But I'm not waiting, Nora. I feel comfortable having sent him the wire. If the detective can track him down, then the authorities in San Francisco can be alerted. They can make an arrest—if that prescription is first tested and proven to contain the same poison that put you on a near deathbed."

She sat still, and quiet.

"You heard Zach. Dr. Bolton is coming here with Ainsworth. It's not about the prescription—unless you told him?" Rafe said.

"No. He would only have wished to claim it. To lock it up somewhere. But I knew I could manage my own affairs. If Clifford Bolton is coming, then Eden's aunt, Lana Stanhope, is likely with him as well, and Eden. I suspect it has merely to do with their upcoming marriage, though this seems to me a strange time in which to mix a happy circumstance into the wretched trouble surrounding the Derringtons."

"What about it, Nora? I want to see this business come to a head and be over with. The longer we drag it out the messier it's going to become—the more upset you and Ainsworth are going to become, and the trial to all the rest of the family will bring frustration and infighting. I'll be on that steamer with Ainsworth and Zach on Sunday for San Francisco. I need that prescription to take with me. I'll need to show it to the authorities there when he's arrested. Otherwise, there's nothing to hold him on."

Nora pushed herself up from the chair and stood erect and sober faced. Her eyes searched his for a moment, and he looked at her steadily.

She sighed. "All right, Rafe. I'll trust you with the evidence. I'd rather it was in your keeping than Ainsworth's, but don't tell him I said so. Unfortunately he's more dedicated to the Derrington name than he is the members of the family." She laid a thin hand on his arm. "You wait here. I'll go up to my room and get the bottle." She glanced toward the lanai. "I believe that's Ainsworth now."

Rafe went to the parlor doors and opened them for her to pass through. He watched her walk across the hall and slowly make her way up the stairs toward her bedroom. For a moment he had an urgent desire to go with her, to make certain the task was carried through without a hitch. Silas appeared on the upper landing, tall, slim, and fashionable. He smiled at Nora, then glanced down at Rafe standing in the parlor doorway watching them.

"Hullo, Aunt Nora, you're looking a trifle under the weather . . . here, please allow me to escort you to your room."

"Nonsense. I'm quite chipper."

Silas chuckled. "I shall play the grand nephew and escort you anyway . . . oh, hullo, Rafe. Say, isn't that Candace who just drove up in the buggy? Looks like Zachary's gone to meet her."

Rafe glanced out the entry hall window. He saw Zachary by the buggy talking to an unhappy looking Candace. Rafe stood there. Something troubled him. He couldn't quite figure out what it was. He heard the voices of Zachary and Candace, and the next thing he knew Silas had an arm looped through Nora's and he was leading her away across the upper corridor.

_____

Kea Lani Plantation House, a white-pillared structure with three stories, was built in the 1830s as a replica of Candace's great-grandmother Amabel's ancestral home in Vicksburg, Mississippi. Great-grandfather Ezra Derrington, a physician, had gone to great lengths hiring builders and shipping materials from Boston, all to make Amabel, who was homesick for her antebellum South, feel comfortable in her new home. When their firstborn, Nora, inherited Kea Lani jointly with her brother, Ainsworth, she set out to transform Kea Lani from a Southern home to an island paradise. The rows of magnolia trees that had been carefully shipped from Vicksburg to grace the long, shady lane winding up to the house were removed and replaced with palms. Banana, mango, papaya, and cherimoya, as well as guavas had to be brought in, being non-native to Hawaii.

Candace, as a young schoolgirl, had been surprised, learning that even the ukulele had been brought to Hawaii by the Portuguese.

As she drove her buggy into Kea Lani's carriageway, the blue-green ocean shimmered in the afternoon sunlight. She stopped the horse in dappled shade near the white residence. Though the warble of birds in the foliage laced the afternoon warmth with tranquility, the true meaning of peace was not present with the family members who had gathered to discuss the grim news of Uncle Townsend.

Zachary, golden tanned, walked toward her as she drove up. Her cousin came from the side of the house with a shady area for hitching posts and water troughs for the horses. Her horse and buggy would be cared for by a Hawaiian boy serving as a groom.

Zachary paused to lend his arm as she stepped down from the buggy seat and gave the reins to the boy.

"Oh, hullo," Zachary said. "Looks like everyone's here, and Eden's aunt came with Doc Bolton."

"Lana Stanhope," Candace offered the name.

"Yes, that was it. A sister of Eden's mother. You know, Doc Bolton doesn't look right, if you ask me. I don't know why Grandfather troubled them to come this afternoon. I could think of more pleasant ways to spend the afternoon." He frowned. "A grim matter, this meeting, if you ask me. Like Halloween, you know? Skulls and ground fog. Depressing."

Candace turned her light auburn head and gave him a steady, searching look. His handsome face was troubled, his icy blue eyes restless.

"You need to get married, Zachary. I think a wife could bring you responsibility and happiness—and you'd forget everything else, including Silas."

Her words must have surprised him, having little to do with his grim surmising. He gave a short laugh. "Why would you say that now, of all times? Though I'd like to marry Bunny Judson."

"What's wrong with Claudia Hunnewell?"

He smirked. "Well . . . she's Oliver's sister. Aren't you sick of Grandfather pushing the Hunnewells on us?"

"Quite," she clipped. "Is Grandfather here now?"

"He's up in his room. Oh, I say! What in the world is *that*!"

Candace followed his gaze to the buggy seat, but with little interest. The one issue on her mind was to speak with her grandfather alone before the family conference. The silver knob on Silas's walking stick caught a ray of sunlight and glittered.

"It's a wolf's head," she said absently. She looked toward the steps and front door. "It belongs to Silas. I picked him up on the road, but he got out early and left it. Is he here now?"

Zachary reached for the walking stick. "Yes."

"Hand it to me, will you?"

"No . . . I'll bring it to him. You go ahead."

She left him examining the walking stick, and hurried inside the house. She saw no one as she entered the wide entryway. Voices came to her from the parlor on her left. She wanted to avoid them now, but took a quick glance in before sneaking past unseen. She saw Eden's aunt Lana with the pleasant and sober Dr. Clifford Bolton. Silas stood behind Great-aunt Nora's chair where she sat sorting through a stack of papers that Candace recognized as the final draft of her book. Eden was seated beside her holding some of the papers, and Rafe Easton moved about restlessly, looking at his timepiece.

She darted up the stairs and across the second floor corridor to Grandfather Ainsworth's room. She tapped on the door.

"Grandfather? It's Candace. I need to talk to you."

"Come in."

She entered the large airy room that had its own lanai overlooking the water, and slipped the door shut behind her.

Ainsworth looked up briefly and smiled his affection at his favorite grandchild, though he was quick to tense his brow as worries resumed their place on his shoulders. Staid and dignified as ever he slipped into a white jacket and checked his gold timepiece.

"You're looking harried, Candace."

She hadn't expected him to notice.

"We've only a few minutes before we go downstairs, so speak your mind."

He looked out at the sea's horizon and picked up a newspaper he'd been reading from the buffet table and tapped it with his finger. "The voyage to the mainland and Washington's already been leaked to Nora's *Gazette*." He dropped the paper onto the table. "If I learn that Zachary did this I shall be greatly disappointed with him."

Candace came to the center of the room. "Grandfather, I'm coming straight to the point. You know how blunt I can be. I came about Oliver."

He showed no concern. "Ah, yes, Oliver. The engagement party is all arranged, I'm told, to take place before I board the steamer. That, at least, will be a consolation."

She moved about, paying no heed to his words. She paused and looked at him. This was going to be difficult.

"I can't go through with it."

His white tufted brows descended.

"My dear Candace, we've been through this, in fact more than once."

"I know."

"He will make you a dependable husband."

"So you keep telling me."

"This is the best decision for your future and that of the Derrington and Hunnewell alliance. You have your duty, and I have mine."

"I know that too. Be that as it may, there are other duties also important."

"You are a responsible young woman. As a Derrington, you simply cannot go off and live your own life just to please yourself. I don't know what's gotten into young people today. No sense of responsibility as they had when I was young. They're not mature enough on their own to make decisions on marriage. Nonetheless they speak about love and marriage as though it were to simply satisfy their own desires rather than fulfill their obligations to the benefit of both family and community!"

While he went on in the same usual vein, Candace pulled herself into a more upright position. She turned the whole thing over in her mind again.

"Where is the obligation to the family name these days? Since when should a young girl be the sole individual to choose the man she should marry? Girls hardly out of their teens!" He took a turn about the room. "Insisting on marrying a certain fellow simply because he may be better looking than someone far more suited to her for a beneficial life!"

"Grandfather, is it beneficial to family and community, as well as the cause of annexation, for a Derrington to marry a British spy?"

He stopped short, turned, and stared at her.

Candace stared back.

"What did you say?" Ainsworth walked up to her.

"You'd better sit down. I've something rather startling to tell you, which you won't like."

He drew his brows together, his sharp blue eyes watching her, showing unease and failing conviction for the first time as she continued to show her own cool assurance.

"I don't need to sit," he snapped.

She recognized that he always became a little snappish when he was beginning to lose his footing.

"One would think I'm ready to be coddled and cajoled by a too-efficient nurse. What are you hinting of? *British spy?*"

"I came upon Oliver and Mr. Symington last night in Hunnewell's garden talking—"

"Hunnewell's garden! I'm beginning to think there's a plan underway to jinx the place! What is the problem now? Did Keno attack Oliver again?"

"He did not attack Oliver the first time. It was planned by Oliver himself."

He paused, but charged ahead. "I don't believe it."

"It's true. I heard what was said, and even more was hinted at."

"I want no 'hints.'"

"Then, the facts as I heard them. Oliver and the Englishman

were alone talking in strong terms under the poinciana tree. I had gone out to have a look at the sunset and came upon them."

"They knew you were walking up?"

"Not at all. I walked on the sand. Oliver made it very plain to Mr. Symington that he was not an annexationist as his father, Mr. Thaddeus Hunnewell, believes him to be. The Englishman already knew this well enough. Oliver said distinctly when speaking of his father: 'He'll stand by me to the bitter end.' Oliver believes the Hawaiian Islands should become a colony of Great Britain, like Canada."

"Do you expect me to accept this?"

"Whether you will or not, Grandfather, that's what I overheard."

"I thought I knew you well, Candace. My every hope has been pinned on you and your cool head to safeguard the Derrington Estate after my demise. But this sounds like a kettle of fish to me. As convenient as anything Zachary might come up with to get me to turn against Silas. Do you both think I'm so muddle-brained that I'll swallow this? Silas, a spy for the gambling cartel. Bosh! Now it's Oliver . . . he's a spy for the English and so the engagement must be postponed. The engagement goes forward, my dear, before I leave for Washington, or I'll be forced to take the strictest measures against the one to blame for all of this nonsense. And you know who that young dapper fellow may be, do you not? Of course you do. He was there the other night spying himself!"

"If you're speaking of Keno, he has nothing to do with this."

"Of course I'm speaking of Keno. He's been cooking up ways to come between you and Hunnewell. Oh I know these things. And my dear, I won't have any of it. Why, Oliver could no more be a sympathizer of England than I could, or Thurston himself."

Candace thinned her lips and stood straight, her fingers twisting into fists at the sides of her long skirts. Her fury burned, but she bit her tongue to silence. She turned and swished her way across the room to the door. She looked back, pale and red cheeked.

"Oliver also stated that if Queen Liliuokalani should be overthrown by the annexationists, England will work with them to put

Princess Kaiulani on the throne. You know don't you, Grandfather, that Princess Kaiulani is in school in England? And that she's married to an Englishman? And that others in the royal family, starting with Kamehameha IV, brought the Church of England to the Islands rather than give way to the rule of the independent churches of the American missionaries? Afterward, they'll naturally turn to Commissioner Wodehouse for support."

Ainsworth stared back at her, his face ruddy with emotion, but saying nothing. Candace went out and closed the door behind her. She swept down the corridor to go to her own room when she met her cousin Eden coming up the stairs. Her green eyes sparkled and her lush dark auburn hair was arranged most becomingly at the back of her neck. Undoubtedly she had just come from speaking with Rafe Easton, who was downstairs.

Eden stopped, and with a knowing glance looked from her toward their grandfather's bedroom door. A hint of sympathy showed in her eyes.

Candace breathed heavily, trying to assuage her temper. She knew what she was going to do. She could always depend on Eden. A more loyal sister she could not have had even if they'd been born of the same father. It troubled Candace's conscience to remember back when Eden, the younger, had lived away from the family and had thought her mother Rebecca murdered. Time and again since reaching maturity Candace rebuked herself. *I should have gone to her. I should have been a sister to her. Instead, I all but ignored her until age fifteen when she came home to Kea Lani—finally.* Eden had belonged here all along, just as she and Zachary had been raised here. Not that Eden had suffered under the good hands of Ambrose and Noelani. Perhaps it was the better upbringing after all.

"Do you have a minute, Eden? I need to talk to you."

"Of course."

"I'd be pleased if you'd pass on what I have to say to Rafe."

Eden calmly affirmed it as they walked quickly toward Candace's bedroom at the other end of the corridor.

Reaching the bedroom door, Candace delayed a moment with her hand on the knob. She had the urge to look over her shoulder, though she wasn't sure why. As she turned her head, she saw Silas was standing on the top stair looking in their direction. He must have been behind Eden coming up the stairs. Candace decided that Silas had a very stealthy footstep. Could he have overheard what she'd just said to Eden? But even if he had, she did not suspect him of anything serious, even if Zachary did.

Candace pushed open the door and they entered.

*R*afe bounded up the stairs and across the corridor toward Silas Derrington as he was leading Great-aunt Nora to her room. Rafe reached the door just as Silas was closing it. Rafe blocked it, then shoved it open.

Nora turned from the divan, surprise written on her pale face. She looked from Silas to Rafe.

Silas stood looking at him, smiling.

Always smiling. But his eyes are as cool as a Northwest winter.

Rafe gave him a measuring look and refused to explain his presence.

"Well, I'd better go downstairs for the meeting," Silas said amiably. "Ainsworth and the others have arrived." He looked at Nora. "Will you be coming down, Great-aunt Nora?"

"In due time, Silas. I've nothing to say about Townsend that I haven't already said to the family, but I should be there. You can tell Ainsworth I'll be down shortly."

Silas gave a nod and started from the room, but paused to look at Rafe who remained.

"Run along, Silas," Nora almost snapped.

He went out, shutting the door. Rafe walked over to Nora and gently took her arm, lowering her to the divan.

"My apologies," he said quietly. "I don't trust him."

"You don't seem to trust any of us," she said curtly.

He smiled faintly. "Not so. I trust you."

She calmed, and sighed. "Give me a moment to collect my wits and I'll get you the bottle. Did you think Silas intended to steal it when my back was turned?"

"Since you're asking me outright, my forthright answer is maybe. At the moment I'm probably being too cautious, but I can't take any chances."

"Well that's undoubtedly wise. I'll get it for you now so you can meet with Ainsworth."

He watched her as she entered the door into her private bedroom and was busy opening drawers.

He waited restlessly until she returned with a bottle and handed it over to him. Rafe read the label, noting the date, the prescribing physician as Dr. Bolton, and the dosage.

"You're certain this is the bottle with the tablets you took?" he asked in a low voice.

"Quite certain. No one knew I had it except Zachary. I've had it locked away. Rest assured there's been no hanky-panky."

Rafe slipped it into his jacket pocket and took her hand into both of his. He held it gently and planted a kiss on her cheek as she smiled, her eyes twinkling. He walked to the door and went out, closing it quietly behind him.

⁓ ১৯ ⁓

When Eden left Candace in her room and came downstairs, Grandfather Ainsworth was pacing the polished wood floor of the parlor.

She entered the large airy room and glanced about to see who was present for the discussion about Uncle Townsend. She knew Dr. Jerome would not be here since she'd left him at Kalihi Hospital working with Dr. Bolton. When she'd brought her father the message that had just arrived from Grandfather Ainsworth telling them both to come to Kea Lani for "the meeting about Townsend," much to her surprise her father became cross.

"My dear, I haven't the time to waste on Townsend. My brother is willfully wayward. He knew the truth while growing up, the same as I did. That he deliberately chose to walk away from God and indulge his carnal appetites, even enjoying the shame it brought, speaks for itself. There are adequate warnings in Scripture on the principle of sowing and reaping."

She now glanced about the room here at Kea Lani. *Where is Rafe? And what will he say when I tell him about Oliver Hunnewell?*

The events in the garden that night took on a new and ominous significance since Candace had explained what she'd overheard between Oliver and the British agent. Had Oliver concealed himself among the trees and shrubs on the night of the annexation meeting in order to pass the stolen manifesto to Silas?

As her gaze fell on her grandfather, the first thing she noticed was how gray and pale he looked. Rather than being angry with him over the recent events, her heart felt a pang of compassion; she loved him and knew he was hurting. Then she realized that the discussion he'd just had with Candace affected him far more severely than Candace had thought. The news about Oliver being a British spy must have shocked him. He'd gone into a defensive denial, but it must have begun to sink into his mind as he struggled with the conviction that it just might be true.

Had I been the one to tell him about Oliver he'd find a way to not believe me, she thought, but Candace posed more of a problem as he had boasted about her sharp mind, and that his "dear Candace had a man's mentality when it comes to hard decisions."

Eden was tempted to feel irritated, for she knew she had as much sense as Candace, but then she realized how vain and unbecoming it was to be offended by her grandfather's biases. She sobered quickly. Was Grandfather serious when he told Candace her marriage into the Hunnewell family must go forward regardless of anything traitorous Oliver may have been involved in?

She watched him move to and fro across the room, silver head bent, hands folded behind his back, staring down at the floor.

Silas stood at an open window gazing outdoors, seemingly absorbed in his thoughts. Recently she had set aside her earlier impressions about him, which had led her to believe he saw himself a mere spectator to what went on in the Derrington family. Things had changed. He was no longer the unemotional observer. He'd been accepted into the family by those who mattered most, Ainsworth and Nora, and he was beginning to feel ties to the enterprise. He was surprised by the acceptance he'd received, even dismayed, as though he had not known how to handle it. Had he come from the mainland only to cause trouble? Was he a spy for a cartel? Was he now developing a twinge of conscience that winced at betrayal? What was it that consumed Silas's thoughts? His reckless father, Townsend? Hardly that. Silas held no affection for him.

Eden came to the conclusion that if Rafe were correct, there'd been something more to the reason that had brought Silas from the mainland to Hawaii.

She couldn't forget that morning when he'd walked out on the lanai where the Derringtons were all having breakfast. With a smile that appeared to be both a smirk and an apology, he'd introduced himself as Silas Derrington, "firstborn son" of Townsend. His announcement had come as a threatening blow to Zachary, had embarrassed Celestine, and at first had even stunned Townsend into silence. Later, he'd decided Silas's audacity was deserving of praise, and even humorous. From that moment onward he had decided to make Silas his firstborn, effectively displacing Zachary.

Was any of this beginning to trouble Silas? Or was Eden only hoping that her prayers for his turning to God would be answered to the praise of His grace and mercy?

She noticed that Zachary still wasn't present, though she'd seen him about Kea Lani when she'd arrived. What was he doing?

As for Dr. Jerome, while he may have been cross about Ainsworth's meeting and so refused to attend, he'd been exceedingly joyful over the news she'd brought him last night about Rafe's offer of a loan to build and supply the clinic. At first he'd been taken aback, but then moved with deep gratitude. "I must say I'm stunned. I completely misread the young man. He's going to make a wonderful son-in-law after all."

Hearing these enthusiastic words from Dr. Jerome himself, Herald had looked up from his desk with a pale, strained face, and his eyes had dropped to his writing.

Rafe entered the parlor, smartly attired and looking toward her as though he had just won the local pearl-diving contest again.

His brisk gaze caught hers and held it. She beckoned him with a lifted eyebrow as she moved toward the piano near the back of the room. She sat down on the bench, her back to the ivory keys, and a moment later he came up and stood beside her.

He rested an arm on the dark polished piano, and spoke in a low voice with a glance toward Ainsworth and Silas, who were enmeshed in their own thoughts. "What is it?"

"I must talk with you," she murmured. "I have something of profound interest about Oliver."

His lashes narrowed. She could almost hear him thinking, *Oliver? What about Oliver?* Again, he glanced unobtrusively toward Ainsworth, then gestured his head toward the lanai. "Let's chance it now. Come."

His strong hand snatched up hers, and in a moment they had slipped out of sight onto the lanai. The warm breezes met her refreshingly, and ruffled her crème and golden taffy colored dress. Her wavy dark-brown hair, glinting with auburns, tumbled in a cascade at the back of her neck when caught by the wind. She reached to protect the belabored work, done with the knowledge that Rafe would be here.

He led her down toward the end of the lanai. A door and window from one of the bedrooms opened onto this section, but it was an empty guest room and it was safe to speak. She turned to face him.

"What about Oliver?"

For a moment she paused to look into his interested eyes.

"Candace went to dinner at the Hunnewells' last night. She overheard Oliver talking to a British assistant to Commissioner Wodehouse. The manifesto was mentioned. Oliver had intended to take it from the library desk where his father left it and hand it over to the British. Evidently someone else got to it first, because Oliver told the agent that he believes he knew who took it, but can't prove it."

"Oliver," he said, more in consideration than in surprise. "So that explains it. Things are beginning to fall into place."

"Is Silas involved? Remember, he was there."

"Yes, I'm sure he's involved one way or another. But later, darling. We haven't much time, and there's something equally as important I need to ask you about. You're the best one to give me some information on Hartley."

Now why would Rafe be interested in Herald, when she'd just passed on such important news about Oliver Hunnewell?

"There's a brighter side to this," she pointed out. "Do you realize these facts about Oliver may give Candace the very opening she needs to end any possibility of marriage to him?" she said.

"Yes, that's true, if Ainsworth acts on his good sense. If he won't, and there's a good chance of it, then maybe Candace will. And Keno will need to act."

"What can he do?"

Rafe gave her a slanted glance. "Let's talk Hartley, shall we?"

"If we must. He's displeased over the loan you've offered Dr. Jerome."

"Interesting."

"My father was most enthusiastic when I told him. He paid you a profound compliment, even suggesting you would make him a fine son-in-law, and he wasn't quiet about saying it. Herald looked as if he were betrayed."

"I'm satisfied your father and I may become amenable to each other after all. I hope nothing turns up to bring further tensions."

"What might happen?" she inquired uneasily.

His eyes searched hers a moment. "I think you'll be able to come to your own conclusion when we've finished our talk about Hartley. Are you agreeable?"

She hesitated, then met his inquiring gaze steadily.

"Yes. I shall tell you what I know, and I admit there are a few things that are sure to confirm your doubts, for I know what you think of Herald."

Again, his gaze searched her face. "And does that displease you?"

"No, not now. You may have been right about him all along. I think he could be untrustworthy. I wouldn't have agreed with you two months ago, but I have my reasons now. If I defended him in the past it was only because I felt defensive about going to Molokai with him and Dr. Jerome. I didn't want you to have suspicions."

"Because it would have supported my wish that you didn't go."

"Yes. Matters are different now between us, darling. I think I understand your motives. You questioned out of concern, not merely to find something against Dr. Jerome."

His gaze softened. He touched her cheek gently with the back of his hand. "That's just what I wanted to hear. Where can we go for a quiet chat?"

She looked about Kea Lani and had a desire to get away for a few minutes. "Remember the old pathway down to the beach?" she asked simply. She could see that he did. Years ago when he'd lived at Kea Lani with Celestine and Townsend, Rafe would walk that route. When she wished to waylay him and discuss some of her own fears with him about her mother whom she'd believed was a victim of murder, she would wait for him there.

"How could I forget our 'secret pathway'? Let's go before

Ainsworth starts his meeting. I don't think he'll begin without me; he'll think I've been delayed."

They went down the steps and hurried off toward the back of the plantation house, toward the palm trees and the sea, to where the pleasant path wound along the hill and stretched out over the cove waters.

The afternoon sunlight shone warmly on the smooth sea and towering palm trees, and the scent from the flowers blooming in profusion in the long flowerbeds wafted to her.

"I must speak with Hartley before he leaves for Molokai with Dr. Jerome," Rafe began. "I'm hoping you can supply me with information you may have picked up through close association. If anyone knows him, it should be you and Dr. Jerome."

"Yes, to a certain degree. But I'm not that friendly with him. If you're convinced he casts a mysterious shadow from San Francisco," she said as they walked, "he may be more inclined to speak to me. I shall see him tomorrow."

"No, darling. I'd rather you *didn't* talk to Hartley now."

"But I thought—"

"If he guesses I'm the reason you're asking, it's likely to put him on the defense. Then by the time I speak with him he'll have arranged a believable story. I want to question him while he's off his guard."

"I see." Then Rafe intended to confront him. She shuddered. "Does Hartley have anything to do with Oliver?"

"Oliver is a different problem altogether, separate from Hartley and Dr. Chen. Oliver was hoping to get his traitorous hands on his father's manifesto. He may still think he can. I wonder whether he's a traitor for personal gain or to hide some scandal, or does he actually have an allegiance to the Union Jack. But Hartley—that's what I want to discuss."

In her heart she'd known that the inevitable narrowing trail would eventually lead back to Dr. Chen and the medical journal. Even so, she put up a mild protest.

"But, Rafe, surely this has nothing to do with Dr. Chen and his journal."

"I think Hartley is up to his ears in it. And it doesn't look good. The worst part is you going to Molokai and working with him. I don't trust him. I intend to look into it when in San Francisco."

She remembered the day Herald had arrived at Kea Lani, not long after Dr. Jerome returned to Hawaii from his long travels. The family had gathered on the front lanai after luncheon when a carriage pulled up bringing Herald from San Francisco. Even her father was surprised to see him in Honolulu, but not nearly as surprised as he'd been to learn that Dr. Chen had died from an overdose of a rare poisonous plant in his house in San Francisco's Chinatown.

Herald had brought the journal containing Dr. Chen's writings on his medical research of tropical diseases encountered on travels in the Far East and India, along with the news that Dr. Chen had wanted her father to have it. Jerome had asked Herald to write it into a manuscript form, and was even now trying to get the Board of Health to publish it.

So far, her father had not been successful in gaining the Board's interest. "It's all a bunch of herbs and snake venom," Dr. Ames had quipped. "And that doesn't grow new fingers and toes."

"Am I such a fool?" her father had snapped. "Do you think I'd recommend sprinkled posy petals? This journal logs Dr. Chen's findings after years of research and travel."

Her father had become so upset over what he'd considered a humiliating insult before his peers on the Board that he had turned and walked out of the meeting.

Eden walked with Rafe beneath the indomitable sun.

"Now, this meeting tomorrow with Liliuokalani. You say Nora will be there with Dr. Jerome. What about Hartley?" He looked toward her.

"Yes, Dr. Jerome will introduce us both as his research assistants."

Eden had a feeling that more trouble loitered somewhere just out of sight.

"Did your father ever ask Hartley about his past workings with Chen?"

"I don't re—Oh," she breathed in an uncertain voice. Eden paused abruptly beside dark lava rocks with the sea and white sand below.

Eden remembered an incident at the breakfast table at Koko Head when her father had made a strange statement about Herald. She turned quickly to Rafe, and his gaze sharpened.

"Remember something?"

"Yes, I'd completely forgotten until just now. It happened at Tamarind House when I was there with Dr. Jerome and Zachary, soon after Nora was ill. Candace had sent me a message asking me to come, that Nora wished to see me."

"Yes?" he said with interest. "I remember."

"I told my father there was something about Herald that puzzled me. He seemed surprised and asked what it was. I told him it was something Herald said to me at Rat Alley a few months ago."

"Rat Alley? The plague, you mean?"

"Yes, you remember how we were there with our medical tents? Well, at one point, Herald's words showed an unexpected burst of resentment toward Dr. Chen."

"*Resentment!* You're sure that's correct?"

"Yes, it seemed quite odd, don't you think?"

"I should say. Did he say what it was about Chen that still riled him?"

"Not exactly. That's why I later asked Dr. Jerome at Tamarind House. Herald had said something about Dr. Chen having 'no courage' when it came to boldness in research. One must 'take risks' was the way he'd put it."

Rafe lapsed into ponderous silence. She might have thought he'd forgotten she was beside him.

"So," he mused. "Dr. Chen lacked the courage to take *risks*. What was Dr. Jerome's response to that?"

"Unfortunately, we were interrupted and I didn't follow through on it, but I mentioned Herald having told me that Jerome had helped him in India. My father agreed that he'd helped Herald, who had worked for Dr. Chen in Calcutta. He'd gotten himself into alcohol and gambling problems. He was dismissed by Dr. Chen, and his reputation was tarnished."

"So Chen dismissed him. On alcohol and gambling?"

"Well, he didn't explain. I assumed it was."

Rafe frowned. "Hartley's resentment seems to go beyond that. He spoke, you said, of a fault as he saw it—of Chen not willing to take risks. Of what kind of risks was he referring . . . medical?"

She pondered, considering. "I see what you mean . . ." She hadn't considered medical risks before, but Rafe could be right. Her thoughts raced. Risks . . . medical risks . . . why was this so glaring to her at the moment? What had happened to make her think there was something more she could mention?

Rafe leaned back against a great lava bolder. "What you've told me strengthens an idea I've had for some time about Hartley. When he showed up at Kea Lani that day, he claimed he'd come from a two-weeklong, warm and cozy visit with Dr. Chen in San Francisco. Remember?"

"Yes, he did."

"He implied he and Chen had shared a deep camaraderie as they mulled over the good old days when, with Dr. Jerome, they'd worked together with heart-to-heart conviction. After having listened to Hartley, one might have thought him to be devoted to Dr. Chen."

"Yes . . . and that was why I was surprised at Rat Alley when he showed resentment toward him. But, Rafe, there's something else I wanted to tell you. At Tamarind House my father made a strange statement. After commenting on leading Herald to Christ in Calcutta, he said something had occurred recently—'in the last few weeks' was how he put it—that now raised a serious doubt."

"I don't suppose he explained?"

"No. He asked me not to discuss it; he intended to look into the matter."

"*In the last few weeks . . .*" Rafe repeated, while looking below. From the mound they stood there was an excellent view of the sea with the wavelets dancing in over the white sand. "The last few weeks from the time at Tamarind House would bring us close to Hartley's arrival from San Francisco."

Eden grew cautious. Her eyes met Rafe's. She saw the gravity in their depths.

"With Dr. Chen's medical journal," she said.

"With the journal and the news that Chen had died, yes. So Hartley told you Dr. Jerome had rescued him from drink and gambling in Calcutta?"

"I do remember Herald once saying that he'd been 'down to grubbing' as he put it, with the untouchables in Calcutta when my father found him and took him in."

"One could almost say Hartley feels indebted to him."

She did not want to say this, but she must. "He told me there wasn't anything he wouldn't do for my father," she admitted.

In the moment of silence that followed she seemed to hear a judge's gavel rap the bar as a harsh verdict was pronounced.

Rafe watched her, his expression unreadable. "I assume Hartley can offer interesting scraps of information on Chen's research into Eastern medicine, herbs and that sort of thing?"

"He's practically an encyclopedia at times. He worked for Dr. Chen in India and, he says, other places in the Far East."

"Does he seem highly educated? Could he be a bacteriologist for instance?"

"It seems unlikely. Otherwise he would boast of it."

"Maybe not."

She looked at him, wondering. "Well, he's not permitted to engage in higher research at Kalihi. One would think if he did have such a degree he would display it."

"Unless he can't."

"Well, there might be something in his medical background or past work that he wished to conceal."

He watched her pensively. Eden suddenly remembered. A slow revulsion crept over her heart.

Rafe drew his brows together and caught hold of her. "Darling, what was it?"

"Oh Rafe, there's something unpleasant. It was yesterday morning when you came to Kalihi. I'd been talking to Herald about improving the environment for the suspected lepers in the holding station—but he showed great coldness of heart in his response, almost as if they were fit for nothing except—experimentation." She could not go on.

"Coldhearted indeed. Would Dr. Chen trust the journal to someone like that?"

She drew her brows together.

"Dr. Chen believed in my father's work, just as my father believed in his. Surely he would not have wanted his years of research to go unnoticed."

"I'm sure he did approve of your father's research, or they wouldn't have teamed up as they did for a time in India. He might have turned his work over to your father in the end, if he'd lived long enough."

If he'd lived long enough? The inference brought her a cold shiver. "Then—I don't understand. You're not accusing my father—Oh! I can't even say the horrid word."

"Murder? Of course not. I'm merely suggesting someone, Hartley in particular, had opportunity to take the journal within the short period surrounding Dr. Chen's demise."

Eden fought against her natural aversion to Rafe investigating incidents that affected her father. "Lord, help me to be wiser," she prayed. "Give me courage to trust in Your plan. Then may truth prevail and lead to repentance."

I can't throw away my future happiness with Rafe to protect wrongdoing, even if the doer is Dr. Jerome.

Eden's heart continued to thud unhappily. *I must face the truth. . . . I must guard my own integrity before God, and not make* excuses for those I love, or causes I care about. If God has blessed these plans to go to Molokai, I will still meet Rebecca and ask her about Kip before she dies. And we can still help the lepers by show-ing mercy and sending the printing press. Rafe is already doing much to assist. I must trust the Lord to work this out according to His plans, not my own. My plans are too easily interlaced with wrong methods and motives. *Lord, help me yield completely to what You desire for all of those involved.*

Her soul grew silent.

She saw then that Rafe watched her with restrained anxiety and compassion. The fact that he understood the distress this situation brought her made her more comfortable in his love. She bravely straightened her shoulders. She didn't want him to think she was the sort of woman who folded up and collapsed at each crisis. Life was filled with earthquakes and storms, and a Christian must find strength in God's promises and His presence. *"My grace is sufficient for thee, for my strength is made perfect in weakness."*

And He has given me a man who will defend me and aid me through a crisis. What more could she have in this life?

The wind rustled the trees. She found her voice again, though her throat was dry with emotion.

"But while there may be something in Hartley's past," she agreed calmly, "it does not prove he stole Dr. Chen's journal in order to bring it to my father, if that's what you think."

"That is what I think, Eden. And it looks as though you've also realized it."

"Yes, but somehow I just can't bring myself to accept it. I can't see my father being knowingly involved in a dreadful theft."

"The present situation is murky enough to permit your heart's opinion," he said gently. "If his comment to you at Koko Head is taken at face value, then he wasn't involved in Hartley's conniving. He may have just discovered the truth some weeks after Hartley's arrival. Though troubled by the implications, he would have been in a quandary over what to do about it. As time went on Hartley would have been able to get by with his illusion of being a dedicated friend to Dr. Chen, because—" Rafe stopped. His jaw set and he said no more.

Eden understood. There could be truth in what Rafe was saying. Yes, she had suspected it all along. Dr. Chen, Chinatown, the journal, all of it had been lurking in the background of her mind. The only other person who knew the truth that day at Kea Lani was Dr. Jerome, and he had kept silent when Herald claimed his devotion to Dr. Chen and produced the medical journal, so esteemed by her father. Had he kept silent because of his desire to have the journal?

She said with measured calmness, "I feared there was something wrong about the journal. I thought you recognized it too."

Rafe looked at her for a long moment. "Hartley aroused my suspicion from the first."

"Dr. Chen would have wanted the written record of his years of study and travel turned over to someone of like mind. Herald claimed Dr. Chen wanted his work brought to my father. We both heard his explanation."

"What was it you told me earlier about Hartley saying there wasn't anything he wouldn't do for Dr. Jerome?"

She recalled her own words with a sigh.

"Yes . . . then, darling, just what are you suggesting?"

"That Hartley had the opportunity to take the journal. He was in the vicinity of Chinatown within a three-week period of his illness and death."

"There was someone else, including Dr. Chen's own cousin," she said.

His gaze sharpened. "Dr. Chen had a cousin from Chinatown?"

"Why, yes, Herald mentioned him once. I can't recall his name."

"Darling, consider the Chinese man—the kingpin that Dr. Jerome met with outside Hunnewell's!"

She stared at him, then drew in a breath. "Rafe—could it be? His cousin stole the journal and sold it to Herald?"

He shook his head, pacing. "If Hartley did buy the journal, then he couldn't have paid much for it. Who pays him? Dr. Jerome."

"Yes, I see. Father doesn't have much money, and Herald even less."

"Certainly not enough to satisfy a kingpin."

"But Dr. Chen was well known," she suggested, "and in certain fields of research and medicine he was thought highly of. So the journal of his life's work might sell for plenty in the right circles."

She could see that Rafe was not convinced.

"We won't jump to conclusions either way, darling. If the kingpin is Chen's relative, I don't think he stole the journal and passed it to Hartley. Our kingpin is in for bigger things, like opium, as Sen Fong was. That doesn't mean the kingpin isn't involved in this journal business in some way if he is related to Dr. Chen. Perhaps Sen Fong brought him to meet Dr. Jerome because there's some connection back to opium. At present, there's not enough time to chase it down in Honolulu. But I have what I needed on Hartley, and if the kingpin is Dr. Chen's relative, I have even more. At present, the sighting of Townsend is important to me, so I intend to board that steamer on Sunday. I'll be able to track down Townsend in San Francisco and then look into Chen's death. Come, we'd best get back to Ainsworth's gathering."

As they walked quickly back toward the plantation house Eden remained thoughtful. Despite the new shadows Dr. Chen and his journal brought to the moment, her heart did feel lighter now that she had told Rafe what she knew. He had been right after all. Sharing, trusting, and reaffirming commitment to each other proved to have bonded them more closely together. Even the news of his plans about looking into Dr. Chen's death and Herald Hartley, though troubling, was better than keeping secrets and retaining a pretense of harmony between two who were to become one.

Eden now understood what had been behind his resolve that she trust him with her secrets. He had realized the need for truthfulness between them and pursued it. She had wanted to keep the door shut and locked, preferring to pretend there was no need to uncover that which was unpleasant.

It's not over yet, she thought. Things were likely to get worse before they became better. On a long journey, however, the act of putting one foot in front of the other was the beginning of moving in the right direction.

Chapter Twenty
Narrowing Path

$\mathscr{G}$randfather Ainsworth was walking the green mottled rug in the parlor when Rafe entered behind Eden. Rafe noticed that all were present except Zach, who did not seem to be about.

Ainsworth then began his discourse about the Derrington name and the importance of its credibility due to their association with the annexation movement while Rafe kept his impatience from seizing control. Great-aunt Nora tightened her lips at the word *annexation* but went on knitting with white yarn as Ainsworth continued:

Townsend had shamed them all, but he would not be permitted to prevail, because Ainsworth would personally see to it in the end. In the meantime it was important to be patient and not allow their concerns to lead them into anything impulsive that would draw the newspapers to the family.

After fifteen minutes Rafe knew he could not keep silent. *Before this meeting is over*, he thought grimly, *I'm going to be seen by the Derringtons as an inflexible avenger with no compassion.* He decided to be forthright, and addressed Ainsworth.

"Sir, I've already sent a wire to Parker Judson last night. I've asked him to hire a Pinkerton detective he recommended two months ago."

As expected, this caught everyone's full attention. Ainsworth looked the most upset. Nora, on the other hand, kept her gaze on her flying knitting needles.

"Most all of you know by now," Rafe said, "that Celestine sent me a wire the other day from San Francisco. She'd seen Townsend watching Parker Judson's mansion on Nob Hill. After all that's occurred, it's necessary that he be tracked down."

"Yes, you must," Great-aunt Nora said tiredly. "He's right, Ainsworth." She looked evenly at her brother, whose face was strained. "There'll be no more of this dallying. I'm supporting Rafe in this. He has as much reason to be plagued by Townsend as I do. I recovered from Townsend's rash and violent behavior, but Matt Easton did not."

"She's right," Candace said coolly. "The sooner this wretched business with Uncle Townsend is over, the better we will all be for it. It's all absolutely horrid. Sometimes I think I'm living in the midst of a nightmare."

Their support did not exactly surprise Rafe, but the strength of their determination did. Silas, however, kept silent. He was over by the lanai as though keeping himself on the fringe of the family. Rafe gave him a measuring glance. *He's struggling. One of these times, and it's going to be soon, he's going to need to decide whose side he's on.*

Rafe turned toward Ainsworth.

The patriarch seemed to know he was outnumbered this time and gave an assenting nod of his head. "I can agree with hiring a detective, but I had a particular man in mind who is cautious in dealing with the newspapers."

"If I hadn't sent the wire, sir, Celestine would have acted on her own," Rafe said. "I don't think you need to worry about the newspapers. Parker Judson isn't likely to act injudiciously. He too views the newspaper men with a skeptical eye. He shares your view on the need to keep us out of the headlines."

"All right, Rafe," Ainsworth said. "It's in your hands. You're right about Parker. He's an old colleague; we've shared a lot together. Just so Townsend isn't turned over to the authorities before I can talk to my son. I'm not asking this for Townsend's sake, my boy, but for yours, understand that. You must not permit anger or even justice itself to disqualify you from a fruitful life. I'm depending on you. We all are. Derringtons and Eastons alike. Ambrose will tell you of the deadly harvest of revenge."

It grew quiet. Rafe was surprised by Ainsworth's affectionate display. *Can I believe him? He's asking this for my sake?*

Eden came over and stood beside Rafe. "Rafe won't step over the line. I know him too well."

But do I know myself? Rafe wondered. He looked at Eden. *I can't disappoint her.*

"And Parker knows what's at stake for the annexation committee going to Washington," Ainsworth added.

"Posh," Nora said, "the annexation committee needs to be unmasked," and flipped her needlework on the white yarn.

Ainsworth's tufted brows inched lower over the light gray eyes as he looked over at her. Unlike Rafe he was not amused. "It is the corrupt monarchy that needs to be unmasked, Nora."

"Now Ainsworth, you're going too far," Nora scolded. "Liliuokalani is anything but corrupt."

"I know you are friends with Liliuokalani, but she is lending an ear to the representatives of the gambling and opium cartels. It's the Reform Party that is voting against her bills that would otherwise impart nothing to Hawaii but further corruption. I'm surprised you continue to stand with her. I invite you to join with those of us working for what's best for the Islands."

Rafe heard the front door open and slam, and window panes rattled. Heavy footsteps trod across the outer hall toward the parlor where they had gathered. Candace stood quickly, looking tense.

Rafe turned toward the archway. Zachary stood, his blond hair tousled, his icy blue eyes homing in on Silas across the parlor. If it were possible for eyes to send out flames, Zachary would have toasted his half-brother. He stood there ready for battle.

Rafe moved toward Zachary, who gripped something in his hand. Rafe saw that it was a walking stick with a silver handle in the shape of a wolf's head.

Zachary held it out toward Silas with a scowl. "Is this murderous weapon yours?"

"Zachary, now what's this about?" Grandfather Ainsworth asked firmly.

Silas showed cynical amusement. "Weapon? You mean my prized walking stick?"

"With a *heavy* silver handle," Zachary accused, holding it out again.

"I must have left it in Candace's buggy. I met up with her on the road earlier and she gave me a ride." Silas arched a brow. "Come little brother, as I told Candace earlier, I'm not particularly fond of the handle, but it's a fine replica of the gray wolf, don't you agree? Done by a famous artist in the Great Northwest."

Rafe watched the fine-tuned interplay, ready to intervene should Zachary lose control and start for Silas.

"Don't play elder brother with me," Zachary snapped. "You know exactly what I mean about this heavy handle."

"I'm afraid I don't, old pal, so why don't you just—"

"I'm not your old pal, and don't say brother either."

"Rest assured, I won't trouble you with such an outrageous claim."

"Hold on, Zach," Rafe stated coming up to him, blocking his view of Silas. "We don't want any accidents here." He took the walking stick before Zachary could react. For a moment their gaze locked while Zachary glared, then he blinked and his eyes faltered. He pointed toward Silas.

"He used that on the back of my skull!"

"We'll find out. Stay calm."

Ainsworth walked up. "Zachary, my boy, what is this? I'm ashamed of your behavior. And with your Great-aunt Nora present, and Candace and Eden. A discussion can take place without angry outbursts. I won't have this in the house. Either calm down and make your case known, or we won't talk about it at all right now."

Zachary grew silent, but as soon as Silas came forward, he flared up again.

"This is what you used at the gate in Hunnewell's garden to clobber me on the head."

Rafe saw the flash of anger darken Silas's eyes as he stared back evenly.

"Say now, wait a minute," Silas said. "You don't know what you're talking about. What are you accusing me of?"

"You heard me!"

"And you're the Christian?" Silas threw the words at Zachary with contempt. "You'll barge into this room without any respect for those present. Hah!"

Zachary looked as if Silas had slapped him.

Silas gripped the walking stick but Rafe held firm. Ainsworth maneuvered Zachary across the room into a chair.

"Until this is cleared up, Ainsworth had better keep the stick."

Silas's face lost all of its suave glibness. Anger tightened his features and his eyes hardened. He began to say something, then stopped. He looked over at Zachary, who sat with his head in his hands.

"I've had enough of this family. I've had enough of the lies, the jealousies, the pretense. I'm leaving!" Silas yelled. He stormed out of the parlor and a moment later the front door slammed again.

Rafe stood looking after him. The silence was heavy with emotion.

Zachary seemed to catch his flyaway emotions and push them back into their cage. He groaned, and as if exhausted, placed a hand at his head. "I'm sorry," he said. "I'm sorry."

Eden looked at him sadly. She laid a hand on his shoulder in a gesture of quiet support. She sat down across from him on a settee and lowered her head to pray.

Rafe's hand had brushed her shoulder before he moved to the window to see which direction Silas was taking. Seeing the lone figure, head bent, hands in pockets, hurrying toward the beach, Rafe left the parlor and went out the front door after him.

—⟡⟡—

Rafe found Silas standing on the sand and staring out to sea, beside a huddle of twisted, leaning palms.

Rafe walked up and Silas showed no surprise. Rafe could see by his tired face that he was a discouraged man, undoubtedly over Zachary's hatred. He was burdened, as well as under conviction.

"If you're considering a swim to the middle of the sea, it won't do you any good," Rafe said lightly.

Silas responded with a wry turn of his mouth. "Out of the frying pan and into the fire, right?"

"Something like that. You need a long talk with Ambrose. He's the one we all go to when we're desperate. Some of us have been doing it since we were boys."

He gave a nod. "You and Keno. I like Keno. He'd make a true friend. They don't come around in life that often. And to some of us, never," he said bitterly.

"You need to do some reaching out yourself."

"There was a time when I didn't care either way. Not about the Derringtons, Hawaii's destiny, anything." He hesitated. "After I arrived last year, met the family, and well . . . became involved, it all began to take on meaning."

"You worked in San Francisco, wasn't it? The *Observer?*" Rafe had his reason for asking, but avoided any hint of it in his tone.

"No, Sacramento. I worked at the *Sacramento Journal.* Then I received an invitation to come to Honolulu to meet the rest of the Derringtons. It was what I'd always wanted. So I came. I haven't regretted it, though Zachary hates my intrusion."

Rafe turned his full attention on Silas. This was the first mention of any invitation to come to Honolulu. He'd heard that Silas came on his own. That he'd been in Hawaii for a month before ever showing up at Kea Lani.

"An invitation from your great-aunt Nora I suppose," Rafe suggested to see his reaction.

Silas met Rafe's gaze evenly, as though he expected a protest when he supplied the answer. "Great-aunt Nora? No. Why did you think that? From Townsend."

Townsend. . . . Townsend had sent for his first son, born out of wedlock, knowing what the shock of his arrival would do to Celestine and Zachary. Why had he done it? It hadn't benefited Townsend where Celestine was concerned, nor Zachary, who had swung his loyalties over to Nora and the monarchy to lash out at his Grandfather Ainsworth for what he considered rejection. So what had Townsend gained by Silas's arrival? Probably the presence of a secret son who brought him more satisfaction than Zachary; now that Townsend Derrington was on the run, he had lost that as well.

"David wrote in the Psalms, 'I said in my haste, all men are liars.' What's the real purpose for your showing up as you did?"

Silas shoved his hands into his pockets and stared at the incoming tide.

"Who do you work for?"

Silas kept silent.

Rafe narrowed his gaze, hands on hips. "Then I'll tell you. Zach's guess was right. You work for the gambling cartel out of Louisiana. You came to play the Derringtons for the fools you thought they were. You wanted to do as much damage as you could out of revenge, and get as much money as you could from Townsend. But unforeseen by you, you began to feel accepted for the first time in your life, and you liked it. You weren't accepted by your half-brother of course, but your grandfather and Nora welcomed you. Even Townsend boasted of you. Eden and Candace welcomed you too. You weren't alone now. You began to like being a Derrington. You could look into a mirror and see more than a gambler. For the first time you could bond to more than a deck of cards and a bottle of whiskey. You still cooperated with the gambling cartel—you had to. They might go to Ainsworth with the truth if you didn't. So you joined your grandfather in the Annexation Club to please him *and* the cartel. They needed a spy to let them know anything going on that might hinder their influence on the queen to pass the lottery bill.

"What was the real reason that brought you into Hunnewell's garden the other night? How about the truth for a change? You came to me about the danger Celestine could face with Townsend. You didn't keep back the fact that he struck her. I don't think you'd have unmasked yourself to me if you hadn't felt a commitment to what's right and decent. How about the truth! Or do you lack the courage?"

Silas kicked the sand and sent it flying. "All right! Clever, aren't you?"

"Just factual."

"I'll tell you. You've got most of it right. I did come to Hawaii for the reasons you said. It's also true, Townsend sent for me. I showed the letter to the cartel in New Orleans—I was a fool. I'd been drinking; I talked too much. Boasted I was a Derrington. Look who my father was. Well, they were excited. They were already making plans to extend the cartel into the Hawaiian Islands. They'd make more money than they'd made in New Orleans and Gretna. They needed a spy, and what better family than the Derringtons, one of the Big Four sugar families of the Islands? It was perfect for them.

"When I sobered up I was angry. Angry at Townsend. It was his letter that put me in this position. Who did he think he was suddenly contacting me at this late hour in my life? Angry, too, at all the Derringtons!"

"I always believed that. You came expecting to fling revenge like thunderbolts and instead collected some back payment. You found you were Townsend's boast around Honolulu, much to Zach's displeasure."

Silas frowned. "If you're aiming to say I've inherited Townsend's nature, you're jumping the gun."

"Ambrose can tell you all about inherited nature from the one earthly father we all have. You know how strongly Zach resents you, don't you?"

"I've a good idea," Silas said, his eyes glinting like steel for once. Even the regular smile, insincere as Rafe thought it to be, was gone.

"Do you blame him?" Rafe countered. "Since you've come to Honolulu, Zach's been pushed back into a corner. Even Ainsworth decided Zach isn't the best qualified grandson to run the Derrington sugar production."

"I take no pleasure in his loss. All this surprised me as much as it did him."

"What have you done to reach out to him? He is, after all, a half-brother. You're the elder."

"You heard him just now at the house. He'd bite my hand off if I extended it."

"Zach is emotional. Building any kind of relationship with him would take time, but he needs a brother."

"Like you maybe, not me. He scorns me . . . a gambler, a drinker, no college education."

"It's my opinion you need each other. Start out by writing a letter and explaining yourself. But let's get back to the main thing. You came here to harass, not make friends."

"You're right," Silas said with a challenge. "Until recently I wouldn't have troubled myself about any of them. When I first came I thought they were all fools and that I was going to enjoy using them. But you're right, it didn't work out that way. I found myself warming to the family. It filled something empty inside. It was good to feel wanted for a change instead of like a rat stuck in a gambling den."

"Who do you work for in the gambling monopoly here in Honolulu?"

Silas hesitated. "Let's just say a certain Louisianan."

"He's here in Honolulu, isn't he?"

"I won't ask how you figured that out. Yes. Fact is, he's got secret access to the queen. Those with him are deceiving her."

"Deceiving her?"

Silas glanced at him. "The queen has a belief in tarot cards. Also, in a certain fortune-teller, a spiritualist. The woman is a German, from Berlin. She advises her to accept offers from the gamblers, to pass the new lottery bill, and allow the sale of opium for revenue for the kingdom. The queen denies it all, of course, to avoid the public outcry."

Rafe thought back to the woman Eden saw at Kalihi Hospital.

"This German woman," Rafe said, "fortune-teller, is she in and out of the Royal Hawaiian Hotel?"

Silas looked at him knowingly. "So you've seen her. Yes, she's the one. A deceiver, but well-practiced at what she does. Spies working for the cartel find out certain facts about people and situations the queen has to deal with. Then, the fortune-teller meets with the queen in secret at Iolani, tells her what to expect from these people, and then arranges it. They're even telling her when to send her cabinet choices to the Legislature for confirmation. The queen would deny it, naturally. Then an anonymous letter, supposedly from a supporter, would be sent to the queen, warning her who could not be trusted, with basically the same information in it that the fortune-teller brought out of her tarot cards. They want that lottery and opium bill passed, you see."

Rafe wasn't fully surprised by the tactics of the cartel when money was involved. The tarot cards, however, were a surprise.

"There's a man with the fortune-teller, isn't there?" Rafe said. *And he hadn't wanted to be noticed.*

"He's the negotiator out of Louisiana. Not that he's informed the queen of it. He's telling her that passage of the lottery bill will bring lots of revenue into the kingdom's coffers. Well, that's how it works," Silas said wearily.

Rafe's interest sharpened. Here, then, the path was winding to its end. He could see the final players; the fog was lifting and understanding was coming to the forefront.

"They followed Sen Fong to Kalihi Hospital that night," Rafe said. "At least the fortune-teller did. Eden noticed her on the front steps. What was she doing, making certain Sen brought Dr. Jerome to Hunnewell's?"

Silas was looking more uneasy now, almost as if he'd come to himself and was shocked over his action of bearing the facts to Rafe.

"Yes, that's it. Look, here, Rafe, I had nothing to do with Sen Fong's murder. That worried me as much as it did the rest of you, and still does. Sen Fong turned to God and was assassinated because he probably wouldn't have gone on playing for the cartel. I guess you know where that puts me!"

"You're already in this, Silas. Even if you don't say another word. If you're serious about the truth you won't turn back now. I, for one, don't think you had anything to do with Sen Fong's death. But we know why he was killed. What I don't know is why the kingpin wanted to contact Dr. Jerome. I have my idea, but I want to hear it from your perspective first. What about your presence in Hunnewell's garden?"

Silas shrugged. "I was the spy, remember? I was told to steal Hunnewell's annexation manifesto. By then I was beginning to be disgusted with myself. I didn't want to do it. I wanted out of the gambling business altogether so I could get accepted into the Derrington sugar business. I liked what was happening to me. Ainsworth likes me; so does Nora, and Eden, Candace—too bad about Zachary . . . and I didn't crack him on the side of the head with that walking stick!"

"So you went along with the cartel in the end, took the manifesto, then what?" *Now it was coming. . . .*

"I was told to pass it on to Jerome, who would bring it to the

Hawaiian queen when he met with her about the clinic on Molokai."

That meeting is tomorrow afternoon.

Rafe felt unexpectedly tired. He looked out at the waves beginning to wash in, getting ever closer to where they stood on the white sand near the palm trees.

"Sen Fong brought Uncle Jerome to talk to the Chinese kingpin," Rafe said thoughtfully. "What did they discuss? Putting an end to teaching the Scriptures to the Chinese?"

"How did you figure that out?"

"Ambrose explained, after Sen Fong's murder. He and Jerome were holding Bible meetings on the sugar plantations. The results are cutting into the opium profits by taking customers away."

"I want you to know I had nothing to do with opium. I was part of the plan to take the manifesto and turn it over to Dr. Jerome."

"So you took the manifesto and passed it to Dr. Jerome on the back lanai."

"How could you know that?"

"Only a guess; I saw someone back there during the meeting. The question that's riling me is why would Jerome cooperate. I have my idea, but I hope it's wrong."

"I don't know the answer to that one."

Rafe remained silent. He thought of Eden and took no satisfaction in the confirmation of his suspicions. Then Rafe remembered his meeting with Zachary and suddenly turned toward Silas. "Zach came to my hotel room the night he was bashed in the garden. Do you know if someone else used that walking stick on him?"

"Oliver whacked him."

Rafe tilted his head. "How do you know?"

"I saw it all. Oliver was behind the gate wall, crouching. When footsteps neared the entry he reached down and scooped up one of those garden rocks Hunnewell has all over his yard. Zach happened to show up at the wrong time. I saw Oliver clobber him. He pulled him over behind some bush trees by the wall. Then he swiftly came through the garden to catch Keno, who was coming in the through the servants' side gate. I witnessed the whole debacle. I didn't like Oliver Hunnewell before this incident, but even less now. It gave me great satisfaction to lift the manifesto before he could take it from his own father and give it to the English. I'm just relieved Eden didn't come through that gate before Zach, though Oliver might have caught himself in time."

"You're right; it's a good thing she didn't," Rafe said too quietly. "Because if he'd 'whacked' her as you say—well, we'd best not get into that."

"I don't doubt it. Oliver might have known Zach would meet up with Keno in the garden and that would spoil things. The two of them together walking along to bring you the message about Townsend would have foiled Oliver's game plan. He wanted to make a big uproar with Keno to cover his own tracks when he stole the papers."

"Did he suspect you as his archrival for the manifesto?"

"Oh, he suspected me all right. He must have learned about me from the English. They're aware of the gambling cartel and what they're trying to accomplish in the Hawaiian Islands. They hope to turn it into a tropical Monte Carlo of the Pacific, or another New Orleans. They see people coming here from all over the world to enjoy themselves. Fancy hotels, island food—add the casinos, the chandeliers, the rich folks—and well, they can scoop in as much money as Monte Carlo. So they're doing everything they can to influence Liliuokalani."

Rafe was aware of the plans to turn Hawaii into a gambling paradise for the world. Moreover, the queen was amenable, since she'd been told that such business would bring untold amounts of money into the nearly empty coffers of the Honolulu government. Thanks to the European elite lifestyle of boastful indulgence, King Kalakaua, Walter Murray Gibson, and others who had observed firsthand the royal elite in London and Paris wanted the same extravagance for the royal line of Hawaiian kings and queens.

"Oliver came to me the other night suggesting a financial payoff if I'd hand over the manifesto his father had written for President Harrison."

Rafe gave him a measuring glance, wondering what his answer had been. Silas gave a twisted smile. "I held him off by telling him I didn't know what he was talking about."

"Did he seem convinced?"

"No. But he had to accept it because Candace happened to come out on her bedroom lanai and looked down in the backyard and saw us."

The tide was washing in, and one large wave threatened to overtake them. They dashed for the leaning palms and held on until the wave receded, then ran toward some lava rock above the beach. Rafe looked at the time. Dr. Jerome would still be at Kalihi. Tomorrow afternoon he would meet with Liliuokalani at Iolani.

"I'll be boarding the steamer the day after tomorrow. I've a last word for you, Silas. The gambling cartel will continue to use extortion to keep you a slave to whatever their wishes may be. As time goes by their demands are likely to grow more risky for you. They'll find ways to take advantage of your position as a Derrington. Get out now. Break away before the chains are too tight. The price will be higher the longer you wait. Tell Ambrose everything you've told me. Ask for his counsel. He can interface on your behalf with Ainsworth. If you're honest about wanting to change your life, there's a way to do it. The Lord can lift you up out of the miry clay and set your feet on solid rock. Now you know what you need to do. Go see Ambrose."

Rafe held out a hand to Silas. Silas looked shocked. He stared at the offered handshake and then slowly he reached and grasped it in a tight, grateful shake.

Rafe turned and climbed, taking the path back toward Kea Lani. His horse waited. He wanted to slip away unseen by Eden and meet with Dr. Jerome. He couldn't tell her the facts as they now were.

He must confront Dr. Jerome before the meeting at Iolani Palace in the afternoon.

Below on the lava rock Silas looked after Rafe Easton until he was out of view, and then he turned and looked toward the beach where the waves were reaching high tide. They'd just barely made it up here to the rock. Silas stared down at the foaming waves as they rushed in, then sucked back to sea again, dragging anything without roots out to deeper water.

"The Lord can lift you up out of the miry clay and set your feet on solid rock. You know what you need to do."

Chapter Twenty-One
A Meeting of Minds

*R*afe arrived at Kakaako detention center near the entrance to Honolulu's harbor and located Dr. Jerome's improvised research laboratory. The bungalow reminded him of a military hut. Just as Rafe neared, the door opened and a man wearing a white medical coat emerged.

Herald Hartley?

It was Dr. Clifford Bolton. Without noticing Rafe, Bolton, unsmiling and haggard looking, came down the rough wood stairs with unusually slow and precise steps. His left foot appeared to weaken, and he grappled for the handrail, but even then went down to one knee.

Rafe bounded to his side and helped him to his feet.

"Ah, Rafe Easton, thank you. . . . I lost my balance there, for a moment."

"Hope you didn't injure your foot. Careful," he said as Bolton began to take a step down. "Your trouser cuff's stuck on that nail head—" He reached down to unloose the doctor's cuff from a protruding nail.

"No!"

Rafe drew his hand back. Bolton's tired face then flushed with embarrassment. Rafe smiled and pretended he hadn't noticed the unusual reaction.

"Er, thank you, Rafe, I'll loosen it." Clifford Bolton bent and tugged at the thick linen cuff, but it wouldn't come free. He refused to pull up the trouser cuff that would bare his ankle as Rafe had begun to do. Rafe saw his hand shake.

Dr. Bolton turned a ruddy color. "Well, if you could just loosen the cuff—"

Rafe reached down and unhooked the caught fabric, careful to not lift the trouser. He straightened and smiled. "You're free at last," he said, adding at once to ease the strange tension, "Is Dr. Jerome in his lab?"

"Er, yes, inside," Dr. Bolton said quietly.

Rafe stepped aside and allowed him to come down the steps. Dr. Bolton thanked him again and walked across the mud flats with yellowing grass tufts, toward one of the holding huts built on stilts.

Rafe looked after him sober-faced. The doctor's tread lacked its usual energy. Rafe experienced a moment of darkening depression, an easy emotion to pick up in an environment so lacking in hope. It didn't take much discernment to guess from Dr. Bolton's strange behavior what might be wrong, and why he'd been alarmed at showing the flesh around his ankle.

Rafe entered the bungalow and glanced toward the front desk, where he expected to see Hartley. The bungalow, however, was quiet and appeared empty. Bolton had said Jerome was here. Rafe walked toward the open doorway of a small room and saw Dr. Jerome bent over some test tubes on a long table. Behind him there were rodents in cages, and a few rabbits and three chickens.

Dr. Jerome looked up at the sound of Rafe's footsteps. An expression of surprise crossed his face, then dissipated . . . one of the few times Rafe could recall when they'd met without tension in Jerome's manner. A smile showed on the lean, craggy face, tanned and leathery from years of traversing the tropics of the world.

"Why hello, Rafe. Come in." His deep-set eyes told of a determination to achieve his goals, a single-minded spirit. They looked past him toward the front of the bungalow. "Is Eden with you, back from the gathering at Kea Lani?"

Rafe sighed to himself. The one time when a relationship with his future father-in-law looked possible, there was Hunnewell's garden and the manifesto to talk about.

"No, she stayed on with the family."

Dr. Jerome's hair remained dark for the most part, but his long sideburns curving inward at the jawline were partially colored by the gray of age.

Despite the unusually genial welcome from Dr. Jerome, Rafe noticed that a look of stress hovered around him.

"How did the meeting go with Ainsworth?" Jerome asked, eyeing him thoughtfully.

"He wasn't pleased that I'd wired Parker Judson to go ahead and hire a Pinkerton detective. He would rather I had waited until we were in San Francisco."

Jerome gave a nod and scrutinized his test tube, then looked over at his "patients" in their cages. "I think you did the wise thing. The matter is an ugly one, and dangerous. The sooner it's resolved, the better for everyone, including my brother."

Sometimes it was difficult for Rafe to remember that Jerome and Townsend were brothers. They were nothing alike in temperament or appearance.

"By the way, Rafe, the news of your loan to build the clinic is deeply appreciated. I can't tell you how thankful I am. I'm certainly in your debt."

"Sir, I'd rather you didn't feel the least indebted. I'm pleased I can be of some assistance. I know what it means to you and Eden. What I came to talk about has nothing to do with Molokai. I'm afraid the subject is apt to heighten tensions between us again."

"Oh? Now why would that be? If it's about Eden—"

"It isn't, sir, not this time."

"Well, that is interesting. Let me put this tube away, then we can talk." He smiled and went to secure the test tube and close the door where the critters were kept.

A minute later Jerome returned, drying his hands on a white cloth. He eyed Rafe, and must have decided he indeed looked grave. Jerome motioned Rafe to a chair, while he sat behind his cluttered desk, pushing things aside.

"No wonder I can never remember where I put things," he said casually. "Unfortunately, the mind can become as cluttered . . . and the heart." Something seemed to pass through his thoughts of a sober nature, for he drew his brows together. Then he looked at Rafe. The frown left his face and a bit of smile showed.

"Well, let's see if we can keep this on friendly terms this time."

"This time" was a reference to the last severe disagreement they'd had over Eden going with him to work at the Kalawao leper camp on Molokai, and previous to that it was over the adoption of Kip.

Rafe had no intention of discussing Kip now. He'd been wondering, even worrying to some extent about how Dr. Jerome would respond to Rafe's gaining the legal right to adopt the boy.

Some months ago Jerome had insisted that Kip was to be turned over to his jurisdiction, but Rafe had refused. Jerome had threatened some kind of punitive action but had never followed through. In fact, neither of them had brought up Kip again. There seemed to be an unspoken understanding either that Rafe had won or that Jerome had decided to relent. Rafe hoped it would remain that way.

Rafe hadn't accepted the chair. He could rarely sit when he was restless or concerned.

He paused in front of Dr. Jerome's desk and looked at him. He dreaded this confrontation. For a brief moment he wanted to turn and walk out, but he couldn't.

"Suppose you tell me what this is about, Rafe. I can see you're disturbed."

Rafe placed his hands on the corners of the desk and leaned forward. He met Jerome's gaze with calm intensity. "Yes, sir, I am disturbed. I board the steamer in forty-eight hours. That doesn't leave much time to retrieve some important papers taken from Mr. Hunnewell's desk the other evening."

Dr. Jerome stared at him.

"I just left Silas at Kea Lani," Rafe said quietly. "He told me he passed the Hunnewell manifesto to you on the back lanai. Don't blame Silas for talking. I'd already guessed most of what happened. I knew Sen Fong brought you to Hunnewell's gate to meet the Chinese opium kingpin. He probably threatened you and told you to stop preaching to the Chinese, and not to warn them about opium addiction."

Dr. Jerome sighed. "Yes, that is correct."

Rafe studied him a moment. "You undoubtedly told him you would do no such thing. Ambrose, too, will keep holding Bible meetings on the plantations with the sugar workers. The kingpin must have known he wasn't dealing with a man who would turn tail and run. Your travels, your work and dedication to leprosy is well known. He would also know that my uncle, as minister of the mission church, would stand like Joshua against a throng of invaders before he stops preaching Christ to those who need Him, just as Sen Fong stood firm."

"Yes, I believe you're quite right so far."

"You were seen in Hunnewell's garden, sir. You were upset, and struggling with a decision that was painful for you. The kingpin had to have threatened you with something other than burning the mission church down, or even sending one of his assassins. Anything of that nature you would have stood up against and refused to cooperate."

"If the mission church is burned to the ground we'll rebuild," Jerome said crisply. He pushed himself up from the chair and began to pace.

Rafe was satisfied. Now it would come out.

"And if he threatened me or Ambrose with a knife in our ribs, we'd have them arrested and sent back to mainland China!"

"Right. Something caused you to do as the kingpin asked."

Dr. Jerome cast him a frown.

"Sir, from the beginning I've been suspicious of Hartley. From the moment he arrived from San Francisco with Dr. Chen's medical journal and the unexpected news that he was dead. The kingpin, I believe, has claimed to be a relative of Dr. Chen. He threatened you with Hartley's theft of the journal and maybe even Chen's death."

Dr. Jerome froze; a look of horror crossed his beleaguered face. He returned to his desk and sank into the chair. He groaned. With an elbow on his desk he rested his forehead against his palm. "Yes, a horrible situation. I couldn't deal with the far-reaching implications of such a dreadful scandal permeating Honolulu. And the Board of Health—I've received little assistance from them since I arrived, at best only sympathetic silence. I couldn't bear the thought of becoming the object of ridicule, or worse. A scandal over Dr. Chen's lifetime medical journal—stolen. His sudden death by rare drugs from Tibet! And Herald accused. If Herald is accused, or guilty, that incriminates me as well. Then what? The clinic will be lost! By the time the newspapers get hold of that story and blow it all out of proportion—followed by the older story of Rebecca being sent to the leper camp—" He groaned again and shook his head. "The Chinese had me dangling over a snake pit."

"Then he did ask you to take the manifesto from Silas and bring it to Liliuokalani when you meet with her tomorrow."

He sighed. "Yes. I went secretly to the back lanai. Silas came after the meeting broke up and gave me the papers. I took them, and during the fracas over Oliver and Keno I was able to slip away quietly and return to Kalihi."

Rafe was thoughtful for some time. He wasn't surprised by any of it. He went over to the small window and looked out, but the scene was so bleak and grim that he turned and came back to the desk where Dr. Jerome sat.

"The Chinese cousin of Dr. Chen, the man you call a kingpin," Jerome said, "has threatened to make all of this known to the papers. He may even seek legal action over the theft of the journal, and he's gone as far as to claim Herald may have poisoned Dr. Chen. I was so overwhelmed that I did what he asked. I've been agonizing ever since because I haven't made any decision what to do about the terrible situation of the journal and Herald's actions."

"What is your opinion on Herald's actions?"

He shook his head doubtfully. "I believe he did take property he had no right to remove from Dr. Chen's house in Chinatown, but murder him? I cannot bear the thought. I've been telling myself he couldn't have."

Rafe looked at him grimly. "You don't sound fully convinced."

"Maybe I'm not. Rafe! This is a hellish experience!"

"Yes, I agree. And I don't want Hartley anywhere near Eden at Kalawao. I haven't liked her working with him in close confines nearly every day here at Kalihi."

Dr. Jerome nodded weakly. "Yes, I intend to dismiss him. I decided on that two days ago, but have been reluctant to carry it through. If I dismiss him now, and he knows why, he may slip out of Honolulu. I thought it best to say nothing yet, though I believe he's very suspicious. He's walking around me on eggshells."

Rafe was relieved that Jerome had come to a crucial decision. "Where is he now, do you know?"

"Oh he's here. He's in back helping Dr. DuPont."

"We need to confront Hartley. Get his confession. Once he admits he deceived you, there's little the opium kingpin can do to your reputation. It's obvious to me, sir, you knew nothing of Hartley's actions beforehand. What he did, he did on his own. That leaves you in the clear. Even if the newspapers pick it up, they'll have nothing on you if Hartley confesses."

Dr. Jerome looked at him. A glimmer of expectation came to his eyes. "Yes, if he confesses."

"I've a notion he will. There's always the San Francisco

authorities to hold over his head if he doesn't come out with the truth—not to mention Dr. Chen's cousin, the opium kingpin."

Dr. Jerome was looking more confident. He nodded. "I agree with you, Rafe. This can be handled much more wisely. I'm afraid I panicked."

"Fear can blind us and cloud our reasoning. In the shadows we may see no way out of a dilemma. The Lord has promised His own, however, that we're never alone. He is our Light and our defense."

Dr. Jerome smiled and thoughtfully studied him. "Ambrose has been a good mentor for you. I don't know why I'm surprised by your spiritual insight, but I'm afraid I've misjudged you. My fault, I know. And even though I'm the one who married Rebecca, I was always a little jealous and insecure around your father, Matt."

"You can throw away any residue of that now, sir. He's gone."

Jerome dropped his head. "Yes . . . I know his death was a great burden to you. You can be comforted knowing he's in the presence of Christ." He shook his head again. "Townsend has much to answer for."

"That leaves us with the Hunnewell manifesto to take care of." Rafe looked at him, hoping his instincts were right.

Dr. Jerome sat still a moment, then he stood to his feet and walked over to his jacket that hung on a peg. He took a key out of a deep pocket, returned to his desk, and unlocked a top drawer. A moment later he pull out a rather thick folder. He looked at it and handed it across the desk to Rafe.

"Now you can board that steamer, and Mr. Hunnewell can bring his manifesto to Secretary of State Blaine and President Harrison."

Rafe took the folder, gave it a brief glance through, and was very much relieved.

"Thank you." *What explanation could Jerome give to not offend the queen?* "What about the queen?" Rafe asked. "Is she expecting to receive this tomorrow?"

Jerome shook his head. "I was under the impression it was to be a surprise. This was planned by the gambling and opium cartels to gain the passage of certain bills in the Legislature."

"They're going to be disappointed."

Dr. Jerome smiled wearily and placed a hand on Rafe's shoulder. "Yes." He sobered and looked directly at Rafe. "Thank God you came, Rafe. I'm going to be a proud man to have such a son-in-law. Can you forgive a temperamental and sometimes foolish old man for taking too long to see how blessed Eden will be to have you?"

Rafe hadn't expected the compliment, but he was relieved that a situation which could have torn them asunder had sealed their upcoming family relationship.

"Thank you, sir. I'm confident the blessing will be mutual. Would this be a good time to speak with Hartley?"

Jerome gave a nod. "Better not go to the back room. I'll have him come here. Dr. DuPont is examining the most recent detainees."

Dr. Jerome was going through the door when Rafe asked, "Is Dr. Bolton well?"

Jerome stopped abruptly. He turned his head, a sorrowful look on his face. He studied Rafe a moment. "You noticed?" he asked in a low voice, troubled.

Rafe gave a brief ascent. "It shows in his walk."

Jerome groaned. "Perhaps the worst tragedy I've come up against since Rebecca. He will soon be going to Molokai. He intends to partner with me at the clinic, so at least some good has come from his tragedy." He drew in a breath. "Lana—knows. She's going through with the marriage next week. She'll come as a nurse to the clinic, and of course, she'll be his kokua."

Rafe kept silent a moment. "Does Eden know?"

He shook his head. "None of us could bring ourselves to tell her yet."

Perhaps that's why Dr. Bolton hadn't wanted him to notice, Rafe thought. *He may have thought I'd mention it to Eden.* Her aunt, Lana, was the likely one to break the news to her.

While Dr. Jerome went after Hartley, Rafe pondered. It would be easy to call for the marshal to haul Hartley downtown, but that might silence him completely through fear, besides involving Dr. Jerome and alerting the newspapers. The marshal was still overwhelmed with the Sen Fong murder, having accomplished, as far as Rafe could tell, little toward locating the opium cartel's assassin. The action to take depended on whether Chen's death was an accident. A blunder by his own hand? A mistaken dosage of his own Eastern medicines? Or did Chen die by the hand of a young man who felt no qualm in rendering vengeance on his employer for dismissing him in Calcutta? If that were the case, Hartley had a mental problem, as well as a sin problem.

Rafe was standing by the window when footsteps coming from the back room alerted him.

A moment later Herald Hartley entered, followed by Dr. Jerome, who shut the door for privacy. Jerome looked stern. Hartley, seeing Rafe, stopped abruptly, his face written with shock. Evidently Dr. Jerome hadn't told him Rafe waited in the office.

Hartley's auburn hair was parted straight down the middle. His lean tanned face turned stiff and uncooperative. His amber eyes surveyed Rafe, and he stiffened visibly.

"What is this? What do you want? I've an important job to attend right now," he said impatiently.

"Herald," Dr. Jerome said firmly, "you'll need to answer some questions."

So Hartley was opting for the aggressive approach. Well, he could do the same.

Hartley threw back his head. "Why, sir? He's not the marshal!"

"No," Rafe stated, "but I can send for him quickly enough if you'd prefer. You'll still have to answer some questions, though probably many more, and anything you tell him will be written down and used against you. What you confess here and now before Dr. Jerome may not go past this room. Which do you prefer?"

"Cooperate, Herald," Jerome urged, again with a firm tone to warn him he'd receive no cover from him.

Hartley drew a long white cloth from his pocket and wiped his face. "I've done nothing evil," he breathed in a low, nervous voice. "Nothing evil."

"The law may have to decide that, not me, Hartley. All I want is the truth. So does Dr. Jerome."

"I didn't kill him, I had nothing to do with his death."

"Then you'd better talk. If you don't, you're not going to waste our time. I'll bring you to the marshal myself."

Hartley stared at Rafe, his mouth growing tight and his breathing quickened.

"I didn't kill Chen," he repeated. "He—he was already dead when I got in the house by the back way. His flesh was still warm. He couldn't have been dead over twenty minutes." His eyes darted from Rafe to Jerome, then back again. "I know who did it. I saw him. I've been afraid to talk—I'd be next."

Rafe gauged his sincerity. He looked frightened all right, probably from the reality of his situation.

Dr. Jerome came around from his desk and peered at him anxiously. "Good grief, my boy! If Dr. Chen was murdered, then out with it! It's your responsibility to tell the truth."

"It wouldn't have done either of us any good, Dr. Jerome. The San Francisco police appear to avoid Chinatown and all its crime. They keep having the tong wars, and who stops them? I was afraid; I'll admit, I was a coward."

Jerome reached a hand and put it on his shoulder. "I know nothing of your cowardice, Herald, but I want to know who killed my friend and colleague."

Rafe narrowed his gaze thoughtfully and looked at Jerome. "Sir, the mention of Chinatown and the tong wars points to the cartel. I've learned that the opium kingpin was Dr. Chen's cousin."

Jerome was startled. "So that could explain the murder of Sen. I thought it had to do with his becoming a Christian and not wanting to distribute the opium."

"He must have also held knowledge about the kingpin that

made it too dangerous for Sen Fong to remain on the scene."

Hartley was wiping his face again. He licked his lips.

"I saw Sen Fong out front of the Chinatown house. The kingpin was coming out the front door, and his face said it all. That's why I ducked behind the hedge. If he'd seen me I wouldn't be here now, I'm sure of that. You've got to believe me."

"What happened next?" Rafe asked.

"I went around to the back, climbed up to a bathroom window and got in that way."

"What makes you so certain the Oriental you saw leaving was the kingpin?" Rafe asked.

"I don't know his name. Sen Fong worked for him. He was the same one who threatened Dr. Jerome about Chen's death and his medical journal."

As Hartley said *journal*, his eyes faltered and his tanned face turned a ruddy color. This convinced Rafe he was onto the truth. If Hartley could feel guilty over stealing the journal but not over murdering a man, he should go onstage.

"So you know about the extortion the kingpin threatened Dr. Jerome with?"

He dropped his head. "Yes, I heard him."

Dr. Jerome showed his surprise. "You were there? I didn't see you."

"I was keeping out of sight in the trees that grow alongside the high wall around Mr. Hunnewell's property."

"But how did you know I would meet with him? Sen came for me at Kalihi and you were not at the hospital that night. You asked if you could have the evening off."

Herald nodded, still looking down at the floor. "I wanted that evening off because I had seen the opium kingpin in Pan Alley the day before. I was scared out of my wits that he'd come to Honolulu looking for me. That somehow he'd discovered I saw him in San Francisco."

"He must have found out," Rafe said. "That's the only reason he'd have to threaten Dr. Jerome."

Herald nodded miserably. "I don't know how he found out, unless Dr. Chen's Chinese cook happened to see me. I thought—maybe—someone might have seen me climb in the bathroom window, but when I looked back, I didn't see anyone in the backyard, but there was a noise in the bushes by the hen house. The chickens, they'd been disturbed."

"All right, you say Pan Alley. Go on."

"I went there to see if I could find the kingpin's den, which one it was. I had an idea to visit each one and, well, just have a quick look inside to see if he was there."

Rafe folded his arms and tilted his head with a wry smile. "Come, Hartley, the truth."

He blotted his face and swallowed. "Well, I also owed a gambling bill . . . I went there to pay it off—that is, to ask for more time—and fortune worked against me! The very den I owed money to was the kingpin's!" Hartley covered his eyes with a shaking hand, and his shoulders shook.

Rafe knew a surge of compassion. Hartley had become enslaved by Satan's chains. Gambling was ruining his life, and Rafe also suspected liquor. Hartley was ashamed before Dr. Jerome, who had claimed to lead Hartley to repentance and faith in Christ back in Calcutta.

Dr. Jerome sank in the chair behind his desk, his chin in his hands. He remained astutely silent.

Rafe drew in a breath. "We now know why you went to Pan Alley, so what happened next?"

"I caught one look at him and fled for my life. I got back to Kalihi just as Dr. Jerome and Sen Fong were coming down the steps."

Rafe remembered how Zachary had come to his hotel room and insisted that he'd followed Silas to the gambling dens and then back to Kalihi. It was clear now that it hadn't been Silas, but Hartley, that Zachary had followed.

Hartley was saying, "I wondered where Sen was taking Dr.

Jerome and followed. I overheard the kingpin's conversation to Dr. Jerome—all about the manifesto, the opium, that lottery bills needed passage in the Legislature. I heard the kingpin threaten Dr. Jerome. What he told him wasn't true—not about Dr. Chen's death—but the journal part was true. I did take it. I knew I was in trouble. But the kingpin was lying too. He was the last one to talk to Dr. Chen alive, not me."

Rafe kept pushing. "So you entered through a back bedroom window. Then what?"

"I knew something was wrong. It was too quiet. I tiptoed into his study and there he was draped over his desk, his herbicides spread all over his desk and on the floor. I took his pulse but he was dead. I was afraid and wanted to get out of there fast but not without the journal. I saw it behind him in a bookshelf. I put it under my coat and left through a door into a garden. It was foggy by then and I'm sure no one saw me, not even the cook. I think he, too, was afraid and stayed by the hen coop. He must have notified the San Francisco police after he entered the house and found Dr. Chen."

"Where did you go with the journal?"

"My room, at the hotel on the wharf."

Rafe didn't want a long lapse of time for Hartley to twist the facts to make himself look better to Dr. Jerome. He asked abruptly: "Why, on the day you came to Kea Lani with the journal, did you pretend you'd developed a friendly relationship with Dr. Chen?"

"Because, as I confessed, I was afraid. I—I was trying to make an alibi. I believed the San Francisco police would eventually come to the conclusion he'd been murdered. Where did that leave me? Especially after taking the journal."

"You were a fool to take it, Herald," Dr. Jerome said. "Especially after what happened!"

"I—I couldn't help myself."

"Why didn't you turn to Christ for guidance and strength?"

Herald dropped his head again. "I—I'm not sure I'm a Christian. I needed your help and so . . . well, I may have said some things to—to make you pleased with me. . . ."

Dr. Jerome turned away and shook his head. He, too, drew out a handkerchief and wiped his eyes.

He's taking the loss of Herald Hartley hard, Rafe thought.

"You had a strong disagreement with Dr. Chen in Calcutta. Dr. Jerome is witness to that. Chen dismissed you and you held it against him. Why would you seek him out at all?"

"For my career. I wanted to come to Honolulu and work again with Dr. Jerome. He'd treated me more than fairly in Calcutta. I was going to apologize to Dr. Chen for what I'd done in offending him in India."

Dr. Jerome sighed deeply.

"And," Hartley said, "ask him if he'd consider writing a letter of recommendation to Dr. Bolton at Kalihi Hospital. I thought they'd never hire me if anything detrimental was ever released by Dr. Chen. I told myself I'd never be accepted into that inner medical circle unless Dr. Chen decided to forgive and forget and give me another opportunity. So I intended to see him first, then catch a steamer to Honolulu with the letter."

"So in reality, Hartley, you had a strong motive to see Dr. Chen dead. You could reap vengeance on a man that destroyed your career, as you saw it, and get a position with Dr. Jerome at Kalihi, but only if he were silent and out of the way."

"No!"

"The journal you could present to Dr. Jerome as a peace offering, making him think Dr. Chen had willed it to him."

"Yes, that part's true, but I didn't murder Dr. Chen. The opium kingpin did. Just as he had murdered Sen Fong. I've no way to prove I didn't kill Chen. Or that the kingpin did, for that matter. Especially after taking the journal—I know it looks bad. It was a foolish move on my part."

Hartley looked ill and miserable. Rafe told himself he didn't need to believe or disbelieve him, that would be left for others, but his own conclusion rendered Hartley not guilty of the murder of Dr. Chen.

Rafe looked over at Dr. Jerome. *What do you want to do?* Rafe seemed to say. Jerome again walked around his desk and came up to Herald.

"There's something I've been meaning to ask you, Herald. The time has come. Your answer will decide your future where my work is concerned. In fact, regardless of your answer I've decided I shall not want you at Molokai with Eden and me."

Herald's head fell again. His hand came up to his eyes. His shoulders trembled. It was one of the worst sights Rafe had confronted in a long while. He turned away and went over to the window. The room was hot and stuffy and he opened the window, but little refreshment blew in.

"What was it you did to so offend Dr. Chen that he dismissed you from his research clinic in Calcutta? You told me it was gambling and drink. I know that you're still trapped in those vices. But there was something more, Herald. Something that upset Dr. Chen in the extreme."

"It *was* the liquor, and gambling. My life spiraled down to the gutter after he fired me. My career, my future, everything was in rubble. Yes, I mulled it over in my mind day after day until I grew bitter. I did end up, literally, in the gutters of India. You know that. It was you who found me; who thought I was worth giving another chance to, and took me in. I've said before, I owe you everything."

Jerome shook his head, sadly. "It is not I who you owe your life too, Herald, but the One who gave His precious life to redeem you from sin and slavery to the Evil One."

Hartley nodded. "I know, I know . . . but I didn't commit murder, I didn't."

"I'm inclined to believe you, but whether we do or not doesn't change matters as far as the law is concerned. My main interest now is in my poor Rebecca, and the many suffering lepers on Kalaupapa, just as for Rafe it's Eden. I cannot trust you again, Herald. I'm sorry, but once trust is broken it's very difficult to restore. No matter your motive, you deceived me about the journal. You nearly caused such a scandal that it would have prevented the queen from granting permission for the clinic!"

Hartley remained silent.

"And there must have been something more to the reason why Dr. Chen dismissed you," Dr. Jerome stated pointedly.

Hartley sighed tiredly. He looked at the floor, at Dr. Jerome, at Rafe, and then back to the floor. "Yes. I followed in the footsteps of the German researcher who used a man as a research tool. I practiced my ideas for a cure on a certain young leper. Unfortunately, something went wrong and the boy died of a great fever. Chen insisted the fever was caused by the herbs I'd used. He was very angry with me. He told me to pack my things and get out. It wasn't fair! The boy was only a leper, the lowest of the low in the caste system. An untouchable from the village dump."

Dr. Jerome slowly drew back from the chair where Hartley sat staring up, indignant. He turned away.

Rafe watched Hartley for a long minute in silence. Maybe he hadn't murdered Chen, but a man's character was surely revealed in how he judged human life.

Rafe didn't want to take a chance and excuse a stolen journal, only to find out one day in the future that a medical researcher named Herald Hartley had stepped over the line and become responsible for another death or disablement through some bizarre error.

At times Hartley had come across as having a tender conscience—such as when he disappointed Dr. Jerome, or shamed himself in stealing the journal. Rafe, however, remembered what Eden had told him yesterday about his hardness of heart. She had read Hartley correctly.

Dr. Jerome, standing behind Hartley, turned his head in Rafe's direction and caught his gaze. Jerome, his face drawn, gave a sober nod to Rafe. He then slipped out of his office and went to send a message to Marshal Harper.

Rafe turned his back and looked out the window.

The interpretation of the law in Hartley's situation was not Rafe's to decide. He had what he needed to know about Hartley, and as far as he was concerned, he was through with the matter. Dr. Jerome had already told him he wouldn't be going to Molokai as his assistant. Rafe could leave Honolulu with a certain amount of satisfaction and peace that Eden would not be in danger from a man who had his integrity as scrambled as his morning eggs.

He looked at the time. As soon as the marshal arrived he was going back to the hotel.

When he saw the marshal alight from a buggy, Rafe left Hartley sitting in the chair, his head still in his hands.

Outside, the sun beat down, and the harbor waters glittered. Rafe explained the issue of the journal. Dr. Jerome was innocent of any knowledge of it having been taken from Dr. Chen's Chinatown house in San Francisco.

"Oh, I'm sure," Harper said, pushing his hat back from his forehead and biting on the end of his stogie.

"Queen Liliuokalani is likely to approve Dr. Derrington's clinic for the leper colony," Rafe told him. "Try and keep this journal business out of the newspapers, will you?"

"No reason for any mention of it, seems to me, Easton. Say—" he cracked a smile. "You wouldn't want to come to work as a detective for the department, would you?"

Rafe smiled. "Only in my spare time, Marshal. Besides, I'm off to San Francisco soon. The work isn't finished yet."

The marshal grew grave. "Townsend, is it? Well, you be careful, Easton. I've had a few street chasers with that fellow when he was younger. Always a wild one. Nothing like the rest of the family. The seed of Cain, that's what those kind are called. As for Hartley, I'll need to contact San Francisco about the Dr. Chen case. I don't know that much about it. But Hartley doesn't seem like a murderer to me."

Rafe then went on to tell him briefly about the Chen situation as he knew of it. "Dr. Jerome can better answer the medical questions. Here's what I've been told:

"There was a postmortem soon after Chen was found dead in his Chinatown residence. A ruling followed of accidental death by a self-inflicted overdose of research drugs. Chen was known to be researching. Here's where the San Francisco police may be wrong: they claim he has no family in the US and there is no certain whereabouts of relatives he corresponded with in Shanghai. But Hartley is certain the kingpin you're trying to locate for questioning is his cousin. He saw him leave Chen's residence not later than twenty minutes after his death."

Marshal Harper was scribbling down notes. "Any talk of a will, legal paper granting the right of personal research papers to Dr. Jerome Derrington, or to the research department at Kalihi Hospital?"

"Good point. I wonder. That would surely help to solve the issue."

"I'll check on it. There probably wasn't any mention in the police file, nor evidence that he entrusted a journal to Herald Hartley for Dr. Derrington."

"I think Hartley is right when he says you need look no further for the murderer than the opium kingpin. The same tyrant who gave the order to assassinate Sen Fong. Hartley saw Sen Fong outside Dr. Chen's house. The kingpin was coming out the front door. They were cousins. Perhaps bitter enemies."

"I'll look into it, Easton. And I'll wire the San Francisco police chief tonight. I think we can get through. Well, good hunting on your trip to the mainland. Keep in touch. I'd like to know what happens."

"I will. If you need me I'll be at the Royal Hawaiian tonight."

Rafe left Kakaako and returned to his suite. He drew out his baggage and stashed the manifesto inside until tomorrow when he would attend the meeting of the Reform Party in the Legislature. It would be excellent news for old Hunnewell to learn his work had been unexpectedly discovered on the eve of their departure to San Francisco. Rafe would omit elaborating on the details. By the time the Reform Party meeting was over in the cloakroom at Aliiolani Hale, Dr. Jerome would already be across the street at Iolani Palace receiving permission from the queen to build his research clinic. Little could go awry now—he hoped. At least there would be no scandal to tarnish Jerome's Christian reputation. And in that, God would be honored. That was the all-important issue at stake in Rafe's mind.

He packed the clothing he expected to use on the voyage to the mainland. He also included the medicine bottle Great-aunt Nora had entrusted to him to take to the San Francisco authorities. When he'd finished packing, he took a bath and changed his clothes.

He would put all this aside until tomorrow. He looked at the time. He would have liked to return to Hanalei for the night for a final oversee of the plantation under Keno's care before the long stay in San Francisco, but there wasn't time.

Keno . . . he was over at Hawaiiana. *I'd better talk to him this afternoon. There's the Oliver situation to tell him about, and Ainsworth's land offer to settle.*

Afterward, a simple and quiet evening with Ambrose and Noelani was just what he wanted leading up to tomorrow. The one thing missing was Eden, but he would see her tomorrow evening for dinner here at the hotel. Her rich green eyes came before him, the lush feel of her hair in his fingers, the soft, warm lips—one day she would be all his.

Irritated by the thought of the long delay till that day, he left the hotel and went in search of his equally deprived and irritated cohort, Keno. At least the news he had was good where Candace was concerned. Oliver was a British spy. Not a likely candidate to sit opposite Candace at the dinner table each evening at Kea Lani while listening to Ainsworth lecturing on the merits of annexation of Hawaii to the US.

Rafe smiled. Keno was going to have some ammunition that could win back Candace.

*R*afe felt an agonizing headache coming on. He was lounging in a chair in the large screened room at Hawaiiana,
furnished with magnificent native woods and green with potted
ferns. Through a narrowed gaze he watched Keno striding back and
forth across the polished floor, his heels making clicking sounds like
a tap dancer.

Rafe shut his eyes, fingers on his forehead, and groaned. "Will
you stop that? It's driving me nuts."

"Stop what?" Keno asked. "I've got to think."

"So do I. That's the trouble." Rafe pushed himself up off the
chair. "Okay, Keno, enough prancing about. You know what to write
her. You're anything but tongue-tied. Now get the letter written and
I'll see that she receives it today."

Keno ran his nervous fingers through his hair. "Imagine the
nerve of Mr. Derrington. Trying to buy me off like that. And thinking he could use *you* as the third party. Why, didn't it even enter his
mind what something like that could do to our friendship?"

"It would have convinced you. That's what mattered to him."

Rafe poured himself a cup of coffee. He looked at the time. "I've got to leave for Iolani in an hour. Dr. Jerome is meeting with the queen. Hartley will be with him."

Keno frowned to himself. "Ainsworth was right about using *you* as the third party—it would have convinced me all right. Say—" Keno looked at him almost meekly. "Were you serious about making a way for me to buy into Hawaiiana?"

"You've known me since we were around ten years old. What do you think? It's past overdue, actually."

"Yeah sure, I knew you meant it, pal. But it's just too generous."

"No. You and Candace need to start off right. We don't want her money to start your successful plantation. This has got to be your endeavor. And we don't want Hunnewell money either—though, if later on, Hunnewell wants to do you justice as his younger brother's son, I'd accept it. It's not charity, you know; you deserve it as much as Oliver."

"He won't offer me anything."

"One never knows. He's a decent man, though not discerning at times. I was going to talk to him on the steamer."

"Well, he's better than Oliver."

Rafe kept from smiling. "And now, the love letter to Candace. Let's see . . . ah! Tell her you're going to have your own plantation as soon as Parker Judson draws the contract up in San Francisco—"

"What if he refuses to cooperate?"

"He won't. Tell her you've won half of Hawaiiana by the sweat of your brow. Just the way a man ought to make his success, not because you were born a Hunnewell. Tell her your sons—which are bound to be many—will grow up to be *men* to carry on the work the that both of you will create together. Your sons—"

"Wait, pal. She'll ask what's wrong with daughters. I know her. She'll *favor* girls."

"All right. Our *daughters* won't be like Oliver, either."

"She wouldn't expect our daughters to be like Oliver."

"Just write the letter."

Keno went to the writing desk and looked back at Rafe. Rafe had leaned his head back and closed his eyes. He looked tired. He had a right to be. If he hadn't chased this mystery down for the last week, where would any of them be now?

Keno picked up the pen and gritted his teeth as he wrote.

⟨⟩

Rafe came to see me today and told me everything. Eden talked to Ambrose and decided it was all right to break a vow if the vow was based on a false premise. So she explained to Rafe what happened at Koko Head between you and your grandfather.

I wouldn't accept land from your grandfather under these circumstances. He knows that, so he tried to use Rafe as a third party to keep his actions in the shadows. I'll earn my own success and land, or I won't have any. But I will get my own plantation. Rafe and I made an agreement before we left for French Guiana—maybe you remember? As soon as Hawaiiana became successful Rafe and I would start the next plantation and this one would be mine and yours. At the time you were happy about it. I believed you.

⟨⟩

Tears sprang to Candace's eyes. Could she ever forget that night when he told her he was taking to sea with Rafe? And that it was to earn his own plantation? *Their own plantation.* Of course she remembered.

Candace wiped her eyes. She sat in her room with the letter on her lap. It had arrived only minutes ago, brought by a smiling Hawaiian boy of around twelve who worked for Rafe Easton. She had seen the boy before, on both Hawaiiana and Hanalei.

Candace read on—

⸻

Now I know why you walked away and told your grandfather you'd marry Oliver. You thought you were doing it for my benefit, also to protect my future in Hawaii. Even so, how could you believe I could be happy without you? That land would satisfy me? It is you in my arms I want. I've loved you for years. I'd rather have you than all of Hawaii at my feet.

⸻

Candace's heart thumped faster. *Keno . . . my darling Keno.*

⸻

So Oliver is a British spy. Well, I have the perfect solution to our problem. Either he gets on the steamer with Mr. Hunnewell for the mainland, or I'm going to have a talk with his father. Oliver doesn't know this, but I remember having seen him in the garden that evening. He was in the bushes by the gate. Now that Silas has told Rafe that it was Oliver who knocked Zach unconscious, and tried to steal the political papers from the Reform Party, I can bear witness against the turncoat. So he'd sell out his father, Hawaii, and the good old USA? Well! Let him go live in London!

Rafe has stated that both he and Silas will be witnesses against Oliver if he doesn't board the steamer for San Francisco. I'm going to have the pleasure of telling him so.

⸻

Oh no, she thought, with an idea that she should do something about it. *This could end in something far worse than the Hunnewell garden fiasco. I must do something, but what?*

My precious Candace, I want to see you. If you love me come down to the beach around five o'clock. Don't disappoint me.
K.

Candace folded the sheet of paper and walked over to the writing desk. Her hands were cold and damp. She picked up the pen, and straightening her shoulders with determination she wrote.

Dear Oliver,
I must see you at once. It's urgent. Come to Kea Lani. I'll be expecting you.
Candace.

With that, she called for Luna, the messenger boy who worked at Kea Lani, and sent him with her letter to Hunnewell's beach house.

Candace looked through the front window. Was Oliver coming or not? She watched anxiously. A few minutes later Oliver drove up in a small buggy. She glanced over her shoulder toward the stairway. Grandfather Ainsworth would be down soon for his late afternoon coffee before the dinner hour.

Earlier, she'd thought the family would be away in Honolulu when Oliver arrived, since Great-aunt Nora and even Zachary had gone with Uncle Jerome to Queen Liliuokalani at Iolani Palace. Eden must have departed earlier for Kalihi, where she would later join them at Iolani. At any rate, by now the meeting should be over and the long-sought-for clinic approved; its likelihood of being turned down by the queen was small. Uncle Jerome had Great-aunt Nora's loyal friendship and support of the queen to be grateful for. Without Nora, the audience at Iolani Palace would still be on the list of delayed items. By now Uncle Jerome and Herald Hartley should be making immediate plans to depart for Molokai, Eden with them.

Also, Rafe would board the steamer on Sunday to the mainland to try to locate Townsend. Grandfather Ainsworth was going, and also Zachary.

The family dealings would certainly be altered at Kea Lani after tomorrow with the absence of so many. If it hadn't been for the discussion she'd overheard between Oliver and the British agent, her life too would have been forever changed. Her grandfather had wanted the engagement and public ceremony to take place tonight, before he departed Honolulu.

Candace slipped out the front door, closing it quietly.

The late afternoon was pleasant. The aquamarine sky appeared windswept, the low tides rolling gently inward across warm, white sand.

Her gaze centered on Oliver, but her heart was for Keno.

Oliver's golden brown coloring contrasted with his unusually dark suit, along with a white ruffled shirt front and a derby hat. She disliked his pencil mustache that was artfully waxed, at the height of city fashion. She descended the front steps and swiftly walked to meet him as he stepped down from his fine buggy with leather seats.

"Well, this is an enthusiastic greeting," he boasted. "My dear Candace, how lovely you look today."

"We must talk. Let's walk toward the beach, shall we?"

Oliver looked down at his boots, polished to a meticulous shine.

"Why not take a pleasant jaunt in the buggy?"

"I'd rather not, Oliver. If not the beach, then let's walk on the path toward the road. I feel restless and wish some exercise before dinner."

The veneer of a smile showed on his wide mouth. "You don't plan to meet someone on the road, do you?"

"Now why would you think so? Such mistrust in the woman you've agreed to make your wife."

He laughed lightly, looked up at the hot sun burning in the sky, and as they set out he noticed she carried no umbrella. "Even young ladies in San Francisco, with all its summer fog, carry pretty umbrellas, my dear. Shouldn't you go back for one if you insist on walking the road—an unpleasant place to be walking, actually, don't you think?"

"No. If I'd thought it unpleasant, Oliver, I wouldn't have suggested it. Would I?"

He was becoming irritated with her. She deliberately tightened her mouth and looked cross. "I was born and raised in the tropics, unlike you. Umbrellas are fashionable in the city, I suppose, but I like the Honolulu weather." Actually, she used umbrellas almost every time she went out. "You're more of a city slicker than you are a true Hawaiian," she said, and drew her brows together. "Do you think you'll ever adjust to beach sand in your shoes and loose shirts, even shirts *unbuttoned* at the neck?"

"My *dear* Candace. I'm a Hunnewell, am I not? Naturally I'm a Hawaiian."

"Oh. There is some word drifting about that you're quite English."

His caramelized brown eyes swerved to capture her gaze. The intensity of that look sought for any meaning that might undermine his charade.

"Well, Keno is a Hunnewell too," she said. "Did you know?"

His smile vanished. A hardness came to his features, and a slight lift of his head.

"Where did you hear such rubbish?"

"I think we should make certain that your father grants Keno his right to a satisfying Hunnewell inheritance, don't you? Something to make up for the disrespectful way your family has treated him since he was born. After all, your father simply must know his younger brother Philip produced a child by Noelani's younger sister."

Candace was walking quickly along the pathway to the road that ran in front of Kea Lani, leading toward the mission church and Hawaiiana—not that she intended to go there! She glanced at Oliver to see his reaction to her blunt words. Was she going too far to goad him out of his façade?

As she expected, his mouth was tightly sealed; a ruddy bloom flared under his high cheekbones. He stalked along beside her, his arms swinging.

"Don't you think so?" she repeated, trying to force an answer from him that he did not want to give. "I mean, Keno P. Hunnewell *is* your half-brother. A little money flowing his way like a bubbling little brook is the just thing for your father to do."

"Stop it. You are deliberately goading me, young lady. I'll have you know I'm going to be one husband who won't put up with a wife whose tongue is going too long and too sharp."

"Indeed. Well, if you're going to be my husband, you'll need to get used to it, my young man, because I'm known to have an acerbic tongue at times. I'm so much like my Great-aunt Nora, you know. She's known for speaking truthfully."

He stopped and confronted her. His eyes flashed with temper. "What's this all about? What are you trying to do? You deliberately called me here just to make insults?"

She stopped and whirled toward him. "Because you're a British spy. I don't care to be married to a man who will trick his own father, and then wear a phony smile as you speak to him over the breakfast table about annexation. You planned to steal your own father's policy manifesto and turn it over to a British agent working for the commissioner."

He looked abashed. "What idiocy is this?"

"Don't pretend with me that you don't know what I'm talking about. I'll let you know right now that I was there on the beach that night when the two of you discussed the manifesto and Keno."

He sucked in a breath and stared at her, searching her face.

"Oh, yes," she said. "I heard every word. You told him how Keno, coming along to the garden as he did the night before, was the good fortune you had needed to divert attention away from you, should your plan to steal those papers have been successful. Unfortunately for you, someone else took them before you could. You deliberately insulted Keno to start a noisy disturbance. The more people that gathered around to see what was happening to you, the better to cast blame on any one of them as being the thief."

His smile was sarcastic. "My, aren't you clever. But you have no proof whatsoever. Who would believe you if you said this? I doubt anyone with an ounce of good sense. I? The son of the leader of annexation movement, a spy?"

"Yes, your same words you said to the agent the other night. Who'd believe Keno? And now, who would believe me?"

"Exactly so. Not my father. And not Ainsworth, if you're so unwise as to go to him with this old wives' fable." He smiled mockingly. "So what are you going to do, my dear? You're only making matters hard on yourself. For regardless of this fantastic tale you've concocted with Keno, you will still become my wife. By such harsh words as these, you are only undermining your own best interest."

"That's where you are wrong, Oliver."

He scrutinized her. "I don't think so."

"Then you shall see the truth. I will let you know now that Keno saw you by the front gate stooping, prepared to knock my cousin Zachary unconscious. Silas also saw you."

"Silas!"

She saw the change as his mocking gaze become sober. "He's willing, as are Keno and Rafe Easton, to tell your father the truth if you persist in this unwise engagement between us."

"What has Rafe Easton to do with this?" he asked uneasily.

Candace saw the opportunity to advance her cause. "Keno is his friend. They're going to become partners in Hawaiiana. Even Parker

Judson is going to back Keno in his own plantation. With Keno and I having allies like these, I would sincerely advise you to board the steamer with your father tomorrow and return to the city where you belong. You'll be the one to tell my grandfather and your father that you don't wish to proceed with our engagement, because you do not love me and will not marry me."

His eyes were slits of anger. His breath came heavily. For a moment she had an uncomfortable awareness that they were alone, and on a lonely road nearing sunset.

He threw back his shoulders and unexpectedly laughed.

"Well, I'm relieved. And you can be sure of one thing you said that's indeed true." His smile vanished and his eyes hardened. "I do not love you at all, Candace."

She lifted her chin. "I'm so glad. That makes it much easier, doesn't it?"

"I shall board the steamer tomorrow, but only because it's what I want to do. As for the decision not to marry, that brings me satisfaction as well. You see, I already have a woman in San Francisco that wants to marry me. Good day, madame." And he turned on his polished boot heel and walked away back to his buggy.

Candace looked after him sober-faced for some time. Afterward she let out a deep breath realizing how near the edge of the cliff she had come. Then, as it dawned on her that she was once again truly free, a joyous laugher bubbled up from within and she smiled and clapped her hands together. Free to have Keno! She whirled about on the path, then abandoning herself to the happiness that enveloped her she lifted the hem of her skirt and ran off toward the warm sand where she was to meet him. She kicked off her shoes and ran freely toward the wet beach as though a young girl again, feeling the merry waters lapping at her ankles.

Candace looked up toward the rocks lined with palm trees and saw her prince standing there watching her. She started toward him at a run, opening her arms. Keno began climbing down.

She waited for him below, laughing, the breezes playfully tugging at her hair.

In another moment Keno had reached her. His eyes searched hers. Her heart was on display, for he came quickly toward her, pulling her toward him.

Candace melted into his strong embrace, and as their lips met in joyful reunion, her heart sang with the Island wind.

Together again. This time, forever.

Chapter Twenty-Three
Stormy Weather

*O*utside Kea Lani sugar plantation, watching . . . hiding . . . waiting within the murky shadows for several days, danger loitered.

Rafe will pay for his meddling, he thought. *This is all his work. He's hated me from the beginning and turned Celestine against me. He stole my rights to Hanalei and the pearl beds. I'll teach that son of Matt Easton! So he thinks I'm in San Francisco, does he? I've fooled them all. I let Celestine and Parker Judson see me, then escaped. The fools will still be looking for me there. Well, I'm in Honolulu to reap joyous vengeance.*

Matt's dead. Rafe's wonderful father, eh? Well, I showed him! He's dead! I'll get even with Rafe for ruining my life in Hawaii. Tracking me down, is he? Then come, Rafe! Come running to save Hanalei from the flames of destruction! Come running to save Eden, the love of your life! By the time I've finished with them both you won't have anything—not Matt, not Hanalei, not Eden! You'll see how it feels to mourn the rest of your life! We're all going up in flames! You can live with the ashes! Let's see how your boasted Christian faith holds together when everything you care about is dust and ashes. My mocking voice will fill your heart for the rest of your days!

—◦◦—

The clinic would be approved today, and the quest Eden sought on Molokai would soon begin. Despite all this, joy was missing, and in its place an uneasy peace held her heart, the foundation of that calm beginning to crumble. For the past two days she'd been ill at ease, though why this should be remained fogged in confusion. "It's as though I'm being watched with evil intent."

That idea, of course, must be fought. *The angel of the Lord encamps round about those who trust in Him and delivers them.*

She had a strong conviction to stop by the bungalow that morning to see Ambrose for a few minutes before going on to Kalihi. She would work with Aunt Lana for a few hours, then change into fashionable garments and join Dr. Jerome and Great-aunt Nora at Iolani Palace to meet with the queen.

"I feel as if someone is following me, Ambrose. I even get an uncanny feeling at the back of my neck when I walk in the garden."

He looked at her thoughtfully. "Well, this is unusual, and troubling. Are you sure it isn't a taste of lonesomeness because Rafe is boarding the steamer tomorrow?"

She smiled wanly. "Oh, that too. But this is something, well, different."

"Let's pray about this. Our all-powerful God is also gracious. He's promised never to leave us or forsake us. So, in fact, you're never alone." He picked up his old Bible and turned its worn pages to Psalm 139 and read it to her in a calm and quiet voice.

After holding her hands and praying for her day of work at Kalihi and the meeting with the queen, he walked her to her buggy.

Eden cast aside her gloom and reflected that the path of obstacles still led in the right direction when God's grace cleared the stony way.

Whatever the future holds, I'll get where I'm intended to go. The others she so cared about could as well if they followed the Truthful way, if they acknowledged that Christ was the Way, the Truth, and the Life.

The faithful promises of Psalm 139 alone were enough to sweep her heart clean of dark concerns.

"Are you attending Dr. Jerome's meeting with the queen?" Ambrose asked.

"Yes, and having dinner with Rafe at the Royal Hawaiian tonight." She reached over to the box beside her on the seat. "I've brought my dress and shoes with me."

"Then tell Rafe I'll be in town tomorrow. I'll stop by the hotel before the steamer departs."

Eden said good-bye, and with a flick of the reins the horse moved down the road.

Ambrose looked after her. The morning was quiet; the wind rustled through the overhead palms. He grew thoughtful.

—◦◦—

Rafe left the Reform Party meeting. He'd returned the manifesto to Thaddeus Hunnewell much to the shock and delight of everyone present, including Ainsworth. A hundred questions had come Rafe's way. He'd adroitly managed to parry each question with an understatement. Someone had tried to steal the papers from the library desk, but Silas had foiled the attempt and turned them over to Dr. Jerome for safekeeping. Dr. Jerome had handed the manifesto over to Rafe to return to the Reform Party delegation on their way to Washington. Only Ainsworth had been silent. He'd watched Hunnewell with a grave face. Rafe believed that once aboard the steamer he would have a long conversation with Hunnewell about his son, Oliver.

After a few last-minute decisions on the political mission to the US Secretary of State Blaine, the meeting had ended and Rafe was taking a waiting hackney over to Iolani Palace.

The bells of Kawaiahao church across the street were striking.

By now, Dr. Jerome, Nora, and Eden would have had their meeting with Queen Liliuokalani. The hackney, as usual, brought Rafe past the Kauikeaouli Gate on King Street. This entrance was used only for visits of state. The wrought-iron barrier was shut and two uniformed native Hawaiian sentries were in their narrow sentinel boxes, watching them pass. The hackney brought him, as required, midway around the eight-foot wall to the Kinau Gate on Richards Street, then turned into the palace yard.

The royal mansion with Corinthian balconies and colonnades seemed to some to be out of place in the tropics. To Rafe, the pillars in the setting of prodigious flora and acres of lucid green with rugged mountains and topaz sky looked at home, being neither implausible, nor of a "grass-hut" ambience.

Rafe went up the stairway through a more public side door, spoke to the Hawaiian guard on duty whom he knew, and asked if Dr. Jerome Derrington's group had met with the queen as yet. He was assured that they were even now in the stately Blue Room with Liliuokalani.

Rafe walked down the corridor, permitted because he was in the Legislature, and waited across from the closed door into the Blue Room. There was so little doubt in his mind about the clinic being approved that Rafe considered the matter closed. Jerome would be a rejoicing man today. Eden too. He was here to talk to Eden and bring her to dinner at the Royal Hawaiian before he left in the morning.

The door opened and Zachary came out quietly, not wishing to disturb the meeting. Rafe was a little surprised to see him, but thought Nora must have wanted him present for the *Gazette*.

Zachary noticed him and walked across the corridor to where he waited.

Zachary looked better today. The strife over Silas at the family meeting had brought him a serious spiritual tumble. Afterward he'd become so discouraged over the walking stick incident that he'd closed himself up in his room.

Rafe had received a note from Eden, which motivated him to return to Kea Lani to encourage Zach to stand up and begin to walk again with the Lord.

Rafe had learned that with Zach, it was important to reassure him, to affirm the fact that he was still accepted, forgiven, and a friend.

In Zach's room, Rafe had calmly explained that Silas did not attack him in Hunnewell's garden. Oliver was the culprit. The walking stick was a red herring.

Rafe had also told Zach that it wasn't Silas he'd followed to the gambling den in Pan Alley that night, but Herald Hartley. The explanations had taken some time to work, but with Eden's help they'd managed to convince him, get him out of his bed of depression, and encourage him to come downstairs to dinner.

Silas, as planned by Eden, had been there waiting, and walked up with a disarming smile and held out his hand of friendship to Zach. For a brief desperate moment Rafe had thought Zach wouldn't take his hand. But he had, and replied with a brief apology for his false accusation. Even a brief apology to Silas meant that things were improving by giant leaps!

Rafe stood now in the corridor at Iolani, leaning his shoulder against the wall as Zachary came up.

"Well, it's all settled. The clinic is approved. Dr. Jerome is leaving for Molokai next week. By the way, Ambrose is in town looking for you."

Rafe assumed he'd come to see him off to the mainland. "He's probably waiting for me at the hotel. I'll wait for Eden, then go meet him."

"Eden? Oh, she didn't come. Just Uncle Jerome, Nora, and me. I'm to write this up for the *Gazette* before I leave with you and Ainsworth in the morning. C'mon. I'll walk with you to the hackney."

Rafe straightened, drawing his dark brows together. "Wait a

minute. She's been looking forward to this crowning victory for months. She wouldn't have missed it. I thought she was inside the Blue Room all this time."

Zachary gave a brief shake of his golden head. "Maybe she's at Kalihi, and she couldn't get off?"

"No. She would have come with Jerome," he said adamantly.

Zachary looked at him, growing sober as he recognized Rafe's concern. "I just assumed something urgent had come up."

"Nobody said anything? Nora, Jerome?"

"No one looked surprised, so I ignored it. What's the matter? Something is troubling you."

Rafe tried to relax. For some reason he was tense today. "I don't know. I just can't see her missing this rare opportunity. Perhaps I'm the only one who knew how much the clinic meant to her. She and I certainly struggled over it! It nearly ended the engagement. Well, if Jerome and Nora aren't concerned, maybe I'm overreacting. Let's go."

"I'll be spending the night aboard the houseboat," Zachary said as they descended the stairs into the grounds. "Someone's been seen snooping about lately, I've been told. There was a light glowing in the houseboat last night."

They entered the warm sunshine. "Some of the Hawaiian boys saw it, and thought I was aboard."

"Anything taken?" Rafe asked absently, still not satisfied about Eden.

"No. Peculiar, that's what it is. I've checked things over and nothing was disturbed. I'd insist it must have been a ghost they saw."

Rafe gave him a sardonic look.

"Oh, well, go ahead and laugh," Zachary said. "Even Eden says she feels as if a ghost is watching her. Ambrose mentioned it. She stopped by the church on her way to Kalihi this morning to talk to him."

Ghosts! Rafe couldn't conceive of Eden thinking of ghosts.

"There's demons, or unclean spirits," Rafe commented, "but

there's no such thing as a ghost. A ghost implies the soul of someone dead hanging around, but every lost person who dies goes to Hades until the Judgment, and every true Christian is present with the Lord."

"Well," Zach said defensively, with a shrug of his shoulder. "You know more about the Bible than I do, but she was scared about it."

Rafe stopped short, hands on hips. He frowned. "Are you serious?"

"Sure!"

"I can't believe it." Rafe walked on. Zachary scowled back as he kept pace beside him. "Now why would I make it up? What about my houseboat? Someone has been there."

"Someone, yes." *Maybe.* Rafe gave him a side glance. "But a ghost in a white sheet . . . with a candle? Look, Zach, whatever form evil spirits may take, don't mess with them."

"That's the last thing I want to do," Zachary said dryly. "What I want is a fancy dinner with Bunny—I mean Bernice Judson—in San Francisco. You know, maybe that's what Ambrose wants to speak to you about . . . Eden, and her ghost."

"Tonight she's having dinner with me at the hotel. I'll take care of any little ghost that wants to spook her."

Zachary laughed. "I'll bet you will."

The bizarre news about Eden was disturbing to Rafe. Why would she, sensible as she was, tell Ambrose—of all people—that she was bothered by something "ghostly"? This was contrary to everything Rafe knew about her. Zach must be enhancing the story because some loner had been hanging around his houseboat.

He paused on the grounds and looked back toward the palace. Uncharacteristic of Eden not to have shown up today. Was her absence somehow connected with Zach's tale?

"Are you coming back to the hotel?" Rafe said.

"No, I'm going to the boat. I'll see you tomorrow on the steamer. Oh! Did Keno tell you?"

"What else is going on that I don't I know about? I haven't seen him since yesterday at Hawaiiana. He was writing Candace a love letter."

Zachary laughed. "Well, she sure must have liked what he wrote. She told Grandfather this morning that she's engaged to Keno and they're going to marry next year. A double wedding, with you and Eden. Now, if I can just convince Bunny to do the same thing. What a triple wedding that would be!"

Rafe was pleased about Keno and Candace. He must be a very happy man today. "How did Ainsworth take the news?"

"He was speechless, because it was Oliver who first wrote him a message saying he was breaking the engagement. There's someone else in San Francisco he wants to marry. The news hit Grandfather like a hammer blow. You know how Ainsworth had wanted the engagement made public before he left for the mainland. Now the entire matter is over. Then Candace comes to him with her firm decision. She says she had a showdown with Oliver yesterday. Told him if he didn't break the engagement himself and board the steamer with Mr. Hunnewell, she'd go straight to his father with the 'British scandal.'"

Zachary was off with a small salute, and Rafe went on, faintly amused over Oliver's plummet from the mountain of pride to the valley of humiliation over his treatment of Keno.

Keno's romantic victory brought Rafe satisfaction as the hackney moved down King Street in the direction of the hotel. This time, the better man won.

His smile didn't last long, though. The uneasiness returned. *Ghost . . . the houseboat . . . unusual.* He pushed the thought aside and entered the hotel.

Rafe unlocked the door to his suite and entered to silence. He closed it softly, pondering things. Most of the questions that had plagued him since Hunnewell's garden were now answered well enough, and the rest he'd leave to the marshal. He was able to put them aside on the shelf. He decided to rest until dinner with Eden.

A new doctor? Eden thought. *Strange, nobody told me about him.* She stopped in the doorway to the nurses' lounge and turned her head to look back down the hall with a puzzled frown. *Am I imagining things?*

She was almost sure she'd seen a man in a white doctor's coat, from the side passage, enter the room at the end of the corridor. She knew all of the physicians on duty and while she'd not recognized this one, she'd gotten an impression of height and shoulders that did not match the older gentlemen.

Her senses must be playing tricks on her. She heard no sound from the examination room. A shadow from the windy moonlit night . . . in a white doctor's coat? Oh, come, Eden!

She smiled ruefully. A ghost? She didn't believe in ghosts.

She looked at the time. Five minutes more and she was off for the day. She would meet Rafe tonight at the hotel for their last evening together for a very long time. Sadness filled her heart. *I won't think about it.* She cheered herself by thinking, *Who knows? My meeting with Rebecca may go so well I might come back early. Maybe I won't stay there an entire year. Or—what if Rafe and I married, and then I went to meet Rebecca?*

She was surprised by her own thoughts. They must have been stirring around in her subconscious all along, ever since she and Rafe had decided that her term on Molokai wouldn't be a long one, as had been her first intention. Well, even if she did not stay long, the work would go on. And the clinic was certain to be approved today when Great-aunt Nora and her father met with the queen. A victory at last! Dr. Jerome was thrilled. So was Dr. Clifford Bolton and Lana. Lana had said, "Now we have a cause to involve ourselves in that could be worth it."

Eden frowned. A strange comment for her aunt to make. Didn't she and Dr. Bolton already have a cause? She had spoken as though the work here at Kalihi was ending, and another door needed opening in order to continue serving God in the medical profession. Come to think of it, neither Dr. Bolton nor Lana looked well recently. Bolton appeared to have aged, with more gray in his hair, and Lana had been losing weight and had darker areas under her eyes as though she was unhappy. Odd, because their wedding would take place next Sunday evening at the mission church, the minister being Ambrose.

Dr. Bolton did seem to be taking great interest in the clinic, spending hours with her father discussing what could be done and how to send equipment to Molokai. Rafe had been most generous with his support, and Ambrose would prepare the printing press for shipment from the *Gazette* office. Keno would arrange getting it to the harbor to be loaded aboard the *Minoa* bound for Molokai. All of that business would take time. Today Rafe would be packing to board the steamer for the mainland. She wondered how long it would be before Rafe would return to Honolulu with Townsend.

Even now her father was making plans to leave for Molokai within a week. After the meeting with the queen he would leave for the day to attend to some business at Kea Lani about orders for medical supplies.

Herald would be remaining in Honolulu under the marshal's jurisdiction until further evidence from San Francisco was supplied. The matter of Dr. Chen's death and the journal remained in the hands of the police. As of yet, none of Chen's relatives had filed complaints about the journal and Herald may not be charged with a crime. She sighed. She was so grateful that Dr. Jerome had not been involved. Her love for Rafe was strengthened, if that were possible, because of his honorable treatment of her father. He'd done everything possible to protect his character and shield him from notoriety.

She looked down the corridor to the examining room. Perhaps Dr. Jerome had hired a new assistant.

Her father was already warming toward Rafe. She could see it in his decisions. He was moving in the direction of finding someone to fill her position in the Molokai clinic, rather than struggling to keep her at his side. That was a tremendous change in his attitude.

Eden finished with her favorite patient, a young girl, and decided she'd best quicken her pace if she were to meet her father and Great-aunt Nora at Iolani Palace. She believed Zachary would attend as well. Her heart beat with enthusiasm. This was the moment she'd long been waiting and praying for.

She went to gather her things, including the box that contained her dress and shoes. She smiled. And afterward, this evening, how pleasant and exciting to have a romantic dinner with Rafe at the Royal Hawaiian. She shook out the modest dress, one of light blue with lace trim, high neckline and tight at the wrist. The windows had no curtains and looked out brazenly into the hall. She decided on her father's little office where there would be privacy in his absence.

She walked down the corridor toward his office, humming to herself. *Mrs. Rafe Easton. Mrs. Eden Easton . . .* well, it didn't quite synchronize, but the man who came with it made up for her new upcoming initials, *E. E.*

She approached the examining room and slowed her steps. The impression of someone having entered there earlier was still so vivid that she hurried to her father's office, anxious to be on her way.

She shut the door and slid the bolt in place . . . there. She was acting silly, but at least she could turn her back to the door now and not worry about her spine tingling.

She shook out the dress, smoothing any slight wrinkle. She looked at her hair in the little mirror, thinking she would arrange it in the cascade of curls at the back for dinner, since Rafe liked it that way. She looked at her diamond engagement ring in the light and it shivered with beauty and excitement.

Unexpectedly the door handle rattled, then a tap sounded on the door. She caught her breath.

"Yes? Who's there?"

"Zach! Eden?"

"Yes, just a moment." With relief she unbolted the lock, opened the door, and stepped back. She blinked hard. *It couldn't be, but it was.* Uncle Townsend stood there in a white physician's coat smiling benignly at her.

Townsend was a big man with wide shoulders and a strong torso, still handsome for his age with golden hair and a cleft in his chin.

He put a finger to his mouth, pushed past her, and shut the door.

"*Shh,*" he said, almost in a boyish fashion, still smiling. "Where's that dear, dear brother of mine, the world's greatest wanderer?"

Her fears dissipated somewhat, but he'd just lied to her, making his voice sound like his son Zachary, and what was the reason for that deception? Maybe he thought she wouldn't open the door if he identified himself. *And what was he doing in Honolulu?*

"Dr. Jerome is at Iolani Palace," she told him without showing any agitation over his presence.

"*Doctor* Jerome? Still can't call him father?"

She hesitated. *Can Silas call you father?* she could have quipped.

"Don't be afraid. For goodness' sake, Eden, I'm your uncle. I've practically raised you from puppyhood."

That wasn't true, but of course he was her uncle, and in her later childhood he was often at the breakfast and dinner table. But still— his smile seemed odd, almost like that of a stranger. His eyes, too, looked hard, as if they didn't see her as Eden. He had changed. It gave her a chill. Had it been Townsend, then, that she'd had small glimpses of watching her?

"What are you doing here in Honolulu?" she asked, keeping her voice calm. "We heard you were in San Francisco."

His smile was oddly rueful with a tinge of wickedness that tightened her spine.

"Smart of me, wasn't it? It was deliberate. I wanted Celestine and Parker Judson to see me there, then I left immediately for home."

"Uncle Townsend, you need help. You must see Grandfather. Let me send someone after him."

"So Rafe can harass me about Matt Easton and poor Nora? Lies, my dear Eden, all lies, and misunderstandings. Your poor old uncle can prove it. Look, I can't let anyone know I'm here right now, not even Ainsworth. But I have contacted Rafe and Zachary. They were surprised to hear from me, but they're pleased, too, especially Rafe. He wants to see me and so we've arranged to meet at Zach's houseboat, then go to Hanalei. Once there, I can explain everything to Rafe's satisfaction. But I need a little help from you. I've got a buggy waiting now to take us to Zach's boat."

Eden didn't believe him about Rafe. Rafe would be the last man he'd want to encounter right now. "Where's Rafe now?" she asked pleasantly. *Don't rile him. Stay calm. Trust in God.* She called on Him quickly, even as Peter while sinking into the Sea of Galilee—*Lord, save me*!

"Oh he's already at Hanalei. He's waiting for us."

He's lying to me. Rafe can't be at Hanalei. He had wanted to go there, he'd told her, but there wasn't enough time. Because he will be boarding the steamer in the morning.

Her heart begin to pound. She mustn't let him notice.

"*My* Hanalei," he said with unexpected bitterness, his phony smile gone. His blue eyes snapped. "I built it. I made it what it is today."

She wasn't about to contradict him.

His eyes widened. Sweat popped out on his forehead. "Rafe will understand before this is all over."

I don't believe either Rafe or Zach is with him. They don't even know he's here. No one does except me.

He's stepped over the line of sanity. He's out for revenge on Rafe and he'll destroy me and Hanalei to hurt him even as he destroyed Matt.

"Uncle Townsend," she said quietly, "I'll go with you. But first, let me get my hat, it's windy out. I'll need my handbag too."

She turned slowly, hoping against hope she could reach the door and fling it open. Even one scream for help might alert Lana.

Every step was an agony of suspense as she drew closer to the door handle while he watched, waiting for her hand to grasp it.

His arm came hard across her collarbone and throat, drawing her back against him, while his other hand clamped a cloth tightly over her nose and mouth. She couldn't breathe anything except the strong fumes. She recognized the odor of chloroform. So that was the reason for the doctor's coat, and entering the examining room— her consciousness was ebbing away. . . .

❧

Rafe, dressed smartly in dinner clothes, looked at the time. Eden should have arrived by now. He paced. Something was wrong. He could feel it.

I should have gone to Kalihi to pick her up, but she wanted to come here.

Frustrated, he left his suite and went down to the lobby and to the desk. "Are you sure there's no message?"

"Certain, Mr. Easton. Is there a message you would like us to send?"

He considered. He looked around the glowing lobby with chandeliers, fancy ball gowns, coats, and ties.

"No, but can you bring a coach around front?"

"At once, sir."

A short time later when he arrived at Kalihi Hospital he found Dr. Jerome away at Kea Lani, and even Dr. Bolton and Lana had left for the evening. When he asked the nurse on duty about Eden Derrington, she raised her brows.

"Oh I heard she left about an hour ago. Lana said her niece would be having dinner with a handsome gentleman tonight. Oh—" She flushed. "You must be him."

"I hope so," he said dryly, and turning left he went down the steps.

He stood in front of the hospital, mulling things over. If Eden left an hour ago she must have gone on to Kea Lani for some reason, and was delayed there, perhaps by Dr. Jerome or her Grandfather Ainsworth. He could either go there or return to the Royal Hawaiian.

Rafe went back to the hotel.

"Any messages?"

The clerk looked at him tensely. "No, sir, nothing."

By ten o'clock that evening when the bells struck on the downtown clock, Rafe, lounging in a chair, looked up and laid down the book he'd been reading—or trying to read. He drummed his fingers on the arm of the chair. He'd come to an earlier conclusion that Eden had chosen not to keep the dinner appointment. She must have assumed that he wouldn't mind, and that "dinner with a handsome gentleman" could wait while she worked with Dr. Jerome on the trip to Molokai next week.

True, the conclusion he'd settled on might not be wholly rational, but some of his dealings with Eden in the last year—at least when it came to Molokai—had not been all that rational. Not that he'd ever tell her so. Nor would he admit to himself that he was extremely irritated that she had broken their date on the eve of a year's separation!

Enough! He tossed the book aside and stood.

Wait a minute. Eden had wanted this last dinner together as much as he had. She was the one who sent a message last night reminding him of it. Not that he needed to be reminded. So what had happened?

Don't let your male pride get in the way, Easton.

Be rational about this. Think it through.

He paced, tapping his chin. She hadn't shown up at the meeting with the queen today. That too was most unusual, not a bit like Eden when she'd worked so hard to get Great-aunt Nora to arrange that meeting for Jerome.

Something was wrong. He had to find out what it was before he boarded the steamer in the morning. He couldn't depart until he was satisfied she was all right. But why wouldn't she be all right?

There was no reason why he should think otherwise except for that absurd talk about Zach's ghost. A ghost aboard his houseboat ... prowling?

He narrowed his gaze. It wasn't just Zach. Eden had gone to Ambrose about an uneasy notion—no, she hadn't told Ambrose she'd seen a ghost. That was Zach's play on words, bringing her unease closer to his own, and what the Hawaiian boys had said about a light, a prowler, or a "ghost."

So Eden's unease in seeking out Ambrose early this morning on her way to Kalihi may have centered around a genuine fear of being watched, or followed by someone of flesh and bone.

He scowled. That changed everything. Why hadn't he thought that way earlier? Why hadn't she come to him about it? She knew he would be at Iolani today. The logical thing was that she'd been *unable* to come. That idea turned him into knots. She'd been *unable* to keep their dinner date. And there his mind slammed into a brick wall. ... Because someone was watching, and following her?

The one thing that gave him a sense of calmness was that the nurse had said she'd left an hour earlier. So Eden had been at the hospital today, perhaps up until five o'clock. Then why had she missed the appointment with the queen? Did the nurse actually see Eden leave at five? Or was she merely stating Eden's routine hour for leaving? The nurse said she'd *heard* that Eden had left around five.

He made up his mind. The ship didn't depart until eleven in the morning. It was now just after ten o'clock. He wouldn't go to bed until he found Eden.

Fool, you've already wasted too much precious time. Wasn't it clear that something was wrong from the beginning?

He grabbed his dinner jacket and his hat and started to leave, then stopped. Fancy clothes slowed him down. Quickly he changed into the comfortable, rugged garb he felt at home in.

If this ordeal turned out to be nothing more than an overreaction over the woman he loved, so be it. He'd rather board the steamer without sleep knowing she was safe than wonder and worry all the way to San Francisco.

Rafe left a message at the front desk for anyone asking for him. He'd return in time to collect his baggage in the morning.

Chapter Twenty-Five
Back to Paradise

*R*afe opened the front door at Hawaiiana Pineapple Plantation, went through the entrance hall, and turned up the lamps as he headed toward the back bedroom. The door was wide open and Keno fast asleep.

Rafe entered and shook the bed. "Up, Keno."

"Huh—what?"

"I need your help. Eden's missing. I've got to find her before my ship leaves in the morning."

Keno sat up, blinking into the lamplight. He shook the cobwebs from his brain. "What! Eden? Missing!" He tossed the cover aside and tumbled out.

Rafe paced, explaining the odd set of circumstances and his concerns while Keno pulled on his clothes.

"Have you talked to Ambrose?"

"Not yet. You do that, and I'll stir up a hornet's nest at Kea Lani."

"What if she's there asleep?"

Rafe narrowed his lashes. "After putting me through all this worry? I'll see she has an 'awakening.'"

Rafe turned and hurried out, calling back, "Meet me at Kea Lani. If she isn't there, we'll need to make plans."

When Rafe arrived at Kea Lani, he was invited in to speak with Dr. Jerome. His concerns only intensified.

"It's after eleven o'clock and she's not home? I was under the impression she was with you," Dr. Jerome cried. "She was to have dinner with you at the Royal Hawaiian. What could have happened?"

"She didn't show up."

At the sound of voices Ainsworth appeared from the library in his dressing gown, book in hand. He looked over at Rafe and Jerome. "What's happening?"

"Eden's missing," Rafe said bluntly. "She could be in danger."

With a shocked expression Ainsworth entered the room. "Missing? My granddaughter? How is that possible!" He turned to Jerome. "Has that scoundrel Herald Hartley been up to something? I never trusted him from the moment he arrived—poisonous herbs and all that."

"He couldn't be involved, sir," Rafe said before Jerome could reply. "He's still under the marshal's supervision. Have you seen Eden at all today?"

"I haven't. I assumed she was spending time with you in Honolulu."

"She didn't show up for dinner, and she wasn't in the meeting at Iolani. That's what worries me most. She wouldn't have missed the queen approving the clinic." Ainsworth removed his dressing gown and snapped an order to the butler to get his jacket. "We'd better go into Honolulu. I want the marshal's men out looking for her."

Rafe turned back to Jerome. "Why wasn't Eden with you and Nora at Iolani?"

"She'd been attending one of the special patients she cares about, a young girl. She was to meet me at the palace. There was a hackney waiting out front, so I knew she'd have no difficulty getting there."

Rafe's hopes climbed. "Then you *did* see her this afternoon, after the meeting with the queen?"

Dr. Jerome's mouth tightened. He released a breath. "In point of fact, no. She'd left a note on my desk . . . saying she would spend the afternoon with you, and then dinner tonight. I thought—" His face tensed and his brows came together.

Taut silence held the room. Jerome groaned and sank into a chair as it dawned on him that *she* might not have written the note.

Rafe's suspicions were growing like a wildfire. "Zach mentioned someone prowling about his houseboat the other night. And Eden told Ambrose early this morning she was being watched."

"Watched!" Grandfather Ainsworth said with alarm.

The door opened and Ambrose walked in with the wind, his long preacher jacket blowing. He swept off his hat. His dark eyes scanned the frowning men. Keno stood behind him by the door.

Rafe, who knew Ambrose so well, understood by his countenance that something was amiss and Rafe stepped toward him. "What is it?"

"Gentlemen, this isn't easy to say. After praying with Eden early this morning I had a strong motivation to go into Honolulu and send Parker Judson a wire. I felt we should inquire if the Pinkerton detective Rafe had hired had any news on Townsend. I stayed in town and Parker's reply just came in a half hour ago." He pulled it from his pocket and read:

Been hunting day and night for T. D. No success. Found out he boarded steamer for Honolulu tenth of October. Danger assured. Notify Honolulu authority.
P.D.A. Charles Morris

The silence enclosed them like a tomb.

For a moment Rafe couldn't move. He was trapped in a nightmare. *Townsend.* His greatest fear, which he'd tried to deny, but which had persisted in the back of his mind, had struck. It felt as if the ground was rumbling beneath him and hot lava was ready to erupt.

Rafe slammed his fist on the table, shaking the lamp.

Keno came to his side. "Take it easy. We'll stop him. God's on our side. Eden belongs to Him."

Rafe struggled to control his rage. *Townsend.* The deed of abducting Eden shouted that this was his wicked handiwork.

"If I get my hands on him—"

Both Dr. Jerome and Ainsworth exchanged quick glances with Ambrose.

"If he's laid a hand on her I'll kill him."

Ambrose came forward, an iron grip on Rafe's shoulder.

"No, Rafe. Don't even entertain the thought. That's what he wants. He knows he's finished. He's planned it this way. He wants to see you go down with him. It was never Celestine or even Kip he was after, and it's not Eden, though he'll use her. It's you. Don't give him a victory, Rafe. 'Wringing his neck,' as you young people put it, isn't worth ruining your life in the process."

"Yes, he's right, Rafe," Dr. Jerome said. "I've known my brother had psychotic problems since we were boys. He was a bully, domineering, selfish, and never willing to accept his own guilt for anything. It's shackled him from humbling his soul before God. He claimed he needed no Savior, and when he did sin, he'd always say it was somebody else's fault."

Grandfather Ainsworth groaned, pacing. "I should have moved at once. I put the Derrington business before the truth. I've been a fool. Dear God! What have I done?"

Rafe walked over to the window and threw it open. He stood facing the darkness, hands on hips, struggling with hate.

How could I have expected him to remain in San Francisco when everything he wants to destroy is right here?

Keno spoke in a low voice. "Look, pal, we can beat Townsend at his own game. We're on to him now. The viper is loose in the garden, but we'll stop him. We've got to outmaneuver him."

"Townsend made one mistake. And it will cost him. He was expecting me to board the steamer in the morning," Rafe said. "He thought it safe to make his move now. He knows it takes two weeks to reach San Francisco. By the time I'd concluded he wasn't there and returned, I'd be looking the fool, with everything I cherish greeting me in rubble."

"But he's blundered," Keno said.

"He should have waited until the steamer was out to sea before taking Eden. He'd been watching her, learning her hours at Kalihi, planning the best time to make his move."

"And when Zach came here to stay at Kea Lani," Keno said thoughtfully, "Townsend must have stayed on his houseboat. He was careful not to touch anything, not to eat anything to give himself away."

"If the Hawaiian boys hadn't seen a light the other night, I doubt Zach would have guessed that something was happening on the boat."

Keno shook his head in dismay. "He's a shrewd one. The more he's pushed into a corner, the more he reveals the nature of Cain."

"He's almost always taken what he wanted, and what he wants now is revenge on me for his losing Celestine, Hanalei, the pearl beds, and his position as Ainsworth's heir."

"Just like evil, isn't it?" Keno said. "Satan wants to take as many to the Lake of Fire with him as he can. Even when he knows he has but a short time left he goes forth with great fury to destroy. There's no repentance, only evil revenge."

Rafe quickly turned to the others. "Since Townsend wants to strike me where it will hurt and destroy the most, where would he take Eden, and what would he do?"

Every head turned toward him. In the silence the wind shook the windows and eaves.

"Hanalei" came a low unison of voices.

"Exactly," Rafe said firmly. "He'd take Eden to the Easton estate. And if he sees no further future for himself in the Islands, as

Ainsworth predicted, then he'll want to destroy Matt Easton's estate and everything on it. I can see him burning it down, just as he burned down Ling's hut."

A groan of affirmation came from the others, as though they too anticipated the worst.

"That's his mind-set, all right," Ambrose said grimly. "Jealousy and pride want to destroy and hurt."

"I've got to search Zach's houseboat to make sure Townsend isn't still there. He could be hiding below with Eden, waiting for morning light to head for the Big Island. If he's not there, I'm heading out tonight." He turned to Grandfather Ainsworth and Dr. Jerome. "Sirs, could either of you alert the authorities here in Honolulu, tell the marshal to send a wire to the police on the Big Island. I want Ling warned to watch his back. And Ambrose—" he turned to his uncle.

Ambrose stood arms folded, blocking his way spiritually with an even stare that only Ambrose could give him.

"I'm coming with you," Ambrose stated firmly.

"If necessary this will be a rough journey by sea tonight."

"Just you make headway, lad, and don't worry about me keeping up. I'll do just fine. We don't know what has happened, or what the purpose of God may be with Eden—so it's not wise you go alone into such a test."

He'd rather go alone. He could handle Townsend. But Ambrose knew that, which was probably why he insisted on going with him. He should be grateful for Ambrose and Keno, but Rafe was too distraught to think about that now.

"Then let's go," Rafe demanded, restless and impatient over details.

The hotel coach was parked in the carriageway. Ambrose was talking to Grandfather Ainsworth on the front steps. Ainsworth's silver hair tossed in the wind. His lean, lined face was solemn.

He's afraid, Rafe decided. *Afraid for Eden this time, instead of the family name or the enterprise.*

Ainsworth came down the walkway where Rafe and Keno stood by the coach.

"I'll have the marshal get his men out. I should have seen it before. Townsend knows the end has come for him, one way or the other."

On the front lanai, Dr. Jerome was speaking to Great-aunt Nora. Nora looked fragile and trembling in a chill wind. Candace came and put an arm around her to lead her back indoors. She glanced over at Keno as if pleased to see he was at Rafe's side. *Stand firm with him*, she seemed to say.

Dr. Jerome had grabbed his knee-length jacket and hat, and came down the steps with Ambrose. The low voice of Grandfather Ainsworth drifted to Rafe, though it wasn't meant to reach his hearing—"And Rafe, we've got to stay with him. We can't permit the young man to destroy himself, which he could do if he gets his hands on Townsend. Townsend would like nothing better than to bring Rafe down with him."

"We can't let that happen," Dr. Jerome answered. "Keno can stop him."

"Yes, Keno—another fine man with character. Candace has made a sound choice. I see that now. I see so many things—when it's too late."

"Maybe not too late, Father," Jerome said. "For Townsend? Yes, unless he comes out of his stupor in time. But not too late for Zachary and Silas. And Candace will remain loyal now that you've seen Keno for what he is."

"Thank God, my dear son Jerome."

Rafe glanced at Keno over what they'd overheard. Despite the dire moment, they exchanged faint smiles.

The moment confirmed to Rafe that even at the darkest hour, the light was never fully extinguished. If the Almighty promised to work some good out of the worst of circumstances, then who was he to doubt Him? Amid the hay, wood, and stubble there may be found a morsel of gold, silver, and precious stones.

Rafe didn't think Townsend was out on the streets, though he approved of Marshal Harper sending his men out to search. Townsend was either on Zach's houseboat or on his way to Hanalei.

"Does your cousin Liho still run his boat?"

"It's tied up at the wharf now. I'll alert him, just in case Zach's houseboat has already set out for the Big Island."

"Will Liho risk it? The wind's picking up."

"He'll risk it."

"Let's go."

—◦◦—

A few minutes later the horse-drawn coach left Kea Lani and turned onto the road to Honolulu.

When they reached King Street, Rafe was swiftly out, and onto the street, Keno and Ambrose with him.

"We're going to the houseboat," Rafe told Grandfather Ainsworth and Dr. Jerome.

"We'll notify the marshal," Ainsworth said.

"Be careful, both of you," Dr. Jerome called out as the coach drove toward the police station.

On the waterfront Rafe hurried along the wharf in midnight darkness, the wind blowing in from the Pacific.

"Looks like a storm," Ambrose warned.

Rafe stopped. His gaze narrowed on the vessels tied up to the posts. Rafe knew the boat to be a white and green yacht that had been turned into a houseboat. When Eden had come to Hanalei from Tamarind House with Zach several months ago, they'd come on this boat, which Zach had named *Lily of the Stars*.

He looked ahead with relief. Zach's houseboat was there. A small light burned like the hope in his heart.

*O*nce aboard *Lily of the Stars*, Rafe walked silently across the deck toward the cabin where a dim light burned above a desk. The door was open a few inches, creaking in the wind. Keno was on the other side of the door in the darkness. Ambrose was some feet back out of view. Rafe gently pushed the door inward. Nothing.

The lamp hanging above the desk swung to and fro as the wind and tides rocked the vessel. Rafe's eyes moved cautiously about the small room, into dim corners and along the flooring. Nothing. He pushed the door against the wall before entering to make sure Townsend wasn't behind it, waiting. He entered, went to the desk, and looked behind it on the floor. He unhooked the lamp and brought it close to the floor. Blood . . . brown, sticky, some hours old. He stooped and looked under the desk, half expecting to see a crumpled corpse, but saw only a pair of slippers, evidently Zach's.

Rafe stood, frowning, hands on hips as Keno entered.

"Blood," Rafe said. "Not much, a few drops. Someone's been pulled from here."

"To the hold?"

"Most likely."

They lifted a hatch and saw steps down to the hold where Zach had some storage.

"Watch those steps," Ambrose whispered.

Below, there was a low cramped space with crates. Rafe had to stoop as he reached the bottom due to the low headroom. He paused by a barrel, and Keno turned up the wicks on several lamps.

"No one here," Keno murmured. "Townsend would have come at us like a growling, mad bear if he were."

Rafe agreed. "This is dark news. We're too late. He must have already taken Eden to the Big Island. He's not a good sailor. I hope he can handle whatever boat he's using."

What about the drops of blood? Rafe refused any thought that would make it his beloved's. *The Lord will keep her*, he kept reminding himself. But always his doubts resurfaced. Would He? Others who had belonged to Him had died. Many murdered. Many through violent deaths. At times He delivered in His purpose, and at other times it was His purpose not to intervene. Always his mind went back to the apostles James and Peter. Peter was led out of prison by an angel. James was killed with the sword. Why? God had His purposes. Did He love Peter more than James? Of course not. He'd given His life for every individual sheep and loved them.

Eden, my love, you are ever in His care. Stay strong.

A groan! A thumping sound. From where!

Keno was looking behind the crates, pulling them out and away from the hull. Ambrose hurried over to a large canvas sea bag.

"It's moving," Ambrose said, stooping.

Rafe drew the knife from his jacket and carefully slit it open.

"Zach!" Ambrose said, and quickly removed a gag from his mouth while Rafe cut a rope that bound his hands and feet.

In a moment Zachary was trying to gain his breath and the use of his vocal cords. In a raspy voice he choked: "Townsend's here. Has Eden."

Rafe grasped his shoulder. "We're onto him. How long ago?"

"This afternoon. He crept up on me. I caught sight of him just as he was about to smother me with chloroform. I got a whiff of it before he could act."

"Did you see Eden?"

"No."

"Whose blood in the cabin?"

"Probably mine," he groaned, reaching a hand to his head. "As I said, I saw him and jumped him and we had a real tussle. He's bigger than me and finally landed me a good one. My jaw's still swollen." He rubbed it, wincing. "That's about as much as I remember. I do recall voices—I'm almost sure it was Laweoki."

"Your sailing captain?"

Zachary gave a nod. "He was due to come this afternoon. I was thinking of having him dock the boat at Koko Head during the time I was away in San Francisco—say! What time is it? That steamer leaves at eleven a.m."

"What happened with Laweoki?"

"Don't know for sure. I think they were in an argument, and another dust-up. Laweoki must've refused to sail the ship for him. I remember something about the Princess Kaiulani."

"That's my cousin Liho's vessel," Keno said quickly. "It's docked here in Honolulu too. Townsend must be using it."

"It's a fast one," Ambrose said. "Liho brought me to Hanalei in swift time when I needed to alert you on Townsend."

Rafe remembered. "Refusing to sail Zach's boat is the best thing Laweoki could have done for us. We need it to reach the Big Island tonight. What do you say, Zach?"

Zach smothered a moan. He rolled over onto his knees and tried to push himself up. Ambrose lent an arm and told him not to rush it. "You've been hit again on the head, poor lad."

"Least it's on the other side," Keno said, and received a smirk from Zachary. "Thanks for reminding me." He looked at Rafe. "He has Eden. We've got to stop him."

Rafe turned to Keno with an arched brow.

Keno ran his fingers through his hair. "Can we do it?"

"After sailing the Caribbean?" Rafe scoffed. "Remember that storm?"

"I remember."

Rafe turned to Ambrose. "Are you up to working those sails with Keno?"

"It's been a while, but I can manage it, lad. You'd better stay quiet and rest that head," he told Zachary. "This is going to be an all-nighter."

Rafe went up the stairs and out on deck. Keno and Ambrose were checking out the sails.

Rafe took the ladder to steerage helm. He looked over the magnetic compass and tested the wheel. All was in order. Laweoki was a careful captain.

He leaned out past the canvas canopy and peered up at the sky. Clouds were rolling in but the moon and stars were still visible. The wind was picking up force, but at the moment it was warm and pleasant. *The Lord is over many waters. The God of glory thunders!*

Chapter Twenty-Seven
Danger at Hanalei

As though a harbinger of what was to come, a blinding streak of lightning stabbed the blackness above Hanalei Plantation House, followed by a loud clap of thunder that shook the glass in the downstairs windows.

Eden heard footsteps in the hall, and they seemed to slow, then abruptly stop outside the bedchamber door. A key turned in the lock and the door opened. She wanted to flinch under her uncle's icy blue eyes. For a moment their eyes locked, and she felt a quell of anger rise above her apprehension. Reality struck with appalling clarity, yet she could only lie down, partially drugged and untidy as she was from such rough traveling. The Scriptures she'd memorized through the years gave her strength and comfort, or she would have panicked. She had awoken, tied up in black darkness, and lying on rough rope and nets that kept swaying and moving. Then she had heard her uncle's threatening voice, "Liho, you man that sail or I'll send you to the bottom." Townsend had put her into the cramped hull of a boat!

The blackness seemed a nightmare. But even then, she'd soon

discovered peace. *Someone is praying for me,* she thought, more than someone, including her beloved Rafe. How precious his love now seemed to her when she understood she might never see him again. Tears filled her eyes. *I should have married him months ago. And if God rescues me from this, I shall marry him immediately! I shall have a double wedding with Aunt Lana.*

Townsend carried her off the boat, leaving her wrists tied behind her while she rode behind him trying to hold on to the back of the saddle. Even then, he had talked incessantly, making excuses, insisting she had always been his favorite niece, and that it caused him profound grief to treat her this way. Her mother, Rebecca, had been a "good" woman. "I am driven to these extremes because of Rafe's jealousy and hatred. He insists I was responsible for Matt's accidental fall from the rocks. Rubbish! I had nothing to do with it. Nora promotes his errors by writing outright lies in her book. As if I'd poison my own aunt. She was old, that's all, imagining things, and Rafe turned her against me. He turns everyone in the family against me; he's finally even turned Ainsworth against me."

Drugged and exhausted, Eden was half asleep, unable to keep from leaning her cheek against his back as they rode toward Hanalei.

Once there, he smuggled her indoors and brought her to a room, and she heard a chuckle. "Rafe's bedchamber. He'll find her here," he mumbled. He went out the door just as she was falling back asleep.

Now that she'd partially awakened again he'd returned and was looking down at her sadly.

"Poor girl," he said again. "I'm sorry to have to treat you this way. It was your choice of Rafe that forced me to use you. Candace would have done just as well, but Keno has nothing to do with all of this. It's Rafe. He's arrogant and selfish. I should have done something about him when he was a boy."

He had something in his hand. Her gaze was a little blurry but it looked like a glass of water.

"Drink this. No need to be afraid. Do as I say and all will be well in the end."

She did not believe him. She had a horrible fear that he would seek to destroy Hanalei and her with it. And yet, he'd appeared quite sane since they'd arrived.

He smiled. "The Hawaiian servants think I've come to surrender myself to Rafe and ask for mercy. I put on some marvelous theatrics for their benefit. I've convinced them. I even had the cook bring me a Bible." He smiled. "They don't know you're here. So you must go to sleep again, my dear. We can't have you yelling out or pounding on the door, or breaking glass. And not one of them would ever open the door to look inside their wonderful Makua Rafe's bedchamber."

His smile vanished in a puff of wind. "Don't worry, this is only a mild sedative. You'll have to drink this or you'll force me to use the chloroform again. Be quick about it, Eden. You're starting to move around. Quiet!"

She turned her face away and held her teeth tightly shut. His strong fingers clamped painfully into her cheeks as she resisted. Having no better alternative while becoming more fearful of his anger, she decided to drink it.

Afterward, Townsend went to the wardrobe and pulled out a jacket. He brought it to her, smiling again. "Here, my pet. Have something to comfort you while you're resting. Here's his jacket." And he laid it over her gently. "Good night, Eden—and good-bye. There, you see, all is well. Aren't you relieved?"

His golden brows lifted. "You see, I'm leaving tonight. I shall no longer hinder Rafe and his greedy plans."

You would know best about greedy plans. If you think you can return to San Francisco and lie your way back into Celestine's arms, you are mistaken.

"If it's Rafe you're worried about, fear no longer," he said. "He can have Hanalei, and he will not be harmed."

Did he mean it? She wondered how he could so quickly act like the old Uncle Townsend she'd grown up knowing. Arrogant, but not profoundly evil. Was he on opium? Could that account for his moods?

"Are you returning to San Francisco?" she asked, her voice raspy.

"I have no intention of returning to Celestine." His face hardened. "I know her well. The woman is after Parker Judson. That's why she's staying in his fancy house on Nob Hill." His eyes were cold. "That's the house that should be turned into rubble and ashes."

A chill ran through her. "Are you threatening Celestine?"

"I'll warn you to keep your wild suspicions to yourself. Ainsworth and I will work this matter out between us by correspondence. I've decided money will answer all things," he scoffed. "Ainsworth will pay a hefty price to see me leave the Islands permanently for parts unknown. Well. I've decided to accommodate him. I'm going to the Caribbean and begin a new life, under a new name. I'll build my own plantation. Better than Hanalei. The Derringtons will never see me again, nor will Rafe."

He truly believes he can get away with all he's done. But I don't believe he means it about not hurting Rafe. He plans to burn Hanalei down, I'm sure of it.

Be still, she told herself. Perhaps it is wiser to let him think he can escape to the Caribbean.

A smirk lingered on his rugged face. "With that, I shall bid you aloha."

"If Grandfather Ainsworth gives you money, how will you get hold of it if you're leaving now?"

He chuckled merrily. "I am more clever than any of you give me credit for, including Rafe. Don't think I'm not convinced he's on his way here now. He expects to find me, and thinks I'm willing to die here. To commit suicide in a blaze of glory. A Custer's last stand, so to speak. Well, I've thought it over in some cooler moments and decided I'm going to enjoy life after all. I'm still a young man. In the Caribbean I can change my name, even my appearance. I could marry. Why not? I could become a big kahuna, say on Jamaica, or

Barbados. I know all about sugar, coffee, pineapples. So, when he arrives here, I shall be arriving at Kea Lani." He smiled. "I will receive my just inheritance from Ainsworth, and some jewels from Nora and Candace. From there I shall leave, and never come back. Does that suit you?"

"If that's true, then—why not let me go?"

"You must be here until Rafe arrives. If I release you too soon—you may be able to alert him of my return to Kea Lani. And I cannot go anywhere until I get the money I need to start a new life."

He opened the door, went out, and shut it quietly. His footsteps filtered away into silence. She heard the wind outside scraping bushes against the side of the house.

He may be going to Kea Lani to see Grandfather for money, but he's just as venomous toward Rafe and jealous of Hanalei as ever. He wouldn't have told me his plans if he anticipated I would live to tell of it!

If only there was a way to escape! The door was unlocked—such irony! He must have found that thought amusing. If she could be sure he had left she might be able to scream loudly enough for someone to realize she was here, but the drug was already taking her strength away.

With great effort she tried to get off the bed, but as soon as her feet met the floor the room seemed to heave to and fro and start to turn upside down.

Dizziness caught hold of her again. *So then . . . this is his solution to prevent my screams and door pounding—I could have guessed it.*

───◦◦───

Outside on the lanai, Townsend stood shielded in the darkness. He'd brought the horse to a place out of sight a mile from here. He must carry out his plans quickly. He would wait until the workers went to bed, perhaps another hour, then light the fires and escape on horseback. Tomorrow he'd locate a boat, or even tonight if he could. Rafe wouldn't be looking for him. He'd assume he was trapped in the flames and dead from smoke inhalation.

He looked down the carriageway and saw no sign of any of the Hawaiian boys. The sky churned with thick clouds. A river flowed by, obscure and silent.

While Rafe and the others were consumed with the trouble here, he would be making his way back to Kea Lani.

—◌◌◌—

Later, Eden tossed restlessly and awakened to a dull, muddled mind with a moan. A brilliant streak of lightning startled her and she came fully awake. She found herself lying on the hard cold floor where she must have fallen as she went out. She managed to raise herself to her elbow and turn over. She looked toward the window, her heart pounding. Fire! She struggled to rouse herself. Hanalei was burning—

What was that odor?—smoke. The plantation house was burning!

In a moment of muddled confusion she managed to get on her feet and stagger toward the door. She found the doorknob and thrust it open—in the hall she called out as best she could. *Hurry! Get out! Fire! Get out!* She wondered if she was really in control of her vocal chords or only thinking the words.

As she reached the stairway, walking, stumbling, and crawling her way, she heard breaking glass coming from one of the rooms. She stopped, horrified the parlor was burning, and Rafe's office. Smoke crept like evil fog ready to smother and blind. Eden screamed below for the servants, for any name that came to mind whether they were there or not. She heard nothing. Had they been able to get out the back door?

Please, Father God! Help us, in Jesus' name!

She turned to crawl back up the stairs when a feeble wail reached her ears from somewhere downstairs in the smoke.

It was a child's voice! A boy's cry of great fear and weakness!

Anguish gripped her stomach. Why was the boy caught? Why was he not with the servants, who must have escaped before she ever awoke?

Eden clutched the banister and stared below. "Where are you?" she shouted. "Can you hear me?"

Nothing. Only the crackle of fire, smoke of acrid fumes, the sputter of rich draperies going up in flames, the crystal chandelier crashing to the floor. The expensive paintings, and those of the Easton patriarchs on the parlor walls sizzling in the heat.

It's the end of the world, her fevered mind told her, *and everything, and every treasure, every cherished memento is being burned to ashes. Seeing that all these things will burn up, what manner of people should we be?*

Oh Rafe, my darling!

"I'm caught!" the boy screamed, crying, and wailing. "Here! I'm caught!"

The voice came from the parlor.

Eden refused to think of the hopelessness of her cause. The boy's terrified wail commanded her heart's response. She managed to get down the last few stairs holding her dress over her mouth and nose.

Hanalei was now wide awake, and from the workers' bungalows and out on the lawn came shouting voices like shadows in the firelight. Horses raced by. She heard the familiar Hawaiian cry of anguish, *Auwe, Auwe,* followed by the cries of frightened birds in the trees and bushes.

Fly away, fly away, her numbed heart echoed. *Hurry, hurry—*

Something crashed in the direction of the hallway. A moment later she heard the boy outside shouting: "There's still someone in the parlor!"

There was the sound of snapping wood, and the heat was becoming unbearable. *The boy is outside safe,* Eden thought, *but I'm trapped.*

She tried to retreat in the direction of the stairway again, but there was so much smoke she could no longer see, or know which direction to take. Her eyes and lungs burned. She crawled and bumped into something that felt like a divan. She struggled in the direction of where she thought the front door should be. Everything was too hot.

She reached her hand out. *Lord, comfort Rafe when I'm gone. Don't let this tragedy destroy his life, his faith in You—*

⸻

Rafe rode with Keno and Ambrose beside him on horses they'd rented in town. The dirt side road was smoother here near the cutoff road to Hanalei, and he turned down it and rode quickly forward. A groan came from Ambrose. Keno pointed. "Look."

The late night air smelled of smoke. Flames were leaping into the darkness, defying the gentle rain that had begun to fall minutes ago.

Eden. Rafe galloped the horse toward Hanalei plantation house, and onto the carriageway, his gaze searching the crowd on the lawn for a glimpse of Eden. His greatest fear leaped with the flames, dancing demonically through openings in roof. For a moment his emotions gave way to panic.

He maneuvered his horse through the crowd, searching. She wasn't there!

A boy came running up beside him, his face dirty and tear-stained, his clothes darkened with smoke.

"Makua Rafe! There is wahine inside!" He gestured wildly. "Inside, she came for me! I get out but she still there, in parlor."

Rafe forced the frightened horse toward the front of the house, reining him at the entrance. The door was down and smoke swirled, burning his throat. *A fool's death*, he thought, but he entered.

"Eden!"

⸻

Ambrose and Keno rode up on horses. They saw men on horses and workers running in all directions. Ambrose could only trust God that he would not lose Rafe now, as well as Eden. Keno, with a desperate face, had started to dismount to enter the inferno, but Ambrose whacked his arm with his horse's whip.

"No! Lad! Do not follow! There's nothing you can do! There's Candace to think of!"

Lightning streaked hot white against the black sky. "Look," Keno cried, his voice choked with delight, looking up at the rumbling dark sky. "It's starting; rain, beautiful rain." Water poured down his face.

The thunder uttered its dominance; the downpour broke in tumultuous streams beating against the land, the trees, the house, the flames, and through the open roof. Ambrose shouted upward to the bursting clouds: "God of Creation! I give You thanks!"

Horses rode by. The cloudburst continued, cooling angry flames, while the smoke and sizzling persisted.

⁂

Eden heard Rafe call her name, and the sound of his strong, urgent voice shot through her like an arrow. She found the hope and strength to crawl forward in the direction of his voice, seeing nothing but smoke that choked her lungs and parched her throat.

"Rafe! Rafe! I'm here!" The call was feeble. Did he hear it?

She heard his steps and struggled to move in his direction.

"Rafe—"

He advanced. "Where are you?"

"Here—"

He moved toward her and now she could just make out his form and reached out both hands toward him. "Rafe!" she cried.

He swiftly swept her up into his arms and ran back in the direction he had come. They emerged into the drenching rain, warm and steamy.

He carried her away from the house toward the shrubs and sank with her to the lawn, where they coughed and gasped, filling their lungs with fresh air.

The rain continued to pour.

Rafe leaned over to where she lay on the grass and drew her head and shoulders to rest on his arm. "You're going to be all right, darling."

"Yes . . . now."

Only vaguely aware of the others out on the lawn, Eden looked into his penetrating dark eyes staring down at her.

The rain saturated her through to the skin, washing away the smell of smoke from her hair and face. The feel of his arm beneath her head, supporting her, seemed to make her alive again. She turned her head to look at him, and her eyes grew languid as the firelight flickered against his wet skin.

"Rafe," she whispered, reaching a hand to the side of his dark wet head. "I've tasted the bitterness of losing you forever in this life. I've learned that I don't want to leave you again, ever. I want to stay with you here, on Hanalei, to help you rebuild. I want to marry you now," she whispered, her eyes clinging to his. "Maybe I could go to Molokai later—just to visit Rebecca—to hear her story, but not to stay. No, never to stay a year. . . . I need you *now*, Rafe."

He stared down at her as though overwhelmed.

She loved the warm glimmer in the depths of his eyes. He smoothed the wet strands of hair from her face and throat.

"Are you sure?" he asked intently. "Do you know what you're saying?"

"Yes. I'm certain, and I know exactly what I'm saying."

For a moment doubt flickered. "What of your father? Dr. Jerome will need you—he will say so. What then?"

She touched his face, his mouth with her fingers. "He doesn't need me. Not as much as I need you. After what's happened he'll understand. He'll want me to stay. Besides, Dr. Bolton and Lana are going to Molokai to work with him. I won't leave you, Rafe. I'm staying."

His arm tightened around her. "Then I'll see we deliver the printing press on the *Minoa*. You could come with me to Molokai. You can spend time with Rebecca. Will that work?"

She smiled, exhausted but thrilled. "It will work, darling, yes."

"Then that's a promise. There's no urgent cause for me to go to San Francisco now. I'll go later for Kip and the adoption business—and to work on getting Keno his plantation."

She looked at him with her heart in her gaze. "That's what I want to do. Maybe . . . we could marry here—look! Not every room in the plantation house is burned out. The rain is putting the fire out."

"You've just removed the ruin and rubble from my heart and filled it with new life and joy. If you become mine now, through all of the rebuilding and struggle ahead here at Hanalei, with God's help and yours, I can conquer anything man can throw at me. As long as I have you, darling, everything else will fall into its rightful place. We'll rebuild what's destroyed."

Tears mingled with the rain falling on her face. "But I don't look or feel like a bride."

He smiled faintly. "You will. I guarantee it."

His lips met hers . . . and the moment merged with greater intensity than the remaining flames. They were oblivious to the downpour, the neighing horses, the shouting voices.

—⟡⟡—

A short distance away Ambrose said to Keno, "The Lord is good to us this night, Keno, my lad. Eden is safe. She's with Rafe. The rain is putting the fire out and keeping it from spreading. Not all is ashes! Out of what is left they will be sure to build again."

"From the looks of things, Doc Bolton's marriage next week won't be the only one. You're going to be busy, Uncle Ambrose."

Ambrose smiled tiredly as the light began to dawn in the eastern sky.

"Looks to me, lad, like I may be attending to three weddings. And the first one may be right here on Hanalei, today."

Keno looked over at Rafe, who was drawing Eden up onto her feet and then embracing her again. From the way Miss Green Eyes was holding on to him and returning his kiss, Keno was sure Ambrose was right.

THE END OF BOOK TWO

Read more about Eden and Rafe, Candace
and Keno, Molokai, and the Revolution
in book three of The Dawn of Hawaii series.